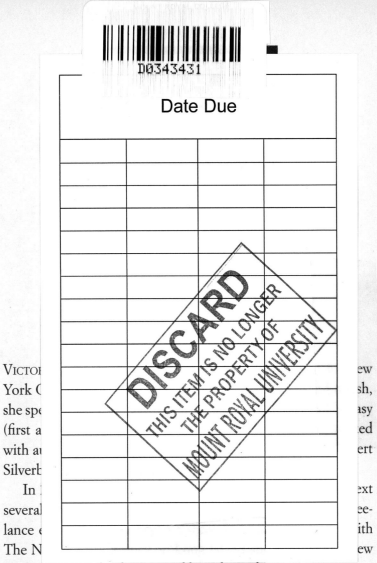

VICTOR   ew
York (sh,
she sp   asy
(first a   ed
with a   ert
Silverb

In   ext
several   ee-
lance   ith
The N   ew
York State, as a fund-raiser and board member.

Six years ago, Victoria made the tumultuous decision to become a writer herself. Her first novel, *Hidden*, was published in June 2006 by Forge Books. She is hard at work on her third novel. She and her husband divide their time between Southampton, New York, and New York City.

STONE CREEK

ALSO BY VICTORIA LUSTBADER

Hidden

STONE CREEK

a novel

Victoria Lustbader

HARPER

NEW YORK • LONDON • TORONTO • SYDNEY

HARPER

This book is a work of fiction. The characters, incidents, and dialogue are drawn from the author's imagination and are not to be construed as real. Any resemblance to actual events or persons, living or dead, is entirely coincidental.

Lyrics from Tom McRae's "Language of Fools" appearing on page 308 are © 2001 Sony/ATV Music Publishing UK Ltd. All rights administered by Sony/ATV Music Publishing LLC, 8 Music Square West, Nashville, TN 37203. All rights reserved. Used by permission.

HarperCollins books may be purchased for educational, business, or sales promotional use. For information please write: Special Markets Department, HarperCollins Publishers, 10 East 53rd Street, New York, NY 10022.

FIRST EDITION

Designed by Phil Mazzone

Library of Congress Cataloging-in-Publication Data

Lustbader, Victoria.
  Stone creek : a novel / Victoria Lustbader.— 1st Harper paperback.
      p. cm.
  ISBN 978-0-06-136921-6
  1. Widowers—Fiction. 2. Healing—Fiction. 3. New York (State)—
Fiction. I. Title.
  PS3612.U79S76   2008
  813'.6—dc22   2007032383

08 09 10 11 12   OV/RRD   10 9 8 7 6 5 4 3 2 1

For Emma and Nicholas

This is all the heaven we've got, right here where we are.

—Mark Knopfler

STONE CREEK

1

In a house in the woods on the outskirts of a small town seventy miles northwest of New York City, Danny Malloy wakes with the dawn. There was a time when he woke gently, rising through the layers of his own soft darkness until his consciousness emerged, whole and round and perched on the radiant horizon of his day. Now he wakes rudely, abruptly, in a recurring state of shock, tangled in his bedcovers. There was a time when he slept without moving, her hand always somewhere on him, stilling any urge to restlessness or disquiet. Now disquiet takes possession of him in those dark hours. There is too much space in his bed and he thrashes in his sleep, blindly seeking what is missing.

It is the end of June and dawn comes early. In the deep shade along the north wall of the house, purple lilacs still bloom. Their sweet perfume floats in the air. The birds are busy, singing and darting to and fro. Bluebirds, orioles, cardinals, finches, jays, nuthatches, thrushes, wrens, catbirds, mockingbirds, hummingbirds. They take turns making hungry strikes at the feeders Danny has spaced throughout the clearing between the back of the house and the woods. Bumblebees drone through the flower-beds, nuzzling into the kaleidoscope of color, coating their little legs and proboscises with sticky pollen. From beyond the edge of the woods comes the sound of the creek. Its clear water rushes over hindering formations of stone and shale. In most years the creek is shallow and serene along the stretch that flows behind Danny's house, but this year it is swollen almost beyond its wide and curving banks from the melt of a winter now famous for its endless snow storms and an early spring full of rain.

Danny frees his limbs and pushes the sheets off him. His eyes linger on the willowy shadows above his head as pale gold light crawls over his face. He turns his head and looks across the empty expanse of bed until his eyes come to rest on her night table. They flutter shut and he turns his head in the other direction. But that is no better, maybe worse, because when he opens them again he is looking into the bathroom doorway. He sits up, puts his feet on the warm wood floor, his hands by his sides on the mattress. The night table is at his back now. A simple cherrywood table with a single drawer. Soon he will have to open that drawer and deal with what's in it; his long reprieve is nearly over. He made a promise and he will keep it, as he keeps all his promises.

He found the book, nearly a year ago, in a box secreted at the back of her closet. It was a lidded box of burled maple wood that he'd made for her twenty-third birthday. There was only the one thing in it: a medium-sized book with sheets of thick, handmade paper. His name stenciled on the embossed ruby-colored leather cover in bold strokes of indelible silver ink. Her cherished Du-pont pen secure in a leather loop at its edge. He had never seen it before. He knew he shouldn't open it, shouldn't look at what was written on the vellum pages. It was far too soon and his pain was too great. He knew there was a chance that whatever was left unshattered inside him would not be enough to hold him together. But at that time he didn't want to be held together. He wanted to dissolve, to vanish into the black cave of his pain. And so he opened it, and he read.

I was ten years old the first time I saw Danny Malloy. He was eighteen. It was toward the end of that year when I was friends with Linda Tompkins. She and I met at Miss Ruth's Dance Academy in Middletown in the fall, two star-struck, dreaming ballerinas, twirling and leaping better than anyone else in our class. Linda and I saw each other three times a week and were inseparable during the ten-minute interludes before and after class, while we dressed and undressed in the moldy locker room. After that day I knew that Linda had come into my life to lead me to Danny.

It was a Wednesday in the middle of June. Class was over and Linda and I were on the sidewalk, waiting to be picked up and taken home. We stood in the sun in our pink tights and black leotards, little black ballet skirts wrapped around our waists, overstuffed dance bags at our feet. We felt so grown-up and important. When Linda's sister Carol arrived, two people got out of her car. Carol and a boy. I knew he must be the boy Carol was dating. Linda had told me about him, rolled her eyes and sniffed when she said that Carol was crazy about him, that she was doing it with him, that she wrote Carol Malloy over and over in decorative columns down the margins of the pages of her school notebooks. We giggled about it; ten years old, we were so clueless. Neither of us knew what it meant to be crazy about a boy.

He was wearing blue jeans and a white T-shirt with the sleeves rolled up, the shortened cuffs turned back high on his up-

per arms. He might have been chiseled from a block of marble, that's how hard and strong he looked. The spring sun had already darkened his fair skin to a light nutty brown and streaked his sandy hair with golden lights. Carol said, And this is Linda's friend, Tara. She's a terrific little dancer. Danny turned to smile at me and that's when I saw his blue eyes. I couldn't breathe. In the space of one heartbeat I fell in love. I wasn't a little girl anymore, even though I still looked like one, staring up at him mute and trembling. His smile broadened and a dimple appeared in his right cheek. He chucked me lightly under the chin, said, Hi Tara. I'll have to come to one of your recitals sometime. He kept smiling down at me until he'd pulled a little upward twitch from my frozen lips, a blink from my wide-open lids.

Late that night, awake in my room long after my parents had gone to sleep, I turned on my little flashlight and opened my diary to a clean page. I wrote our two names one under the other. I crossed out all the letters our names had in common and then I counted off the letters that were left. Not with numbers. With a repeating litany of possible fates: Love, Marriage, Friendship, Hate, Love, Marriage, Friendship, Hate. And I put the results next to our names:

D A N N Y   M A L L O Y – M
T A R A   J A M I S O N – M

It came out exactly as I knew it would. It didn't matter that I hadn't understood anything before that afternoon. It didn't matter that I would remain a little girl to him for such a long time after. When the time was right, I would come and find him.

He closed the book and thrust it from him with a violent jerk of his hand. An automatic motion that originated somewhere in the middle of his chest. He sat on the bed gasping, then staggered into the bathroom and tried in vain to rid himself of the small breakfast he had eaten an hour earlier. When finally his gorge settled and he was able to breathe normally, he found a large padded envelope and put the book inside. Then he put the envelope in the drawer of her table. He closed the drawer and promised her that in eleven months he would open it again and read every word. On the anniversary of the day she died.

There is no point in trying to go back to sleep, the day is already calling to him. Danny stands up and stretches his arms slowly and hugely over his head. He can get a lot done in these quiet early hours. Still, he takes the time to make the bed, smoothing the sheets and tucking them under the mattress at the foot where his tossing has wrestled them loose. He fluffs his pillow. He pads across the room to his dresser, opens the top drawer, and exclaims, "Oh shit," with a small, mournful laugh. He is out of clean underwear and he forgot to move the laundry from the washer to the dryer last night. It's been nearly a year but he can't seem to get it all under control. He sleeps naked, no matter the season, and so his jeans go on over his bare ass. He discovers that it's actually comfortable. He doesn't bother with shoes or a shirt.

As he crosses the threshold of the bedroom and no ghostly words follow him into the hallway, a faint sigh escapes him and he thinks that today will be a decent day. He peers into the open door of the first room down the hall. Caleb is a small mound under the covers in the middle of his bed; one exposed bare white foot dangles over the edge of the mattress. Danny takes the little wooden hammer he carved from where it hangs on the doorknob and moves it to the hook set in the middle of Caleb's door.

It's a signal they devised months ago, so that if Caleb awoke and Danny wasn't in the house, the boy would know to look for him in the studio. Danny goes into the sun-bright kitchen and puts up coffee. He goes into the mudroom where the washer and dryer are and transfers the damp ball of clothing.

When the words follow him he can't think clearly about anything, he can only feel, and what he feels at those times is her; she is a fog that surrounds him. When they leave him alone, when she releases him, he is able to recapture his own memories. He is convinced that he must hold on to them or he will never be able to separate himself from her. If what he remembers of their coming together is forever melded to the adoration she gifted him in her every word and act he will remain as possessed by her dim shade as he was by her brilliant substance.

As he listens to the gurgle and drip of the coffeemaker and watches the glass pot slowly fill with liquid, his mind wanders back seventeen years, to that day in June and the time that followed.

It was a hot beginning to what turned out to be an even hotter summer. Mid-June and already the skin on Danny's nose had peeled off twice and he had taken to smearing it with titanium dioxide cream when he was on an outdoor job. He was earning good money, working hard for Tom Gallo, the best general contractor in the area. He'd graduated high school with an undistinguished history, survived his mandatory education careening between As in subjects he liked and Ds in those that bored him. College was as far off his radar screen as a blip could get. Starting in first grade, his frustrated teachers held frequent meetings with Danny's gentle, affable parents in the hopes that they might help rouse their son to use his obvious intelligence more fully. John and Teresa said, Oh yes, of course, and then privately told him to do what made him happy. John was head of the janitorial staff at Stone Creek Elementary School, Teresa was a breakfast- and lunch-shift waitress at The Kitchen on the corner of Elm and Main streets. When they considered the shortcomings of their own lives, they calculated that what would give Danny the better life they wanted for him was finding the thing he loved best and being allowed to make it his life's work.

Now Danny was in the exhilarating throes of discovering that he had an innate talent and love for building and shaping things. He had a feel for wood and marble and granite and glass and their versatility and malleability. He'd been in Gallo's full-time employ only four weeks but already Tom was moving him around, letting him work on homes in various stages of completion, attaching him to different subcontractors, quietly watching to see how deep Danny's talents went. As though he were a piece of wood or marble or granite or glass, Danny was beginning to shape his own life.

Mid-June. Danny's world rotated in harmony with the universe. It would be several more months before he spun slowly away from Carol Tompkins, as he had from the two girls he'd dated before her, regretfully leaving her to cry all throughout the fall and winter. It would be more than a year before his mother, the welcoming smile at The Kitchen for twenty-five years, was diagnosed with the lung cancer that would kill her slowly and turn John and Danny into anguished custodians of her flickering life. It would be three years, after his twenty-first birthday had come and gone, after his mother had been dead four months, before his father gave him money and ordered him to go somewhere far; far enough that he could put the sadness and the smallness behind him, where he could learn his craft, where he could absorb enough of the wide world beyond Stone Creek to know that he had choices.

But none of that had happened yet. It was still mid-June and he was happy where he was. Late one afternoon he drove to Middletown, twenty minutes northwest of town, with Carol to pick up her kid sister after ballet class.

"Would you just look at the two of them," Carol said as they pulled up at the curb. "Are they not the cutest things you've ever seen? The little ballerinas."

"They are pretty damned cute," Danny obliged. He looked through the window at Linda and the other girl. Linda was quite a good little ballerina, but you couldn't tell from the way she carried herself outside class. She was just another shy, slouchy kid standing on the sidewalk, slump shouldered, fidgety, and slightly pigeon-toed, strands of mousy hair straggling across her face. In unfair contrast, the other girl was as poised, as posed, as if she were onstage. Back straight, shoulders down, chin up, gleaming mahogany-colored hair neat in its high ponytail. One small foot, still in its soft ballet slipper, pointed forward and slightly turned out, as though she were about to glide across the hot cement. "Who's the baby Maria Tallchief over there?"

"Yeah, isn't she just? That's Tara. She's a Harmony brat, lives up the ridge road. Her parents won't let her come to our house and, of course, Linda has never been invited to hers." Offense on her sister's behalf tightened Carol's voice. "Tara actually seems like a really nice kid, though. Linda loves her." She softened.

Maybe Tara was a nice kid, maybe she wasn't, it didn't matter to Danny. He didn't know her. She was just another kid growing up on the rich side of town, a different world from the one he lived in. He said hi, smiled, and looked down at her. She was a tiny, formless thing, her body all bone and her face all dark round eyes. Dark round eyes fixed on his face with a stricken look in them.

He didn't have a lot of experience with little girls, but he knew enough to want to be kind to one who looked at him with that look. So he smiled a little longer into the oval cameo of her face, said something about watching her dance and when he got a small smile from her in return, he looked away and forgot about her.

After that afternoon in June, she materialized like magic where she had no reason to be, like a word you hear one day for the first time in your life and then hear everywhere. Over the next three years he'd see her zipping by on her bike; she'd show up and linger at the construction sites where he was working, even ones miles from where she lived; he'd come upon her drinking a vanilla Coke or a strawberry milkshake at The Kitchen, where he would sometimes take his lunch break even after his mother had become too ill to keep her job. She'd appear in an aisle of the bookstore, on the sidewalk outside the hardware store, at the post office. And in the same way you might not ever say that new word although you'd become used to hearing it, Danny got used to seeing little Tara Jamison around and speaking a few words to her when he did, although he never thought of her between times.

They ran into each other on Main Street a week before he went away. Teresa was dead; John had given Danny five thousand dollars and a plane ticket to London; Tom Gallo had arranged a trial position for him with a company that restored historic buildings. Too dazed to be kind, Danny bluntly told her he was leaving for Europe and didn't know when he'd be back, then turned and left her, tearful and open-mouthed, the autumn sun glinting off the metal braces on her sweetly crooked teeth.

As soon as the coffee is done, Danny pours it into a Thermos. He brews his coffee very strong, and he adds a little half-and-half to mellow out the flavor. He balances the Thermos, a mug, a container of peach yogurt, and a spoon in his hands and he pushes aside the screen of the double-wide sliding glass doors that make up the south wall of the kitchen and that have been standing open all night. He slides the screen closed. He steps off the teak deck onto the bluestone path and crosses the gravel expanse to the square barnlike building behind the house. He unlatches the oversized wooden plank doors and swings them against the exterior wall. The opening is wide enough for him to drive his pickup truck through when he has something to load into it. He leaves these doors open as well so that Caleb can find him easily.

The pungent smells of wood dust and paint, glue, oil, and turpentine ride the eddies of the fast-warming air. He puts his breakfast down on a bench, strides across the painted cement floor, and opens the windows in the back to get some cross-ventilation. Now the bright aerated tingle of frothy water lightens the earthy scents. He turns and surveys the projects awaiting his attention. He anticipates with pleasure the work he'll do today. There are many things that give him pleasure. He is aware of that, and yet he knows, too, that he is stuck. Not paralyzed. He was never paralyzed. That was not a state he ever had the luxury of succumbing to. But he is stuck, and without her to help him he doesn't know how to become unstuck. It's starting to feel like another pleasure—living stuck—but no one has to tell him that that's not a good thing.

He fills his mug with hot coffee and sips it as he walks slowly around the interior of his workspace. Soon, the caffeine kicks in, his pace quickens, and his brain comes to full attention. He makes his choice from the many possibilities and goes to work.

2

PAUL SPENCER REQUIRES no human or human-devised assistance to wake him at the proper and necessary hour. He never has, not from his youngest days. He was born alert and his fifty-four years of life have acted as a strop to his keenness, honing it to a fine edge. This June morning, his eyes open exactly at 6:15 despite the drape-shrouded dimness of the bedroom and the lullaby hum of the apartment's air-conditioning. These mufflers of light and sound are for Lily's sake, so that she will not be disturbed by the traffic noises from Central Park West or the intermittent white flaring of headlights and the red and blue flashing of police cars and ambulances. New York may be a city that never sleeps, but Lily is a woman who likes her rest. And although she was born and raised in the city, since they've had the house in the country she sleeps better there. Paul was raised in the country, a different country from where their house is, but he can sleep anywhere.

Sleek and silent as a panther, Paul gets out of bed and goes into his bathroom. He closes the door before turning on the light. He'll be gone within twenty minutes, in his office by 7:10, with enough time to eat a good breakfast in the partners' dining room before the firm's 8:00 a.m. meeting with SynTech's CEO, CFO, general counsel, and their justifiably very worried board chairman. He shaves, rinses his face, strips off his undershorts, and turns on the shower. While he waits for the hot water to work its way through the San Remo's historical pipes to his twenty-second-floor south tower apartment, Paul dispassionately considers himself in the floor-to-ceiling mirror across from the sink.

Except for a pragmatic understanding of the obvious—that what he has experienced and accomplished in his life by necessity took time and are not the experiences or accomplishments of youth—he cannot make sense of the fact that he is fifty-four. He can identify no familiar or believable quality of himself in that number; it is too large and unwieldy. He is still an ambitious, tightly coiled spring and in his mind he feels no different than he did at thirty-two, the year he made partner after only seven years with Chaikin-Gibbs. Or than he did at forty-six, when he was named managing partner, the youngest ever in the firm's 117-year history, and met, wooed, and married Lily Margolies, the warmest, most nurturing, most beautiful woman he has ever known. Or than he did at fifty, when he was taken with an uncharacteristic ambition that he pursued zealously for a short time but dismissed unconditionally when that pursuit produced only discord in his life.

That's the way Paul is. He sets his sights on something or someone and most of the time he gets what he's after. And when he doesn't get what he's after, he stops wanting it. It's a trick he taught himself when he was too young to understand the whys and wherefores of his own behavior. Being exceedingly bright and clever, he has learned the trick down to the bone. He has never continued to want what he can't have. He considers that a waste of time. There is always something else to want.

He gazes into the mirror but his reflection only heightens this puzzlement of his age, this feeling of being unfamiliar to himself. He looks a damned sight better than most men in their fifties, or even their forties, but he certainly doesn't look thirty-two. His body is good, lean as ever, well formed and athletic. His face, too, with its wide mouth and strong nose below a high forehead, is still lean; it's a deceptively ascetic-looking face, or so numerous women have told him. His skin is lined, but gently, no deep grooves between his eyes or around his mouth. A little shadow beneath, a touch of puffiness around the eyes, but the eyes themselves are clear, dark, and piercing. He still has a full head of hair, although there are delicate wings of silver at his temples and silver strands peeking through the dense black here and there.

Lily doesn't seem to mind the lines or the puff or the silver strands but, to his chagrin, Paul does. Not because he is vain. An hour three times a week in the pool at the New York Athletic Club, reasonably healthy eating, and some skin care products that he lets Lily buy for him comprise his arsenal in the war against aging. He is a powerful and charismatic man, his compelling presence and attractiveness undiminished by the inevitable signs of maturity.

It isn't the signs themselves that make him feel as though he doesn't know himself. It's that every time he is unexpectedly hijacked and held captive to the reality of the physical changes in himself, he senses those other changes, the ones hovering out of sight, the ones he doesn't know how to think about. He has let them become part of what surrounds him these past few years, like the dust mites that inhabit his pillow and his mattress, that he breathes in with every breath he takes but never sees and can ignore until the day he coughs and sneezes in allergic response. He'd need his microscope to see them and Paul has never turned his microscope on himself or anyone else. To examine life that way, that intensely, is not the way his mind works.

The shower is steaming. Paul turns his gaze from the mirror and settles his uneasy mind with thoughts of the new, killer case that may be coming to him. He showers, towels dry, and steps quietly into his dressing room. He dons a pale blue shirt, his favorite black Hugo Boss suit, and a boldly patterned Japanese hand-dyed tie. He pulls something from a shopping bag on his dressing-room floor. He steals back into the bedroom, smiling to himself, and gingerly places what was in the bag on his pillow. Lily is sleeping turned toward his side of the bed and Paul positions the object so that she will see it immediately when she opens her eyes. He stands a moment, leaning over his pillow, arrested by the way her long dark lashes spread like miniature fans against her creamy pale skin. He wants to kiss her, to rest his lips on the curving grace of her neck and absorb into himself the steady, sedating throb of her. He wants it, but he doesn't do it. As he straightens and turns away from the bed, he gets that odd feeling in his stomach and chest that he's been getting lately, not a pain really but a tight, heavy, twisted feeling. He wonders again if there could possibly be something wrong with him, if he should go see Bertram for another checkup.

He goes into the kitchen and sets the coffeemaker to grind and brew at eight o'clock. He collects his wallet, watch, and briefcase from the table in the entryway and he's out the door and in the elevator. He says good morning to Sean, the midnight-to-eight doorman, turns right out of the building onto Central Park West, right again west onto Seventy-second Street to the Seventh Avenue subway. He takes the number 2 express train all the way to Wall Street, where his office is. He's there by 7:10 on the dot.

*   *   *

By the time Lily wakes up, Paul has been in his meeting for nearly fifteen minutes. She has become something of a slug-a-bed, which doesn't make her feel all that good about herself. But she has come to like that lazy, torporous feeling, caught in stasis between buoyancy and leadenness, her body transformed by the opposing pulls of gravity and a top-of-the-line Tempur-Pedic into that of some neomythical beast—half goddess, half mattress.

There is no particular reason for her to get up, in any case. There's been no job to rush to for more than three years. She loved her work and could start again anytime, but she doesn't want to. More and more she seems not to want to do much of anything. Time feels as though it's standing still and yet her days pass too quickly, one after the other.

The magical bio-bedding connection doesn't last long, sadly, and after a few seconds Lily opens her eyes. Something is staring back at her, a foot from her face, and she bolts upright with a shriek. She grabs what Paul has left on his pillow, hugs it to her chest, and laughs out loud, a throaty, happy laugh. It's a stuffed animal, a child's plush toy. A stuffed bat, to be precise, with a furry mottled brown body, black Alfred E. Newman ears, black button eyes and a soft, slightly off-center nose, enormous velvety wings that wrap the creature like a luxurious black cape, and two white fangs protruding from the idea of a mouth in a wacky-looking overbite. It's adorable and begs to be cuddled. Lily loves bats. Paul loves Lily. Lily loves Paul. For the moment, life is a perfectly balanced equation.

Clutching the bat in her arms, her nose buried in its soft, squeezable body, Lily gets out of bed and rushes into the kitchen.

The aroma of coffee fills her nostrils and the equation becomes weighted on the side of Lily loves Paul. She picks up the cordless phone and hits 1 on the speed dial.

"Mr. Spencer's office."

As soon as his secretary answers, she remembers that he is in an early meeting. "Oh, Diane, it's Lily. I forgot, he's in a meeting, isn't he?"

"Good morning, Mrs. Spencer. Yes, but he left instructions to put you through."

"No, I know it's an important meeting. Don't disturb him."

"He wants to talk to you. He was very definite. Hold on a moment."

While she waits for Paul, feeling childish for taking him from his work because of a stuffed animal, she cradles the phone between ear and shoulder and pours herself a cup of coffee. The bat's silky little face snuggles into the other side of her neck.

"Hey, sleepyhead. What's up?"

"You have to come home. There's a bat loose in the apartment."

Paul laughs. "Do you like him?"

"I love him. I just love him. Where on earth did you find him?"

"He was in the window of a kids' clothing store. He flew out and followed me home."

Paul does things like this, spontaneous, generous, thoughtful things. Unselfish things. When he does, Lily melts with love for him. But even though she melts, her love can no longer find its way into the secret core of her, that place that Paul, and only Paul, once touched. A fireproof brick wall has built itself around it over the past three years. A million little unselfish acts won't tear it down. She knows it's there, knows even that it's a bad

thing, a hurtful thing, but here is where she and Paul are unfor-
tunately too much alike: fear prevents her from thinking about
it, from examining it too closely, from admitting to anyone, often
even to herself, that it exists. It is easier for both of them to hold
themselves ignorant and helpless—even Paul, a man who has
rarely if ever felt ignorant or helpless in his entire life—than to
face the disturbing changes in their marriage.

"I wish you could come home now." With him several miles
downtown, she would like to put her arms around him.

"I like the sound of that."

His tone is neutral, but Lily hears criticism and complaint
and the melt begins to freeze over. "I'm keeping you from your
meeting. Go back to work. I'll see you tonight."

"In a minute. This meeting just started and there's already
more bullshit in the room than in the Staten Island land-
fill. It won't hurt them to cool their heels a little longer. The
Whitemans"—the mister being one of Paul's law partners—
"want to have dinner with us next Wednesday. I told them yes.
Okay with you?"

Exasperation geysers up in her. "I told you four times, Paul.
I'm going up to the house Tuesday to get ready for the holiday
weekend."

"Ri-i-ight. Sorry."

"You do remember that Mona and Chuck and the kids are
coming?" There is an unpleasant edge to her voice. The inap-
propriateness of her response and the sound of her voice shame
her, but she can't control herself. "And Rick and . . ."

"Yes, I remember." Paul cuts her off. Several seconds pass in
silence. "Did I not do a nice thing this morning?"

Guilt and contrition make her throat ache. "You did. You
did a wonderful, lovely thing. You should have heard me scream

when I saw him. I'm sorry. I'm turning into a pre-coffee bitch. The coffee is delicious, by the way. Why is it always better when you make it?"

"You're afraid to make it strong enough. And you could never be a bitch. So, what are you going to call the little darling?"

She holds the bat at arm's length. He looks startled by the bright kitchen light, his bead eyes seem larger and more shiny. "I'm going to call him Blinkie," she says. "Or maybe Floyd, as in Count Floyd, you remember, that Joe Flaherty character, the cowardly vampire from Second City TV?"

"I don't think I ever saw that. They're both cute names, though. How about a last and a first, Mr. Blinkie Floyd."

"*Count* Blinkie Floyd to you." Lily laughs, instantly happy again. "I love you."

"I love you, too. I guess that means I'm forgiven for whatever I did before." He doesn't wait for her to respond. "Uh-oh. Gotta go. SynTech's board chair looks like he's about to throw something."

"Well, don't let him throw it at you."

"Don't worry, it's his CEO he wants to kill. Don't eat too much today. We'll go to Jean Georges for dinner and celebrate BF's arrival."

As the line goes dead, Lily's bubble of happiness bursts. He's going to take her to one of the fanciest restaurants in the city to celebrate their getting a stuffed bat. She knows it's just a silly excuse to go out, but that's what he said, as though it would mean nothing to her: we'll celebrate his arrival. As if it were something real. Her eyes fill with tears and she has to put her mug down. Blinkie Floyd is looking at her with concern. She holds him against her shoulder as one would a newborn and lumbers back to the bedroom. The sheets are still warm from her body, the pillow still holds the impression of her head; she could just climb back in, take Blinkie Floyd with her. She whimpers softly, then goes to the window, draws back the drapes. Sunlight floods the room and captures Lily in its dazzle. From twenty-two stories up she can see a long way up and down Central Park West and far out over the park, all that life on the other side of the glass.

She will not spend her days in bed. It is too pathetic and there is simply no reason for it. There is nothing wrong with her own life; far from it; it is a better and more fortunate life than 99.9 percent of the planet will ever know. And no one has everything, despite how things look from twenty-two stories up. *For crying out loud, get over it, Lily. Just do it.* The Margolies family credo, coined in a masterful joint effort of philosophic expression by Max and Ada Margolies, long before any sneaker company thought of it. It was a given that Lily, their firstborn, would live, as they had, by its harsh and lonely teachings. Like most firstborns, Lily was not destined to be the rebel in the family. She was serious and dutiful. It was Mona, five years younger, who got to be bad.

Lily turns from the window. The first thing she has to do is find a day-time cave for her bat. There are sets of glass shelves recessed into the wall on either side of the bed. She arranges him on the second shelf on her side, well out of the sun, so that his feet dangle slightly over the beveled edge and his wings drape his body. She plants a kiss between his ears and heads for her bathroom. The feel of his fur is soft and cool on her lips.

A little after ten, Lily emerges from the San Remo's lobby onto the sidewalk. Ivan, the 8:00 a.m. to 4:00 p.m. doorman, holds the door for her and with utter gentlemanly politeness, he, being a happily married sixty-five-year-old Estonian possessed of old-fashioned values, tells her she looks lovely. Which she does.

She can't help it. Even in a simple summer dress and sandals, her only makeup a light foundation with a good sunscreen in it and a swipe of sheer lipstick; even though she has attained that certain age, Lily is an undeniable beauty. That Paul finds her the most beautiful woman he has ever actually seen in the flesh is, of course, his opinion, but it is an understandable one. Lily smiles fondly at Ivan and crosses Central Park West. She will walk through the park and spend the morning at the Metropolitan Museum, and for lunch have an enormous cup of decadent hot chocolate at Sarabeth's. Then she'll go back into the park, find a quiet bench around the lake or Turtle Pond, and read. By two o'clock she misses Paul and is hungry just thinking about what she's going to eat at Jean Georges. She has *done* it. She feels much much better.

3

EVE COMES TO SIT BY Tara's grave most every day. No one realizes that she does, not even Lester. They come together every Sunday after church, but the other days she comes alone. She comes when it is time to come, when necessity overtakes her. She is sure that Daniel comes often, too—his hand is evident in the meticulously tended plantings around the headstone—but in nearly a year they have never surprised each other. Not that they haven't been there at the same time. That would be statistically improbable. She assumes that he has arrived to find her there more often than she has arrived to find him there and that it is discomfort that prevents him from showing himself, as distaste prevents her. She does not want to commune with her dead daughter in the presence of the man who stole a lovely, unknowing girl from her family, ruined her future, and let her die on a bathroom floor. She has to deal with him; she will likely have to deal with him for the rest of her life. She has no choice. As a well-brought-up Savannah belle, in the manner of generations of Foster women, she knows how to be coolly civil to those she does not care for. Daniel has been a challenge, certainly, but for Tara's sake she has always done her best. As she will do now for Caleb. But she does not have to, she will *not*, share her grief with him.

At least he will never lie beside Tara in her eternal rest. Eve and Lester will, and there is room for Tara's child, as well. But not Daniel. When they bought the family plots, they didn't buy one for him. *Your people are Catholic, Daniel, are they not? Surely, you will want to be buried with your own*, she said. He laughed at her and said that he didn't intend to be buried anywhere, that he wanted to be incinerated and his ashes scattered on the wind.

Eve sits on the stone bench, four feet beyond the foot of Tara's grave. Even on a warm day such as today, the stone feels cold beneath her skirt. She sits with her legs together and her hands folded on her linen-covered thighs. Her back is straight. She wears sunglasses and a close-weave, wide-brimmed Panama straw hat to keep the sun from her face. From behind her glasses, her eyes are fixed on Tara's headstone. She allows no tears to distort her view. This is what she does every time she is here alone. She stares reverently at the incised granite block and she silently tells Tara a story that no one has ever heard. No matter how many times she tells it now, the story is never over.

4

LILY SHIVERS AS SHE REACHES into the overly chilled dairy case for a gallon of organic low-fat milk. She rubs at the goose-flesh dimpling the skin of her bare arms and thinks, too late, that she should have thrown a sweater into the car to put on over her halter top. Even out of the frozen food or refrigerated aisles, it is always unnecessarily cold in Dreiser's Market. Paul jokes that it has nothing to do with maintaining the fancy high-priced food they now carry along with the every-day fare; it's so that the horny, trollish local guys who work there can get their jol-lies ogling the popped nipples of the good-looking city women who shop there. She looks quickly around to make sure no one is staring at her and her nipples, which are, in fact, pushing in protest against the thick cotton of her top. A few women paying her no attention; one man far down the aisle, his head perhaps just turning away.

She puts a dozen assorted organic yogurts into her cart. Mona and Chuck's kids are eleven and seven and belie the myth that children don't eat a lot; these two eat like locusts and are possessed of innocently, ignorantly expensive tastes. They'll eat peanut butter and jelly sandwiches if that's what there is, but let them see lobster or caviar or a wheel of twenty-dollar-a-pound imported sheep cheese and the PB and J goes to the dog. Metaphorically, that is, since neither the Spencers nor the Golds have a dog. Lily loves to indulge her niece and nephew, so she has a lot of shopping left to do. She hurries into the slightly warmer part of the store. As she makes her way down a long aisle dedicated to nothing but pasta, rice, grains, and cereals, plucking things off the shelves, racking her brain to remember what Joshua's favorite cereal is these days, her cell phone rings.

"Hey baby. Where are you?"

"I'm in Dreiser's, quaking with cold, walking proof of your nipple theory."

Paul's laugh comes through the static-laden connection. "When are you going to admit that I'm always right? I'm glad I caught you. You're shopping for the weekend? Can you hear me? Jesus, why can't they get decent cell service up there?" His rapid-fire mouth has trouble keeping pace with his ricocheting thoughts. "That's better. Don't move."

"I can hear you fine. And yes, I'm shopping for the weekend."

"Listen, I hate to do this to you, but buy extra everything. I'm going to be bringing a couple of the associates up with me."

"What? Oh, no, Paul! It's July Fourth weekend, we have a houseful of company. Mona and Chuck are coming all the way from D.C. Please don't tell me you're going to be working the whole time."

"Pretty much. It's official. We've been hired by SynTech's board to carry out an independent probe of the company's accounting practices and revenue reporting. The SEC and Department of Justice finally told the board that their employees weren't cooperating and they'd better hire their own lawyers. It's looking ugly. We've got a year's worth of federal investigation documents to go through by yesterday just to catch up. Hold on. Hey, Diane, where are you going with that frigging file? I'm taking it with me! Wake up, would you?"

Lily takes the phone from her ear while Paul barks at his secretary and Diane murmurs *Sorry, Paul*. She wants to be annoyed at him, for the one-dimensional, black-and-white way he makes decisions, always according to his own needs. But it would be unfair in this case. He is the reigning king of corporate law in New York, he loves his work, and she knew the amount of time and attention his job required of him when she married him. She takes a breath, brings the phone back again. "Hello? Paul?"

"Yeah. I'm here."

"Stop traumatizing the woman."

"Can't be done. I've tried."

Lily snorts lightly. "You're impossible. Are you going to have any time at all? You know I can't be trusted at the grill."

"I'll put the peons to work round the clock and take most of Sunday off. That's the best I can do, okay? Everyone finds you more entertaining than me, anyway. I know I certainly do."

"I should hope so." Lily capitulates. There is nothing else to do. "So, which unfortunates are coming with you?"

"Terchunian, the aspiring Armenian, and Steinberg, the jovial Jew."

"Oh, God, Paul!" Lily cries, giggling, her hand to her mouth. He can make her laugh like no one else on earth. "Well, at least they're fun."

"Hey. Don't be having too much fun with them. I don't like the way they look at you. Well, truth be told, I do—my gorgeous young wife. Just don't let me see you look back."

"Don't worry. They're too young for me," she teases.

"Like hell."

"Like hell to you, too. It's going to be a hot weekend. I'm going commando and you'll just have to—"

"Ah . . . sorry, baby, I've got to go." He tramples over her bantering; he's through. "One last thing. Pick up a bunch of steaks at Pekarski's."

Now Lily bristles with annoyance. Pekarski's is forty minutes from the village, out in the countryside. "Dreiser's meats are excellent, Paul."

"Pekarski's are better. Get some big fat porterhouses, I have to feed the animals."

Lily's hand tightens around her little pink phone. "Fine."

"Are you pissed? Come on. You know their meat's the best. Anyway, it's a scenic drive and it'll give you something to do tomorrow."

Lily closes her eyes and slowly counts to three. "Right. It's a lovely drive."

"Be nice. I'll see you tomorrow night. The car's coming at eight thirty, so we should be there before ten. Have some sandwiches ready, pretty please? I love you."

"If Big Vinnie is driving you, make sure he stays awake this time. I love you, too."

She holds her phone and stares sightlessly into her shopping cart. *Be nice.* That's all he wants from her; it's not so much and yet it's becoming harder to manage it, to damp down the unreasonable irritation she feels so much of the time. He's nice to her, why can't she be nice back? Maybe she's starting menopause. She should go see her gynecologist, get tested.

She exhales a big, puffy breath, slides the phone into her purse, and marshals her thoughts. Serge and Ira, the eager associates, are both dark, skinny, hyperactive Paul clones and will eat everything put in front of them. She swings her cart around, heading again for the dairy section, but at the end of the otherwise vacant aisle a man is standing, watching her. The man she'd seen earlier, while she'd been shivering. She becomes flustered and glances at him for just long enough to capture a sense of him. A local, certainly, but no troll. Young and well-built, square-shouldered and slim-hipped, light-eyed and bearded, dressed in jeans and a T-shirt so well worn its faded black fabric appears dusty. His expression as he watches her, even seen so briefly and from a distance, is openly appreciative but somehow stark and strangely unsettling. A flush of embarrassment paints her throat and she quickly swings back, glues her attention to the fifteen different granola options on the shelf in front of her. She feels his eyes stay on her as he comes up the aisle. She doesn't turn her head, not even a fraction, as he passes behind her, but she steals a swiveling peek at his retreating back. It isn't like her to notice or care about the attention she gets from men other than Paul, but the way this one so obviously planted himself where he could see her gives her a visceral thrill.

She finishes her shopping without spotting him again, but as she pushes her laden cart across the front of the store, past the rows of checkout lines, she notices him at the head of the counter closest to the door. His purchases are bagged, his head is down, and he's pulling cash from an old, squashed-looking wallet. Lily's heart begins to beat fast as she walks by him and, stupidly, she is upset when he doesn't look up. She looks straight ahead and keeps walking, out the automatic doors into the blessedly warm air of the parking lot. She loads her bags into the trunk of the BMW, gets behind the wheel, puts the key in the ignition, and then stops, the flexing motion of her wrist and arm left uncompleted. The engine remains dormant while, through the tinted windshield, she sees him emerge from the store, a bag in each arm.

Now he can't see her but she can see him, etched in clear lines in the sparkling afternoon sunlight. She tells herself to start the car. It's hot and she should get her groceries home. She has other errands to run. But she sits, frozen in place, leaning forward, her hand still holding the key, her eyes on him. She studies him with breathless deliberation, as though he were the perpetrator of a crime and she the unwilling sole witness.

She'd been right: he is young. Somewhere in his mid-thirties, a decade her junior. He balances one of the bags on a bent leg to free a hand, draws a pair of sunglasses from his back pocket. The dark glasses hide his light eyes, but not the substantial crow's feet at their sides, and his beard doesn't mask the lines around his mouth. He is young but weathered and slightly beaten-looking, as though life has been harsh with him or he a little too hard on it. His hair is a confusing color, on the cusp between blond and brown. It is cut short, blunt and choppy, boyishly tousled on top with ends already burnished gold from the sun. His beard is a shade lighter than his hair, close and neat. A tattoo of intricate design encircles his right biceps. His clothes, the worn jeans and soft, shrunken-looking T-shirt, hang loosely on his slight frame, hinting that he has recently filled them out more fully. They reveal the contours of his body more absolutely than if they hugged him tight, for they drape him like an artist's cloth purposefully laid over a sculpture of an ideal male form. He walks down the row of cars to a silver Dodge pickup truck and lifts his bags into the open back. The T-shirt floats up and away as he raises his arms and Lily sees the smooth, solid muscles of his side and stomach move beneath their covering of pale skin.

It would be a mistake to say that he is handsome; he isn't.

Paul is handsome. But it would be a lie to pretend then that he isn't attractive. Lily watches him swing himself up into the cab of his truck. He's very attractive, in the way that men of his type so often are. And in Lily's alarmingly fevered imagination there is no doubt about what type he is. *He works with his hands: a house painter, a garage mechanic; there is a six-pack of Bud in one of his shopping bags. He never went to college. He took and discarded a dozen girls, then married his high school sweetheart, had a bunch of kids, and settled down a stone's throw from where he grew up.* In one swift, competent maneuver, he cranes his neck, backs the long truck out of the parking space, pulls out of the lot, and peels out. To the left, toward the old part of town. Where the generations-old locals and the less well-off newcomers live.

Still, Lily doesn't move. Her last glimpse is of sunlight skidding off the curve of his arm as it emerges from the truck's open window to rest on the silver doorframe. She continues to see him in her mind's eye, cataloging and registering every detail, preparing her private testimony. She recalls his exposed stomach, and suddenly she is imagining drawing her tongue across the pale skin, down the smooth muscles until she finds the sharpness of his hip bones. His truck is fast disappearing down Route 5W. Lily sees her BMW parked next to it in the back lot of the shabby Creekside Motel four miles down the road, sees herself lying with him on a lumpy bed.

"Mrs. Spencer? Mrs. Spencer?"

Lily jerks erect as she hears her name and the sound of knocking on the closed driver's-side window. The interior of the car is stifling and lines of itchy sweat crawl down her back and between her breasts. In a daze, she completes the twist of her wrist and the car purrs to life. She opens the window and looks up into the peering face of one of the young bag boys.

"Oh. Peter."

"Hi. Sorry to disturb your daydreaming there, Mrs. Spencer, but you left your credit card in the store."

"Oh, my. Thank you."

"No sweat. Glad I caught you. Have a great weekend."

Lily puts her card away. She leans forward and rests her head against the steering wheel, waits for the car to cool down. Her breathing is a little ragged and the air she draws sticks in her throat. Nothing like that has ever happened to her before. Never has she looked at a total stranger and been catapulted into a raw, erotic fantasy so vivid she can all but taste him. And in the nine years she's been with Paul, she's never once entertained sexual thoughts about another man. Why would she? What in God's name was that all about? Stunned and a little frightened, holding the steering wheel with a fierce grip, Lily pulls out of Dreiser's lot. She turns right onto 5W and speeds off, in the opposite direction from the silver truck, toward the high ground of the wealthy side of town; but even as the miles between them grow, she feels him at her back.

5

DANNY IS RUNNING LATE and he takes the turn onto Old Stone Creek Road a little too fast. He hears one of the shopping bags fall out of the mesh basket in the back of the truck and he winces, hoping it wasn't the one with the eggs and peaches in it. He delivered George Copley's furniture and was kept there for an hour, Copley taking all that time to lavish on Danny his praise and thanks for Danny's skilled restoring of a family heirloom, an Edwardian highboy negligently left to molder in an attic for twenty-five years. Danny had worked on it for two painstaking months, given new life to an elegant piece of furniture, and made a lonely old man very happy. He spent more time at Dreiser's than he had intended as well, skulking in the aisles, halted and mystified by his hope of catching another glimpse of that woman.

He slows down on the winding, hilly road, heading north out of town. The first five miles are punctuated on either side by a string of housing developments with names like Birchwood Estates and Pine Run. The newest and last, the Willowbrook, is not yet completed and sits baking in the sun, a livid scar on the landscape. Its beckoning sales signs leer out from the churned-up dirt in front of a long, low stone wall meant to look like a relic of the Revolutionary War era and failing mightily. Once beyond it, however, the inevitable future cedes way to the clinging past. There is nothing yet but a scattering of old, neat houses widely set among the rolling fields and dense woods, all unchanged since Danny's childhood. Out here the air is cooler and clearer and he leans his head out the window like a happy dog, inhales the smell of grass and roses.

He drives past the house he grew up in. It is a rambling affair separated from the road by a sprawling lawn and a clean, white picket fence. His great-great-grandfather built the original core of that house back before the turn of the last century, when the first Malloys settled in this part of the state. Succeeding generations filled and expanded the house. But by the time Danny was born the family had been diminished by early death, barrenness, and exodus, reduced finally to just his parents and him, rattling around the big, old house. He left, too, for a while, and when he came back to bury his father, the house and the family's twenty-five acres of land belonged to him alone. He spent a year renovating the house, updating the wiring and the plumbing, modernizing the kitchen and bathrooms, putting in new hardwood floors, custom cabinets, built-in shelving, and wood-framed windows. Then he sold it, along with ten of the acres, to the first people who came to see it. He kept the other fifteen acres for himself. That was seven years ago, and he is still here.

Several hundred yards past the old house, he turns left into his driveway. Although the roadside is overgrown with thick, heavy shrubbery and overhanging trees, his driveway is impossible to miss, what with the shiny black-and-yellow striped, white-winged flying-bumblebee mailbox all but buzzing in the foliage at its head. Danny made it in strict accordance with Caleb's garish, immature vision, but Danny has to admit that he loves it. The truck crunches its way down the long gravel drive, through gradually thinning woods filled with the myriad colors of early summer and the sounds of songbirds. After five hundred feet the woods give out onto a large clearing that undulates away in all directions until it meets the surrounding woods again. In the forefront of the clearing is his house, 2,500 square feet of wood, glass, and stone open to the air and the sun and the sound of fast-running water coming from the woods beyond, from Stone Creek, the tripping current that provided the town its name.

The Volvo is parked out in front. It was Tara's college car. It's getting a little temperamental, but it still runs okay. There's a Princeton parking sticker on the rear bumper, faded now. Danny grunts in frustration as he drives by it. Once again, he forgot to take out Caleb's car seat and clean it of the spilled grape juice and mashed banana that resulted from Monday's little accident. He parks the truck around the back, between the house and his studio, and unloads the groceries through the unlocked back door into the kitchen.

A quick glance at the kitchen clock tells him that he has ten minutes before Caleb gets home from nursery school, enough time to get his snack ready before walking to the road to meet the school's private bus. Danny fills one of his son's plastic Pooh plates with ten bite-sized cubes of organic Cheddar cheese, five red grapes cut in half because Caleb likes to lick their watery surfaces before popping them in his mouth, and ten whole almonds. He smiles as he counts and cuts. Caleb has inherited his looks and his soft nature from Danny, but he has Tara's lightning fast intellect and her almost disdainful preference for strict order and mathematical symmetry in all things. He puts the plate on the kitchen table. He mixes up some chocolate milk in Caleb's favorite mug, the bright yellow-and-blue plastic dinosaur mug they bought at the Museum of Natural History. He puts the mug next to the plate. He quickly checks the answering machine. One message, and when he hears his mother-in-law's voice, he immediately hits the STOP button. He'll listen to it later, after Caleb is asleep.

He walks down the drive and is waiting by the mailbox when Caleb's teacher's minivan pulls up. A moment later Caleb flies out the door, his backpack bouncing and a piece of drawing paper bunched up in one hand.

"Daddeee!" Caleb flings himself at Danny's legs and wraps his thin, monkey arms around him.

"Hey." Danny bends and kisses the top of Caleb's head, then lays a protective hand over the spot where his lips had been. "Lauren, what are you doing driving the kids home?" Three more noisy children are strapped into the minivan's back seats.

"The battery in the bus died."

"Someone should have called me on my cell. I would have come to pick him up. You didn't have to drive all the way out here."

"I don't mind, really. It's not that far, and it's good to see you." She leans over the front passenger seat with a hopeful smile. Her long blond hair swings across her face.

Danny knows that Lauren would drive Caleb home every day if she could find an excuse to. So that if she saw him often enough and smiled hopefully often enough, he would ask her out. He likes her. But even if he liked her more, he wouldn't ask her out. She wants something he isn't ready for.

"Good to see you, too." There is nothing in his voice to encourage her. "Should I bring him to school tomorrow?"

"No. They're putting in a new battery this afternoon." Still she sits, smiling at him.

"Okay. Well, thanks. Take care." Danny waves at the kids in the back, takes Caleb's hand, and starts down the driveway.

The van door slams shut behind him and then comes the discontented sound of tires spinning on the gravel. They walk at Caleb's pace, Danny holding tight to his hand. As has been the case for the past month, they make it to the house, onto the porch, into Caleb's bedroom to put away his backpack and to-day's artwork, to the bathroom sink for the washing of hands, to the kitchen table for the eating of the cheese and grapes and almonds and milk, all without Caleb looking at him in childish misery and asking him if Mommy is coming home today. But Danny sees Caleb's drawing as the boy places it in the drawer of his child-sized desk, atop the other drawings he's done in the past year. He's the son of an artist and his drawings are remarkably well rendered for a boy who just last month turned five years old. This is another one of a boxy house with two small figures stand-ing together at a window and a third figure, much larger, in the air above the roof, where the others can't see it. Danny knows it's normal, that Caleb is searching for a way to cope with the loss of his mother. Danny knows it's good. But every time Caleb draws this one, Danny's heart misses a couple of beats.

It has been nearly a year since Caleb napped in the afternoons. Now, if he doesn't have a play date or if he isn't visiting his grandparents, he and Danny spend the time before dinner in the studio. Often he draws while Danny works, or creates elabo-rate setups with his dinosaurs, or plays with a toy or puzzle. But Danny knows that what Caleb likes best is helping his father.

Danny is perilously close to having more work than he can handle. He is defenseless and has ceded his ability to say no to the pointlessness of saving himself for anything besides Caleb and work. He is doing the finishing woodwork for two home renovations; there are several pieces of furniture in the studio in various stages of restoration; and he has taken on commissions for three pieces of his own design. Today Danny wants to make some progress on the glass mosaic tabletop that Mrs. Williams, a demanding but loyal customer, requested for the end of July. He assigns Caleb an important job, sorting the smooth-edged pieces of glass into colors and sizes, while he works on sketching the template for the table's design.

"What are we going to do, Dad?" Neat little piles of rain-bowed glass—blue, red, yellow, green, black—are already grow-ing, at equal rates, on the low counter.

"She wants something classic, something Roman-looking, she said." Danny kneels on the floor, a large sheet of sketch paper laid out in front of him, a pencil in his hand.

Caleb says, "I know what, let's do a horse, a head, like on those coins in that book."

Danny turns and looks at his son's mouth, his beautiful baby's mouth, lips pursed with purpose and deliberation as they work hard to form the correct adult words to express his precocious thoughts. Sometimes Danny just can't believe the things Caleb comes out with.

"Daddy? What do you think?"

Danny blinks and smiles. "Wow. What a great idea. But we can't. She doesn't want any animals."

Caleb looks back at him, disbelief widening his eyes, clear and light like Danny's. "She doesn't like animals?"

Danny winks at him. "She's a vegetarian."

Caleb grins. "That's funny, Daddy." He turns his head and continues sorting.

Danny watches him picking through the jewel-hued glass and says softly, "Be careful."

Caleb doesn't look at Danny. He just nods very slowly. "I will."

A little later, Danny feels small, strong arms come around his neck from behind, a small warm body press against his back. They stay like that for a few moments, quiet and snug together, and then they both go back to work.

Danny pours himself a glass of wine and, thus fortified, rewinds and plays the message from Eve. A knot forms in his stomach as her precise, imperious voice with its honey-sweet Southern lilt comes through the machine's tinny speaker. She doesn't identify herself; she doesn't have to. She doesn't begin with a friendly or respectful *Hello, Daniel,* but then she never does. She says what is on her mind, throws it down the line like a poison dart, and leaves it for him to pluck out of his flesh.

When you drop Caleb off on Monday you really must sign the application for the Harmony School, Daniel. The principal is holding a place for him, even though it's now frightfully late because of your stalling. The public school was adequate for you and your friends, but Caleb should be exposed to a better class of children and more educational options. Bring him here before eleven, please. We have tickets for the holiday puppet show and picnic at the club.

Eve has always referred to him as Daniel, never Danny. She is a cool and reserved woman, the sugar-slow lilting cadence of her voice at times in curious conflict with the formality of her words. But Danny is sure that she calls him Daniel not because it's his proper name but because she loathes everything that is Danny about him and doesn't want him to ever forget it. Before, every time she spoke his name it was to remind him of the damage he'd already done her daughter and to warn him he'd better not do any more. Since, it is to tell him that she blames him—unscientifically, illogically—and that now it is all about Caleb.

He erases the message, turns off the kitchen light, and stands in the dimness for a moment, his eyes closed, breathing deeply. Tara was thick-skinned and competitive and she did well at Harmony, although she didn't like it, didn't like passing through twelve years of her life in Stone Creek in a guarded bubble of privilege. Caleb wouldn't do well. He would hold his own academically, but he would be bruised and baffled by the harsh social order among the children of the wealthy, the elitism, the lack of diversity and acceptance. Danny and Tara talked about it and decided that he would go to the public school. It is a good school: modern, well funded, well staffed, and nurturing.

He brings the glass onto the porch and sinks into a wicker chair at the far, dark end, away from the light that spills from the living room windows. He removes his cell phone from his pocket and puts it on the glass-topped rattan table. Summer insects call to one another and from somewhere in the distance comes the mysterious sound of an owl's breathy hoot. He leans his head against the chair back and for a brief but necessary moment allows a curling wave of frustration and self-pity to tumble him. Then he sits up and blots his eyes with the hem of his T-shirt. He sips his wine.

The cell phone rings, a harsh, invasive sound, and the vibration from the ringing rattles the small phone against the glass. He snatches it up. He knows it isn't Eve again; she never calls his cell, only the home phone, only during the day. Too much chance otherwise that she might actually get him, have to talk to him directly. When he sees the number of the caller, he quickly thumbs the phone on.

"Danny boy, how's it hangin'?"

"Beats the hell out of me, Will."

"You'll have to do better than that. You don't sound good. Bad day?"

Danny shrugs in the dark. "No, not really. I'm getting ready for a final face-off with Eve and Lester about Caleb's school. She just won't quit about it. I'm tired, Will, that's all." His voice falters a little. He can't help it. He is tired. Tired of feeling that his life has been forever reduced to one unspeakable day and its endless aftermath.

"I know. I know what you're saying, Danny. But listen to me. You've got to get your life started again. Really. She wouldn't want you going on like this."

His gaze unfocused, Danny looks off into the stand of oak and beech beyond his front yard. "I'm living, Will. I'm working. I'm taking care of Caleb. I have moments of happiness. Life goes on."

"You know what I mean, Danny."

Danny groans. "No, you're too subtle. Yeah, I know what you mean."

"What about Lauren? She's cute. Take her to dinner. What's the harm in that?"

"I don't want to take Lauren to dinner. I don't want to take anyone to dinner."

In the spaces between the trees, elongated shadow shapes sway like dancers. With a sudden leap of his heart, without wishing it, he recalls the woman he saw in Dreiser's earlier in the day. She looked like a dancer, petite and graceful, in tight black capri pants, a well-filled-out white halter top, delicate ballet-slipper shoes. Her dark hair was swept up in a ponytail, and she wore little gold hoops in her ears.

He gives a low laugh. "You want to hear something funny?"

"From you, most definitely."

"I saw someone today, in the store. A stranger. I didn't talk to her, she didn't even see me. But I'm sitting here thinking about her. I don't want to ask Lauren out, but I felt like I wanted to know that woman."

"Hallelujah, it's about time. Go back to the store, find out who she is. Track her down."

"No. That's not the point. I'm not going to track her down. She's probably married and nothing like what I imagine."

What he imagines. What does he imagine? What does he think he saw when he looked at her? A creaminess, a richness that had nothing to do with her evident wealth but everything to do with the way she held herself, the way she moved. With the way she took in everything around her with wide-open dark eyes. With the sound of her delighted, girlish laugh when the voice coming through her cell phone said something that amused her; the sad loss of her delight when the voice said something that upset her and anger stiffened her back. He noticed her with an aching acuity and for the first time in all this time he was betrayed by a yearning for a contact that was more than physical, more than temporary. And now he can't deny what else he saw in her, what the shapes in the shadows make him think of, what he imagines. He sees Tara, he is imagining Tara. Imagining a dark-haired, dark-eyed woman, small, curvy, and delicate, quick to show her emotions, holding nothing back. He pictures her walking down the aisles, stretching up, bending down, talking on her phone, and although she is older and has a different face and a different voice, the woman reminds him of Tara.

"How do you know *what* she is if you don't even try to find out?" Will cajoles.

"Will, I'm telling you. She was talking to someone on her cell who pissed her off in the way only husbands know how to do. She's married to some loaded city guy and lives in a big house out Kensington Ridge Road with hundreds of thousands of dollars of landscaping and an enormous kidney-shaped pool in the backyard." Danny imagines more. She belongs to the club and plays golf and tennis. The young pros ogle her in her brief shorts and tops and flirt with her in a semiserious way but she doesn't see them—just as she hadn't seen him today—and she doesn't respond to their flirting. She plays to win, and she blows Eve into the clubhouse. That last thought brings him some small pleasure.

"Leave me alone with this, okay? I just want to try and let myself feel what she made me feel. I can't think about anything else. It hasn't even been a year." But in six weeks it will be.

Will is quiet for a moment. "Okay. It's a good first step. Let yourself feel what's coming to you, Danny, don't kill it with guilt." He pauses again. "Danny. Next month, when . . . If you need anything, if you need to be with friends, you know Sue and I are here for you."

"I know. I know you are, and I appreciate it."

"Okay. And one more thing. I've said this before but it's worth repeating. You don't have to put up with this shit from your in-laws. I know why you do, and I respect you for it, it's admirable. But listen to the voice of experience. It's going to become a problem. For you and for Caleb. When you're ready to deal with it, let me know. I'm very good at what I do and we can get serious limits put on their visitation rights if they don't behave themselves, believe me."

"Thanks. But I'm still hoping it will work itself out. I'm sure no one's going to want things to get to that point. Hey, you feel like going hiking on Monday?"

"Sure. Sue won't miss me. Harriman Park or the Gunks for some rock climbing?"

"Let's do the Gunks. I won't be able to worry about Eve while I'm dangling off the side of a mountain."

Danny replaces the phone on the tabletop. He finishes his wine. After a time his mind and body become slightly anesthetized and everything inside him sinks into stillness. He knows he should get up and go to bed, but he knows he won't make it farther than the couch. Tonight has become one of those nights when the emptiness of the chair beside him, the absence of her voice in his ears, the words dying in his throat, are just too much, and there is nothing he can do about it.

He puts his glass in the kitchen sink, goes to check on Caleb. He gently pulls the boy's thumb from his mouth and tucks the damp hand under the covers. He moves a mound of stuffed animals away from Caleb's face, angelic in unbreachable five-year-old sleep. On a number of nights after Tara died, Danny slept on the floor by Caleb's bed. He'd wake up to find himself in bed with Caleb or Caleb on the floor with him. He can't slip too far down when he's with his son. Danny's love of life may have dimmed, but his love for Caleb flares more brightly than ever. He can see Tara in its glow. Danny bends and kisses the pointy tip of Caleb's ear.

He avoids his own bedroom, washes his face and brushes his teeth at the sink in the hall bathroom. He peels off his clothes, leaves them hanging on a hook behind the bathroom door. He turns off the lights in the living room, lies down on the couch, and covers himself with the cotton quilt. He doesn't want to close his eyes. Images of intolerable beauty and indelible horror lurk behind his lids. The shadows have swayed and danced their way into the house and perform for him in the corners of the room, lit by a high moon spilling its light through the row of clerestory windows above him. A lone, forlorn audience, he peers deeply into the shadows in the hope that they might transport him somewhere where the images won't find him. After an unknowable amount of time, he falls asleep.

6

T WENTY-FIVE YEARS AGO there hadn't been one house on Kensington Ridge Road. Actually, there hadn't been a Kensington Ridge Road back then, just Kensington Ridge, a rising swell of shale and schist that, continuing on to the northwest, eventually bled into the foothills of the Catskill Mountains. The ridge had been traversed by a narrow, rutted, well-used dirt road, braved by hunters, agents of the forest service, and hormonally haywire adolescents, all in search of a primitive experience of the Divine. It wasn't until the first of a succeeding flood of small and mid-sized companies discovered that they could relocate from New York City to the gentler, cheaper counties nearby and take the best of their workforce with them that the dirt road acquired a name, a two-lane width, and a covering of asphalt. It was called Kensington Ridge Road after what it had always been, because calling it what it quickly became—Executive Mansion Ridge Road—didn't have that bucolic ring to it. Before long, the town being a reasonable commute from the city and well along the path to rural sophistication, Stone Creek additionally became a second-home haven for people with money who wanted some sleepy country—sleepy but civilized—as a counterpart to their frantic urban lives.

The Spencers' house, with its five acres of manicured land, sits upon the very peak of Kensington Ridge Road, on the highest ground in all of the incorporated township of Stone Creek. The property commands sweeping views of the countryside, of fields and woods and streams and even a small lake off in the distance, and it is hard to believe that it is a mere eight miles from Stone Creek's quaint, two-hundred-year-old village center. In the months of full foliage, none of the other houses that dot the ridge or nestle in the wooded hillsides are visible from the house or grounds; in the bare months, picturesque rooftops and smoking chimneys peek through denuded branches. The house itself is a 4,800-square-foot gem, thoughtfully designed and skillfully built, unpretentious and thoroughly livable. An understated twelve-room ultramodern white-shingled, green-shuttered farmhouse full of light and charm. It is *the* property in all the township. Six years earlier, the area Realtors warred like hyenas among themselves to get an exclusive listing from the seller, the CEO of an investment firm that had decided to relocate once again, this time to Arizona. The victorious hyena's husband happened to be the cousin of one of Paul's law partners. Lily loved it, Paul wanted her to have it, he made an unrefusable cash offer, and the deal closed in three weeks.

It's late Sunday afternoon, the holiday weekend is passing quickly. Paul has been as true to his promise as is possible for him; after being holed up with the hermitically sequestered Serge and Ira since 6:00 a.m., he emerged from his office around two o'clock, bleary-eyed and distracted and happy as a clam. It is not hard to discern the effort it's costing him to not renege, to not make a perfunctory apology and disappear again until dinner. This is the kind of case he lives for: a muscular winner-takes-all case involving revoltingly immoral and blatantly stupid behavior among people who should know better, a game of hide-and-seek played with billions of dollars, the fate of one of the tech field's corporate giants on the line. Thousands of SynTech employees and shareholders, an incensed and fed-up public, the business media vultures—not to mention corporate wrongdoers every-where—all avidly watching the show. And the one thing, the only thing, that everyone is likely to agree on is that SynTech's board made a brilliant defensive move in hiring Chaikin-Gibbs and its uncompromisingly ethical megabrain managing partner.

As Lily watches Paul at the wet bar built into the outdoor mini-kitchen talking to Chuck—undoubtedly about the case, one lawyer to another—and mixing up a pitcher of margaritas, she can see how happy he is. Anyone could. But she sees some-thing that no one else does. He is not just happy, he is relieved. She can practically feel his relief coming off him in waves and racing toward her across the lawn. A veritable tsunami of relief. He has been handed an unassailable alibi for his whereabouts as he is about to go AWOL from conventional life and thus from her and her moodiness and the tension it is causing. She can hardly blame him. After all, she is relieved, too, although her re-lief is, as it should be, impure and feels like grit, like gravel under her skin, whereas his, she is sure, feels simply like relief to him.

Lily is watching Paul from inside the gazebo, a delicately carved wooden octagonal confection Paul had built for her a few years after they'd bought the house. It is set on a rise of ground well beyond the flowerbeds that divide the pool and deck from the backyard. She is there waiting for Rick to join her so that he can finally talk to her about whatever it is that's been making him nervous all weekend and unable to meet her eye for more than the occasional doleful glance. He has always tended to be a worrier and so, as she sees him coming across the lawn, she prepares herself to be reassuring and calming. She and Rick, at least, have always been kind to each other, despite everything.

She stands as he steps up into the gazebo, puts her hands on his shoulders, and kisses him lightly on both cheeks, in the European fashion. It makes him smile at her for the first time in two days, which was her intention. There is an unspoken message in her kissing him that way. What began as a youthful affectation shared by two insecure college kids wanting to appear worldly has since become a soothing ritual greeting. It serves to remind them of the longevity and tenacity of their friendship.

Before they sit, Lily rubs her hand playfully over Rick's shaved scalp and its patchy grey-brown fuzz. His eyes turn upward and he says, "I'm ready for a trim. It's getting long."

"Yes. It must be at least one thirty-second of an inch. You'll be happy to know that I think I'm starting to like you without hair."

"I'm cautiously ecstatic. You *will* notify me when you're sure."

"Oh, go to hell." Lily laughs. "Learn to take a compliment."

"Thank you. I think."

Rick has brought two glasses of chilled white wine with him. He hands her one and they sit, side by side, and sip. They look out at the bright summer landscape. They spent a great deal of their time together not talking and they are used to it. But this is not a comfortable silence.

"The garden looks positively fabulous after all that spring rain. I particularly love what you've done with that perennial bed. Those orange poppies just pull it all together."

Lily puts her glass down on the bench seat. "Okay, Rick. Out with it. You don't want to talk to me about poppies, lovely though they are. Would you please tell me what's going on?"

He nods. He is still not looking at her. "There's something I've got to talk to you about, without everyone else around."

"Of course," Lily says. "Rick, you're not ill or anything?"

"No, no. Nothing like that." He pulls on his left earlobe, an old nervous habit. "I'm a little worried about how you're going to take what I have to say."

"Darling. You were worried when you told me you were leaving me for someone named Alan, and I took that rather well, as I recall." She says this drily and with humor, although it was not all that funny when it happened sixteen years ago. When Rick doesn't even smile, she leans playfully into his shoulder. "Do you know that until the day she died my mother harbored the belief that I made you gay? Because I didn't give you what you needed in bed."

Lily sits up and masks her natural sympathetic expression with one of unforgiving censure. In uncanny imitation of Ada Margolies's pinched, world-weary voice, she whines, "What did you do to him? Why would such a brilliant, good-looking Jewish boy, a doctor no less and from the Bronx, become a fegele? I told you, you were always cold, Lily. It's no wonder."

Rick's attention is riveted on her and now he smiles, albeit a bit warily. "Wow. That was scary. What, is she, like, insulting people through you now?"

Lily laughs. "You know the saddest thing, though? Until I met Paul, I thought she was right. You were the only boy I'd ever slept with and I was terrible at it. And I was terrible at it with everyone who came after you."

"Duh. Hello. We were terrible at it because I was gay and

wished I were screwing some Tom, Dick, or Harry. Which I was during the last two years when I wasn't incompetently screwing you anymore. And you weren't sexually attracted to me in the first place. That was your thing, Lily, running from the guys who actually turned you on. Until Paul, of course. The one irresistible force in your life. For better or worse."

"That was an unnecessary qualifier, if I may say so." Her brows lift in feigned annoyance.

Rick shrugs. "When you get older, you're allowed to say what you really feel."

"You're not that old," she says pointedly.

They smile at each other and their eyes automatically drift toward the object of their contention. As if on cue, Paul chooses that moment to cross the deck to where Mona and Chuck's daughter, Lisa, lies sprawled on a chaise in the full afternoon sun. He is bringing her a very grown-up-looking cocktail glass filled with fruit juice. He has stuck one of those tiny paper Polynesian cocktail umbrellas into a piece of pineapple and it floats above the rim. With a flourish, he puts it down on the table next to her. She pops up and yelps "Oooh, Uncle Paul!" loudly enough for Lily and Rick to hear. Paul bows to her and then heads for the deep end of the pool. He sheds his khaki pants and white shirt as he goes, until he is down to a black Speedo, and he dives in. Rick and Lily track the arc of his body as it enters the water without a splash; they watch his dark head and long arms flash in and out of the sunlight dappling the pool. They sigh in unison.

"An irritatingly likable and very sexy man, your husband, for a domineering, self-absorbed control freak."

"I quite agree." She watches Paul swim, watches the water sliding away from him as he pushes through it with steady, strong movements of his arms and legs.

Rick chuckles, then turns to look at her. "Jesus, Lily, I don't know how you could have thought for one second that it was your fault we didn't stay together. We only got married out of fear. When are you going to stop blaming yourself for everything?"

There is a flub-dub of her heart when in her mind she hears him say *When are you going to stop being afraid* instead of what he does say. She turns back to him. "Oh, I don't know. Maybe when Papa Max dies and there's no one left to remind me of my guilt."

"That might not be for a long time. I think bile is keeping him alive. Please don't wait."

"Bile, the lovely Sylvia, and, according to my father, his daily grapefruit, the elixir of life. My mother couldn't get him to sit in the sun or eat a piece of fruit for love or money, but for Sylvia he moves to Florida and eats a grapefruit every morning." She smiles ruefully. "Go know. All right. Enough. Look me in the eye and tell me what you have to tell me."

Rick takes her hands and looks her in the eye. "Lily. Alan and I are adopting a baby."

Lily doesn't appear to move but her eyes vibrate, her hands twitch in his, and her lips part slightly. She doesn't say a word.

"Lily, say something, please."

She smiles like a puppet and says, "Well, it's a shock, of course. But a lovely one. It's lovely, just lovely." Her voice is bright with incredulity.

"Save that for later. Say something honest. Say how unfair it is. Tell me you hate me."

Lily turns her head and slowly disengages her hands, which have gone cold in Rick's warm grasp. She takes up her glass again. "Don't be absurd. I don't hate you. I'm delighted for you. How are you going to do it?"

"We've been working for a year with an agency in Texas.

They say they'll have a baby for us within the next few months. Probably a Mexican or mixed-race baby." Though there is no one near enough to hear them, Rick lowers his voice. "Lily, you can't not be upset by this. It's me. Who are you trying to fool?"

Lily's heart balloons inside her chest. She feels like she's going to gag. She drinks some wine. She pats Rick's cheek. "You are so melodramatic. Rick, I'm not trying to fool anyone. Honestly, I'm not upset. A little surprised, perhaps. That you didn't tell me sooner and that you want to be a father. You didn't when we were together."

"I waited to tell you because if it wasn't going to work out, there was no reason for you to know anything. And it's Alan who wants it. I'm not really sure how I feel. Decades of treating sick and traumatized kids in the ER have left me kind of gun-shy to have one of my own."

"You still worry too much." The sounds of Paul lapping the pool are as clear as if she were sitting on the deck next to him and not a hundred feet away. "But you're doing it anyway. For Alan." Lily can't keep the tremor from her voice.

"Yes. Because he wants it badly enough for both of us. And because I love and trust him and he believes it will be all right. You and I never had children for obvious reasons, Lily, but if you had ever actually asked me, I would have done it." Rick looks across the lawn toward the pool. "I would have done it for you." He looks back at her. "Did you and Paul ever discuss the possibility of adopting, after he decided you weren't going to keep trying?"

Lily stands up. Wine spills onto the floor of the gazebo. "Yes, Rick. We did. Of course we did. And you know we stopped trying because it wasn't working." Lily's brain is going numb. She is never going to have a baby to raise and love, but her gay ex-husband is.

Rick is on his feet now, too. He opens his mouth to say something else but then closes it.

"Rick, please." She smiles, kisses his cheek. "Believe me, I am happy for you. You and Alan will make wonderful parents."

"I think we probably will, too. But we want you to have a meaningful role in this child's life, Lily. Girl or boy, it's going to need a woman."

"Well, yes. We'll see. We'll see what happens."

"Yeah. There'll be time to work that out." He takes her hand and tugs at it gently. "Come on, let's go take a swim. It'll clear our heads."

"You go. I'll be along in a minute."

He hesitates for a second and then says, "Alan and I can leave tonight if it would be easier for you."

"No! Of course not. What are you talking about? You're not going anywhere." She hands Rick her empty glass. "Tell Paul to pour me a margarita. I'll be right there."

Lily should not stay there with her arms wrapped around a supporting pole of the gazebo. She should go with Rick and resume her role in the family play being enacted on the stage of her backyard, with its clever set of free-form gunite pool with gently trickling waterfall, expansive multilevel mahogany decking, expensive charming house in the background. Gracious hostess, doting aunt, understanding ex, admiring older sister, forgiving and thankful wife, overall good sport good friend good girl. But she is suffering such a dizzying sense of dislocation that she has missed her prompt. And her eyes are filling with tears. They do that so often lately; they are untrustworthy, they have become a cracking dam struggling to hold back a reservoir swollen with tears. So she is compelled to remain in the wings and watch.

Mona and Alan are laughing together, safely flirting with each other, as they open and tilt the two market umbrellas on either end of the outdoor dining table and start setting it for dinner. Chuck is chasing Joshua, his blue-lipped, shivering son, around the deck, letting the boy's prancing keep him just beyond his father's grasp. Lisa deserts her sun-blasted chaise and her copy of *Teen Scene Magazine* to stand in her bone-dry bikini with her hip cocked, petulant and terribly put-upon by the disgusting male noise and tumult; after a moment she reverts to the eleven-year-old child she is and flounces off to help her mother fold napkins. Rick squats down by the deep end of the pool, waits for Paul to complete his lap, says something to him, and then continues on toward the house. Paul looks in Lily's direction and pulls himself out of the water. He puts his pants on over his wet suit, his wet skin. He goes to the bar, rims a cocktail glass in salt, adds some ice cubes, takes the pitcher of margaritas from the mini-fridge, and fills the glass.

A full stage, a satisfying amount of action, a goodly complement of players. Lily's character is missing, of course, and from the perspective of her distant remove she sees yet another gaping absence in the cast. There should be a toddler. As comic relief, perhaps. Somewhere amid all that sizable flesh and bone there should be something about three feet tall with outstretched chubby arms and pumping chubby legs and wild dark foolish hair, alternately ignored or avidly gathered up, stumbling after everyone and trailing gleeful laughter. There should be their child. But all there is is the shadow that only she can see.

Paul starts across the lawn toward the gazebo. Paul. Her irresistible force. Rick is right. That's what he was. That's what he is. He comes toward her the way he did that night at Chuck and Mona's, his eyes on her, making for her like a heat-seeking missile. His skin gleams red-brown in the lowering sun. He told her once that when he was a child he'd imagined he was part American Indian; looking at him now she wonders if he was right. She loves his rich-colored skin. She loves the muscle and bone beneath it. She loves him. But not the way she used to.

"Rick said you wanted a drink." Paul smiles down at her and holds out the sweating glass. "Are you okay?"

"I'm fine. Thank you, it looks delicious." She takes a sip. It is delicious. He makes his drinks the way he makes coffee, with skilled, controlled aggression, so that they will kick ass as they are meant to. It's the way he does everything.

"What were you two talking about?"

She wants to love him the way she loved him when they met, the way she loved him until the day he pulled the ground from beneath her feet and left her hanging there all alone. "I'll tell you later." But she doesn't know how she can, and if she can't she doesn't know what will happen.

His dark eyes glitter in the slanting light. It occurs to her that they look like Blinkie Floyd's eyes looked in the kitchen light, shiny with concern. She doesn't want to see it, it demands a response and she has none to give. She lowers her gaze from his face. She caresses his arm. "You're cold, from the pool. You should change. You'll get chilled."

"I will." He takes her face in his hands and kisses her, softly. Twice, three times. His lips linger on hers and their breaths quicken. "Lily," he whispers, "I love you. Do you still love me?"

He has the lawyer's uncanny knack for asking his punchline question at the ideal moment for eliciting the response he is looking for. "Oh, Paul." It's a yielding sigh, a little mew of a sound. "Of course I love you. What a question."

"I wouldn't be doing my job if I didn't ask. If I didn't get all the facts."

She groans as though at a bad pun and shakes her head inside the gentle restraint of his fingers.

"I'm not going back to work after dinner. Let's leave our guests to their own devices and get to bed early."

Her heart is beating hard in her chest. She raises her eyes and his are dark magnets drawing at her resistance. One hand is going numb with cold from the icy glass, the other is tingling with heat from the feel of his flesh. She rises up onto her toes and finds his mouth again.

It's not as though she wasn't warned about him. She most certainly was. Not once, not twice, but three times in rapid succession on that fateful night.

Warning number one, the pre-introduction warning, was from Mona, Lily's outrageous-flake-turned-überwife-and-mother of a little sister: *That's the infamous Paul Spencer, over there, the tall dark handsome guy talking to the blonde in the black dress. He's already spotted you. He's going to hit on you, I guarantee it, as soon as he figures out that you're the prettiest woman in the room. For Chuck's sake, don't be cold, Lily, okay? Like you always are to good-looking men who hit on you? Be pleasant, but don't let him get too cozy with you either, or he'll move right in. He's a major Don Juan.*

Warning number two, the post-introduction, mid-seduction warning, was from Chuck, Mona's surprisingly serious, conventional, reliable, respectable husband, upon spotting her transfixed in the corner of the room where Paul had just left her: *Oh lord, you've met Paul, I see. Listen, Lilykins, he's a great guy, an incredible guy, actually. But he's way hard on women, not very . . . good at intimacy, shall we say, definitely not long-term relationship material. He's not for you, trust me, you don't have the cyni-*

cism it takes to handle someone like him. If he asks you out, just say no thanks. He won't fire me.

Warning number three, after the terrifying kiss on the terrace, was from some woman she didn't even know who waylaid her outside Chuck and Mona's powder room: *Honey, you don't know me and this may be none of my business, but be smart and take a little friendly advice. Stay away from Paul Spencer. Believe me, it's not worth what you're going to feel when he dumps you.*

I guarantee it; trust me; believe me. The problem was, they all warned her about the wrong thing.

Paul Spencer, Master of the Universe, Chaikin-Gibbs's newly named managing partner. Litigator. Shark. Inveterate bachelor. Womanizer. Predator. Wolf. He looked like a wolf when she first saw him, staring at her from out of black, hooded eyes. With his long, bony body and strong, bony face, his stare fixed and penetrating. He was fifty feet away, across the full length of the living room of Mona and Chuck's TriBeCa loft, a crowd of people between them, but he captured her eye as though there was nothing but air separating them and began moving toward her. Mona's words repeated themselves in her ears as she saw him coming and she grew woozy with fearful anticipation of doing something that might embarrass Chuck. Or at least she told herself it was from fearful anticipation and not from her inability to take her eyes off him as he came nearer and nearer.

It was the last dinner party the Golds gave before they moved to D.C. Chuck was thirty-five and had just made partner at Chaikin-Gibbs; Paul was his mentor, his idol, and with Paul's support he'd gotten the transfer to the Washington office that he wanted. Chuck and Mona didn't usually mix business colleagues with friends and family at their gatherings, but this was a special occasion.

"Hello. I'm Paul Spencer, I don't think we've met."

She took his proffered hand. His fingers were long and slender and strong and he held her hand captive in his a beat longer than he should have.

"Hello. No, we haven't. I'm Lily Milstein." In response to his questioning arch of the brow, she added, "Mona's sister, Chuck's sister-in-law?"

"Ah. Milstein, not Margolies. You're married."

"Divorced. Some time ago."

He smiled with blatant pleasure at the clarification. She blushed.

"I should fire Chuck for not introducing us before this."

"Please don't. I'm sure he was just protecting me, since I have no husband to do that for me," she teased.

"Do you need protection?"

"From what I understand, all women need protection from you. You have quite a reputation, Mr. Spencer."

He gave a little grunt of a laugh. "It's Paul, please. And people tend to exaggerate. I just haven't met the right woman yet."

She rewarded him with a slant-eyed, disbelieving smile. It wasn't as difficult as she thought, being charming and flirtatious with someone like him. It was just a game. He was good at it and he made it easy for her to be good at it. It was like playing tennis doubles with a stronger partner who naturally elevated the level of the weaker partner's play. She found zinging shots inside herself she didn't know she possessed.

"And would you know the right woman if you did meet her?"

She waited for his next clever line. But it didn't come. He just looked at her and looked at her, until all the humor faded from his eyes and her smile wobbled and collapsed and then he said, "Yes. I think I would."

Someone came to borrow him then, a matter of business. He slowly backed away from her and said, "Don't go away." Then he smiled disarmingly at her muteness and added, "Please." He was gone a good half hour and the entire time he watched her from amid the changing groupings that surrounded him, so many people vying for his attention. She stood in the corner—there was nowhere she could go now—and tried to not look back. She heard again Mona's and now Chuck's words of caution, but they were neatly decimated by the constancy of his intense, dark gaze, replaced by a heavily accented, impish voice in her head telling her, *Resistance is futile.* She began to laugh. She gave up and looked straight at him and he smiled at her, a confident, un-quizzical smile, as though he knew exactly what it was that had amused her.

He came back to her and took her out onto the terrace. It was January but not impossibly cold, and the sky was hard and black-bright with stars and there was moonlight on the Hudson River, and he stood in such a way as to shield her and warm her with his own heat. They talked, about whatever it is two people talk about when they are spellbound and the world around them has faded to drabness. About Lily growing up in New York, Paul in Michigan. Her years at Barnard and Columbia, his at Ann Arbor and Harvard Law. Lily told him about her family, how she felt like a failure in her parents' eyes, how close she was with Mona despite all the ways in which they were unalike. Paul told her about his career, how much he loved his work. They compared places they'd been, things they loved, things they didn't. When she told him about her work—assisting families who were grappling with the trauma of a terminal illness or a failing elder by guiding them through the morass of doctors, hospitals, insurance companies, social workers (a private career that grew out of a year spent managing her mother's death)—Paul grew completely still for a moment and then said, "Where do you find the compassion to do that?" She answered, "From the people I help. They're all special." He looked at her in fascination and said, "I think perhaps it's you who's special." Then he drew one finger along the side of her face, murmured, "You're so beautiful," took her face in both his hands, and kissed her.

It was a simple kiss. A serious kiss that didn't know when or how to end. And so it went on and on until one of his hands crept like a silken spider from her cheek to the back of her neck, and along the short journey one slender finger found its way briefly into the delicate opening of her ear and Lily split apart. From her toes to her eyes, she split apart and screamed softly with the shock of it. The kiss ended then. As she pulled away from him, Lily saw something reaching for her from behind his dark, heavy eyes, and although she had been warned all about him, and not yet for the last time, she knew it to be an eruption of hope and fear. When he asked her to have dinner with him the following Saturday, she said yes. An immediate, incautious yes.

It wasn't until after their sixth date, some four weeks later, that he took her to bed. By then they were so delirious, so inflamed with passion for each other, that the first time was over too quickly. But they made up for it during the course of the night and by morning Lily had given up counting the number of her orgasms; given up despairing that it had taken so long to find the man who could release such wildness in her, whose confident devoted ardor gradually unearthed her own; given up fearing what she would do if she couldn't make love to Paul for the rest of her life. She was crazed and blinded with love for him; he had stolen her sanity. As they lay for the moment quiet and exhausted in each other's arms, Lily remembered what the woman outside the powder room had said to her. She knew it couldn't be true. There couldn't be anything, anything, that wasn't worth being the one Paul Spencer loved and needed.

It's the middle of the night. The house is alive with gentle nocturnal creakings as its inhabitants, all but one, serenely slumber inside its sheltering walls. It's warm, it's going to be a hot summer, but the air-conditioning is off in Paul and Lily's bedroom suite and the windows are open. There is almost always a breeze up here on top of the ridge, and, besides, they enjoy making love in the heat. Paul is on his side, one arm flung out and lying heavily on the mattress now that Lily has carefully slid herself out from under it. She has drawn a light cotton robe around herself and is sitting, knees to chest, on the thick cushion lining the bay window. She can't sleep.

Paul never did ask a second time what she and Rick talked about. The conversation is running in an endless loop in her head but she has somehow managed to forget to tell Paul about it. She watches the regular, minuscule movements of her beloved husband's back as he breathes; that long back so sleek and hard inside the urgent grip of her arms and legs. Earlier, while she'd lain awake pinned under the weight of his arm and listened to the whisperings of her dreaming house, she decided not to go back to the city after the long weekend. She wants to spend the summer here at the house in Stone Creek. She needs a change, time alone somewhere quiet. Paul will be so busy with the SynTech case he won't miss her, anyway. She'll tell him in the morning. He can come up on weekends, as he did the last time. But she knows it won't be like that summer, nothing again will ever be like that summer. Records were set for the most days of unseasonably cold weather from June through August since 1937, but it was the hottest summer of their lives.

The wide curved bedroom window faces out over the valley that lies between the ridge and the village. From this high up Lily can see the gently rolling hills of the land on the far side of town, coolly limned in the moonlight. Something else has been looping through her head since the conversation in the gazebo, a charged visual and visceral accompaniment to her and Rick's charged dialogue. It is as unwanted and as firmly embedded and as impossible to make sense of as what Rick said to her. It's a memory of that man, Paul's opposite, that fair-haired, light-eyed, pale-skinned man. And now, as she looks out into the night, in the direction of his disappearing truck, she thinks, *That man is out there*. He is out there, sleeping in a bed somewhere not far from where she sits, awake, thinking about him. There is a woman sleeping by his side, or maybe she is awake, too, watching him sleep and growing weak with love at the sight of him while she thinks about her life, lets fly thoughts that she will call back to her in the morning and won't share with him when he wakes. She wonders who he really is, why he was watching her, why he looked at her the way he did, why she felt what she felt when she looked at him. Why she is thinking about him at all.

7

Five hours of rapturous brainlessness and brutal physical exertion has had its usual salubrious effect on Danny's state of mind. There is tremendous benefit in the impossibility of thinking about anything other than not doing something dumb and killing yourself when you're rock-climbing. You really can't dilute your attention to the job at hand wishing your mother-in-law would disappear, as heartily as you might like to.

He's on his way home from dropping Will off. The breeze blowing through the truck's open windows has dried the salty sweat on his skin and his muscles ache in that hard-used way he loves. He drives past Schiller's Farm Stand and sees Carol Schiller, née Tompkins, with one of her little girls hanging on to her skirt. She's carrying a flat of strawberries out to a customer's car. Her heart had mended by spring of that long-ago year and by the time Danny left for London she was engaged to John Schiller. The three of them had become friends and when Danny returned home seven years later, their friendship resumed as though no time had passed, as had his friendship with Will Pollack, unshakably solid since second grade.

Danny hasn't seen Carol and John in weeks, he's been turning down their invitations to dinner, but today he's glad to be alive and he's missing them. He puts the truck into a squealing U-turn, spends a few moments talking with Carol, then drives away with three quarts of lush local strawberries on the seat next to him. He and Caleb will be spending part of tomorrow putting up jam. The sweet smell of the berries is driving him crazy; half a quart finds its way into his stomach before he finds the turn into his driveway.

He is still full of energy, but he doesn't have a lot of time before he has to get Caleb so he doesn't open the studio. There is plenty to keep him busy. The flowerbeds behind the house are full of weeds, the bird feeders are nearly empty, the lawn is threatening to become unkempt. An hour later, his nails crusted with dirt, his skin flecked with specks of grass, and his stomach still full of strawberries, Danny is lying on his back in the sun, on the pungent mowed lawn, drifting into unconsciousness. The sound of the creek washes over him and bears him downstream. *Danny. Danny. Take me down to the creek. I want to make love with you in the water. I want to feel you all wet and slippery when I hold you.*

Danny opens his eyes. His heart is hammering and he is blanketed in sweat. He could let the day go dark. Despite the indisputable fact of the sun strong and hot on his face he could let his bright day go dark with the memory of what he's lost. He desperately does not want that to happen. He wants to get through one entire day feeling as good as he's felt today. There will be other days when he won't manage it, but today he believes he can. He feels strong enough to hold her that close. He gets up and walks back to the house. The sun is still shining. The day is still bright.

He almost decides not to shower and change before he goes to get Caleb, knowing that the sight of him in such a rank and primordial state will drive Eve to an early martini. But that's just childish, and he's not a child, although Eve rouses a powerful urge in him to revert to arm-flailing immaturity. He showers and puts on clean clothes and gets in the Volvo and drives across town to the Jamisons' house at the east end of Kensington Ridge Road.

When he walks into the kitchen, Caleb is sitting at the round glass table licking the last of a bowl of rocky road ice cream with caramel sauce off his spoon. There is a trail of watery brown liquid on the clear glass and a drying blob of brown on his yellow polo shirt. He's too sunburned and there's a sugar-doped glaze over his eyes. Eve is sitting at the table as well, one manicured hand resting on the Harmony School application, still there on the table, exactly where it was when Danny walked out nine hours earlier. Muffled noises come from the den, evidence that Lester is in there watching something on the enormous wall-mounted plasma-screen TV.

Danny doesn't see much of Lester. For the past twenty-five years, Lester has been the administrative director of the generously endowed Mid-Hudson Medical Complex outside Newburgh, thirty minutes to the northeast, with satellite clinics spread over two counties. Every weekday he leaves Stone Creek early and gets back late. Since Tara died, Lester's weekends consist of activities meant to occupy his time and his attention as fully as work does his weekdays. Saturday mornings it's golf or, in the off-season, indoor tennis; afternoons and evenings it's subdued social drinking at the club, dinner with his wife and friends, an early lights-out. Sundays it's church and Tara's grave, then a mind-numbing afternoon in front of the TV. He makes sure he spends time with Caleb when the boy comes to visit, but mostly he leaves his grandson in his wife's hands. His son-in-law he leaves entirely in his wife's hands, although he is always polite to Danny when he sees him, and there have been hints, especially in the past year, that if Eve weren't there to disabuse him of the idea, Lester might find something to like in the man his daughter chose to marry.

Danny doesn't sit. Eve doesn't invite him to. Caleb's bag is on the table, his damp bathing suit wrapped in plastic and set neatly atop the change of clothes Danny packed for him.

"How was the puppet show?" Danny leans on straight arms against the back of a chair.

The question is addressed to Caleb but Eve answers. "It was thoroughly delightful. He loved it. And he had a good time in the pool, and with the other children there, didn't you, sweetheart?" She tips her upper body toward her grandson as she speaks. She strokes his head and pushes his hair behind his ear; her fingers trace the outline of his upper lobe. "He needs a haircut, Daniel. His hair should not be falling over his ears."

"He likes it long. He's into being a cowboy these days." He and Caleb smile at each other.

"He needs a haircut."

"Right. Okay, kiddo, ready to go?"

Danny reaches for the bag but Eve moves it away. She taps a red-tipped finger on the school application. "We aren't done, Daniel."

"Yes we are."

"No. We are not."

"I told you this morning, Eve, he's not going to Harmony. He's going to the local elementary school with all of his nursery school friends."

"Why do you do this? Really, I don't understand. Are you so proud of your educational record that you hope your son will follow in your footsteps? You are making a mistake."

Danny stares at the shining black helmet of Eve's chin-length hair, her large brown eyes set in her ivory-skinned, oval face and he marvels at how she could look so much like Tara on the outside and be so different on the inside. For the umpteenth time, he scrolls through the list of reasons he puts up with Eve's blatant antagonism. He reminds himself that Tara was the focus of her life for twenty-six years and that she is suffering a grief that even he, perhaps, cannot truly comprehend. That Caleb is the focus now and in her unyielding way Eve wants what she believes to be best for him, just as she did for Tara. He reminds himself that Tara loved her; and not just loved her but felt responsible for her mother's happiness in some profound, tangled way that she could never adequately explain to him. He reminds himself that for Tara's sake, because she and Eve were so tightly bound to each other and there was a baby coming and because he would do anything for her, six years ago he let Eve cast him in the role of crude, lowlife seducer. So that Tara would remain forever blameless, at her core a pure and obedient flower who would never have made such a bad choice uncoerced.

It hurt Tara more than it hurt him, his accepting the part, but he convinced her that he didn't care if Eve hated him, he didn't care if he never saw the Fosters or Jamisons again after the reception Eve and Lester threw for them at the club several weeks after their hasty marriage. His only condition was that Eve never disparage him in front of his son. Now that Tara is no longer here to absorb their enmity and Danny and Eve must confront each other directly, Eve is beginning to cross that line. But he remains too compassionate at his own core to be the one to shatter her world into even smaller pieces. For Tara's sake, he's willing to give her more time.

"He's my son, Eve. It's my mistake to make."

He pulls the application from under Eve's pinioning nail and shoves it into Caleb's bag, swings the bag onto his shoulder. Caleb has gotten to his feet and is standing next to Danny. His thumb is in his mouth and his eyes are open wide. He is listening to every word. Danny takes his hand.

Eve glares at Danny with angry eyes and a clenched jaw. They stare at each other for a stony second and then Eve grimaces and looks away and Danny pulls on Caleb's hand and walks out without saying good-bye.

As he's buckling Caleb in, Danny kisses him and says, "I'm sorry if I sounded angry back there. I'm not angry at you, you know that."

Caleb plays with the strap at his waist. "I know. It's okay." He doesn't sound okay. He lolls in his car seat. After a long silence, he moans softly and says, "Daddy, I don't feel so good. My tummy hurts. I think maybe I have an illness."

Danny nearly chokes from trying not to laugh. "I think maybe you ate a little too much ice cream?" Danny keeps his expression somber, not wanting Caleb to hear and perhaps misinterpret his amused reaction to such a serious statement.

Caleb kicks his feet lethargically against the back of the passenger seat. "Yeah. Maybe."

Danny has no doubt that he did, that Eve let him eat himself sick on rocky road covered in caramel sauce and who knows what else. But he's equally sure that's not what's really making Caleb's tummy hurt. It's the constant tension between his father and his grandmother.

"How much did you eat?"

"A lot. I had vanilla at the puppet show and then Grandma

said I could have rocky road when we got home." The boy's voice is pitifully fuddled and apologetic.

Danny smiles at him in the rearview mirror. Caleb knows that Danny doesn't want him to have that much sugary food; but Eve knows it, too, and she's the adult. "But I bet it tasted good going down."

Caleb gives back a little smile. "Yeah."

"Tomorrow it's tofu and rice for dinner, okay?"

"Okay." He sighs.

"Caleb? Do you think you could do me a favor?"

"Sure. What?"

"I'm not feeling so great myself—too much sun probably. Do you think you could lie in the hammock with me for a little while when we get home?"

"I could do that, Dad." He strains against the restraint of his car seat and stretches out his arm. He pats Danny's back then slumps into his seat again. "Dad?"

"Yes?"

"Do I have to go to that school if I don't want to?"

"No, you don't." Glancing into the rearview mirror again, Danny sees what he was hoping for. A look of peacefulness is spreading across his son's sun-flushed face.

The soft padding of the hammock has molded itself to Danny's back. Caleb is sitting on his abdomen. They are holding hands and using the joint motion of their bodies to set the hammock swaying gently back and forth. Danny smiles up at him.

Caleb bounces up and down. He swings their arms a little faster and a little wider. He says, "Tell me about when I was three and I swam with Mommy in the creek."

So Danny tells him, again, about the time when he was three

and he swam with Mommy in the pool formed by the big rocks and Daddy took a picture of them and the picture is in a heart-shaped frame on top of his dresser. Caleb never tires of hearing the story and Danny never tires of telling it to him.

Satisfied, Caleb lets go of Danny's hands and falls off him. He flops and flounders around for a few minutes, then falls sound asleep curled up into his father's side. Danny's body relaxes, his vulnerable parts—his shins, nose, testicles—all safe for the moment from the sharp weaponry of Caleb's arms and legs in motion. He caresses the boy's fair head. Everything about Caleb fills Danny with joy. Every look, every smell, every movement, every word. Everything everything everything fills him with joy. He wants more children. When he fell in love with Tara he realized that he'd grown up lonely. Even though he was close to his parents and he had friends, he was alone too much and like most only children he wished he had brothers and sisters to keep him company. He doesn't want Caleb to be lonely. It's another reason, perhaps now the only real and lasting reason, that he works so hard to sustain a relationship with Eve and Lester—so that Caleb will at least have grandparents. He doesn't want to be lonely, either. He wants his house to be full of noise and mess. He doesn't want to live the rest of his life as he had before she came and led him through the looking glass: deaf and blind, a haphazard inhabitant of a padded, muffled world. But her love was a drug—*Drink me, Eat me*—and he became addicted to its wild blissful high. He doesn't think he could survive such bliss a second time.

So close still to the year's longest day, there is pearly light in the sky although it is nearly nine o'clock. Nocturnal insects are starting to make themselves heard. Danny's body settles into the hammock and his eyes want to close. He lets them, and when nothing bad happens his mind relaxes and goes as limp as his muscles. As he begins to doze off, he wonders if he drove past her house tonight, on his way to and from the Jamisons'. If she really does live up on the ridge, if she's really married. Or if there is no husband and the voice on her phone was a mother, a sister, someone else who could both please and irritate her and she is alone right now, thinking about loneliness and its dangerous opposite, just as he is. He falls asleep to an image of dark hair in a high ponytail and small feet in black ballet slippers.

8

THE REALTOR THROUGH WHOM the Spencers bought their house is not a hyena at all but a very lovely, uncarnivorous lady named Joan Trachtenberg, whom Lily likes quite a bit. She is about Lily's age, also Jewish and also from the Bronx, although she and her husband, Sidney, have lived in Stone Creek for twenty years. They have two children, whom Lily has met several times: a bright son who's a sophomore at NYU and a severely learning-disabled daughter who is struggling through the local middle school and about whose future, Lily knows, Joan and Sidney worry constantly. Joan and Lily haven't become friends, exactly—Lily hasn't spent enough consistent time in the community to develop deep friendships—but they have a meaningful acquaintanceship, dating from four years ago. That was the other summer when Lily stayed in Stone Creek.

That summer Lily was a pulsing bundle of raw nerves, a bouncing ball of fevered anticipation from Monday morning, when Paul left to go back to the city, until Thursday night, when he returned to the country. The waiting for him, four befogged

days of it every week, was torture of the most exquisitely painful kind. It was a clawing, screaming heartache of the sort she
had only dreamed existed and she couldn't get enough of it.
She wallowed in it, throbbed with it, roamed the house at night
from the adrenaline rush of it, and when she did sleep—with
Paul's pillow in her arms and the smell of him on her face—her
dreams were invaded by it. Every Monday, the moment his car
turned out of the driveway and disappeared from sight, the waiting began anew and she thought she would die of it before she
saw him again. She craved distraction. Big time. She couldn't
read. She couldn't listen to music. She craved mindless, prefer-
ably physical, distraction. So she took adult ballet classes at the
legendary Miss Ruth's Dance Academy in nearby Middletown;
she gardened with a vengeance and grew enough cut flowers and
basil, parsley, tomatoes, zucchini, green beans, and lettuces to
open her own farm stand; she took solitary hikes on the trails of
nearby Harriman State Park. Tuesday and Thursday mornings
she played tennis with Joan on the high school courts.

She is playing tennis with Joan again this summer, Tuesdays
and Fridays this year, on the old Har-Tru courts of Stone Creek
High School. Lily and Joan would enjoy playing on the fabulous
fifty-thousand-dollar synthetic grass courts of the Kensington
Ridge Country Club, but that would require their public conver-
sion to a dainty, plaid-blazered, pink-skirted form of Christian-
ity, and Joan would most certainly have to get a nose job. Actually, the club's membership committee would tolerantly overlook
Lily's Jewishness in favor of her spiritually inoffensive husband's
significant wealth and professional reputation, but Joan, whose
husband is the proprietor of Stone Creek's first and only bagel
emporium, doesn't have a prayer, Christian, Jewish, Muslim,
Wiccan, or anything else. One of the things Lily and Joan like

about each other is that neither would be happy at the KRCC. They greatly prefer playing at the high school. It reminds them both of growing up near Fordham Road and practicing their girlie serves against the cement wall of their schoolyard handball courts.

Lily is playing tennis with Joan again, just like before. She is driving to Middletown for ballet class. She is gardening. She is hiking. She is pushing herself to keep busy because what she really wants to do is get in her BMW, strap Blinkie Floyd into the passenger seat atop a value pack–sized box of Devil Dogs, and drive until she is too far away to turn back. She is a bundle of raw nerves again, but this time the pain is not pleasurable.

She has been waiting for Paul for nearly three weeks. He is finally taking a short break and coming up for the weekend for the first time since the Fourth. He'll be here tonight. She is thinking of him every minute and she is missing him, but that doesn't mean she is looking forward to seeing him. When she imagines him walking through the door, what she feels is so shockingly different from what she felt four years ago it frightens her. There was nothing separating them then. The minute he was through the door she was in his arms. It was never too late; they were never too tired. There was no possibility of sleeping, or even talking, until they'd done what they'd been waiting four days to do. There was rarely the possibility of climbing the stairs to their bedroom. By the end of that summer they were intimate with every couch and guest bed and plush rug and shower stall on the first floor. She knows that nothing like that is going to happen tonight. They may want it, but they are being pushed apart as if by a strange wind blowing in two directions at once, a wind that they have conjured, each of them, in the mistaken belief that it would buffer them from hurt.

So, once again, Joan is providing some necessary distraction. She has invited Lily to have an early lunch with her after their tennis game. Another thing Joan and Lily like about each other is that neither of them is afraid to eat like a healthy, hungry human being. They are sitting in a booth at Rudy's, both with overstuffed tuna-on-rye sandwiches in front of them and a plate of thick, hot, salted french fries for sharing.

Around a mouthful of Bumblebee deliciously saturated with full-fat Hellman's mayonnaise, Joan says, "It's fun to be playing with you again, Lily. Your backhand still stinks, but your forehand made me want to run for cover."

Lily laughs. "It *is* fun. We are equally bad and don't give a damn." Lily dips a fry in ketchup and pops it into her mouth. "I like walloping the *kishkes* out of that little fuzzy thing."

"Great for getting out those aggressions. What made you decide to spend the summer?"

"Oh. Paul is involved in this big case . . ."

"Ah, the SynTech scandal. I've read about it. The bastards." Joan picks up the salt shaker. "Okay if I salt these a little more?"

"No, go ahead, I love retaining water. So, anyway, he hasn't been busy like this in years, it's hot in the city . . . it seemed like a good time to enjoy the house and a little solitude."

"I know what you mean. I long for international bagel seminars so Sidney would disappear from time to time. We love them, but it's nice to get rid of them for a few days."

"Mmmm." Lily has never before wanted to get rid of Paul for any length of time. She takes no comfort from Joan's desire to ditch her husband occasionally; they are not talking about the same thing. She picks up the second half of her sandwich, knowing that if she eats it she's going to feel like a beached whale for the rest of the day. She takes a big bite.

"So, Lily. I didn't ask you to lunch just so we could keep our cardiologists in business. I have a favor to ask you." Joan pushes her plate aside. The second half of her sandwich is untouched. "Lunch tomorrow. I can't believe you're eating that whole thing." She waves at the waitress to wrap her leftovers. "Okay. So. You have such a way with people, and such great organizational skills, and all the right experience . . ."

"Flattery will get you everywhere. What's the favor?" Lily puts the sandwich down. Joan has unintentionally embarrassed her. She shouldn't keep eating when she's not even remotely hungry.

"We could really use your help getting The Doorway up and running."

"What? How? I mean, I've waded through the swamps of the health care system but only on behalf of individuals. The Doorway's a great project, Joan, but I don't know anything about group homes or mentally challenged kids."

"You don't have to know anything. All you need is time and brains—both of which you have in abundance—to wade through the bureaucratic swamps of the county and the state, so all the i's are dotted and t's crossed by the time the renovations on the house are done. Insurance, filing staff licenses, procedures for referrals, whatever."

"Gosh. I don't know, Joan."

"Lily, you told me you're looking for something to do. You can do this with your eyes closed and I know you'd enjoy it. You'd be working with Dr. Beth Marcus, who you will love. She's a pediatrician with a practice here in town and an affiliation with the Mid-Hudson Medical Complex. She's setting up the services end of things and will be our liaison with the medical world, but she doesn't have time to do the phone calls, the paperwork."

Lily already knows that she is going to do it. Her days have to have some purpose. She hasn't been able to make it happen for herself, but here it is, being handed to her. While Joan has been talking, Lily has been remembering Jennifer, a friendly, endearing girl whose interface with the world is indefinably off kilter. Just enough that the normal kids don't know what to make of her and the possibility of an independent life is not an option. Lily's heart already hurts at the thought of a houseful of Jennifers with a chance for happiness. And why should Paul be the only one who gets to do what he wants? If this means staying in Stone Creek into the fall, too bad. He didn't ask her permission to take on the SynTech case and disappear for the next God knows how many months.

"What do you say, Lily? It's familiar, it's for a good cause, it won't take up that much of your time, it will keep you out of trouble for a couple of months . . ."

"I say okay. I'm your girl. What do I do?"

"Oh, Lily, thank you. Just call Beth, here's her number. I'll take you by the house in a few weeks. It's a wreck now, but the contractor who's doing the work, for the cost of materials—Tom Gallo, what a guy—says it will be worth seeing by then. No, no, lunch is on me."

Lily puts Beth Marcus's number in her pocket and graciously lets Joan pick up the check.

She has to buy lightbulbs, and so she has left her car at the other end of Main Street, in front of the hardware store. As she struts down the street, feeling unencumbered and willfully pleased with herself, a young man, no more than twenty-five, gives her a lewd slit-eyed once-over and says, "Lookin' good, babe," as he passes.

She responds with a flirtatious smile, aware of how out of character that is for her and enjoying it immensely. She is wearing a pair
of cut-off jeans shorts and a red tank top—the lack of dress code
another reason she likes playing at the high school—ankle-high
tennis socks, and sneakers. From a distance she looks twenty-five.
From up close she looks thirty-five. The boy's reaction to her is
ridiculous, of course, but it makes her feel good, very good. She
is airborne in her sneakers as she crosses Main Street midway between Elm and Maple. At the far corner, she spots a silver Dodge
pickup truck, parked in front of The Kitchen.

They have never eaten at The Kitchen in the entire six years
they've had the house. It's a worn old place with cheap, old-
fashioned food that, Lily has always assumed without bothering
to find out, must also be bad, as in *You get what you pay for,*
another Max and Ada–ism, although they then had to muddle
things with the addition of *But if you can get it cheap. . . .* In any
case, The Kitchen is where the locals eat and Rudy's—newer,
spiffier, fancier food, twice the price—is where folks like the
Spencers or even the Trachtenbergs eat. That's just the way it is.
Where else would he be but at The Kitchen.

She crash lands; her sneakers are nothing but clumsy blocks
of rubber on the sidewalk. That youthful, buoyant sensation is
being pressed out of her by a weighty, merciless desire to see
him again, to see him look at her again with those pale eyes filled
with . . . with what? His look stopped her breath; it was what
compelled her to watch him in Dreiser's parking lot, but she
doesn't know why. She glances quickly around her, down the
block ahead, absurdly afraid that he's going to be there, catching
her in his sights when she is unprepared for him. It might not
even be his truck. He can't have the only silver Dodge pickup
truck in town.

She advances slowly up the street. Her legs, strong and sturdy on the courts just an hour ago, threaten to fold under her. She draws abreast of The Kitchen's large window and cautiously peeks in. He is there, at the counter, facing away from her. From the back, he could be mistaken for some other hard-bodied blond man, but not by her. She has been carrying a detailed, three-dimensional picture of him in her mind for weeks. She would know him in a crowd.

An older woman, a waitress, is behind the counter, pouring him coffee. She laughs at something he says, ruffles his hair, and moves on to another customer. The brimming reservoir behind Lily's eyes starts to overflow. He peers into an obviously empty creamer, then swivels on his stool, slides off it. He is heading toward a vacant table, to borrow its full creamer. He is heading toward the window, toward Lily. As though pulled by an unseen string, his head turns and he is looking at her through the glass. He slowly takes in all of her, her short shorts and skimpy top, then brings his eyes back to her face. There is nothing about his look similar to that smarmy boy's. It is not a look filled with sex; it holds much more complex desires and a terrible vulnerability, and there is again that stark, unsettling quality about it, and it makes Lily ache and burn with longing. It makes her want to be young again, but not the way she was. It makes her want to be different, with everything still possible. But she's not young, and there are too many things that are not possible anymore. Hot tears spill onto her cheeks as she hurries along Stone Creek's charming Main Street.

She is drifting in the gentle current created by the waterfall, on a thick foam float, around and around the pool. She has been

drifting there for hours. The afternoon is giving way to early evening and she has been found by the long, stippled shadows cast
by the honey locust tree just off the western edge of the deck.
When the currents swirl the float so that she is facing the decking between the pool and the house, she catches a glimpse of
Blinkie Floyd. He goes with her everywhere now, around the
house, out by the pool, out on the grounds. She is vigilant about
shielding him from the sun, so he is sitting on the round white-
resin table, the small one on the kitchen-level deck that they use
for themselves, beneath an umbrella, with a towel that Lily has
hung from its spokes as an additional barrier between him and
the afternoon's far-reaching rays. Each time his sweet, silly face
comes into view, Lily starts to cry again.

There is music coming from the outdoor speakers. This summer Lily is listening to music. When she is in the house there
is music in the air almost all the time. And it is always of the
same sort: sinuous male voices singing songs of the blind joy of
new love and its inevitable end, of heartache and loss. They are
masterful songs, lyrical, poetic, and true. They collude with her
growing despair and encourage her tears. She can't listen to anything else.

She has been thinking throughout the hours of her drifting,
and her thoughts, like the music, are all of the same sort. They
are bewildered, disbelieving thoughts about herself and Mona
and how it came to be that she, the obedient good girl, became
a divorced, childless disappointment to her parents *and* putative
stepmother, then dismayed them further by remarrying an aloof
goy and not even producing a child from that scandalous union.
While Mona, the unmanageable embarrassment with school
suspensions, Ecstasy in her purse, two abortions by the age of
twenty-two, became a happy stay-at-home, synagogue-joining

mom and the apple of her parents', *and* putative stepmother's, eye. They are thoughts of herself and Rick and how it came to be that her closest ally throughout her agonizing adolescence and timid young adulthood, her best friend, left her to love and live with a man and is now leaving her again to become a father. They are thoughts of lost years and discarded opportunities and unrealized desires. She has been drifting and crying and listening to sad music and thinking about the myriad forms in which betrayal can cloak itself, although that word has not been in her thoughts at all.

She has not been thinking about Paul, the love of her life. Not consciously. She will have to float and drift in her sadness a while longer, into much deeper waters, before she is ready to do that. But he is the subtext beneath it all. Soon he will be here and she, with or without conscious thought, will have to find a way to get out of the pool, stop crying, turn off the music, greet her love when he arrives, and then appear to let him in.

9

THE NURSERY SCHOOL DAY camp is unexpectedly closed on the last Friday of July due to a burst water pipe in the main activities building. Caleb is scheduled to spend the weekend, so Eve is happy to take him a day early when Daniel, with too many appointments and too much work, calls to ask if she can.

He could have somehow managed to keep the boy with him all day, which Caleb would have loved. Or he could have dropped him with the Schillers or the Pollacks. He did not have to give her this extra day with him. She is aware of that. She is aware that he never denies her time with her grandson, despite the escalating disagreements over how Caleb should be raised and the ongoing skirmishes in the undeclared war for his heart and mind. She is not obliged to be grateful to Daniel for this. He is not being generous. He simply cannot take care of the boy by himself and she is his grandmother. Daniel is capitulating, admitting his weakness. She would not be generous, either. If the situation were reversed, she would be quick to put him in his place. She would not let him find the weakness in her to exploit.

Nothing Daniel could do now will ever make up for how unendingly difficult it has been to have him for a son-in-law. It is her right to treat him as she does. He deserves it for being so callous in his desires and unheeding of a young girl's susceptibility. Eve could never and will never think one bad thing of Tara; Tara will always be the embodiment of the greatest love that Eve has ever known. But it has always been possible for her to think ill of Daniel. And now more than ever it is possible to place him where he will remain as nothing to her so that she can punish him without remorse. There must be punishment somewhere for mistakes that were made, promises unkept.

All that is left to her now is Caleb and she will not lose him, not from cowardice or relinquishment or illness or anything that is in her power to prevent. It used to bother her that he looks so much like Daniel, but that never had anything to do with the boy himself, and she has let it go. It is the others in Caleb that she chooses to see now, that she must nurture and keep alive, for they are there, too, very much so. Daniel will move on. He is too vital a man to remain forever subdued by his grief; and yes, she gives him that, that he grieves for Tara. But it won't last; she is surprised he has not already begun to search for a new woman to take Tara's place. He will replace the life he had with her with another, and it will be so much easier for him if Caleb forgets what came before. It is up to Eve to make certain that he never forgets. That he remembers always where he came from, what blood runs in his veins, who his mother was.

Contrary to the weather forecast, which promised an end to three days of rain by Thursday evening, it is still pouring late Friday morning.

"Why can they never get it right? I had hoped we might spend the morning in the park."

Eve and Caleb are standing at the window of his bedroom, a large, light room that was once Tara's. They are watching the rain bombard the surface of the pool and form miniature lakes on the lawn.

Caleb shakes his head. "You know, Grandma, it's not an exact science."

Eve slowly turns her head from the soggy view and smiles down at him. She vaguely remembers Lester using that very phrase about something or other several weeks ago. "No, it most certainly is not." She puts a hand beneath his chin and directs his face toward her. "Do you have any idea how adorable you are?"

"Yes." He grins at her with a mouthful of baby teeth.

"Well then, Mr. Adorable, why don't we make some brownies on this rainy morning. You may pour the batter into the pan and lick the bowl."

The kitchen is beginning to fill with the irresistible aroma of warm chocolate, Caleb's hands and mouth have been wiped clean of batter, and he is at the table, on his booster seat, chewing his lip in concentration as he labors over an *Animals of the Jungle* coloring book. Eve has gone into the den to get something, and now she stands in the kitchen doorway watching him as he removes one crayon at a time from the forty-eight-crayon Crayola box, uses it, and puts it back in its place before choosing another. He is exacting, just as Tara was, and he has learned from his father to take good care of his tools and keep a neat workspace.

"Those are very colorful creatures you are creating, sweetheart. I never knew that lions could be such a lovely shade of green." Eve places a photo album on the table. She checks the brownies. "Another ten minutes I think. And look, the sun is coming out."

Caleb's eyes dart rapidly to the window, to the closing oven door, to the album, then back to his coloring. "Lions aren't really green. I'm being artistic. Daddy says it's okay."

"Is that so?" Eve sits down and turns back the album's cardboard cover. "Caleb, shall we look at pictures of Mommy? We can talk about her a little. It's been some time since we've done that together. Come, sweetheart, come sit on my lap."

Caleb's head remains bent over his green lion as he shakes it. "I want to color."

Eve looks at the top of his blond head, at his reluctance to meet her eye, and her throat constricts around an upwelling of anger. She coughs and takes a sip of water. "You can color more later, Caleb. I would like it if you would come and look at the pictures with me now."

He raises his head. His bright blue eyes are damp and his mouth is twisted.

"I don't want to, Grandma."

Her anger spreads into her chest and she looks away from him so he won't see it. This anger is not for him, it is not honestly for any man.

"All right, Caleb. Another time."

Although she tries to disguise her displeasure, her words come out harsh and clipped. Caleb's head drops like a stone back to his coloring book and his careful hand this time makes a violent green mess of a lion's tail. Eve rises and walks to the sink on the pretense of refilling her water glass. She looks out the window. There is vapor rising from the drying slate around the pool.

"Look, sweetheart, the rain has stopped. Why don't you put on your bathing suit and go play on the swing? I will join you as soon as the brownies are done and we can go into the pool."

A few moments later his lean little body in its bright orange bathing trunks scuttles through the kitchen. Before he goes out the back door, he stops and says, "I'm sorry, Grandma. Don't be long."

His tremulous voice resonates in Eve's ears. Her hand tightens around the faucet and she closes her eyes. She senses a shadow sweep across her lids and her eyes open.

The swing set is at the bottom of the sloping lawn beyond the far end of the pool. Caleb has emerged onto the pool deck and is running past the kitchen windows. Eve leans over the sink, pushes the window open, and yells out at him.

"Caleb, don't run! The slate is slippery after the rain. Caleb, do you hear me? Do not run!"

But it is no use. He is an energetic little boy and he is upset and he is running fast. He rounds the corner of the pool and his feet go out from under him. He flies a short distance in the air and lands on the deck and slides into a pile of chaises, turned on their sides so as not to catch three days of rain in their cushions. His bare white skin drags across the slick slate and his right leg slams into the jagged metal foot of an exposed chaise leg.

"Caleb!" Eve shrieks and drops her glass into the sink. Blood is pouring from his leg. She can see it from where she stands. "Caleb! Oh my God!"

After a second of shocked silence, he begins to scream. "Daddy! Daddy! Daddy!"

Propelled by instinct, she gets a beach towel from the closet near the kitchen, snatches her purse off the counter, and rushes to where he is lying, sobbing for his father. She kneels at his side. She is afraid to touch him.

"Your head! Did you hit your head? Caleb, stop crying and answer me! Did you hit your head?"

The boy stops howling for an instant and stares at her in terror as he shakes his head back and forth. She realizes that she is screaming at him, that he can hear the hysteria in her voice.

"No, no. It's all right, darling. Grandma is here." Calmer now, she quickly looks him over and sees that his right arm and side are abraded and there is an ugly-looking gash in his leg, just below the knee. The leg is covered in blood and there is blood on the grey stone. His face and his head are untouched. Eve tries to wrap the towel around the wound. Her hands are shaking and he won't lie still. "Stop thrashing! Let me do this. Caleb!"

"I want my daddy!" He starts to howl again. His eyes are popping with fear and pain.

"Caleb, stay still! Daddy is working. We don't need to disturb him. Grandma will take care of you."

"I want Daddy!"

He is screaming, but the words are barely intelligible, he is crying so hard. Tears and snot are running down his face. He is beyond comfort, stunned that such a thing could happen to him. It wouldn't matter if Daniel were here. He would be screaming all the same.

"Now, sweetheart. We don't want to worry Daddy, do we? He's so busy and there's nothing he can do that we can't do ourselves." She secures the towel, picks him up, and carries him to her car. "I'm taking you to Dr. Marcus's office. It's a five-minute drive. Everything will be fine."

She cannot be bothered expending the precious moments to strap him into his car seat. She buckles the front passenger seat belt around him and orders him to sit still. There is blood pooling on the Lexus's soft beige leather and dripping onto the beige carpeting beneath. Caleb's screeches ricochet off the window glass. As she runs to the driver's side, her cell phone falls out of her purse onto the gravel. She picks it up and it lies in her hand with the weight of a reproach. She doesn't want to, but she knows she has to call him. She hits the voice dial button, reluctantly says *Daniel,* and when his message comes on after four rings she hangs up. She tried. It's not her fault that he doesn't answer his phone.

Two hours later, Eve and Caleb are on the sofa in the den. The house smells of burned brownies. Eve has the television on, tuned to CNN, but she has turned the sound off and is watching the hypnotic crawl of words across the bottom of the screen. Caleb is asleep, his head in her lap. There are eight stitches in his leg, ointment and more bandages on his right upper arm and over his ribs on the right side. Dr. Marcus, who Eve admits has proved to be an excellent pediatrician for being young and a woman, gave Caleb a spoonful of Panadol and sent her home with enough of the painkiller for the first twenty-four hours, and some liquid ibuprofen for afterward, if necessary.

Dr. Marcus and Caleb are obviously very fond of each other. Her gentle hands and soothing voice gradually stopped his tears and he has since remained courageous and dry-eyed. Eve is curious as to whether at least some of the loving attention Dr. Marcus gives to Caleb stems from her feelings for Daniel. Eve knows more about Daniel than he thinks. She knows that he dated Beth Marcus that first summer he was home from Europe, when she was Dr. Mills's new associate, before he turned to Tara. Why couldn't he have gotten *her* pregnant and left Tara alone?

She has not called him again, and she is not going to. He will be furious, but she can handle him. She and Caleb have already conspired not to say anything when he calls; it is their little secret adventure now, and Daddy will be so proud of his bravery. She threads her fingers in his hair as he sleeps. A child must have a mother. Tara is gone, the years collapse into the void where she once was, and Eve is his mother now. She will keep this child safe. No one and nothing will prevent her. No one can keep a child safe the way a mother can.

Normally when he is with them on a Sunday, Eve and Lester take Caleb to church and to his mother's grave, although he pays very little attention to his surroundings in either place. She knows he is too young to understand their significance, but his disinterest dismays her nonetheless. This is one thing she must be grateful to Daniel for, that he allows her to try to instill faith in Caleb despite his own agnosticism. Today, however, they stay home and he and Lester spend the morning in the den, eating raisin toast with cream cheese and laughing at SpongeBob videos.

Caleb is his usual sunny self when Daniel comes to take him home in the late afternoon. Eve and Caleb have come out of the house to meet him, and the three of them are standing on the shallow front porch. Eve has Caleb's overnight bag in her hands.

"All right now, Daniel. Don't be upset with us. As you can see, we had a little accident on Friday, a nasty spill on the deck. I tried to call you, but I was rushing to Dr. Marcus's and you didn't answer and I was just so flustered. . . . In any case, all is well and we decided afterward not to disturb your weekend."

Caleb excitedly thrusts out his bandaged leg, smiles up at his father, and says, "Look, Dad. I have eight stitches in my leg. Dr. Beth took care of me. She says hi."

Daniel is rigid. Only his eyes move, from his son's leg to Eve's face. He has very expressive features, especially his eyes, and in them she can clearly see his conflicting desires: to not make a scene in front of Caleb and to strangle her.

"You should have called me, Eve."

"He was in good hands with me, Daniel. I know how to take care of an injured child. I knew you had a lot to accomplish and we didn't need you."

"Do you think I don't know how to take care of him? He *did* need me and you should have called."

Now there is pure fury in his eyes. She smiles serenely, aware that he knows exactly what she is thinking, what she will not say in front of the boy. *You did not take good care of my daughter, did you, Daniel? Why should I trust that you will take good care of my grandson?*

"You are overreacting."

He wrenches Caleb's bag from her hand. "Don't ever do anything like that again."

Eve gives him a mock-staggered look. "My goodness. Are you threatening me, Daniel?"

"Don't yell at each other!" Caleb cries. They are not yelling, but no matter how calm their tones or how seemingly controlled their words, the spark and crackle of hostility between his father and grandmother showers down on him. Eve bends toward him, but Daniel is too quick for her. He scoops the boy up.

"I'm warning you," Daniel says quietly. "Don't ever do anything like that again."

An unexpected prick of fear pierces Eve's composure. For the first time it occurs to her that there might be a hard place somewhere in his heart, after all, hard enough to push back if she pushes him too far. She nods and says, "I will heed your warning."

*   *   *

Lester has gone to bed earlier even than usual. SpongeBob just plain wore him out, apparently. She can barely remember the last time they went to bed together, even just to sleep. She is almost always up for hours after he has retired. It has been months since they have had sex. Neither of them has been able to regain much interest in it since Tara died, at least not with each other. Eve has no idea what might be on Lester's mind in that regard, she knows only what has been on hers. They do, however, wake up together every morning to find that their bodies are in contact in some tender way.

She didn't have her time at the cemetery today, so before she goes to sleep there is something she must do. She climbs the stairs and tiptoes into the bedroom. Lester is snoring lightly. As he always does, he has left her bedside lamp lit for her and donned a silken sleep mask. With his thinning hair and blandly pleasant face, the mask makes him appear like an inept, apologetic bandit. She smiles to look at him. Lester is a good man and he has loved her devotedly for nearly thirty years. She has not always been easy to love, but he has loved her regardless.

They both come from economically and socially dominant Southern families with rich histories and strict codes of conduct and so he thinks he understands her. He thinks he understands her antagonism toward Daniel and he doesn't interfere. But then he can afford to be lenient in his attitudes. His parents are long gone, and as the youngest of a large brood, his defection north and the subsequent marriage of his daughter to a low-class Yankee did little to tarnish the Jamisons' luster back in Charleston. But for the Fosters of Savannah, with Eve their only daughter, Daniel's existence has remained a source of never-ending humiliation. Eve's parents, when they refer to him at all, do so as *that-uneducated-atheist-Irish-laborer-your-daughter-married,* all in one breath as though that were his name, and have never once that she can recall uttered his real name, neither Danny nor Daniel. Her two older brothers once in a while derisively ask *How's the carpenter?* Both families met him once, at the wedding reception, and a second time when he accompanied Tara with an infant Caleb to Charleston and Savannah. He never went visiting with her again.

So what Lester does understand is to a large measure correct. But it is merely the tip of the iceberg. The cold, ruinous bulk that lies beneath the water is invisible to him and she will go to her grave making sure it always remains so.

She removes the jewelry box from her closet and takes it into the bathroom. There is no jewelry in it anymore; it is where she keeps certain special artifacts from Tara's childhood. She doesn't always open the box; sometimes it is enough just to touch it. But not tonight. She raises the leather-covered lid and lifts out the full tray. In the open space below there is a folded page ripped twelve years ago from an issue of *People* magazine, which Tara read obsessively when she was a teenager. She would have read this. Gingerly, Eve takes the page from its velvet nest. It is folded neatly across the middle, the crease directly below the photograph that comprises its upper half. Any caption or accompanying text is hidden on the tucked-under side. Tonight she wants only to look at the photograph. Another time she may reread the article that describes it. Or them, to be more accurate. The photograph is of a family, a husband, a wife, a little boy, and a little girl. They are a beautiful family, posed before their big, beautiful home set in the unmistakable landscape of northern California. The husband is fair-haired and he sports an impish grin that sparks his light eyes. His hair is thick and long—it is California—and it covers the tops of his ears. He has one arm around his blond wife and the other around his two blond children. Eve touches a finger to the reduced image of his face. It is an easy face to look at, very open, very alive. He looks happy, so very happy. He looks like a man with no memories to haunt him.

10

P AUL, SLOW DOWN!" Lily thrusts her hand out and clamps it on Paul's forearm.

Paul is behind the wheel of his midnight-blue Porsche Boxster convertible, barreling down the steep driveway—the one thing about their house the Spencers do not love—toward Kensington Ridge Road. He pushes hard on the brakes and the car slews to a stop just as an old-model white Volvo shoots by, also moving a little too fast on the narrow, hilly road.

"I see him. I see him. Asshole."

Lily heaves a sigh as if to say *If he's an asshole, what does that make you?*

Paul pulls out and snaps, "Lighten up, would you? When have I ever had an accident?"

"Never," she snaps back. "You have never had an accident. You're a wonderful driver." She can't sustain the sarcasm in her voice, misplaced in any case since they both know that what she says is true, and her next words are uttered in a conciliatory tone. "Just slow down a little, okay? Forty in this car feels like ninety." She removes her hand, but slowly, with a light stroke of his wrist.

Paul slows down and turns to look at her. Her hair is unbound and it is blowing around her face in a dark cloud. He extends his arm and gathers the flying strands in his hand, holds them at the nape of her neck. "You should tie your hair up," he says softly. "I love to see it wild like this, but it will be one big knot by the time we get there."

"Why don't you just hold it for me?" She smiles at him. She rummages in her purse for a big tortoise-shell clip and secures her hair in its teeth. A few stray tendrils continue to whip around her ears.

Paul is gradually free-falling into a state of confusion so thoroughly unfamiliar to him that the only way he can live with it is to first turn it into something familiar. This ability to transform, to rationalize, to create a reality of choice, is a uniquely human mental exercise that Paul is very good at. It fits well with his trick of not wanting what he can't have. Thus his distressing confusion, brought on by the undecipherable mixed messages flying at him fast and furiously from his wife, is being transmuted into withdrawal and impatience, two states that Paul has long been comfortable with. At the same time that he is retreating from Lily's erratic behavior, he is striking back, attempting to reassert control over her.

Starting with his very first romantic relationship, his prepubescent stalking of pig-tailed Pamela Babcock in the third grade, which won him his heart's desire of holding her hand and kissing her cheek during recess, Paul's instincts for dealing with women have been based on his compulsion to position himself at the center of a woman's universe. He's not aware that that's what he does, that that's what his being controlling and demanding and selfish is all about. If someone told him that the manipulative behavior he has employed in all of his liaisons stemmed from his unconscious attempt to make up for having been discarded by the woman who gave birth to him and shoved aside by the woman who raised him, Paul would tell that someone to go take a flying fuck. Since no one has told him that, however, he remains free to tell his confusion to take a flying fuck.

So. Paul is taking Lily to dinner at The Farmhouse, a restaurant with an uninventive name but very inventive food in a tastefully restored farmhouse about fifteen minutes from their own tasteful farmhouse. They have a six o'clock reservation, not the most fashionable time to dine, but for the second weekend in a row, he is heading back to the city early on Sunday evening. He'd rather spend the night at the house. For one thing, he likes getting up at five thirty and driving into town ahead of the worst of rush-hour traffic. At that hour on a summer morning it's an easy run on the Thruway, across the Tappan Zee Bridge, and straight down into Manhattan, and it's even a picturesque drive until Yonkers. For another thing, he'd prefer to lie next to Lily one more night. Make love one more time and fall asleep with her warm, soft body nearby. Paul is a very sexual man and his libido has always remained separate from his thinking, or unthinking, brain. Like being able to sleep anywhere, Paul can get it up anywhere or anytime and he always knows what to do with it once it's up and the more frequently he does it the happier he is. He's actually starting to have trouble sleeping in the apartment—he can't imagine why—but his ability to enjoy sex, and a guaranteed good night's sleep, is untarnished.

For all those reasons, Paul would rather spend Sunday night at the house. But Lily has somehow managed to make him feel that she'd just as soon he not, and so when Sunday evening rolls around, he thinks he would just as soon not as well. He's not quite sure how she's done that, or even *if* she's really done that. She didn't look at him and say, *I want you to leave.* But there is a jumpy atmosphere in the house and it's pushing him out the door from the moment he arrives on Friday night. She seems happy to see him then, but very quickly she gets testy with him for no reason and when he looks at her for an explanation she laughs and says some variety of "Oh, just ignore me" or "I get used to being alone during the week. I have to adjust to your being here" or "It's hormones, I'm probably going into menopause."

Paul has reserved a table on the veranda. It's the best table, on an outside corner, private and romantic. It's the same table at which they had dinner every Sunday night from the middle of June until the middle of September four summers ago. It's been a long time since they've been back and now that they are here, Paul wonders if perhaps it was a mistake to come. Nothing feels the same.

"This is nice, isn't it? We shouldn't have waited so long to come back here." Paul lifts his head from his perusal of the wine list.

"Mmmmm." Lily is smiling at him but she looks away as soon as their eyes meet. "I'd forgotten what a lovely view this is."

Paul takes a quick glance over the porch railing. It's a very fine view, out over an apple and peach orchard, but it hardly deserves the intense attention Lily is giving it.

"Red or white?"

"Red, I think." She inhales contentedly and turns back to him. She puts her hand on his arm, softly this time, as she exhales. "This *is* nice, Paul. Thank you."

"You're welcome." He leans over and kisses her hand. When he looks up again, she doesn't look away. They look at each other for a long silent moment. An intimate yet awkward moment ended for them by the waiter's coming to take their wine order and leave menus.

The moment of contact ends, but the silence continues. They've already spent too much of the weekend not talking; Paul casts around for an innocuous subject and says, "So, it sounds like you're enjoying this little job you've taken on."

"It's not a *little job,* Paul." She all but leaps down his throat.

"Oh, man. Give me a goddamned break. I didn't mean it that way."

"Then you shouldn't have said it that way." Lily studies her menu.

Her pissiness is unrelenting and he's getting annoyed. He's trying to be patient with her but she's sniping at him every chance she gets. And he really hates being told what he should or shouldn't do.

"You're not even getting paid, for Christ's sake. If you want to work again, why don't you come back home and go back to work for real?"

"What's the matter with you? Who cares about getting paid? This is real, Paul. There are real people's lives involved here. I feel good about doing this and I don't appreciate your making me feel like it's not important."

There is a steely tone in her voice but she looks like she's about to cry. Paul tries to take her hand, but she pulls it away and drops her eyes to the menu again.

"Fine. It's important. It's important. I get it. And I'm glad you're doing it."

Paul admires every single thing about Lily, down to the fact that she obsessively begins using a new toothbrush every four months. He doesn't intend to make her feel small or to hurt her and even now he doesn't think that he did. He thinks she is just being prickly. Making her feel small is the last thing in the world he would ever consciously want to do. He never intended to do it in the past, although he did; and he won't intend to do it in the future, although he will. There are two reasons, both of which operate behind the back of Paul's consciousness and are beginning to clash with each other. The first has nothing specifically to do with Lily. It is that Paul never learned the art of compromise except as a legal strategy, and even there he tries to avoid it. In the personal realm he equates compromise with lethal exposure; it reveals a dangerous degree of desire or need. And so, when he wants or needs something, he doesn't ask or negotiate, he pursues with dedicated, single-minded intent. The second reason has everything specifically to do with Lily. He thinks she's too good for him, he's waiting for her to fall out of love with him, and therefore he's afraid of her.

"I just think if you're going to work, you should come back to the city where you belong, get your career going again. I mean, how long is this job going to take, anyway?"

Without looking up, she says, "I don't know, Paul. How long is the SynTech case going to take?"

Paul closes his menu. He lowers his voice and talks to the top of her head. "You know, you *are* turning into a bitch."

Lily looks up and fixes him with an unfeeling, catlike stare. Her warm brown eyes have gone cold and hard. An unpleasant rush of blood to his head dizzies him.

"I'm sorry. I didn't mean that. It's just . . . okay, look, we've both got a lot on our minds and it would be nice if we could just have a civil dinner together before I go home and we don't see each other for another couple of weeks."

The glassy film over Lily's eyes dissolves in wetness. Tears are standing on her lower lids and she is biting her lip. "No, I'm sorry. I don't know what's wrong with me."

"Lily." He feels like he's inside a pachinko machine, flipping off the bumpers. "Maybe you should come back into town and see your gynecologist. I mean, you are forty-six, no kids . . . maybe you are going into menopause or something. Bob says his wife has had PMS for ten years." He flicks lightly at her hand with a finger. "Hello? Joke?"

She gives him a lame smile. "I will, after the summer."

"Why wait? Tell him it's important and—"

"No! I don't want to come back now. I'll do it after the summer."

"Okay, okay. Could we please call a truce for the rest of the night?"

She plucks her napkin off her lap and swings the crisp white cloth in the air, a childlike grin on her face. He laughs and shakes his head. "I love you."

"I love you, too." She starts to laugh, but her laughter collapses into tears and she puts the napkin over her face.

Paul is not a stranger to women crying in restaurants. He's terminated more than one relationship over an expensive meal. In those instances it was no mystery why they were crying or how the night would end. He knew exactly what to say, how to extricate himself with kindness and a gentle reminder that he never promised forever. But he doesn't know why Lily is crying or what to say to her, his wife to whom he did promise forever and meant it. He knows how he'd like the night to end, but this time he's not in control of what happens. He wants to ask her if he can stay, if he can take her home after dinner and take her to bed and if she thinks she might ever come to him again the way she did four years ago. If they could try to make each other that happy again. But if the answer is no, he doesn't want to hear it, so he doesn't ask. He pours her a little more wine and when, after maybe ten or twenty seconds, she composes herself and places her napkin back on her lap he clears his throat and says, "I think I'm going to have the bouillabaisse, what looks good to you?"

It wasn't just the heat between them, or that she greeted him at the door in lace panties and sheer negligees, or that their hands were in each other's clothes before he'd even put his bags down. It was the feel of their lovemaking. He'd never experienced anything like it in his life. There was something about making love with no barriers, nothing at all—no condoms, no diaphragm, no pills, no *intent* to keep part of him separate from part of her—that placed the act onto a transcendent plane. He was six months into his fiftieth year, but that summer he felt like he was twenty again, having sex eight, ten times in three days and feeling like he could do it nonstop if he didn't have to sleep or eat or work or breathe. He thought he and Lily had experienced as great a degree of intimacy with each other as was possible between two people, but he'd been wrong. And it wasn't just the sex. They were making love even when they weren't having sex, that heavenly connection was there in everything they did. It was there when they did nothing more than sit in the same room and read.

They were trying to have a baby. Some months after he turned fifty he got it into his head that he wanted an heir. It started when his estate lawyer asked him, as he did every five years, to review his will for any changes he might want to make. Lily now got everything after he died, but he started thinking about where it would all go after she was gone. There were bequests to her niece and nephew, and the rest went to charities. Suddenly it seemed a waste. For the first time the thought of leaving a piece of his physical being in the world took on a tremendous appeal to him. Not being an introspective man, he didn't stop to think why, that it might not be so much about wanting an heir to leave his money to as it was about having arrived at an age where he was closer to his death than to his birth and that not knowing whose blood he came from was something he had never made his peace with; that he wanted his blood to endure beyond him. All he knew was that something was gnawing at him and he named it Let's Have a Baby, undoubtedly because it was the most unexpected thing he could think to do. He could have named it Let's Retire and Travel Around the World for a Year, or Let's Buy a Vineyard in Napa Valley, or Let's Go to Africa and Bungee Jump off Victoria Falls. And Lily would have said yes to any of them. But not as eagerly as she said yes to the let's have a baby request. In her eagerness, Paul saw what he had chosen to see in the actions of all of his women: a desire to please him.

By October, after four months of no results and a secret talk with Lily's gynecologist, Paul concluded that the odds of success were poor. From one day to the next, the urgent gnawing that had started the whole thing disappeared. He didn't stop to think why, that maybe once again it wasn't about having or not having a future repository for his wealth but rather about the consequences to one's soul, and the effect on the soul's desires, of being connected to another human being as he now was to Lily. He wasn't likely to get this thing he thought he wanted and so, as he had done time and time again, he applied his formidable will and stopped wanting it.

By October, four months of failing to conceive had begun

to wreak its insidious damage on Lily, but to Paul she merely seemed as eager to keep trying, to give him what he'd asked for, as when they'd started. All he wanted was to suspend time and remain forever in this ecstatic, private place he and Lily had created together. If letting her continue to try to give him a baby would do that, then he would let her continue. Even after it all fell apart, when they failed and failed and the ecstatic connection was broken, he never saw that the need that had possessed him briefly had not actually disappeared; he had exorcised it from himself, yes, but it had cleverly seeded itself in a more hospitable host, from where it could damage both of them. It had taken possession of Lily, and there it would stay.

11

CALEB, GO SIT IN THE waiting room. I want to talk to Dr. Beth for a minute. And save that for later."

Caleb is brandishing his reward, an organic fruit roll, as Danny pushes him firmly down the hallway. The stitches have come out today, the scrapes are nearly all healed. There is nothing wrong, yet Danny is uneasy.

"Come on in."

Beth smiles at him as she closes her office door. Neither of them sits. He leans against the door and she leans against her desk.

"I'm so glad you said yes to helping out with The Doorway project. No one could possibly do a better job than you will, Danny."

"Yeah, well, what were the odds of my surviving saying no to you *and* Tom?"

Beth laughs. "Not great." She is still smiling but her eyes have turned thoughtful. "I think you'll enjoy it. You work alone too much. There are warm, wonderful people involved in this project; it will be good for you."

"I'm not doing it to meet people, Beth." It's a churlish response to a purely generous thought and Danny is immediately sorry he said it. "So, how is your end of things going?"

"Very well. Joan found me the loveliest woman, someone named Lily Spencer, to help me. She's got a master's in social work and she negotiated the medical bureaucracy in New York for private clients so she really knows what she's doing."

"Lovely? Come on, she must be a pit bull if she's good at that sort of thing," Danny jokes.

"Well, then she's a very lovely and sweet pit bull. And I'm sure you'll meet her at some point, whether you want to or not."

They look at each other. Danny smiles apologetically and says, "I'm sorry, that was uncalled for, how I reacted before. You're right. It will be good for me, and it'll be fun."

"It's okay. I understand. So. You looked worried. Should I have given Caleb a cherry fruit roll instead of a grape?"

He laughs. "You shouldn't have given him anything. I promised I'd take him for an early dinner at The Kitchen. He wants a hamburger, which is code for a chocolate milkshake."

Beth touches his arm with a light, swift motion, like a butterfly. "Danny. Caleb is fine. He won't even have a scar."

Danny nods but doesn't say anything.

"Are you all right? Did you talk to Will? I still can't believe Eve didn't call you."

"Yeah, I did. I called him the next day right after I called you. He wants me to start documenting everything. How much time Caleb spends with them, what they do with him, anything I don't like or approve of. If he comes home upset." Danny laughs without humor. "He told me he doesn't want to go to the cemetery or look at pictures of Mommy with Grandma." Danny can easily imagine why. No matter what they do, Tara is still not there

when they're done and Eve's misery, her unyielding and expect-
ant eyes, make Caleb believe it's his fault that his mother is gone.
Eve can even make Danny feel that way. "Poor Caleb. If Eve
doesn't upset him, I do."

"I'm sure you're handling Caleb just fine."

"No, Beth, I'm not. I'm so pissed off at what she did I'm
walking around with smoke coming out of my ears for a week
and I'm probably scaring the crap out of him. He's been a little
too well behaved, if you know what I mean. Man, I really hate
this."

Beth puts her hand on his arm again. This time she leaves it
there. "Danny. I'm sorry."

Danny shifts subtly against the door and the offer of Beth's
warmth and comfort falls away. "Beth, I have to ask you something. It's not just that she didn't call me. It's that she always
makes me feel that I'm not taking good enough care of him. Tell
me, really, should I be worrying more? Should I be getting him
tested for . . . you know . . . for what Tara had?"

"Danny, what happened to Tara was unpredictable. She was
healthy, she was young . . . it was a freak accident of fate. We
talked about this before. Screening for aneurysms is a bit of a
grey area, but most practitioners would not recommend it in a
case like this, where only one first-degree relative—a parent, sib-
ling or child—is affected and there's no family history of other
unusual medical problems that have a strong relationship to cerebral aneurysms, such as polycystic kidney disease. Aneurysms
are extremely rare in children. Screening is very expensive, trau-
matic for a child, and no one knows how often it would have to
be repeated."

Beth delivers her opinion with absolute professional confidence, which Danny greatly appreciates. It's calming and en-

courages him to stay rational, but he requires more; he requires a deeper sort of reassurance. He doesn't register the tiny flicker in her eye when he asks, "If he was your son, what would you do?"

She shakes her head. "Nothing. I would do exactly what you're doing. Danny, you could not be a better father. Please stop beating yourself up over this. He's fine. The odds of what happened to Tara happening to him are infinitesimal."

"I could stand to be reminded of that every so often."

Beth smiles. "You're in luck. I think I could stand to do that for you."

"Are you going to eat that?" Danny tries to fork one of Caleb's remaining french fries.

"No! Daaaaad!!!"

Caleb deftly parries the attack with his own fork and they fence across the table, silverware clashing.

"Come on. Take pity on your old dad. Where are you going to put it, anyway? You look like you swallowed a basketball."

Caleb has eaten his entire hamburger and drunk every drop of his chocolate milkshake. He looks down at his belly, bulging beneath his Yankees shirt, and dissolves in a fit of giggles. Danny grins, sneaks in, and spears a fat fry.

"You cheated!" Caleb yells. He snatches the fry off Danny's fork and shoves it in his mouth. "You're a poopyhead!" White and brown potato paste flies from his lips.

"Yeah? Well, then you're the son of a poopyhead. And that's a pretty sight," Danny says, and flicks another fry at Caleb's mouth. Caleb shrieks and throws it back.

From behind the counter, Arlene calls, "No fighting in here, you hooligans! Don't make me come over there and tickle you!"

Caleb clamps his hands over his mouth. His eyes bug open in make-believe fear and he nearly flops off his seat.

"Uh-oh, kiddo. We're in trouble now. We'd better get out of here, fast."

Caleb scrambles to his feet and, clutching a french fry in each fist, laughing and screaming like a banshee, runs out the door. Danny is three paces behind him.

Lily is hurrying to the post office before they close to mail her niece, Lisa, a darling pair of earrings she found in a way cool shop in New Paltz, the college town about an hour north of Stone Creek. She is also out of stamps and hopes they have sheets of those bat stamps she's been getting in the city. She leaves her car in the small lot at the side of the building and emerges onto Main Street. The Kitchen is diagonally across the street, but there is no sign of the silver Dodge. Lily stands by the post office door for a moment, searching in both directions, relieved and despondent all at once. Reluctantly, she turns and goes inside and gets on the surprisingly long line to do her business.

At five thirty she is back out on the street. She pauses to put the receipt for the insured package into her wallet and tuck the sheet of stamps into her bag's outside pouch—no bats but some cute snakes, turtles, and frogs. She is thinking about how much Lisa is going to love those earrings and how much fun she had shopping for them and maybe she should drive back up to New Paltz one day next week, and maybe even go on to Woodstock. As she raises her head she hears a shriek from across the street. She looks over and sees a little boy come barreling out the door of The Kitchen, waving french fries. Quite the delightful spectacle. She smiles and starts to turn away but stops when a man emerges behind the boy, takes the fries, wipes the boy's hands, wraps the fries in the napkin, and gives it to the laughing waitress standing in the doorway. He takes the boy's hand and heads toward the curb. The little boy is blond and blue-eyed and has a big bandage on his leg. As the man steps off the curb he swings the boy up onto his shoulders. The boy settles himself there as if he were terribly tired and digs his fingers into his father's spiky sun-bleached hair.

It's him.But how can it be? Where is his truck? Disoriented, Lily frantically looks around, dumbly thinking that if the truck isn't there it can't be him. And he isn't dressed right, either. Where are the jeans, the T-shirt? This man is wearing neat black pants and a dark blue short-sleeved shirt. Lily is frozen on the sidewalk as he comes toward her, just as she was rooted into the corner of Chuck and Mona's living room by the sight of Paul the night they met. As he nears the curb on her side of the street, he sees her. Their eyes meet and his seem to leap out at her from his craggy face, their light pure blue color set off by the dark blue of his shirt. His gait falters as though some force in her is pushing at him, driving him backward, but he doesn't take his eyes from her. It is Lily who moves her unblinking gaze, upward, to take in every inch of the bandaged child with his father's eyes and hair, who is drooping now from fatigue, from the aftermath of whatever happened to him, from the meal he just ate.

The man steps onto the sidewalk, no more than ten feet from her. He has been moving slowly and all but stops now. The little boy sags and the man effortlessly slides the boy off his shoulders into his arms. Lily can almost feel the small limp body in her own arms and her body trembles, as though a tiny earthquake is shaking the ground beneath her feet. All the while he is staring at her and at one point he opens his mouth slightly, and she thinks he is going to say something, put into words the unreadable question in his imploring gaze. Lily can't look away from him; she is caught like an animal in the blue beacons of his eyes. For a second they reveal to her what it is he wants. Solace. But he doesn't say anything and the illumination dulls and he begins to retreat. She stares after him as he backs farther and farther away, a ghost of a smile on his lips, and disappears around the corner.

"What do you want to do when we get home?" Danny lifts Caleb onto his shoulders as they step off the curb.

"*Finding Nemo*!!!"

For the fortieth time, but he'll be asleep before it's half over. "You got it."

His talk with Beth and an hour of lunacy with Caleb have subdued his chaotic thoughts. Tara, Caleb, and Eve have stopped chasing one another around in his head. His mind is peacefully blank as he crosses the street. There is nothing there to fend off the impact of the unexpected sight of her, that woman, standing on the sidewalk in front of him, staring at him. She is wearing a short black skirt and a cinnamon-colored sleeveless top that hugs her body. She is all curves and smooth tanned skin and one shapely foot in its thin-strapped sandal is on its way down the block but she isn't moving. Danny missteps, then catches himself. He meets her eye and in that first second of contact, standing so close to her at last, he sees things about her that he was not able to see from a distance. Obvious things, but also things he has no reason to know and yet believes he does. That she is older than she appeared, and prettier. Beautiful. With the sort of fragile beauty that can turn a woman into an object and put too much distance between her and the world. It makes her seem unapproachable but Danny intuits that she is not, that she's been lonely, her looks and her private fears keeping all but the most aggressive of men away from her. That she has never learned how to offer herself or to ask for what she wants.

During the no-time it takes him to conclude these things, she is looking at Caleb, following his trajectory as Danny takes him down off his shoulders and lets him snuggle against his chest. When her gaze returns to his face, to his eyes, which have been fixed on her the whole time, she stares directly into them but he knows that it is the twined unit of him and Caleb, father and son, that she is seeing. And in her eyes as she stares at him there is such devastation that it is painful to look at her. She has lost something she loved, he has no doubt of it, something as precious to her as Tara was to him. His arms tighten around Caleb and he thinks, *She lost a child.* And as hard as it is to think about that and to look at her, he can't turn away because he recognizes that devastation, no matter that it's the first time he's seen it anywhere but in his mirror. Except for their soft, dark color, he could be staring into his own eyes. He shrinks inside to realize that this is what the people who love him have been seeing when they look at him. She must be seeing it too. Her pain reflected in his eyes, in the eyes of someone who should feel like a stranger but doesn't. This is what has been pulling them toward each other, this bond of private catastrophe, and the despairing hope of finding someone who will cherish the other's pain as lovingly as they each do their own.

He wants to speak to her but the encounter has taken on the surreality of a dream and he feels himself no different from most men and he can't imagine how to approach her. He smiles timidly as he continues to back away but there is no change in her expression. He backs all the way to the end of the block, around the corner, then turns and walks quickly down the street to where he's parked the Volvo, his heart beating so hard and fast that Caleb feels it and climbs higher on Danny's chest to get away from it. As he drives away, he realizes he saw one other thing about her. She was wearing a wedding ring. There is a stab of regret in his gut so sharp it makes him gasp and Caleb perks up at the sound and says, "Dad?" He shakes his head and reaches back to squeeze Caleb's knee. The regret is intense, and yet it is followed immediately by an equally intense feeling of relief. She is unavailable. Whatever treacherous, traitorous thoughts he has had or might yet have about her or about his own availability are going to remain safely inside his head. That little gold circle will protect them both. The dissonance of his regret and his relief is like sandpaper in his brain. She is unavailable.

Lily lurches in the opposite direction, toward the post office parking lot. She has to guide herself with a hand on the rough redbrick wall. It is a fortunate thing that Stone Creek's citizenry are an honest lot and that Lily has grown accustomed to leaving the car doors unlocked. She is so blinded by tears she would never be able to find her keys. She gropes for the handle of the door she comes to first—the rear driver's side door—and yanks it open. She drags herself into the car, pulls the door closed, and slowly topples onto the seat. She puts her hands over her face and moans and the sound seeps through her fingers with her tears.

He has a son. A sweet little boy who looks just like him. He's a father. A tender, loving father who carries his child on his shoulders when he's too tired to walk, and holds him close to comfort him. He's a father.

*   *   *

Paul promised to take her to Paris for their fifth wedding anniversary. For the first time since their honeymoon he was going to take off two entire weeks so that, for the first time since
their honeymoon, they could spend more than a week alone
together. Two weeks in Paris in June with Paul! Lily bought
and read a dozen guidebooks and mapped out walks and side
trips and dinners and every romantic picnic spot in the city.
One-third of her suitcase, already packed ten days before the
trip, was taken up with lingerie, and there was plenty of room
for the new frilly things she planned to let Paul buy for her.
She wound down her responsibilities with her existing clients
and didn't take on any new ones after February so she could
be totally free.

She was disappointed, of course, but didn't complain when
Paul told her, a week before they were scheduled to leave, that
they couldn't go. The important case on which he was lead at-
torney had been put on the court calendar sooner than anyone
expected and he couldn't get away. She never complained about
the enormous bite his work took from their time together, although she hadn't been quite prepared for how deprived of him
she felt because of it.

When he told her, she was mindful to react in such a way
that wouldn't make him feel bad. His announcement was made
with sincere expressions of regret and apology, but he couldn't
suppress his predator's excitement at the prospect of going full
out after prey and it made her feel as though she, their anniversary, their time together, paled to insignificance for him in
comparison. She told herself she was being foolish and didn't
let her feelings show. She said she understood, which truly she

did, that it was all right. She unpacked her suitcase and as she was putting her lingerie back into the drawer she decided that, having worked hard for twenty years, she would take the entire summer off and, since he was going to be so busy, spend it in Stone Creek.

The day of their anniversary fell that year on a Thursday. Paul had so much to do so quickly that he couldn't even take a long weekend. But he did come home from the office that day by six thirty, in time to change and to keep their seven thirty reservation for dinner. He took her to The Boathouse, which would not have been his first choice as it didn't have the best food in New York. But it did have one of the loveliest settings anywhere in the world, on the easternmost bulge of the amorphously shaped lake in Central Park and Lily thought it one of the most romantic places in the city. She knew he was taking her there to make up for not taking her to the actual most romantic city in the world and she loved him for trying.

They were led to a table by the railing on the wide outdoor patio. Boaters moved idly through the lily pads out on the dark water. Beyond, at the far end of the lake, Bethesda Fountain, topped by Emma Stebbins's 1873 sculpture, *Angel of the Waters*, soared into the clear blue sky and sent delicate circles of water cascading into the enormous pool below. A billowing wind blew droplets onto the grand brick and stone terrace that surrounded it. The Boathouse was not a formal or fancy place and the weather was warm and a little sticky, so Lily wore a simple white dress with a bustier top; the square-cut emerald pendant Paul had given her that morning hung just below the hollow of her throat. Paul wore black slacks and a black short-sleeved shirt. Heads turned as they crossed the patio and because she thought Paul was the handsomest man on earth she assumed it was him they were looking at. She was wrong, of course, it was both of them, but then she had had a lifetime of practice not noticing people's interest in her.

It was after they had finished their dinners and a bottle of wine, their espressos and a shared hot banana-coconut bread pudding with hard sauce that Paul gave her the anniversary gift that made her forget all about Paris. He moved the smeared plate aside and took her hand. They looked into each other's eyes. They sat like that for a few minutes, in the moist summer darkness, muted lights and sounds of the city all around them, not talking, just looking at each other. His fingers moved over her hand, grazed her palm, slid in and out of her fingers; his thumb traced small circles on the inside of her wrist. She felt his touch deep inside her and she grew lightheaded with her desire to lie down with him. Then he leaned across the table, his eyes boring into hers, and he smiled and said, "Lily. My beautiful Lily. Let's have a baby."

Her head swam, with wine, with lust, with the belief that she must have misheard him. *Let's have a brownie? Let's halve the navy?* "What?"

"I said, let's have a baby."

"What are you talking about? I don't understand. I thought . . ."

He tossed his head, dismissed her bewilderment. "Yeah, I know. But I don't know. I'm fifty. You're going to outlive me. I don't want you to forget me when I'm gone." He laughed and then shrugged. "Look. I want to try. If it works, it works. If it doesn't, we move on. It might be fun. We'd have one smart, great-looking kid, that's for sure. I don't want to talk it to death. Let's just give it a shot."

She sat there looking into the eyes of this man she loved, all her senses heightened by alcohol and the seductive pull of the night, her brain and body already consumed with the thought of him, and she imagined the feel of his child growing in her, a boy who would look just like him, and her insides pushed and twisted with the need for that to be. She was forty-one. No one had ever wanted to have a baby with her.

"I know what I said before, but just say yes, Lily, don't think about it. Think about what a good time we'll have trying. I'll come up every weekend and we'll fuck our brains out every minute I'm not working and whatever happens happens."

She didn't think about it. She didn't have to. She hadn't wanted a baby before because she had been asked not to and she was brought up to do what people stronger and surer than she, in other words everyone, asked of her. Now Paul was asking her to want a baby. She wanted what he wanted and that was as far as her thoughts took her that night. He wanted a baby and she would give him one.

"So. Should we go home and take our first run at it?" His hand crept up her arm.

She didn't answer, she just nodded and stood up.

He laughed. "Hey, sit down. They really like it when you pay the bill before you leave."

The check was lying discreetly on the table, on a brass tray. Lily picked it up and said, "That's fair, I suppose." She opened her purse, took out her wallet, and placed two hundred dollars on the tray. She extended her hand to him and said, "Happy anniversary. Now take me home."

The next morning, Lily drove up to Stone Creek in a state of bliss and when she arrived at the house had no memory of how she'd gotten there. The world had changed and would never be the same again. When she'd told him to take her home it was to tell him that he could have from her what he wanted, whatever he wanted. If she had understood then that she was telling him what *she* wanted, their world would still have changed, no doubt, but it might have changed for the better instead of for the worse.

12

"Okay, Spencer, put your clothes on and come into my boudoir."

Paul is at Dr. Henry Bertram's office for the second time in the past two weeks. Bertram is an internist with a brain and mouth as sharp as Paul's and has been his doctor for sixteen years. There has been the occasional sinus infection, one very nasty and resistant parasitic problem after a business trip to Asia, and two occurrences of walking pneumonia brought on by sheer stubborn neglect, but otherwise Paul is disgustingly healthy and his annual physicals are typically brief and boring in the examining room, relaxing and clever in Bertram's office. Paul had his last uneventful annual physical six months ago. He's here now because he's not sleeping, that heaviness in his stomach and chest has become more persistent, and he is experiencing intermittent episodes of shortness of breath and racing heartbeat.

"Sit." Bertram waves a hand at the chair across from his desk. He gets up from his own chair and goes to the barred ground-floor window facing out onto Park Avenue. He perches on the sill and pushes the window open. He fishes a pack of cigarettes

from the pocket of his white coat. "You mind?" He ignores
Paul's gesture of amused permission and lights up. "Don't tell
the witches of Eastwick out front. They yell at me."

"They should. You're overweight and you smoke. You're an
embarrassment to your profession. So, what's wrong with me?"

"I could look like you and not reek of tobacco if I wanted to.
I do this because it's important that people feel their doctor is
human. It inspires trust." He takes a folder from the desk and
resettles on the sill. "All right. All your tests came back clean."
Bertram riffles disinterestedly through Paul's file. "You don't
have an ulcer, your lungs are clear, your blood work would give a
vampire a hard-on, your urine is potable, your cholesterol is low,
you have the heart of a twenty-five-year-old. Whoever your fore-
bears were, they gave you a hell of a set of genes, and you didn't
have to put up with their nagging you to clean up your room. A
little high blood pressure today, but that's atypical of you and it
doesn't mean anything."

"Where did you buy those diplomas, Doctors R Us? These
symptoms have to mean something, Henry. I'm not imagining
them."

"No, you're not. You couldn't be. You have no imagination.
Plenty of brains but no imagination." He stubs out his cigarette
in a dirty GlaxoSmithKline mug and sits down behind his desk.
"Knots in the stomach, a heavy feeling in your chest, insomnia, a
sense of doom. Schmuck. You're having anxiety attacks."

Paul is dumbfounded. "And you're an idiot. Who said anything about a sense of doom, for Christ's sake?" Even as he denies it, he recognizes that a sense of doom is exactly what he's
been feeling lately. He jumps up from his seat and starts pacing
the small office. "What the hell do I have to be anxious about?"

"You tell me."

Paul is silent. He is displeased with his sparring partner's diagnosis. Not that he wants to have an ulcer or plaque-ridden arteries, but a rare viral infection would have done nicely. The pain in his stomach feels worse.

"So, how's work? You're the go-to guy on the hottest case since Monica and the married man's fantasy that a blow job isn't really sex." Bertram leans back in his chair. "You're under a lot of pressure to find the smoking gun, right? Sit down, you're making me queasy."

Paul laughs and sits. "Oh, yeah. A Mount Everest of pressure. But I love it, you know that."

"Who's the idiot? All right. And how's the lovely Lily? How are things at home?"

"The lovely Lily is as lovely as ever. She's fine. Everything's fine. I'm so damned busy, she's spending the summer up in the country."

Bertram leans forward and fixes Paul with a detective's challenging stare. "Ah, so. As I recall, you do not enjoy sleeping alone."

Paul's rancorous glare has no effect on Bertram's scrutiny and he averts his eyes.

"And you do not enjoy being told things you don't want to hear. Okay, Paul." He pulls out a prescription pad and starts scribbling. "I'm giving you a prescription for Ambien—it's a sleeping pill, very effective with no morning-after hangover. And one for lorazepam, for the anxiety. You can take both of them as needed. If in a few weeks everything is still *fine* but you aren't feeling better, call me and I'll give you a few names and you'll go talk to someone."

*　*　*

There isn't a snowball's chance in hell that Paul is ever going to go talk to someone, or that he's going to fill these prescriptions. For all the insulting banter, he has faith in Bertram's skills and if Bertram says there's nothing wrong with him then there's nothing wrong with him. So if his problems are all in his head, he'll use the plenty of brains that Bertram graciously acknowledges he has and logic himself out of them.

Bertram was right about the brains but wrong about the imagination. Paul does have an imagination. However, since he was never able to identify a justifiable or positive use for it, he locked it safely in the barn some time during his young adulthood. He blames what imagination he has for some of the greatest unpleasantnesses of his life. Such as when he was six and imagined that his dark dark coloring, his red-tinged warm skin, and his distinctive nose proved that he must be at least half a Michigan Chippewa Indian who had been stolen from his real mother off a reservation in the far north of the state and given to this pale pale family outside the city of Kalamazoo in the far south and that she had been searching for him ever since and was going to come rescue him on the exact day of his seventh birthday. Or the years that followed her crushing nonappearance when he imagined that even if he wasn't a Chippewa, but was Greek or Italian or Armenian or even a Jew instead of the Spenglers' thoughtlessly proud Aryan German, his being the smartest kid in town, the valedictorian of his high school graduating class, and the winner of a full scholarship to the University of Michigan at Ann Arbor, would make his adoptive mother look at him with the same pleasure and dumb love she bestowed on her four biological sons.

He blames his imagination for this ridiculous anxiety. Chaikin-Gibbs's workload has been singularly unchallenging for him for

the past year, and having his brain in idle has never been good
for him. He creates problems that aren't there just to keep his
mind busy, to give him something to assault or solve or conquer.
These worries about his age, about Lily, they're crazy. Happily,
he now has a focus for his straying attention; thank goodness for
corporate greed. The SynTech case will corral his imagination
back into the barn and allow his creativity—his expertly trained
titanic intellectual creativity—to run free. Once it's in full gallop
all these foolish thoughts will stop and the anxiety will disappear.

It's nearly six o'clock, but Paul tells Big Vinnie, his favorite driver, to take him back downtown, back to the office. He
is putting in fourteen-, sometimes sixteen-hour days, getting to
Wall Street by seven and not leaving until nine or later. Some
nights he just gives it up and sleeps there, on the pull-out sofa
in the cozy library attached to his office. And screw Bertram's
innuendos; he's glad that Lily decided to spend the summer at
the house. Why should she stay in town in the steamy fume-
filled heat when most of her friends are away and her husband
is buried in work? She would just be worrying about him worrying about her being lonely and bored. She's obviously finding plenty to do—although for him a week up there has proved
to be as much consecutive time as he can tolerate—and if their
weekends haven't been what they were four years ago, so what?
They've been married nine years, he knows things can cool down
at times, for a while. It doesn't mean anything. He's got a lot on
his mind and she's giving him some space. She's having some
hormonal problems. That's all.

The SynTech investigation is an eighteen-wheeler going
downhill without brakes, just the harrowing speed Paul loves, no
runaway truck ramps in sight. In the five weeks since Chaikin-

Gibbs was handed the case, his office has sifted through enough previously gathered information to assure him of the high probability that the software company's senior officers went rogue in royal style. That they stole money, cooked the books, back-dated contracts, misreported earnings; that they cheated their employees, screwed their shareholders, and used their ill-gotten gains for egregious acts of self-indulgence.

For starters he is going to have to redo much of the work the Feds already did. Not because they didn't do a thorough job but because they didn't find the proof. Those same senior officers everyone knows had fun playing criminal have managed to cover their asses for nearly twenty months now. Subpoenaed documents that they claim don't exist and similar obstructionist crap. Piling one illegality on top of another. But the truth is out there and Paul's going to find it. He's scheduling new depositions of company executives and board members all over the country. He's writing up official requests for the immediate delivery of hundreds of cartons of company records. He's hunting for an outside software genius who will be able to retrieve past company e-mails, where, Paul has found, people tend to blatantly incriminate themselves in the ignorant belief that hitting that little DELETE button makes it all go bye-bye.

Normally the frenzy of a case like this keeps him manically happy during the day and knocks him out at night like a tranquilizer-darted bull. And the days are not bad. It's the nights that have been the real problem. The nights he sleeps at the office are a little better than the nights he goes home to the apartment, but neither are good. For the first time in his life, he just can't sleep. The deserted office feels sterile and full of strange light and the bed in the apartment feels too large and arid.

Big Vinnie is driving downtown on Park Avenue from Bertram's office on Ninetieth Street. The wide avenue's planted median is a river of color between the elegant buildings on either side. There is a clear line of sight all the way down to Forty-fifth Street, where the avenue is interrupted by the architectural grandeur of the nearly one-hundred-year-old Grand Central Terminal and the unfortunate modern MetLife building, once the PanAm building, rising above it. Paul likes the house in Stone Creek well enough. He likes having a place in the country. But to him there's nothing better than this incredible city. He rolls his window down and takes a sedating breath of the warm, carbon-dioxide-filled air.

He rolls the window up and turns to his briefcase beside him. The car is moving through the wide intersection of Seventy-second Street and Paul catches his reflection in the rearview mirror just as a bolt of sunlight floods the car from the west. In the unforgiving harshness of the full sun, he sees an old man looking back at him. His scalp and palms break out in a cold sweat and a thought-obliterating panic sweeps through him. He gasps to get breath into his lungs.

"Mr. Spencer? You okay?" Big Vinnie's head swivels as he tries to see Paul in the mirror.

"Yeah, yeah. Just some reflux or something. Listen. Take me home, would you? Go across at Sixty-sixth."

Paul retrieves his cell phone, calls his secretary, and tells her to messenger the files on his desk up to the apartment. He has Vinnie drop him in front of the San Remo, but he doesn't go in. Before Miguel, the 4:00 p.m. to midnight doorman, spots him, he veers away west. On Broadway he finds one of those huge, anonymous pharmacies, a Duane Reade or Rite-Aid, he doesn't know which, hands them both prescriptions, and is told that they'll be ready in an hour. Obviously they keep a lot of that shit on hand; he guesses he's not the only anxious jackass in New York. He kills the hour in front of the magazine rack at the Barnes & Noble on Sixty-sixth Street, reading nothing. He picks up his pills, stops in the dental care aisle, and downs a lorazepam without water.

When he gets to the apartment, he goes into the living room, pours himself a vodka, and stands at the windows with his back to the room so he doesn't have to see the walls. He doesn't care if he's not supposed to drink with this stuff. By the time the messenger arrives, the panic and the sweats have subsided. He finishes off some leftover Chinese takeout and works until midnight. He's very tired and he wants to sleep but his brain is humming so he takes an Ambien. The last thing he thinks before the drug knocks him out is that he wishes Lily would come home.

The night they made love for the first time, Paul knew his hungry shark days were over. He knew it the night they met, at that singular moment right before he kissed her. He'd zeroed in on her at the Golds' party because she was the prettiest woman there and he'd always thought it a crime to leave a pretty woman unclaimed. And at first she'd seemed exactly his kind of woman: young and lovely, but old enough and clever enough to not bore him, in or out of bed, and to have been sufficiently hardened by experience to weather a go-round with someone like him. But even as she bantered with him so charmingly, he saw in her guileless eyes that Lily was a different kind of woman. She was an emotional virgin, a sleeping beauty awaiting the man who would awaken her. As he looked down into her, and then watched her from across the room, all he could think of was how amazing, how frightening, it would be to let go his grip, fall into her softness, and be enveloped by her innocence. To let himself be seen by such accepting eyes as hers. To start over, from the very beginning. With a woman like Lily, he could.

Still, he had to fight it for at least a little while so as not to feel that he had been reduced to a common variety infatuated middle-aged moron thinking with his prick. Although in a way he was. It had been his hard head and heart, not that other hard organ, that had chosen, time and again, to move on to the next woman. However persuasive what was going on below his waist might have been, it never had influence above the belt line. But with Lily, everything everywhere inside seemed to pull and push and merge somewhere in the middle of him, in his gut—the body's unthinking brain. In that same spot where he is now having those odd, twisted feelings. It wasn't that Lily had bedroom skills so exotic that they could go where no one had gone before. What she lacked initially in crude technical prowess, however, was mysteriously rendered maddeningly erotic by her utter lack of restraint, her pure, unadulterated passion. By the avidity with which she absorbed his patiently offered education in how to please him and, most exciting to him, how to let him please her. By the unguarded love for him he felt and heard in her every touch and moan. The result of it all was that he fit into her in a way he had never fit with anyone else. And he didn't have to be inside her to feel it.

But still, it took him four months to accept that he had to marry her. The inescapable truth of it was made manifest when, one predawn morning in May, after they had made love, he found himself confiding his childhood history to her, a history that only his doctor, his estate lawyer, and two of his closest colleagues knew. He told her that he had been born nameless, adopted in infancy, and raised by the Spenglers of Kalamazoo, Michigan.

Beginning when Paul was a year and a half old, Mrs. Spengler's previously uncooperative uterus disgorged four sons in six years. By the time she was done, Paul knew he wasn't loved or needed anymore. He was just a jagged speck of dirt clinging to the pod case that contained the real Spenglers: six featureless peas, blond, beefy, good-natured, and of exuberantly average brain power. He left home when he was seventeen. He took with him his striking looks and piercing intelligence, the two assets he could count on to win him love and admiration, despite their being belittled by his father and brothers and ignored by his mother, who could not find a way to reward Paul for qualities her own sons lacked. At twenty-one he changed his last name to Spencer, left Michigan for the East Coast, and never went back.

He told Lily the facts of it. And all the while he spoke, her hand caressed his body and her eyes caressed his face, and the flesh of him, lain cold and dormant for years on the bare bones of what he presented to her, warmed and came to life.

He proposed a week later, on the night of her birthday, May 9, at the luxurious, romantic inn in Massachusetts where he had taken her. His proposal, his final and best gift, was not made timorously on bended knee; he may have been reduced to desiring a conventional union but he was still the same Paul Spencer who never begged favors from any woman. He proposed forcefully while on top of her, in her and on her in every way he could find to be, penis deep in the heat of her, breath and tongue in her mouth, stretched arms skin against skin and fingers entwined in a struggling grip. The question, expressed, naturally enough, as a demand—"Marry me. I want you to marry me"—was unfairly popped during the susceptible seconds between her third and fourth orgasm. He felt her come as he moved to the rhythm she had set for them; he felt rather than heard her moan and cry out into his mouth. He freed her to find her breath, moved his mouth, and whispered it into her ear. Although he'd been thinking about nothing else for a week, the words gushed out of him unexpectedly, spontaneously. As he willfully held back his own release, the punitively controlled animal he was tore loose from its cage and howled that *she* was the one thing he wanted that he would never stop wanting. It was time to make sure he had her. Paul Spencer may certainly have been all the things Lily had been warned of, but, as of that moment, he became something more, something more than he'd ever been. He became a man in love. The seconds it took for her to reply ballooned to an eternity. But, of course, he had nothing to worry about. She said yes. She said yes a dozen times and clung to him and cried.

The next morning, over breakfast in their room, she asked, "Why me? You've had so many women in your life. There's nothing special about me. Why do you want to marry me?"

"I don't know why you. How can I answer that?" But then he paused and found that he had an answer of sorts to give her. "Because when I'm with you I feel safe. When I touch you everything goes quiet inside me, like . . . like the scales are all finally in perfect balance." He studied her face and he thought, *This is the face of my wife. This beautiful face belongs to me. She belongs to me.* His eyes roamed over her delicate features and came to rest on her melting brown eyes, eyes in which he had never seen so much as a shadow of secretiveness or deceit. When he looked into those eyes, he could believe himself lovable.

"You're a better person than I am, Lily. You have such generosity and compassion in you. You know how to give people what they need and you *want* to do it. I don't. I wouldn't even know how. I've spent too many years alone, watching out for my own needs."

"You have me to help you now. And you give me what I need." She shook her head, smiled at him lovingly. "It's not your fault that you don't see what others see, what I see. When you doubt yourself, all you have to do is look at me. I'll show you how wonderful you are."

He knew by both that smile and those words that Lily believed, mistakenly, that the very honesty of his confession belied its truth. She thought he was saying that he expected her to make a better person of him. He didn't. He didn't want to become a better person in those emotional vulnerable-underbelly ways. It had never bothered him when he was accused of being selfish or controlling or demanding. He was what he was. It had worked for him for forty-six years. He didn't see why he should change now, or imagine how he even could. What he meant by what he'd said was that he didn't have to be a better person if he had her to be that for him.

By this time, his previous women had figured that out. It always took at least a few months. The one place where Paul wasn't selfish with women was in bed. Neither was he controlling or demanding. Skilled and a bit aggressive, yes, but these were traits that were appreciated more or less everywhere. All his women started out convinced that any man who was as generous, sensitive, and patient when his clothes were off as Paul was most certainly had it in him to be generous, sensitive, and patient when fully dressed, as well. In time they realized that he didn't. Which convinced them that being such a good lover was just another form of his selfishness, as it brought him great, immediate, and heavenly rewards. In this, however, they were wrong. His selfless attentiveness was genuine. He liked making women happy. Using his body to do it was direct and uncomplicated. It wasn't his fault, either, that he wasn't as proficient at using his heart and his mind. You could teach yourself how to be good at sex. But you had to be shown how to be good at love.

Paul thought he could do better with Lily, give her enough so that it wouldn't matter that he couldn't change, that he *wasn't* as good as she was and never would be. He made no comment on her optimistic assessment of him, merely smiled and said, "Why me?"

She answered without hesitation. "Because I know now that I've never truly loved anyone before. I didn't know a person could feel this way in real life. You have unbalanced the scales for me. I'm not frightened of what might happen if I let myself love you. I'm frightened of what will happen if I don't. No one will ever make me feel this way again, it's not possible."

"I'm glad to know you're not frightened of me."

"I didn't say that. I am frightened of you."

He gave a gentle laugh of admonition. "Lily."

She laughed lightly in response. "Well . . . maybe I'm not frightened of you, exactly. But by how easily you abandoned all your other women. That you might do that to me, if I stopped pleasing you."

She was smiling, but he saw that she was serious. "That will never happen. You could never stop pleasing me." He leaned over the small table and kissed her. "There is one thing we should talk about before we send out the invitations."

"That sounds ominous. What? Do you want me to sign a prenup or something?"

"No, of course not. Whatever I have is yours. No. It's something you've probably already figured out. It's about kids. You've never said anything, so I assume it's not going to be a problem, but you should know that I don't want children. I don't want a family. It's not something I've ever been interested in. All I want is you. Okay?"

She drew in a surprised breath, and a look of disbelief passed fleetingly across her face.

"I'm serious about this, Lily. Is it okay with you?"

"I . . . okay. Yes. Yes, it's okay. Of course it's okay. I stopped thinking about having children long ago, while Rick and I were still married. I think maybe I'm just not meant to. I don't even know if I could. "

"You'd better be sure. I don't want this to come up and bite us later."

"What if I'm not sure? Will you withdraw your proposal?" Once again, she was smiling, teasing him, but her questions begged to be answered.

"No. This is your call. I want to marry you. I want to spend my life with you. But a life with me is not going to include kids. If I misjudged what you wanted, if you can't live with that, you'll have to be the one to withdraw your acceptance. It's up to you, Lily."

He got up and knelt beside her chair. He knew he had her, and now that he did he could appear to bend before her. He took her hand and played with her fingers, kissed her palm. "I love you. You are all I want. You are enough for me, forever. Am I enough for you?"

She let her palm rest on his cheek. "Yes. You're enough."

Five weeks later, Paul and Lily were married in a simple civil ceremony in Paul's apartment in front of their closest friends and family. The next week he took her to Venice for their honeymoon. And for five years thereafter, they were indeed enough for each other. And he has only himself to blame for why that changed.

13

When he wakes up on the morning of Friday, August 18, Danny is in one fucking ugly mood. Since he's basically an emotionally steady and easygoing guy, this is rare for him, although certainly not unheard of. Like anyone else, he has his moments. This morning's fucking ugly mood is partly a result of the ample amount of Grey Goose he drank in order to get to sleep last night, also rare for him. The real culprit, however, is the reason for the Grey Goose, which is that August 18 is the day. The day he's been waiting for and dreading in equal measure. So when he wakes up yet another morning alone in his bed with the summer sheet half on the floor and the first thought that enters his brain is *A year ago on this day I watched the woman I love die,* and the second is *Tonight I have to read the rest of her journal,* he feels like he wants to kill someone. Or maybe just have someone kill him.

He has spent most of the past year counting down to this day as though to a private Armageddon, but that didn't stop him from berating himself as he finally fell into inebriated sleep for the folly of his own melodrama. Doesn't he live on in a universe unchanged from one day to the next in its indifference to the mortality of Tara Ann Jamison Malloy and the ruination of Daniel Patrick Malloy? Arriving at August 18 will not change him or release him or inform him or destroy him. He can't miss her any more profoundly. He can't recall that night any more vividly. The uncaring cosmos won't hand him an epiphany that will reveal to him why she died or what he is meant to make of the rest of his life. It will just be the start of another summer day.

That's what he told himself last night but when he wakes in his ugly mood he knows he was wrong. Something *is* going to happen today. External reality is unchanged—the sun is coming through the window and the birds are singing and the universe is undoubtedly indifferent—but his internal universe has undergone a jarring realignment. His heart flutters; he feels flushed as with fever and the objects in the room shimmer before his eyes. He's very frightened. He sits up and curls himself over his legs. He turns onto his belly and slithers across the bed to Tara's night table. He opens the drawer and stares into it, at the padded envelope that has been waiting for him all these months. The fear ratchets up until he is nauseated with terror. What if after he reads the remainder of what Tara wrote, tonight when he is alone in the house, he realizes that he hasn't even begun to miss her? What if something does indeed happen today but it's not what he hopes, what he's hoped for a year? What if after today it is all only going to get worse and not better?

Danny half crawls and half rolls out of bed. In the bathroom he scrubs his face with cold water then sticks his head under the faucet and lets the chilly water run over his hair and down his neck and arms. He turns his head and gulps down thirsty mouthfuls. He straightens up and shakes his head, sends a spray of cold water in all directions. He's calming down. The feverishness is withdrawing from his skin and his eyes. His heartbeat is slowing. He takes a quick shower, gets dressed, makes his bed, and puts the envelope on his pillow. He closes the door as he leaves the room. He won't open it again until it's time.

He wants the day—until tonight—to be a regular day. He'll take Caleb to camp, spend the morning in his studio, and after lunch meet Tom Gallo at The Doorway house and get an idea of what he's got to do there. Pick Caleb up and go to Will and Sue's for dinner. Then he'll leave Caleb there, come home, and do what he has to do. In the morning, back to Will and Sue's for breakfast.

He wakes Caleb at 7:15. His inner turmoil is shunted aside as he watches for any sign of unrest, any indication that the child might have picked up an adult knowledge of what day it is and be disturbed by it. But there is nothing. Caleb is happy and peaceful, as he has been since their good time at The Kitchen. Danny was worried about Eve, but she must have done as he requested and not said anything.

Since the weekend of Caleb's accident, she has been on her best behavior. When she asked if she could have Caleb today or for the night and Danny said no, she didn't argue. She hasn't baited him or insulted him or challenged him once in the past two and a half weeks. She hasn't been warm, but neither has she been disagreeable. She hasn't sent Caleb home with a tummy full of junk or a head full of things he doesn't understand or so much as a mosquito bite that she hasn't told Danny about. She hasn't asked Caleb to look at photos or go to the cemetery. She has left Danny nothing to make note of in the log Will told him to keep. For the first time that he can remember, he is even finding her soft drawl pleasant to listen to. It's a lovely change but he doesn't trust it. He can't help but think that he's being deliberately lulled into a state of false security and that any day now he will feel the point of a thin blade between his shoulder blades as she skewers his heart from behind.

As soon as he pulls out of his driveway his turmoil reasserts itself. Too many of the people he is going to see today are aware of what August 18 means to him and he already feels exposed just turning onto Old Stone Creek Road. He is calmer than earlier, but his mood is not much prettier. The fear is still there and so is an agitated anger that he thought he'd gotten under control months ago. He doesn't know which is worse, that old anger or the new dread. They're not a good combination, that much he does know.

Caleb is singing an alphabet song and keeping rhythm, energetically, with his hands against the arms of his car seat and his feet against each other; he loves camp and he's eager to get there. His constant movement and his innocent happiness grate on Danny's jangling nerves. He has a perverse urge to take Caleb's idyllic day and smash it. To turn around and yell at Caleb to stay still, to make him cry, to make him fearful and miserable so his father doesn't have to be fearful and miserable alone. Of course he doesn't do it. Instead, when he takes Caleb out of the car he overrides the boy's impatience and hugs him so hard that Caleb says, "Ow, Daddy!"

Danny loosens his hold. "Sorry. I just had to do that. You know, the way sometimes you hug Zilla so tight?" He sets Caleb down.

Zilla is Caleb's stuffed dinosaur, for whom he is often overcome with love. "I know. He doesn't mind. Bye."

Caleb runs off, leaving Danny still ripe to whack someone to ease his psychic discomfort. Poor unwitting Lauren comes up to him with nothing but the best of intentions and gets hit with both barrels.

"Hi, Danny. How are you?" And then she makes the mistake of turning a pitying, slightly damp set of grey eyes on him.

That's all he needs. Rage rumbles like thunder through his chest and comes out of his mouth like the unexpected strike of a rattlesnake. "Don't look at me like that, Lauren. Don't *ever* fucking look at me like that."

She turns bright red and whispers, "I'm sorry, Danny, I didn't mean . . ."

He doesn't give her an inch and her eyes go from damp to wet. She whirls around and hurries away, her blond hair whipping across her flaming cheeks.

Danny feels like a shit but he doesn't go after her to apologize. He gets in the car and drives back home. He goes directly to the studio and puts the new Garbage album into the CD player. The music is raw and aggressive and he turns the stereo up loud. He has some fine finishing work to do on several pieces of furniture, but he shuns that in favor of a more violent job, sanding down the pocked and stained oak of an old hutch. He works at it until his stomach stops asking politely and starts demanding to be fed. By then he's a sweaty, dusty mess. He can't go back into his bedroom or bathroom so he cools down and cleans himself in the creek and dresses in fresh clothes from the laundry room. It's somehow gotten to be two thirty and he's supposed to meet Tom at three. He stands at the open refrigerator door and wolfs down some grilled chicken and tomato basil salad left over from last night's dinner, throws the fork into the sink, wipes his hands on a dish towel, and heads out again.

The hours are ticking down and he is doing everything possible every minute to not think about Tara. That was the point of his plan. To stay busy and not think about her until tonight, when he can be alone in that place where she died at the hour that she died, and perform the ritual her memory demands of him so that he might this time, after failing time and time again, succeed at saying good-bye to her. He understands that he has failed because he has wanted to fail. He still wants to fail, but it's getting harder and harder to live with her ghost clawing at his heart and if he continues like this much longer he will end up living like a ghost himself.

He knows the old place that will house The Doorway. It's on the edge of town, about ten blocks off Main Street, not quite in the countryside, not quite in the village. It's a good location for the group home, quiet and private but close enough to civilization so no one will feel banished or ostracized being there. The now-derelict house, with its equally derelict acre of once well-tended land, belonged to the O'Connors, a large family whose youngest son, Dennis, went to high school with Danny. He's been in it a few times, but not for nearly twenty years. Everyone in town knows that Dennis became a bad drunk, like his father, lost his wife to another man and the family house to the bank, and then disappeared. No one's seen him in nearly four years. Danny remembers the house being a fine one, inside and out. It's going to take a lot of work, but at least there's a former glory waiting to reemerge.

When he pulls into the rutted driveway he sees a few familiar vehicles, including Tom's white panel truck with GALLO CONSTRUC-TION stenciled in blue on its side. There are people here who are going to be thinking things when they see him, but it should be okay. No one is likely to do or say anything stupid or outwardly sentimental. These guys all belong to the same secret society of men who are respectful of another man's privacy, which is to say balls-shrivelingly embarrassed by unmanly displays of emotion, and it would take at least three or four beers before any of them would so much as clap a hand on his shoulder. Tom is not like that, but he knows Danny too well to intrude on him today.

He grabs his tool belt and is buckling it around his waist as he enters the house. He hears Tom's voice coming from off to the left, from what was the formal living room when the O'Connors lived here, and a woman's voice answering him. He walks into the room and standing at the far end, by the fireplace, are Tom, facing him, and two women with their backs to him. Tom sees him and smiles and says, "And here he is, right on time." The women turn to look at him and one of them is her.

He feels wheels turning in his head and in his ears there is a *snick*-like sound as of gears falling into place and the fear and the anger settle out of his brain like dirt churned up from the creek bottom, left to drift back to the muddy floor. The indifferent universe is not indifferent to Daniel Malloy after all, not on this day. From the moment he saw her in Dreiser's she has been in his thoughts, surrounded by an aura of inevitability. He should have known that he would meet her today and that somehow, in a way he cannot yet see, everything will begin to change. He comes across the room and before he turns his attention and his eyes to Tom, he glances at her for the briefest of moments with a look and a smile that say, *Thank God.* She gives him a tremulous smile in return.

Joan is giving Lily the promised tour of the house. The renovations are not that far along yet, but Lily has been wanting to see it. She is becoming emotionally involved in the project and developing an appreciation for the community that she's never had before. She thinks that she could really become friends with Joan and with Beth. It feels so good to be doing something to help people again and she loves that it has nothing to do with Paul and he has nothing to do with it. When she's hard at work on this, she doesn't think about him, doesn't miss him, doesn't believe she needs him.

He has started traveling for his case and has come to Stone Creek only three weekends since July Fourth. He was here again last weekend. The truce they had called at the end of the previous visit two weeks earlier held. It held because they were subdued and cautious with each other and talked about nothing of significance. They kept a palpable emotional distance from each other, unavoidably collided once or twice but quickly withdrew. Familiar endearments were uttered, there was no fighting or sniping. But there was a strained and wearying self-consciousness in their behavior. Lily felt again that sensation she had had for a moment over July Fourth of observing her life as though it were being enacted on a stage and she was working from a script she had not written. When they'd made love, she felt trapped in her mind, watching herself making love to Paul from a distance, from far outside the body that he kissed and caressed and penetrated. She responded to him as she always did, but at one point she had the thought that if she moved away just a little more, she wouldn't feel anything at all.

Joan and Lily have spent an hour going through the house with Tom Gallo. Tom has described to them in detail what will be fixed, changed, replaced, rebuilt in every room and he is so eloquent in his excitement that Lily can almost see what the house will look like when it's done, down to the colors of the walls. Lily likes Tom. His enthusiasm is contagious and his generosity toward the project is clearly from the heart. He's probably not much older than Paul, but he's bald, pot-bellied, and grizzled, his skin leathery from years of sun damage. He looks like a wise and friendly gnome and Lily gets a kick out of how pleased he is with himself for having talked everyone working on the house into donating their time. The further into this project she gets, the happier she is that Joan asked for her help.

The tour is nearly over and the three of them are standing in the living room in front of a fireplace whose surround and mantel even Lily can see were once masterpieces of wood carving but are now criminally cracked, chipped, and scorched.

"Ladies, you won't believe what this will look like a couple months from now." Tom runs his hand over the disfigured mantel. "Joan, I told you I was going to get you the best woodworker there is, and I did."

"Oh, fabulous. Um. Who was that again?"

"Danny. Danny Malloy."

Tom announces the name with such unabashed pride that Lily smiles and says teasingly, "If I didn't know your name was Gallo, I'd suspect you of fatherly pride there, Tom."

Tom narrows his eyes and says, "Well, Lily, I'll tell you. You're not far wrong. He's not my son, but he's my boy. I've known him since he was sixteen, his folks are long gone, and I couldn't think more of him even if he were mine. I like to think I helped some in putting him on the right path back twenty years ago."

"How sweet." Tom's words wipe the smile off Lily's face. Her jest has turned on her.

"Yes, ma'am. And I'm thinking he could use a little help now, too."

"What do you mean?" Joan asks. "Is he having trouble getting work? I thought you said you were afraid he would be too busy."

"No. He's turning jobs down. No. It's that he lost his wife last summer and he's having a real hard time getting back on his feet. Good for him to be part of something, you know?"

Lily does know, only too well.

"And here he is, right on time."

Tom's face lights up as his eyes travel toward the living room entry. Lily hears Danny Malloy's footsteps coming across the room and she begins to turn toward the sound. As she does, facts like the clues to a riddle rush together in her head: a man who would be in his mid-thirties now, a woodworker whose hands might be brown with wood stain, a soul drowning in grief. She hasn't the slightest doubt who it is she's going to see when she is finally facing the doorway. A hot wire of trepidation and excitement threads itself through her bloodstream. Her pulse pounds at her temples. It's going to be him.

She completes her turn. Her eyes are clouded by the blood in her head but as soon as she sees him the haze drops away, the room drops away, Joan and Tom drop away, and there he is. He is looking right at her and for the briefest moment he smiles at her with an expression of such relief that her fear of what she feels when she looks at him evaporates and there is a burst of happiness in her heart. She smiles back at him as though to say, *Thank God.*

Lily and Danny are leaning against the peeling exterior wall of the house while Tom and Joan stand on the decimated lawn, debating what color to paint the wooden siding. They've locked eyes on the street, seen down beneath each other's skin, but they find now that they can't look directly at each other. The air around them is full of static and whenever their eyes meet there is a flash and a shock and they both flinch and have to look away. But they look back, taking each other in in quick, sporadic glances as they chat.

"Lily Spencer. I have to apologize. I called you a pit bull."

"What?"

He laughs. "Beth told me about you. She said you were lovely and I said you couldn't be if you were good at wringing results from bureaucrats, that you had to be a pit bull."

Lily laughs too and says, "Well, I can actually be very aggravating when I want to be. So you're a friend of Beth's?"

"I am. She's my son's pediatrician."

She looks at him for a second then lowers her eyes to the ground. "Danny, I don't. . . . Tom told us about your wife. I don't want to pretend that I don't know. I just want to say that I'm so sorry."

He is quiet for a moment. "Yeah. Thank you." He glances at her and her head is still down so he watches her profile. He wants to tell her that it was on this exact day a year ago. He wants her to know that and to ask her what it means that he has met her today. But he can't say any of that so he says, "You're married." Beth had told him, but she didn't say anything about Lily Spencer ever having had children. He was wrong about what he thought he saw in her eyes that day on the street. He saw something, but he guesses now it wasn't that.

"Yes. I am."

"And your husband's a hot-shot lawyer in New York?" Out of the corner of his eye he sees her shake her head slightly and bite at her lower lip.

"Yep. The hottest there is."

She says it proudly but there is a melancholy undertone to her pride and the contradiction between her words and the way they are spoken makes him turn to look at her. She looks back and they smile tentatively before looking away again.

"Very understanding guy not to mind you spending the summer up here without him," Danny says jokingly.

Lily is about to say, *He's fine with it, he's so busy*, which is what she has told anyone who's asked, but what she says to Danny is "No, I think he's actually quite upset with me." She rushes to change the subject to cover her own embarrassment and so he won't feel obligated to respond to her inappropriate admission. "This is a wonderful thing to be involved with, The Doorway, isn't it? Joan and Beth and Tom, they're all such terrific people."

Danny's attempt at banter has worked about as well as it usually does. Frothy conversation is not his strong suit. "Yeah, they are. Stone Creek is still a good little town. People care about one another. I'm so busy, I was going to say no but I'm glad I didn't."

"I can't wait to see what you do with this place. Tom thinks you can turn water into wine."

"Tom drinks Thunderbird, what does he know?"

They can't help it then, they look at each other and laugh. Danny holds Lily's eye and smiles and softly says her name. "Lily. Lily Spencer. I'm glad we finally get to meet."

Lily doesn't look away. "Me too." She tries to smile but her lips refuse to turn up.

Danny looks at her struggling mouth and he wants to kiss her. He is more ashamed of himself than he's ever been in his life. He turns away.

"Hey, Tom! Come on, I don't have all day. I've got to pick Caleb up at four." He levers himself away from the wall and starts walking back to the front door.

Lily is suddenly leaning against the house alone. He's turned his back to her and walked away, just like that. A pit forms in her stomach. She follows after him. "Caleb?"

"My son." He glances back at her but doesn't stop.

"Is he all right? What happened to his leg?"

"He's fine. He fell, gashed his leg, took a few stitches." Danny stops. He can't manage being this rude twice in one day. This is all his problem, not Lily's. "Lily, it's really nice talking to you, but I've got to get going."

"No, of course. I understand. I've got to go, too. I enjoyed meeting you."

And then he vanishes into the house, Tom following after him, and Joan is at Lily's side, pulling her down the driveway.

"Hello, Earth to Lily? What's with you? He's not *that* cute and he's a baby, for God's sake."

Lily shakes Joan's hand off her arm. "Nothing's with me. It's just so sad, about his wife. And he has a little boy. I feel bad for him. It makes you think, you know?"

"Oh, I know. He does seem a little shell-shocked, doesn't he? Tom said she was only twenty-six, his wife. What a terrible thing. God, we're lucky, aren't we?" Joan shivers, then plants a kiss on Lily's cheek. "So, what do you think of the place?"

"I think it's going to be incredible. And I have to thank you, truly. I am so happy to be part of this. For the first time since we bought the house I feel as though I belong here."

"Well, good. You know that sweet little east-facing room off the kitchen? Why don't you go back inside and tell Tom and Danny what you want done to it."

"What *I* want done to it?"

"Why not? It could be your office."

"Joan, have you lost your mind? I live in the city. I can't take a job up here."

Joan shrugs. "Just a thought. Are we playing tomorrow morning?"

"You are a pistol." Lily shakes her head and smiles. "Sure. I'll be there at nine."

Lily walks toward her car, but as soon as Joan's Audi is out of sight she heads for the silver Dodge. There is a child's traveling bag in the back, packed tight. She peeks into the cab of the truck through the open window. There is a insulated cup in the cup holder, pens and crumpled papers and a few CDs in the hollow between the seats. A child's car seat rests on the floor well and tossed into it are a small box of apple juice and a plastic container filled with almonds and raisins. A bulging bag from Ex Libris, the local bookstore, is on the passenger seat. Lily looks around, then opens the truck door and surreptitiously checks out Danny's choice of reading material. She doesn't know what she's expecting, but she's surprised to see a biography of the abstract expressionist painter Willem de Kooning, which she herself read and enjoyed a couple of years ago. A few children's books and several literary-looking novels by authors she's never heard of. No shallow escapist drivel, no *Advanced Carburetor Digest*, no girlie magazines. She remembers what she thought of him the first time she saw him. She was an idiot.

She slides Danny's books back into their bag and closes the door to his truck. She gets in her car and pulls out of the driveway. The pit in her stomach is opening up into her chest. He's a giver, not a taker, anyone could see that about him with one look, and he knows she's married.

Lily turns the BMW around at the next corner and returns to the house. She doesn't think, she just goes inside and walks from room to room until she finds him, in the kitchen, taking measurements of the cabinets. He's alone for the moment. She can see Tom on his cell phone right outside the kitchen door.

Danny puts his measuring tape down on the counter and watches her come toward him. Her dark hair is loose around her face. She's wearing a scooped-neck black leotard with a denim skirt pulled over it, the same thing Tara would wear during the summer when she went to dance class.

She stops on the other side of the counter from him. "I forgot something."

"What's that?"

"I forgot to ask you if you'd like to have a cup of coffee with me sometime." There's a hesitation in his eyes and her heart jumps.

Her face has gone pale beneath her light tan. He nods slowly and says, "Yes. I'd like that."

"Okay. I'll call you?"

"I'm in the book."

Lily's heart is still jumping as she walks away. She can't believe that she just did that.

"Lily?" He calls after her. "What made you remember?"

She turns back to him. "I don't know. Is that all right?"

He picks up his tape. "It's fine. I don't know either."

14

Ninety minutes of exacting, unnatural body movements that no forty-six-year-old woman in her right mind should ever attempt, done in an unair-conditioned ballet studio smelling of thirty years of female sweat is just what the doctor ordered. The disorderly roil of Lily's thoughts, of Danny and Paul, of the possibility of staying on in Stone Creek permanently, of what happened this afternoon and of how empowered yet out of control she feels, is beaten into submission by the precision and unwavering concentration required to do what she's doing. By the time Miss Ruth—who at sixty-seven is as regal, eagle-eyed, and pitiless a teacher as she ever was—is finished pushing and prodding and positioning Lily's protesting but supple body, Lily's soaring brain has fallen back to earth.

When she walks into her big, lovely, lonely house at six thirty she is mentally and physically exhausted. She doesn't wish for anyone to be there with her, but the quiet is oppressive. Before she does anything else, she puts the David Gray CD six-pack on the stereo and blasts his sexy, growling voice all throughout the house. *In your eyes, I start to see / A starry veil, the ocean of infinity*. She goes into the laundry room beyond the kitchen, strips off her sweat-drenched dance togs, and puts them directly into the washing machine. Naked, she goes outside and jumps into the pool.

Her thoughts are soaring again and her heart is racing. Danny Malloy. What did she do? She fills her lungs and slides fully under the water. The heavy bass vibrations from the outdoor speakers flow through the liquid and find her there in the deep. The cool water and hot music seep over her bare skin. She rises for air, swims to a spot shallow enough for her to stand. She runs a tentative hand lightly over a buoyant breast. Her nipple comes instantly to attention and there's a rush of electricity down to her crotch. She closes her eyes and imagines Danny's calloused brown-stained hand on her soft white flesh. *Feels like lightning running through my veins, every time I look at you.* Her eyes fly open. She shouldn't be doing this. It's just a fantasy in her head, but she shouldn't be doing it. It's Paul's hand she should be imagining, not Danny's. She takes her hand away, lets it drop back into the water.

She stands there until her excitement subsides. She climbs out of the pool and goes inside to dress and make herself some dinner. While she waits for the pasta water to boil, she goes into the laundry room and takes the local phone book down from the shelf. *Daniel Malloy. 587 Old Stone Creek Road.* She stares down at the letters and numbers, then touches them, sets his address and phone number in her memory. She tries to divine him through her trembling finger as she conjures him in her mind. She needs to know why he looks at her as though he knows something about her that no one else does. She needs to know what his love for his son has done to him, what it means to him, why it isn't enough for him now. She needs to know why he can't get over his wife's death, what his grief feels like, if it's different from the grief that's overtaken her. She needs to know if it's worse to lose something you've had or never to have had it at all. By the time she frees herself and returns to the stove, a third of the water has boiled away and she has to add more.

By nine o'clock, Lily is falling asleep on the couch, the only music in the air now the song of the crickets in the grass and woods around the house. The ringing of the telephone rouses her. With slow guilty steps she walks to the phone. Paul is in Dallas. If it's his cell number on the caller ID, she's not going to pick it up. She doesn't want to talk to him tonight. It's not Paul, though, it's Rick. She hasn't seen him since July Fourth, but they've spoken several times. He hasn't mentioned the baby again and she hasn't asked. The subject has filled every silent second of each conversation. It pulses at her through the ether like incoming enemy fire, but her defense system has remained unassailable. The Pentagon could learn a thing or two from Lily on the matter of securing one's borders.

"Hi, Rick." Her voice is heavy with fatigue.

"Hi, honey. Did I wake you? It's only nine o'clock, are you asleep already?"

"Yeah, I think I am." She yawns into the phone. "I've had a tiring day."

"Oh, really? Try a ten-hour shift in St. Vincent's emergency room and then tell me how tiring your day was."

"Sorry. I'd love to join you in a pissing contest but I don't have a dick."

"Oooh. Someone's cranky. Speaking of not having a dick, are

you missing your hubby? Is absence making your tender heart grow fonder or are we talking out of sight out of mind?"

"Neither, you talking greeting card."

Rick breaks out in peals of laughter. "Ah, Lily, you're still the most fun person to spar with. So, what does neither mean? Don't tell me Paul doesn't make your knees weak anymore."

"Neither means just that, Rick. He is very much on my mind and my heart is as fond as it was a month ago." An accurate statement but not a true one. The truth lies in the unspoken explication of *why* Paul is on her mind and *how* fond of him she was a month ago. "And I'm sorry to disappoint you, but yes, he does still make my knees weak." An accurate and true statement, although with several pieces missing.

"Oh, come on, Lily. I may consider it my right and obligation to point out his shortcomings from time to time, but you know I would never want to hear that he's stopped doing it for you. I like Paul."

"Oh yes? You like domineering, self-absorbed control freaks? Your words."

"Sure. There are some things I don't like about Paul, and there are things I don't like about your relationship with him, but I can say that about nearly everyone I know. I could say that about me and Alan. But you know I like Paul. He's a very contradictory, domineering, self-absorbed control freak. There's plenty to like, not the least of which is that he loves you."

Lily doesn't want to talk to Rick about Paul. She doesn't want to hear about all the things there are to like about Paul beneath the minefield of his opaque surface: his intelligence, his wit, his honesty and reliability, the interest he takes in people and the kindness he shows them, unless they happen to ask the wrong things of him. His generosity with his knowledge, time, and money. She certainly doesn't want to hear about how much

Paul loves her. She doesn't want to think about the unfailing notice he takes of the littlest things she likes; about his child-like willingness to sing Puccini arias to her when they are alone, even though his voice stinks. She doesn't want to think about how much of her love she has willfully withdrawn from his soft places, those deepest, softest injured places whose location only she knows; how she has abandoned them to fend for themselves against the superior force of Paul's self-denigration.

"Rick, do you think I could be going into menopause?"

"Aaand, once again, ladies and gentlemen, she changes the subject. Well, the average age of my patients is somewhere around six, so I don't qualify as an expert, but I know a few things. You could be, sure. Women start having symptoms years before their periods actually stop. What's going on with you?"

"I don't know. I'm terribly moody lately. I'm snapping Paul's head off for no reason. I'm having trouble sleeping. My head feels foggy a lot of the time."

"Hot flashes? Loss of libido? Headaches?"

"No. Just what I said."

"It could be perimenopause, or it could be that you're upset about something." When Lily doesn't respond, he sighs and continues. "Or it could be both. Who's your gyno?"

"Same as ever, Dr. Maibach."

"Oh, right. No good. He'll do blood tests, you'll be within normal parameters, and he'll tell you it's all in your head. Or he'll put you on Premarin or some other horse-urine shit. I'll find you someone with a more open mind. In the meantime, go to the health food store and get a progesterone cream, see if that does any good. Or, wild guess here, tell Paul he fucked up and see if that makes you feel better."

"I don't know why I even talk to you."

"You *don't* talk to me, that's the problem."

She used to talk to Rick about everything, but three years ago things changed. It was to protect herself from Paul that she had built her brick wall, but she'd built it too well. Now Lily fends Rick off with quips and barbs. It's hard work. Their recent conversations deplete her energy and leave her feeling sad and lonely. And soon he and Alan will have a baby and she'll be even sadder and lonelier.

"I'm going to miss you, Rick."

"What do you mean? Where are you going?"

"Nowhere. Nothing. Forget it. I have to go to sleep. Did you call for an actual reason?"

"I actually did. I'd like to come up and spend a day with you, maybe the Monday of Labor Day weekend? Could you take some time for me?"

"Of course. I'd love that. I'll ink you in."

"Good. Sweet dreams. I'll see you soon."

She hangs up, shuts off the downstairs lights, and climbs the stairs to the bedroom. It is ridiculously early to go to bed, but she is too tired to do anything else. Paul left a shirt draped over the arm of one of the chairs in the sitting area in the corner by the windows. She hasn't moved it, hasn't put it away. It's the one she most loves on him, a plain black short-sleeved summer shirt. She sits in the chair and takes it up, buries her face in the sleek cloth. It smells of his shaving cream and of him. He is so far away. Not because he's in Dallas. They are so far away from each other and the distance seems to grow week by week. She should call him. It's not even eight o'clock where he is. She pictures him eating a lonely dinner in some fancy restaurant or sitting alone in his hotel suite. There is a phone on the table next to her. Before she can talk herself out of it she picks up the receiver and dials his cell. He doesn't answer. When the beep sounds at the end of his efficient message she says, "Hello, darling. It's me. I hope you're not perishing from the Texas heat. I just called to say hello. I miss you. I'm going to sleep now, so call me tomorrow. I love you."

She quickly does her nighttime cleansing and moisturizing regimen. She puts on a short, feather-light nightgown. She has screwed two hooks close together into the shallow face of one of the bookshelves that line the wall behind the chair where Paul's shirt lies and attached a looped length of blue ribbon to each of them. It's for Blinkie Floyd, so that he can hang upside down every so often, as a bat must do. He's hanging there now and she hates to disturb him, but it's time to go *schluffy*. She takes him down and carries him and Paul's shirt to the bed. She lays Blinkie Floyd next to her with his head on Paul's pillow. She drapes him with Paul's shirt. She turns off the light.

As tired as she is, as soon as she's supine between the sateen sheets, sexual longing shoots through her as it had in the pool. It is an insistent longing and she doesn't think she can push it away this time. She reaches into the bottom drawer of her night table for her vibrator. She wants to do it quickly, so there will be no time for her thoughts to wander somewhere they shouldn't go. But there's no escaping it. As she climaxes, and for those seconds loses all control of her thoughts, Danny sneaks into her head. Would his touch be the same thrill on her skin as Paul's? What would he smell like? Would he fill her inside the way Paul does? What would his body, smaller than Paul's but denser, more muscular, feel like within her limbs? Would they fit together the way she fits with Paul? For nine years Lily knew she couldn't love making love to anyone else the way she loved making love to Paul, that no one could make her feel the way Paul does. She doesn't know that anymore.

She casts the vibrator to the floor and rolls over onto her side. She puts out a hand; it brushes against Paul's shirt. She moves it aside and pulls Blinkie Floyd from Paul's place in the bed. She holds the uncomplaining bat against her chest, smooths his cape-like wings and the downy spot on the top of his head. She murmurs into one of his long, silky ears, "Come to Mommy." And with the loving little thing cradled in her arms, she falls asleep.

Lily failed to conceive the old-fashioned way six months in a row. From high summer to Indian summer to fall, she failed to conceive and the heat was leaching out of their lovemaking just as it was leaching from the earth. Lily knew, although he hadn't said it yet, that Paul no longer cared about having a child. But from the moment her half-drunken, love-besotted brain heard him say, *My beautiful Lily, let's have a baby,* her years of holding that desire at bay came to a permanent end. She wanted a child. She had always wanted a child. She wanted a child with the man she loved and she wanted him to want one, too.

She wasn't like Paul; she couldn't make herself stop wanting something simply because she couldn't have it. So she pretended to believe that Paul did still want it and that his growing impatience stemmed from his own disappointment and not from her increasing obsessiveness or from the way their sex life had become hostage to the misfiring of her ovaries. In November Dr. Maibach confirmed to her that at forty-two her ovaries were no longer producing enough eggs for a viable chance at conception and it was unlikely she could hold a pregnancy even if she did conceive. Her options were fertility drugs, adoption, or acceptance. But in December, the month Paul turned fifty-one, her period, regular as clockwork since she was thirteen, did not arrive. After ten excruciating days she took a home pregnancy test. It was positive. Paul was something less than happy but Lily was too elated to notice. When she aborted spontaneously six weeks into the pregnancy, he was not terribly upset but Lily was too devastated to notice. It was only much later that she would remember how devoid of real feeling were his words of excitement and sympathy.

In February, when she'd recovered sufficiently, she discreetly consulted with a highly regarded fertility specialist. He was gently discouraging despite the one conception, but concurred that a few rounds of artificial insemination might be worth the hardship and would at least give them the information necessary to make a rational decision about going further, to in vitro. What he was suggesting required that Lily be injected daily in the first part of her cycle with Pergonal, a fertility drug that stimulated the ovaries to produce eggs, and that Paul accompany her to the doctor's office at the time of ovulation to contribute his sperm, which would then be artificially introduced into Lily's uterus.

When she came home and, her heart in her mouth, explained this to him and asked if they could please try it, just for a couple of months, that she knew it could work, he said, "No. I'm not going to jack off into a cup in some doctor's office. I don't have time for it, for one thing—I'm in the middle of this trial, you know that—and also, I'm just not going to do that. Lily, we're done with this. We tried, it didn't take. That was the deal."

She couldn't let it go. Not yet. "Paul, please, just once. It's hard for a woman to just turn this off. You said you wanted a baby, let me try a little longer."

Maybe he saw something unusual in her eyes, or maybe in his objective ethical judgment he felt he owed it to her, or maybe it was just that he loved her enough at that moment for so wanting to please him, or maybe it was that he had nothing to lose because he had no doubt it wouldn't work. Whatever the reason, he relented, but on his own terms, as always.

"Okay. You can take the drugs, but we do the rest the natural way, here at home, in bed. We do it once. If it doesn't work, I want your promise that that will be the end of it."

"I promise."

It didn't work. The Pergonal made her butt ache, gave her a three-week migraine, made her feel as though her womb were going to explode if her nerves didn't combust first, but it didn't make her ovaries produce any more eggs. It was as though there just weren't any left from the store she'd been born with. She had wasted twenty-five years of fertility and a million eggs. All of them offered and rejected and now all used up.

She had promised Paul and she didn't ask to try again. There was no point. She knew what his answer would be and how angry he would get at her. She made a belated New Year's resolution to be gracious about her fate, to be grateful for the joy she and Paul had had for those few months of trying, to put the past nine months somewhere where they wouldn't interfere with their happiness, to go back to work. But by the time May came and Lily was staring her forty-third birthday in the face, she still wasn't working, she still wasn't happy, she still wanted a child, and her fury at Paul for opening this Pandora's box and then ignoring what flew out was seeding itself in her heart.

On the night of her birthday, after they'd returned home from dinner and the opera, Lily presented him with her last argument. She had tried two of Dr. Maibach's three options—fertility drugs and acceptance—with no luck. That third option was still out there and she couldn't stop thinking about it. So she allowed herself the misguidedly wishful notion that Paul might be willing to consider it and, as they were undressing for bed, she gave him a final opportunity to fail her.

"Paul, why don't we look into adopting a baby?"

He stopped dead in the middle of pulling off his tie. "What is this? Are you kidding? I thought we understood that we were done here. Why are we even talking about this again?"

"Because I need to."

"Lily, sweetheart. No. We can't have our own and adoption was never on the table. You should know better than to even bring it up to me. Let's leave it alone now, okay?"

"Why, Paul? Why can't we at least—"

"I told you very clearly that I hated being an adopted child. I don't want to be the father of one. Let's stop talking about this."

Paul's lamentable childhood history moved Lily, but now it was standing in the way of something she wanted, wanted so badly that desperation gave her the courage to press him.

"Not all adoptees feel the way you do, Paul. Or have bad experiences. And you don't know what the alternative might have been for you."

"Well, how's this for a novel idea? How about the people who conceive a child taking responsibility for what they did and keeping it?" Paul was all at once rigid with anger. He seemed to Lily to swell with anger, to the size and weight of an unmovable statue blocking the door to his dressing room. "Don't talk about things you don't know anything about, Lily."

"Okay, okay." Blood coursed into her brain. Her courage was failing. She was losing her ability to think clearly, to articulate her arguments. "But, Paul, we're different from the Spenglers. We're not going to have any little replicas of ourselves. Whatever child we would get will be our only one. It will be ours."

"It won't be ours. It will never be ours. And we will always know it. And he will always know it. And he will always wonder who he is and why his real parents didn't want him."

"Paul, please, just—"

"No! What is the matter with you, Lily? What are you not understanding about what I'm saying? I told you before we got married that I didn't want kids and you said you were all right with it. Were you lying to me?"

Lily could no longer make sense of the conversation. Chuck had been right, she didn't have the strength or the courage to stand up to this Paul, the one she'd been warned about but had never truly seen. This was the Paul who would not be demanded of, denied, told what to do, or argued with. The one who might not toss her away as he had all the others but who would let their relationship disintegrate and let her fall away rather than be forced to acquiesce to her needs when they didn't match his own. *You fucking bastard!* You *were the one who said let's have a baby, not me!* She was screaming inside, but all she could do was hang helplessly by her side of the bed and look at him and well up with tears.

His high color faded instantly and all traces of his ire vanished. He strode across the room and took her in his arms. "Lily. I feel like you've disappeared. I love you, you're all I want. All I ever wanted was you. You know that, don't you?"

She did know it. Knowing what Paul wanted was never the problem. "Yes. It's just . . . it's just going to take me a little time to . . . this has been so hard, such a disappointment . . ." She began to cry.

"Sweetheart, don't cry. It's okay." He wiped at her tears with his fingers. Then he took her by the hand and led her into his dressing room.

"I was going to save this as a surprise for our anniversary, but I don't want to wait now." He pulled a stuffed oversized yellow envelope from a shelf and removed a folded wad of architectural drawing papers. "Look." He pulled her down to the floor and spread the papers out in front of her. "When we bought the house you said all it was missing was a gazebo on the back lawn. Now you're going to have one."

He knelt behind her on the carpeted closet floor, wrapped his arms around her, and put his lips to her neck. "Lily, don't cry. Everything's going to be okay, it will be perfect, like it was before. We don't need a child. The trial is over. How about I arrange things and take some time off and we'll go to Paris? We'll get away for a few weeks, forget about everything, put this all behind us, then come home and start over."

And now here was the other Paul. The mesmerizing magician so skilled at sleight of hand. The one who dangled his love in front of you, so warm and real, so impossible to walk away from, and so dazzled you with its promise that you didn't realize he was stealing it back at the same time and holding it captive to your obedience. Lily felt herself split apart once again, but not in the ecstatic way she had the first time he'd kissed her, when everything inside her had broken free and rushed madly through her to lavish itself on him. This was horrible. This was a sundering of her heart, which now held inside its walls the two unrenounceable desires of her life: Paul and a child. She could not have both. Choosing one desire meant forfeiting the other. And in truth she had made her choice years ago, when she'd married him knowing he didn't want children. She had thought it was all right then. She had to make it all right now. She did love him, and she did want them to be happy again the way they had been. That was what she had to remember. That she loved him. That he loved her. That she was the one who could bend without breaking. That his inability to give her this thing she wanted wasn't from a sparsity of love for her, he simply couldn't help who he was.

She let him take her to Paris. How could she say no to someone who loved her so much? Two weeks. The fifth anniversary trip they had never gotten to make. They stayed in a suite at the San Regis. They walked miles every day. They ate sinfully good food and drank sinfully expensive wine. Paul bought her gorgeous clothes and sexy lingerie. He let her drag him anywhere she wanted to go. He treated her like a princess, made careful, tender love to her every night. And she had a wonderful time. She really did. Except for those nights when, after they'd made love, she had to creep into the bathroom so she could cry without his hearing her. Or when they were out walking and she saw a baby and wanted to throw herself into the Seine. She had a wonderful time except that she didn't want to be Paul's princess anymore. She wanted to be somebody's mommy. And he didn't care. He just didn't care at all. Why hadn't anyone seen just how clever he truly was and warn her that even if she were the one he kept, he would find a way to break her heart nonetheless?

15

Dinner was delicious, Sue, thanks."

"You're very welcome, Danny. It's a pleasure to cook for someone who likes good food." Sue grins and pats Will's stomach fondly. "Will would eat kielbasa and boiled potatoes every night if I let him."

"It's what I grew up on. I love that stuff." Will is a solidly built fireplug of a man whose stomach is neither fat nor flat. It bulges over his belt just far enough to ensure that he will say yes every time Danny asks him to go hiking or rock climbing with him.

"Yeah, well, that stuff'll kill you. Listen to your wife and eat your vegetables."

The adults are standing on the Pollacks' back porch watching their children play. Caleb and Sue and Will's seven-year-old twins, Ellen and Jack, are running around the floodlit yard, playing Frisbee with one another and with Daisy, the family's golden retriever. They are none of them overly adept at the nuances of the game and, in fact, Daisy is by far the best Frisbee player of the lot. At least on the catching end. Jack has a pretty good throwing arm. Ellen runs the fastest. Caleb yells the loudest. They are having a wonderful time.

Sue links her arm through Danny's and pulls him to her. "Are you sure you don't want to stay here tonight? Maybe it would be better?"

"No, Sue. I have to go home." It's time to leave. The pretense of today being a normal day cannot sustain itself any longer. Danny feels his house beckoning him to return. It's time for him to go home and be with Tara. "I'll be back early, before the kids wake up. I'm sorry to leave you to put the monsters to bed."

"Don't be silly. I'm going to toss them into the big Jacuzzi and by the time they've soaked and splashed a while, Will will have to carry them into bed. Caleb won't even miss you."

"No, he loves staying here with you guys." He disengages his arm. "So do I, but I've got to go now."

Sue kisses his cheek. "I love you, Danny. I'll see you in the morning. Kids, say good night to Danny!"

All three of them sing out, "Good night, Danny!" and Danny hears Caleb giggle.

Will walks with Danny to the truck. The driveway is lit from above by a bright three-quarter moon and from below by a row of knee-high lights.

"You've got yourself a good girl there, my friend."

"Yeah, she's not bad for an Ohio transplant. If I could just get her to eat kielbasa and explain to me how in hell she files things in the office, she'd be perfect."

Danny laughs. "I think you two are perfect the way you are." He looks back toward the welcoming house. "I don't know how I'd have managed without your help this past year. I owe you a lot."

"You don't owe us anything. This is what friends do, Danny. You'd do the same."

Danny puts his hand on the door handle and takes a shuddering breath. "I've really got to go, Will." The fear and anger are starting to lift off the bottom again and fill his head.

"In a second. Eve is still being good?"

"Yeah, she is."

"Did you talk to her or Lester today at all?"

"No. I haven't spoken to her since the weekend. We didn't even go near the subject of today. She's such a fucking difficult woman, but today's got to be hell for her, too. It's a pity, isn't it, that we can't share anything about this with each other?"

"It is, but it's her doing and her loss. I'm sure she's not musing to Lester what a pity it is that they can't share this with *you*. Danny, look, I'm glad she's behaving well lately, but I'm going to warn you not to get too comfortable with it. It's not going to last."

"You have an enviable faith in the innate goodness of human nature, I see," Danny says wryly. "Don't worry. I'm far from comfortable with it."

"Good. You're a pathetically nice person and I don't want you blindsided the next time she decides to wedge herself between you and Caleb. Don't stash that notebook away."

"No. I won't. Will, really. I've got to go."

"I know, I know." Will pulls Danny into a bear hug and kisses him on the cheek, just as his wife did. "I love you, man. Call me if you need me."

"I'll be fine. Tuck the kids in, kiss them for me, and go to bed."

The woods around his house are filled with the noises of the summer night, just as they were a year ago. He sits in his truck, the motor off, listening. He is looking for the strength to get out of the truck and go inside and he's hoping he'll find it in the fa-

miliar sounds of the clacking of insects and the soughing of wind
in the trees and the babbling of the creek. Even with his dread
of this moment, he didn't expect it to be this hard. He misses
her with a fury that makes him want to curl up and scream and
rail against the world. He missed her so much tonight, at Will
and Sue's. There was a void where she should have been, there
with her friends, her husband, her son, and as the hours passed
the void grew and grew until all the warmth and the light disappeared. He knows he has to go back to go forward, but going
back now feels to him like stepping into quicksand. But he made
a promise, not only to her but to himself.

The house is dark and he leaves it that way. He designed and
built this house and he knows every inch of it as well as he knew
every inch of her body. He could navigate both in pitch blackness if he had to. He goes into his bedroom and closes the door
behind him. He switches on the lamp on his night table. The envelope is still on his pillow. No angel of mercy came and took it
away while he wasn't looking. He stands by the bed, indecisive,
then he picks up the envelope and walks into the bathroom. He
turns on the lights around the mirror then backs into the opposite wall and slowly slides down the cool tile until he is sitting
on the floor, his legs out straight before him. He removes her
journal and places it on his thighs. He puts his hands on the red
leather and stares down at his silver-scripted name. He doesn't
hear the summer sounds anymore. His mind is turned inward,
his senses shut off to the outside world.

He opens the book and hesitantly fans the pages. To his surprise, there isn't as much written as he thought, or feared. She
didn't fill the book, there are only perhaps twenty pages written
on; the rest are blank. And yet, though it's not so much to read,
he is beset by the awful, shameful fear that he made a promise he

will not be able to keep. That he expected too much of himself eleven months ago. It was a reasonable expectation, that he would be ready by now, but life and death and grief are not reasonable. Although she's been gone a year, and in surprisingly many ways he has grown used to her absence, he has not found his way to that further shore where the promises of the future hold sway and not the betrayals of the past. He is still adrift somewhere out on a cold, misty ocean, waiting to catch sight of a safe place to land.

But he tries. He starts at the beginning, rereads the entry he read before. At first it is not too difficult, the words are so familiar to him, but by the time he comes to the end he feels much as he did the first time, weak and shaken. Seeing the words written in her even, slanting script is so much harder than hearing them in his mind. He is compelled to imagine her hand holding the pen, her head down as she writes, and then he can't not see the curving back of her neck and then he can't not remember how many times he kissed her there. How much he loved kissing her there and how the sweet scent of her neck and her hair filled his nose and mouth. . . . *I will come and find him.* That was what she did. Metaphorically, truly. She came and found him. And now he's lost again. He tries to go on, thinks that if he takes just one more step then perhaps he can take another and another. He turns the page and begins the second entry. *Then was the fall of my senior year. Danny had been home since July, returned from France the day of his father's heart attack, but I was working at Princeton that summer and there was no one to tell me. . . .*

He slowly closes the book. There she is, standing in the dining room of his family house on a brilliant October day, having come for him, risking everything to fulfill a destiny she'd believed in since childhood. He knows he won't read more tonight. And it's not that he can't because it's too painful. He can survive the pain. He's still here, isn't he? He can't because these unread words are all he has left. They are the only thing he has of her that he hasn't touched or looked at or dreamed of or revisited in his mind a million times. He can't use them up too fast. Because when he comes to the end of her words she will be gone with a finality unlike even the finality of death. Tonight is not the night he is going to say good-bye, after all. He is going to fail again.

It was a still and sultry August night. The woods were brimming with life, bursting with it; fecund nature in furious denial of the decline that waited not far ahead, when summer would turn to fall and fall to winter. The very earth steamed and the moist air reverberated with the frenzied clicking and hissing of unseen crickets, katydids, and cicadas. Moths and beetles, lured by the light, forsook the safety of the dark night and flung themselves, pinging and whirring, against the tight wire mesh of the screens. Into the warm bedroom of the house in the woods that Danny had built, a light breeze slid easily through the mesh, leaving the defeated insects trapped on the other side. It brought with it the cooling smells and sounds of the creek, the water low now in its bed but still running swiftly.

They had been hungering for each other all evening. From the moment he'd come home, her eyes had barely left his face, her hands repeatedly settled fleetingly on his arm, his back, his head. During the hours of preparing and eating dinner, of clearing and washing dishes, of getting Caleb ready for bed, Danny revealed his need again and again, helpless to do anything else, with a firm hand on her hip, a lingering kiss on the back of her neck, a brief, tight embrace. Each time, she melted against him and quickly kissed him. His anticipation of their lovemaking quickened and rose from deep inside him to his surface while, as if in harmonious response, the heavy summer heat settled onto his skin and sank into him through his pores. Internal and external heat melded and mingled inside him, warming and thickening his blood. He hid his impatience as he read Caleb his stories, calmly reading one after another while willing the boy to go to sleep. Until finally, in the middle of yet another tale of Curious George, the boy passed from wide-eyed attentive wakefulness into unshakable sleep, as though his own innocent curiosity had at last been found and subdued by his father's powerful, urgent will.

Now she was in the bathroom, naked at the sink. In the soft light reflecting off the wood-framed mirror a dewy sheen of sweat gleamed on her tanned skin. Danny watched her from inside the shadows of the bedroom, from where he stood by their bed waiting for her. Enveloped in the throbbing night sounds, mindless and breathless with happiness, he watched her. His eyes followed her every graceful gesture. She raised a hand to her hair, and the small movement of her breast lifting sent a tingling shiver through him. He groaned, a soft exhalation. She heard and turned her head. As if in response to him, she playfully plucked the full pack of birth control pills from the medicine cabinet and tossed them with a flourish into the wastebasket. She looked at him, her full mouth curving into a sly, conspiratorial smile. As she turned back to the mirror her head jerked and she winced; her raised hand flew to her brow.

Danny took a step toward the bathroom doorway. "Tara, what's wrong?"

She held her hand out to him. "Nothing, it's nothing. The headache just seems a little worse. But that's good . . ." She smiled again, ". . . it probably means I'm ovulating. And August was lucky for us the last ti—" She didn't finish the sentence. In the middle of a word, she doubled over and vomited into the sink.

"Tara!" A rush of adrenaline roared through him, spasmed his stomach, and squeezed his heart. He leaped into the bathroom.

"Oh, God!" There was alarm in her voice. She straightened and turned toward him, but her movements were awkward and graceless. She clutched at her head, pressed her palms into her temples. "Oh! My head! It hurts!" She staggered sideways, her hip banged hard into the sink. "Danny, something's wrong with me!" She took a lurching step toward him. Her face contorted and she screamed in pain.

"Oh, no. Tara. I'm taking you to the hospital."

Nearly blinded with fear, his blood now thin and cold, Danny groped for her robe, which was hanging on the back of the bathroom door. Before his arm had stretched its full length to find the soft cotton, he saw it happen. He saw a bomb of agony detonate behind her eyes. Her panicked gasp froze them both but only for a fraction of a second. Then her head shook and her eyes filled with terror. She thrust out a hand and touched his face with an open palm, like a sightless woman desperate to see her lover. Her eyes rolled and opened hideously wide and she cried out his name. Her body twisted to one side and she fell against him, twisted further, and dropped to the floor at his feet. As she fell, he saw his life collapse and fall down with her. His knees buckled and he was on the floor beside her, his hands grasping her face, his cheek near her mouth, praying to feel her breath on his skin. It was there, faint and moist. He scrabbled into the bedroom for his cell phone and dialed 911. When he returned to her side, less than a minute later, he couldn't find her pulse or feel her breath anymore. She was gone. Her final utterance resounded in the barren air and echoed in his ears like the last beat of her heart. *Danny!*

*   *   *

The house is so empty. Danny wonders if there is actually anything but black space beyond the closed bedroom door. Long minutes tick by and he is still sitting on the bathroom floor with the book in his lap. Old guilt rips through him. How did he not see that she wasn't right, that she didn't feel well? If he hadn't been so impatient, so focused on getting Caleb to sleep, on getting her into bed, he would have noticed that her head hurt and taken her to the hospital before it was too late. But there *was* nothing to notice until it happened; she asked him to get her some aspirin before dinner, that's all. How many times is he going to sift through this handful of shifting sand? How much reassurance will it take to convince him that it wasn't his fault?

He was so sure he had to be alone tonight, so sure he wanted it, but he doesn't. What he wants more than anything on earth at this moment is to crawl into Lily Spencer's arms, crush her to him, and do whatever it takes to still her struggling mouth and wipe that look from her eyes. From both their eyes. New, freshly potent guilt assails him. He fumbles for his phone, still in its clip on his belt. Will answers before the first ring ends.

"Danny."

"Will, I'm sorry, it's so late . . ."

"I'm up. Are you all right?"

"Uh . . . uh . . ." That's all he can make come out of his mouth, some inarticulate grunting.

"I'll be there in ten minutes."

"No, no. I just needed to hear—"

"I'll be there in ten minutes. Don't argue. I'm a lawyer. You'll lose."

Danny slides back up the wall. He is facing himself in the mirror, but he's seeing Tara reflected in the lighted glass. He takes a step, picks up the brushed-steel soap dish from the sink ledge and smashes it into the mirror with a murderous force. The wood frame smacks against the wall and the glass crazes wildly outward from the point of impact. Small chunks fall into the sink. Danny drops the soap dish on top of them.

He is sitting on the bed, facing the bathroom doorway when Will arrives. Will sits down next to him and puts a thick, strong arm around his shoulders. The pale red hair that coats his freckled skin tickles Danny's neck.

"I'm here, Danny. I'm here." Will tightens his arm and gives Danny a little shake. He looks into the bathroom. "Oh, man. I should not have let you do this. You should not be sitting here." He shakes Danny again. "Good thing Home Depot is open tomorrow."

Danny tries to laugh, but it's a feeble sound that emerges from him.

"Come on. I'm taking you back home with me."

Danny nods. He turns his head from his contemplation of the bathroom floor and looks at his friend. "What am I going to have to do, Will? Burn my house down? Move to another country, somewhere I never was with her?"

"No. You're going to have to live like this a little longer, but it will get better. All you have to do right now is get up and walk to my car. I'm going to give you a sleeping pill, and you're going to take it. You're going to go to sleep, and in the morning things will look different."

"Yeah? And how is that going to happen? How will things look different?"

"Because the sun will be shining, and you'll see your son. And you'll be with people who love you. Sue's going to make her famous cinnamon French toast and you'll be hungry and you'll eat it. And you'll know that you lived through another worst day. Nothing stays the same, Danny, and neither will you."

16

LILY ISN'T PERTURBED when she comes partially awake during the night, dimly aware of movement and a momentary shift of the mattress, a hand falling onto her hip. Paul has come home from Dallas in the middle of the night, as he has done from other trips many times in the past. Semiconscious, untethered from time, she is free to feel the same instantaneous joy at his return that she always does, and to then spiral serenely back down into sleep. It isn't until she comes fully awake in the bright and early August morning with Blinkie Floyd snug in her arms and herself snug in Paul's that the disturbing reality of his unexpected presence makes itself felt. Her waking thought is that she is thankful he didn't make love to her, as he often does at such times, and that he will be gone again in two days. She is coming to savor his frequent absences. Her distress over their growing emotional rift has found a counterbalance in her relief at the ongoing physical separation. That relief has evolved since July Fourth from a contained, prickly shock of an emotion into a virtual drug, one she manufactures in ever-increasing strength to subdue the distrust and dislike that have taken their place beside the love and need she has for him.

She eases herself from his hold and out of the bed. Her vibrator is still on the floor, the drawer of her night table open. She squats down to put it away and glances guiltily back at the bed. Paul is on his side, his head half on her pillow, his arms flung out toward her across the sheets. His eyes are closed. Feeling like a thief who has snuck back to the scene of the crime to return what she had stolen, she quickly replaces the vibrator and closes the drawer. Blinkie Floyd remains cradled in the crook of her elbow. She kneels on the floor at the side of the bed and looks at Paul. He didn't answer his phone last night because he was on a plane, flying home from Dallas a day early so that he could come to Stone Creek and sleep in the same bed with her, so that he could spend a day or two with her.

She takes in his face with her eyes, then leans over the bed and combs her fingers through his black hair, long enough now to be falling over his cheekbone. He has been so busy he hasn't had time to get it cut. His hair is thick and straight and warm to her touch. It feels like velvet that has been baking in the sun. Danny's hair would be cool. It would be like cool pale silk and run like water through her fingers. She draws a finger along the length of Paul's jaw; a day's growth of beard scratches her skin. Danny's beard would be soft. She sits back on her heels. Paul hasn't moved; his breathing is slow and steady. He must be exhausted. There is a tear forming and swelling at the side of Lily's eye; in an instant it will spill over onto her face. She wipes it away, then carefully lifts Paul's arm and places Blinkie Floyd under it. He still doesn't move. She arranges one plush wing so that it rests protectively on Paul's bare shoulder and she tiptoes out of the room, her clothes bundled in her hands.

*   *   *

It's ten thirty by the time Lily hears Paul coming down the stairs. She ate breakfast hours ago, cleaned up the omelet pan and her dishes. There's laundry to fold and weeds to pull but she is sitting at the kitchen table nursing a third cup of half-decaf coffee, unable to do anything but wait for him to wake up. He has slept a solid eight hours. Still, when he walks into the kitchen in a pair of shorts, the creased cotton stark white against his ruddy skin, his eyelids are at half-mast. Lily doesn't remember him ever looking so tired; the shadows under his lazy eyes are nearly as dark as his unshaven cheek. Her attention is immediately seized, however, by the sight of Blinkie Floyd riding on Paul's still-naked shoulder. The bat's wacky smile and round shining eyes radiate naïve pride as his master bears him aloft. Paul is holding him delicately by the wing. The soft round black feet dangle over Paul's hard, straight collarbone. Paul stops just inside the kitchen's wide doorway with a questioning smile on his face. He waits for her to come to him.

Are you happy to see me? Lily doesn't know how to answer his unspoken question any more than Paul knows how to ask it. She doesn't know what she feels. Three hours ago she wished he weren't here. Now, as she sees him standing in the doorway with a tender hand on her beloved Blinkie Floyd, Lily's need to believe in him asserts itself with a vengeance. And with the need comes the desire to love him. She leaves her chair and crosses the room. She puts her hand over his. She smiles up at him and says, "Hi."

"Hi." Paul puts his free arm around her and holds her loosely. He hesitates a second, then leans forward to kiss her. As he does, Blinkie Floyd loses his balance and begins to fall. Paul quickly removes his hand from under Lily's and catches Blinkie Floyd in his arm as he tumbles off his perch.

Lily feels the small body settle into the space between them, feels Paul's flexed arm supporting it. She is instantly transported to that day on the street outside the post office. She sees Caleb listing on Danny's shoulders, Danny reaching up to catch him and bring him into the safety of his own body. She feels Blinkie Floyd like a child against her breast, the way she imagined she felt Danny's son. Her eyes close and she returns Paul's tentative kiss, feels it deepen in response. They could have had this. This little body nestled in their arms, helpless and adored, could have been their child. Paul draws her closer to him. He is thinking what she is thinking. How could he not? They could still have it. She and Rick are the same age. It's not too late. Finally, she wants to tell him about Rick and Alan and the baby they are going to adopt so that he can help her be happy for them, so that he can see what's possible. She raises her head to speak, her brain denuded of rationality by the brute strength of her yearning. All at once she realizes that Blinkie Floyd is now in her arms. Somehow, as they kissed, Paul managed to rid himself of him, to abandon him to Lily. As soon as their eyes meet, he lets them both go and steps back.

"That was cute, you putting him in bed with me like that. I would rather have woken up with you there, but I have to say he made me laugh. Thanks. And thanks for letting me sleep in. There was a screaming baby on the flight last night, I couldn't even close my eyes."

Lily's imaginary world vanishes as quickly as it appeared. He wasn't thinking what she was thinking. Could she be anymore stupid? She is not going to tell him anything, lay herself open so he can extract another piece of her just to toss it away. He didn't want to hear three years ago that she wanted a baby. He doesn't want to hear it now. He won't help her find a way to love Rick and Alan's child. How can he, when he is still a child himself, a stunted child inside a fifty-four-year-old brat who throws tantrums to get what he wants—grown-up tantrums, calm, cold, and calculated.

The narcotic of relief—adequate to dull her fears when he is away from her—fails to smother the panic that blooms in her as she looks at Paul and cannot identify what she loves about him. She hugs Blinkie Floyd against her pounding heart.

"Is there enough coffee for me or should I make a fresh pot?"

The half-full carafe is visible on the counter. He can see it, he's not blind. The question is his oblique way of telling her that her coffee is lousy. *Is that your usual feeble brew? Do I have to make a pot of good stuff myself?* "There's enough. It's part decaf but it's quite strong."

He walks past her as though he's done nothing wrong. Lily's agitation wafts after him like a wave of heat rising off the summer pavement. She stands very still so that he won't see or feel it, this perceivable aura of her anger and her panic. If he sees it, he will be displeased and he will batter her with his displeasure until her thoughts and emotions are dust.

Paul was born aggressive and bold but Lily was born passive and fearful, intolerant of domestic turmoil. Turmoil frightens her, makes her cower inside. There was too much of it in the Margolies household. Ada yelling at Max, Max yelling at Ada, both of them yelling at Mona, Mona yelling back. Lily never yelled at anyone and no one ever yelled at her. She never gave them any reason to. She did try to be bad once, when she was around twelve, when it became clear to her that Max and Ada loved Mona for her badness. They tore their hair over Mona's contrariness, fits of temper, lying, carelessness, but they loved her more than they loved Lily. Lily didn't blame them. Mona was more interesting. Bad was always more interesting than good. So one day Lily lied about something, but Max just laughed and Ada shook her head and said, "No, Lily. That's not for you. You don't want that kind of attention."

And Ada was right. Lily wants to remain below the radar detection system of her fellow beings. She wants to fly low and silently, take off and land neatly, keep her flight path clear and calm and devoid of all turbulence. She doesn't want to get caught in the sights of anyone's anger. She does not want Paul angry with her. She can be angry with him, inside, privately and clandestinely. As long as he doesn't see it, as long as he doesn't turn his anger on her, the human explosion can be indefinitely contained.

"Are you hungry? I made myself a goat cheese omelet earlier. Would you like one?"

He leans against the kitchen counter. He smiles at her gratefully. "I'm starving. An omelet sounds great. Any bagels around?"

"In the freezer. Why don't you take one out and defrost it in the microwave while I put Blinkie Floyd away."

"How long do I nuke it for?"

"One minute at eight. Then you slice it and put it in the toaster."

"Good coffee, by the way," he says, with unintentional demeaning surprise.

Lily doesn't thank him. She turns and goes upstairs. As she climbs she hears the crackle of the small kitchen television and the rapid changing of channels. She won't be playing her music today. She sits heavily at the foot of the bed and listens to the muted sounds of CNBC coming from downstairs. Paul has straightened the sheets and pulled the light summer comforter taut and neat. His black shirt is nowhere to be seen. He's hung it up along with the clothes he was wearing when he arrived.

"Where's Daddy's shirt?" She drops her head and mewls into Blinkie Floyd's pointed ear. Lily is dizzy with careering from one feeling to another. She wants Paul to put on his Armani suit and go back to the city. She wants Paul to put on his black shirt and hold her. She wants to love him. She wants to blame him. She wants to forgive him. She wants to hate him. She wants him to understand what he's done but she doesn't want to tell him what it is.

Lily hauls herself to her feet and returns Blinkie Floyd to his shelf, upright. She doesn't think he's in any shape to view the world upside down. Things are hard enough right side up.

Back in the kitchen, Paul is standing in front of the TV, holding one of Sidney Trachtenberg's crusty everything bagels in his hand. It's still frozen. Lily plucks it from him and throws it into the microwave, punches at the keypad.

"Sorry. I got caught up in—"

"It's fine. I'll do it."

She gets the eggs and goat cheese from the fridge and sets about making his omelet. Moments later, the bagel is in the toaster, the omelet is about to be turned, and Paul comes up behind her, puts his arms around her waist, and nuzzles his cheek against the side of her neck. His touch is light but Lily feels imprisoned by his embrace and abraded by his stubbled skin. She stiffens and moves her head away. She immediately turns and with a smile says, "Not now, silly. I'll burn your breakfast."

Paul doesn't smile back. He drops his arms and goes to sit at the table. He points the remote at the TV and turns the volume up on the weekend business report.

*   *   *

Paul didn't sleep on the flight to Newark, but it wasn't the fault of some anonymous crotchety baby. There was no baby. Paul said that only so Lily wouldn't find his sleeping like a dead person until the middle of the morning overly suspicious. He doesn't want her to know that his decision to come to Stone Creek this weekend had him popping sleeping pills and anti-anxiety pills, his new best friends, like they were candy corn. He didn't decide to come because last weekend was just so wonderful he couldn't wait to repeat it. It was actually pretty grim. Both of them on their best behavior, so good and polite. He felt lonelier during the two days he was with her than he had during the two preceding weeks without her. He doesn't want Lily to have any suspicions about him, but he's got one about her. He's beginning to suspect that she hates him.

Until recently, when Lily looked at him it was with soft, guileless eyes infused with love; the same eyes he'd succumbed to the night they met. Nothing has ever both thrilled and soothed him in quite the same way that possessing Lily's love has thrilled and soothed him. When she looks at him lately it's with sharp, ambiguous eyes that puncture him and then slide away. They slide away just as Bertha Spengler's eyes slid away, just as his real mother's eyes would have slid away if she'd ever seen him, with disinterest and a stomach-turning instant of nonrecognition.

He's not going to be able to see her again for a month. He is going flat out with the final round of meetings, interviews, and depositions with SynTech board members and ex-employees and officers of companies that bought from or sold to SynTech in the past five years. They are scattered all over the country and his travel schedule is horrendous. It will be mid-September before he'll be home again. When he thinks about their being apart for so long, that pesky sense of doom starts playing havoc with his entrails. He doesn't want to leave things with her the way they were last weekend. His goal for this weekend is to satisfy himself that his suspicions are groundless. He's tackling the task like the canny lawyer he is, with the most effective protocol he knows. His job is to get his client off and to that end it's often best not to ask or answer too many questions. Paul requires that his client be not guilty, but he doesn't have to prove it to the jury. It's reasonable doubt he's after. If he acts sufficiently lovable, Lily's suspected conviction of his hatefulness will suffer reasonable doubt and she will have no choice but to exonerate him.

The day has gone well so far, after a shaky start. She did look at him for a second this morning the way he wants her to, but the veil came down quickly and she barely looked at him at all while he ate his breakfast. He was a little thrown, but he stuck to his game plan and it seems to be paying off. She was sweet and even affectionate as they wandered the streets of Woodstock. She linked her arm in his. She let him buy her a bracelet in a hippie jewelry shop and kissed him as he slipped it onto her wrist. They had a leisurely dinner at the Blue Mountain Bistro and she dozed in the car on the way home, her hand resting on his thigh.

Lily is already in bed, at his request wearing a naughty black teddy he bought for her in Paris. Paul is feeling hopeful as he brushes his teeth and prepares to make his closing argument. It is his forte, after all. The day went well, but as he shuts off the bathroom light he admits to himself that *well* is really relative only to worse days they've had in the past weeks. He feels the chill. He knows things are delicate and that his performance has to be compelling.

He steps out of the dark bathroom into a candlelit bedroom.

Lily has got a scented candle going on her night table. She is lying inertly on her back looking up at the ceiling. Her head doesn't turn to him as he emerges into the flickering shadows and, despite his having snuck a lorazepam after breakfast, a stab of anxiety pushes his breath audibly from his mouth. She loves me, she loves me not. Her head turns at the sound, she smiles, and the anxiety subsides. He slides out of his briefs and into bed.

Paul caresses her cheek, tries to grab her eyes with his but she quickly hides her face in the guise of rearing up to kiss his chest. He strokes her head and her back as she insinuates herself against him, uses her body to push him down and continues to kiss his chest, his throat. He likes when she takes charge like that, and she hasn't really done it much lately, but her mouth feels tense on his skin. And when her hand moves down to his balls, too soon, he has the disturbing sense that she's not into it, that she's trying to get him to sprint to the finish line. That's not what he wants, not at all, so he takes her hand away, rolls her over onto her back, and dedicates himself to getting her attention.

He caresses her from throat to mound while he kisses her and he keeps at it until her lips soften under his and her breath fills his mouth. Very slowly, he undoes the satin loops on the teddy's covered buttons, one by one, and he teases the silk away from her breasts, replaces the slinky fabric with his hand, then with his mouth. She gasps and grasps at his hair. He stays there, cups the heaviness of her breasts in his hand, draws slow circles around her erect nipples with his tongue, plays the pad of his thumb over their hard pink-brown tips. He takes his time. He wants to make sure she feels how much he loves her body, how much he loves her. With his mouth still at her breasts, he brings his hand all the way down and this time slides it beneath the tiny V of satin that still covers her. She moans and the space between her legs widens, just enough so his hand can fit between them. Now, sure that he's won his argument, he begins to relax, his blood pounds through him, rushes to pool in his loins.

He's not planning to do anything with it yet, but his penis rises quickly to pulsing readiness and it pushes insistently into Lily's belly. Suddenly, Paul can't sense her; it's as if she's not there. Her arms are still around him, she is touching him and he is touching her, but he can't *feel* her. From one second to the next, the life in her has just disappeared. Her breath, her voice, her body, all gone silent. All that lovingly induced arousal evaporated like unwanted sweat off her now clammy skin. His blood surges from his crotch into his head. He wilts. Her hand slips between his legs and when it closes over his once-again flaccid penis she makes a little noise and reverses position so she can use her mouth on him. She goes to work, puts some really serious mechanical effort into it, but it's no good. She's still not there. Paul shrivels completely and with finality, and Lily lifts her head and gives him a startled look.

"Shit!" Paul pulls away and practically jumps off the bed. "Fuck!"

"Paul, come on. It's okay. It happens. You're tired."

"It's not *okay*, Lily! This does not happen to me!" He fumbles in the shadows for his briefs.

"Paul, calm down, please. Don't make such a big deal out of it. Let's just go to sleep."

Her voice sounds weary. Paul can't find his underpants. He straightens up and looks at her. Even in the warm candlelight, her expression is cold and flat. She looks as though she couldn't care less. She's not disappointed, she's not sympathetic. She's sitting cross-legged, the teddy gathered across her chest, looking tired and distant.

In his shock, humiliated to be standing in front of her naked and shrunken, Paul trips over that line between fear and anger and lands on the wrong side. He lashes out at her.

"If you don't want to fuck me, goddamn it, just say so instead of lying there like a corpse. I don't know what the hell is going on with you, Lily, but you'd better figure it out by the time I get home next month." He picks up his pillow. "I'm going to go sleep downstairs."

"Paul! Paul!"

Before he's halfway down the stairs he knows he made a big mistake. This has never happened to him before. It's not the pills; Bertram promised him that neither one had any such side effects. It's Lily, the chilly shitty way she's been acting toward him, but still, he knows he shouldn't have said what he did. He has to apologize. First thing in the morning; and then he'll have to leave. He can't deal with her now. He has work to do and he has to be 100 percent on top of it. A month apart will probably be good, anyway. Get some distance. Cool down. Miss each other. Deal with it when he gets home. He calls the car service and arranges for Big Vinnie to pick him up at eight o'clock.

He takes an Ambien and lies down in one of the two single beds in the guest room behind the kitchen. He's crawling with anxiety and his lungs don't seem to be working right. The fundamental givens of his life have plumb gone and given in. He can't sleep. He can't get it up. He can't pretend it doesn't matter whether this woman loves him or loves him not. He wants Lily's love but now he thinks he can't have it. If he can't have it, then he has to stop wanting it. He can't stop wanting it so he has to maintain his pursuit. But his pursuit strategies aren't working. What he did before, yelling at her like that, he wants to take it back. But it wouldn't be good to let her see his need or his fear, to have her think him vulnerable. That's not the man she loves. He doesn't know what to do. And so the only thing he can do for the moment is retreat even further. Retreat, regroup, try to figure out what's wrong and what to do about it. He can't wait now to get on the road.

All those good tricks he learned when he was young, all those things he's relied on, are now balled up in a fierce, tight, undo-able tangle in the middle of his superbly intelligent, unimagi-native brain. He turns onto his side with his arms around the extra pillow. While he sweats out waiting for the drug to render him unconscious, he strains to hear Lily's footsteps on the stairs. He listens in an agony of wanting her to come find him. Fifteen minutes later he falls asleep to the sound of his blood whooshing past his ears.

17

By WEDNESDAY MORNING Lily can't take it another minute. She has to either hammer her cell phone to cyberbits or use it to call Danny. She told him she would call; it's all up to her. It's all she's been able to think of since the weekend; calling him, seeing him. She entered his number into her phone's memory as soon as Paul drove away. Now that modern miracle device, so tiny and innocuous-looking, hangs before her with all the heady allure of the forbidden apple that got Adam and Eve thrown out of paradise. The landline doesn't have the same evil serpentine draw. Although technically she could pick it up and call Danny with it, actually she can't. It's the house phone, Paul's phone. The cell is hers. It's not attached to the house. It's not attached to Paul. It can take her anywhere. It can take her to 587 Old Stone Creek Road if that's where she wants to go.

She can't think coherently about what happened with Paul on Saturday, how she lay awake half the night crying, waiting for him to come back upstairs to her. Words and images keep skittering around her brain like a cageful of hysterical hamsters.

What happened; the terrifying truth of the vile things he said. He fumbled through an apology before he left. He avoided her red, swollen eyes and directed his awkward excuses somewhere in the vicinity of her ear. It made everything worse. Something *is* going on with her. She didn't want to fuck him. For a few moments her body went its own way, forming itself into the volcanic puddle that his hands and mouth, the smell and feel of him, always reduce her to. But when she felt his demanding penis push against her and she imagined herself splayed wide for him and him thrusting into her, something shut down inside her and all her desire died. The possibility she had glimpsed the weekend before—that she could remove herself so far from him in her mind as to feel nothing when he touched her—became reality.

He called Monday, before leaving for the airport, to say good-bye and to apologize again. They were both calmer and it was better. He reassured her that it wasn't her, that he'd been too quick with his anger, that she had to understand how upsetting it was to a man to be unable to make love to his wife. It was better, but it didn't reassure her. Even if she hadn't heard the distance in his voice it wouldn't have reassured her. It's her own feelings she's worried about now, more even than his.

He's gone for a month. Lily has been clutching and tearing at her relief, but it's been fatally tainted. She requires the narcotic of a more powerful emotion, a more giddy emotion, to hold her nightmares at bay. She requires a huge hit of happiness.

It's eight o'clock and she is sitting at the small table on the deck. On the pebbled glass top is her cell phone and a mug. She isn't afraid to make her coffee strong anymore and she is wired from caffeine and anticipation. She has been sitting there for an hour, rubbing the pink metal case of her phone and drinking coffee. She flips the phone open, finds Danny's name, and hits

SEND. His answering machine picks up after four rings. Lily's pulse is in her ears and she doesn't really hear his message but she hears his voice.

"Danny. Hi. It's Lily Spencer. I was wondering if maybe we could have that cup of coffee sometime this week. I'm free most anytime, so call me." She leaves him the number of her cell phone. "Bye."

Danny is taking Caleb to camp when Lily calls. He returns at eight thirty, hears her shy, shaky voice, and he's dialing her number on his cell, adding it to his phone's memory, before his answering machine clicks off. He wouldn't call her first, try to explain to Beth why he wants her number, but he's been waiting four impatient days for her to call him, hoping she won't change her mind. He gets her voice mail.

"Lily. Sorry I missed your call. How about today? Can you meet me for lunch? The Kitchen at one? My cell number is 845-555-3990. Let me know if that works for you."

Lily is in the shower when Danny calls. At 8:45, wrapped in a towel, her hair dripping water down her back, she dials his cell number, saves that, too, in her phone's memory. She gets his voice mail. "Oh, this is ridiculous! Maybe our cell phones should meet for lunch! Hi, Danny. The Kitchen at one. I'll be there. Bye."

At one o'clock Lily walks into The Kitchen. It's busy, she doesn't see Danny, and she stands uncertainly inside the doorway, not knowing whether to sit or stand outside or inside. The older waitress who tousled Danny's hair, the one who was laughing in the doorway, is waiting tables and she glances up as the restaurant's screen door bangs shut. She comes over and looks at Lily searchingly, emits a *tsk* sound, and smiles.

"You must be Lily."

Lily's eyes open wide in surprise.

"Danny described you very well. He just called. He apologizes, he's running a little late. A squirrel got into his house. Come, I saved him a table by the window."

"Thank you"—the woman has a plastic name tag pinned to the bodice of her uniform, an old-fashioned yellow shirtwaist dress with a crisp white collar—"Arlene."

Lily sits. She looks around. The place is friendly and welcoming. She can sense its history, the generations of Stone Creek families who have sat at these tables and stools talking with their neighbors about their children, their parents, their jobs, the weather, over pie and coffee. The room is filled with the indistinct sounds of conversation and the smells of good food. She loves it. Her assumptions about so many things are falling like dominoes.

"Here you go, dear. Danny thought you might like this while you wait." Arlene sets a chocolate milkshake down in front of Lily's astonished eyes—an enormous glassful with a refill in the icy, moisture-beaded metal canister.

He's not just inside her head, he's inside her heart. Chocolate milkshakes are Lily's enduring childhood comfort food. She loves them but they are not to be had just for fun; they are for special occasions, for necessary occasions. Somehow, he knew. She draws her initials in the frosty condensation on the stainless steel, as she did when she was little: *LMM.* Lily Maxine Margolies. Not too many people know about the Maxine. There is a red-and-white-striped straw in the glass, upright in the thick liquid. She puts her lips to it and drains the entire glass. It's the best chocolate milkshake she's had since she was fourteen years old. She sits back in her chair and watches for him out the window.

Fifteen minutes later the truck pulls into a parking space in front of the post office. Danny jumps out and hurries across the street. His sinewy body weaves through the gaps in the traffic. Arlene is at the door the moment he walks in. She gives him a motherly hug and a kiss and tosses her head in Lily's direction.

"Sorry I'm late." He slides into the seat across from her. His eyes skid off hers and take refuge on the canister.

"It's okay." Her eyes attach to a recent scrape on his forearm. "I had good company while I waited." She taps her straw. "Thank you. It's delicious."

"I'm glad you like it."

Their eyes meet and hold but only long enough for them to smile at each other. That shock of contact is still there. They don't yet know how to absorb it, how to let it move through them so they can relax with each other. Danny taps his fork against her glass.

"You still hungry?"

"Unbelievably, I'm starving."

"Good. So am I." He has only to turn in Arlene's direction and she's on her way.

"Arlene seems very possessive of you. She gave me quite the once-over when I came in."

Danny freezes in mid-twist, unable to turn back and look at her. He looks instead at Arlene as she comes toward them, as her gaze lingers a moment on Lily, as she smiles at him worriedly and with too much knowledge. Danny's back is to Lily but he sees the truth in Arlene's eyes. How easily Lily might remind someone of Tara. Arlene puts down menus. She touches his cheek and says, "Blueberry pie today, sweetheart," then leaves them to decide.

Beneath the camouflage of his beard, Danny's cheek feels branded. He commands himself to complete his turn. Lily is watching him with quiet curiosity. He takes a drink of water. He has to swallow a few times to get the water down before he can speak. "Arlene was my mom's best friend. I don't have any blood family left here. She and Tom Gallo, they're like my aunt and uncle."

"It's easy to see how fond of you they are." She tilts her head a little and smiles again.

They manage to look at each other for a little longer this time before they both drop their gazes to the menus.

"Everything's good here. What do you like?"

She is about to say, *I've never been here before, why don't you order for me?*, she even opens her mouth, but the words don't make it to her throat. In the early days of their relationship, Paul would often order for her when he'd take her to a place he knew well and she'd never been. She wanted him to; she reveled in feeling helpless, in being led and sheltered by his greater experience and his unassailable control of the environment and of her. She can't believe now that she ever wanted that.

"I love shrimp salad. I'm going to have a shrimp salad sandwich and potato salad."

"Sounds good. I'll have the same thing. Let's get some coleslaw, too."

The tension that's encased her since she called him lets go its hold. She points to the scrape on his arm, smiles for real. "The squirrel won, huh?"

Danny gives her a confused look and then laughs. "Oh. Yeah, kind of, I guess. I scraped myself chasing it out the door."

Lily surveys the restaurant's bustling interior. "You know, I've never been in here. You come often, don't you?"

"Very often. All my life. My mother was a waitress here for twenty-five years, practically until the day she died."

"You've spent your whole life in Stone Creek?"

"Except for the seven years I spent overseas." Lily can't hide her amazement and Danny looks down at himself with a disparaging grunt. "Still don't look very sophisticated, do I?"

He's wearing a snug orange T-shirt, olive green pants, and work boots. He doesn't look sophisticated at all. "I try not to judge people by what they look like," Lily says. But that's just what she did the first time she saw him. She saw what she wanted to see. "Where were you?"

Danny doesn't answer right away. He is staring straight through her.

"Danny? What is it?"

"Nothing. Nothing." He shakes his head and refocuses his eyes. "My father sent me off after my mom died, with Tom Gallo's help—I was three years in England, one in Japan, three in France. Came back with a profession, a beard, and a tattoo."

Lily laughs delightedly and studies the tattoo. "That's from Japan I'll bet."

"How did you know?"

"Because the Japanese are such consummate artists and that's an unusually beautiful tattoo." Unusually beautiful and an unusual color, a dark earthy brown that makes the complex woven braid seem to have risen from some warm place beneath his cool, light skin. "And where's the beard from?"

Danny smiles and blushes a little. "France. I grew it for a girl, naturally. Juliette."

"Ah. *Juliette aimait les barbus?* Did it work?"

"*Mais oui. En réalité, un peu trop.* She wanted me to stay and marry her."

"But you didn't want that."

"No. She wasn't the one."

"Well. At least you got the beard out of it. It suits you. And so does the tattoo. It really is beautiful, and it looks wonderful on you."

"Thanks. I'm glad you like it. Not everyone appreciates a bearded man with a tattoo."

"I like it." They look at each other with fathomless understanding. "Danny. How did you know I needed a chocolate milkshake?"

"You sounded a little frail," he says softly. Every simple exchange is loaded. Danny hears compressed years of information, questions asked and answered. *Can I trust you? You can trust me.*

Their eyes hold. They are both a little frail. That's why they're here.

Lily sighs and bites at her lip. Danny remembers she did that before, when they were talking about her husband.

"My husband and I are having a hard time. It was a bad weekend. He's away for a month now and I'm quite glad of it." The thing she can't say to the people who have known her forever she has said to Danny without a second thought. She and Paul are having a terribly hard time.

Danny doesn't fake surprise. He just nods. "I'm sorry to hear it." He doesn't ask her to elaborate. The tone of her voice makes him think that she probably hasn't said even that much to anyone before. He pours the rest of the milkshake into her glass. "I hope this helped a little. You look like a chocolate kind of woman."

"It helped a lot, actually. And what woman isn't the chocolate kind?"

Danny smiles. "My wife liked strawberry milkshakes. I mean,

give her a piece of chocolate cake and she was a happy girl. But when it came to milkshakes . . ."

They smile gently at each other. Finally, Lily says, "You and your wife never had hard times, did you?"

"No. Not between us, anyway. We weren't married long enough."

Lily knows Danny is making a joke, but his eyes aren't laughing. "Very funny. But that's not why, is it?"

"No. That's not why." Danny doesn't believe he and Tara would ever have had times as hard as whatever it is Lily and her husband are going through, not if they'd been given fifty years.

"How long did you have together?"

"She died right before our fifth anniversary."

Lily winces. "What happened to her?"

"She had a cerebral aneurysm. One night it ruptured. Just like that. Two minutes. She was gone in two minutes." He sees the shock in Lily's eyes, and he waits for her to look away in embarrassment for him or fear for herself, as so many people have done in the past year. But she doesn't look away and the shock fades quickly. Danny's own fear, never far from him, moves off a little bit. "I still can't believe it."

"Oh, Danny, I'm so sorry. And I'm upsetting you with all these questions."

He's about to agree, as he has to deflect so many people in the past year, but he's not upset. "No. It's okay. Actually, if you don't mind, I'd like to be able to talk to you about her."

"No, I don't mind. I'm happy you feel you can."

He stares hard at her, seized once more by that sense of inevitability. "Lily. Why do I feel as though we know each other?"

He has read her mind. Again. "I don't know, Danny. But I feel it, too."

They are leaning toward each other across the table. They pull back, smile again, a little timidly this time, and settle into their chairs.

The table has been cleared of the remains of shrimp salad sandwiches, potato salad and coleslaw, and, of course, blueberry pie. Arlene startles them when she reappears at the table and lays down the check.

"Danny, it's three thirty. Don't you have to pick Caleb up?"

They've been talking for more than two hours. It feels like no more than ten minutes have gone by. In a disbelieving rush Danny pays the bill, over Lily's protests, and they are on the street. Neither wants to walk away before they have ensured that they will see each other again.

"I'd love to meet Caleb sometime." Lily takes the leap.

Danny exhales in relief. "Yeah. I'd love you to. I'm taking him to the playground after camp Saturday afternoon. Why don't you join us?"

It's midnight. Danny isn't tired but he craves dimness and quiet, so he is sketching in a small circle of light directed onto his worktable. A bedframe and night tables for the Morgans. The studio's wooden doors and back windows are open. It has been a warm, still night but suddenly a water-cooled breeze flows softly through the room and rustles the paper beneath his hand. Danny lifts his head and looks back through the doors, toward the house, as if expecting to see someone standing there, the source of the wind that has roused him. There is no one, and yet he gets up and walks out onto the bluestone path and halts inside the rectangle of light cast from his bedroom window. The wind gusts. The treetops are moving. Murmuring.

I'll pick you up— you live up on the ridge road, right?

Yes, but don't come for me, I'll meet you here.

Why?

It would be better if my parents didn't know I was going out with you.

They wouldn't be happy to see an older guy with a beard and a tattoo fetching you in a truck, huh?

No, they wouldn't. Don't judge me by them, Danny. I love them, but I'm not like them.

I try not to judge people by anything but who they are.

He listens for a moment, remembering. He nearly failed to do that with her, to judge her only for who she was. He had so much to lose if he was wrong that he almost let her go rather than risk himself. But she wouldn't let him. The wind stills and he goes inside, to the bedroom, and takes her notebook from his night table. He's not going to read it tonight. But he will, very soon.

18

In ONE HOT, HEADY WEEK, Lily's life in Stone Creek, a previously fragmented, impersonal, part-time life, has become more meaningful to her than her supposed real life. Danny and Caleb. Her work with The Doorway, the people she's getting to know. She's spent several evenings at the Trachtenbergs' and soon she wants to invite Beth to dinner. The house feels like hers in a way it never did before, filled every moment with her choice of music, food, flowers. The rooms lit or left in darkness at her desire. The TV rarely on. The freedom to dance like a dervish around the living room. The peacefulness of her garden and her pool with no one else in them. She has never enjoyed being on her own this way.

Paul called again on Thursday. They are talking every two or three days, as they always do when he's away. They are talking, but they aren't connected when they talk. Before, he would call her from New Jersey and California and Washington, D.C., from China and Russia and Iceland, and no matter where he was, near or far, as soon as they heard each other's voices they were together. They could spend minutes happy just to listen to each other breathe. Now Lily is aware of every mile of high-tech fiber-optic cable wire that separates them. With every day that passes without feeling him near her, he seems to move further away and the days themselves seem to grow longer and longer. Her days in Stone Creek are flying by, but her days without Paul, those same winged days, are stretching into an eternity.

At 3:45 Lily gets ready to go out and meet Danny and Caleb. It's the last week of August and the weather is miserable—hot, hazy, and humid, the upstate New York summer mantra. She breaks out in a sweat just looking at the vaporous silver sky outside the window of her air-conditioned bedroom. She puts on the coolest clothing she has: a pair of loose, very short rayon shorts in a blue and green palm tree print that she bought for seven dollars in a surfer shop in Florida, and her white halter top. Blue plastic flip-flops on her feet. In the bathroom, bending over the sink, she brushes her hair over her head and catches it up in a ponytail. She turns to leave but is momentarily stopped by her reflection in the bathroom's mirrored wall.

She is showing a lot of skin. A narrow band of midriff peeks through the gap where the shorts droop away from the edge of her top. Bare legs, bare arms and shoulders, bare back. A little slice of bare bosom. She looks young and awfully sexy, in a Daisy Mae kind of way. She imagines Danny seeing her like this and her heartbeat jumps into her throat. She puts a trembling hand on her chest, as if to push her pulse back down where it belongs. Her gold wedding band shines and tingles against her skin, right over her heart.

"Caleb, this is my friend Lily."

Lily bends down and smiles at Caleb, who is half-hiding behind Danny's leg. "Hi, Caleb." She holds out a hand. "I'm really happy to meet you. I *love* your shirt, by the way. Aren't dinosaurs the best?"

Caleb is wearing a T-shirt from the Museum of Natural History. He smiles shyly and takes a step toward her. He studies her for a second, then takes her hand and heads off, pulling her with him. "Let's go to the sandbox."

"Caleb, maybe Lily doesn't want to go to the sandbox just yet." Danny is ready to smile an apology as she turns toward him, but there is that look in her eye again. He notices how her hand tightens around Caleb's. "Maybe for a few minutes?" He smiles an invitation instead.

"Yes, for a few minutes. Come on, Caleb. Let's take the shovel and pail."

"*You* wait here, Dad." Caleb points, his little finger aimed unerringly at Danny's chest.

Danny obeys. He doesn't mind being excluded. It's going to take a few minutes for him to calm down. To get the sight of the swell of her breasts and the contours of her toned arms as she bent toward Caleb out of his mind. He wants to watch her from a distance until it's safe for him to take off his sunglasses and let her see his eyes. He doesn't want to scare her. He doesn't want her worrying that he's going to hit on her. He sits down on the wooden bench and observes his son playing in the sandbox with the new woman in their lives.

Lily and Caleb are making pail-shaped sand castles while they talk. Lily asks him what he did at camp today. He asks her if she has a dog. She tells him she loves bats. He tells her he loves sushi.

She's squatting, patting the sides of their newest mound. She's definitely into it. She's actually trying to make it look like a castle. Caleb is sitting in the sand next to her, digging a hole in preparation for burying the pail. He puts the shovel down and comes to stand in front of her, leveling several structures on the way, including the one Lily is working on.

"You're pretty."

Lily wipes her hands on her thighs. "Thank you. What a nice thing to say."

"My mommy was pretty."

"I'm sure she was. You must miss her a lot."

He doesn't respond. He lifts both hands and touches the diamond studs sparkling at her earlobes. "I like those."

"Me, too. They were a birthday present from my husband."

"For when you were five?"

She smiles. "No. For when I was forty."

"I'm five."

"I know. Your daddy told me. You're a big boy." She can't help herself, she reaches out and caresses his head. Her hand shakes a little as it lingers on his cheek. He's a precious child, his blue eyes enormous in his face as he stares at her intently.

"Did your husband die?"

She places her hands on his bony sides and draws him toward her. "No. He's in New York City, working."

"At the Museum of Natural History?" He gives her a hopeful look.

She shakes her head ruefully. "No. He doesn't work there, but he likes it, very much."

"Me, too. I like the dinosaurs."

"Oh, yeah. Who wouldn't?"

Caleb puts his hands on her shoulders and gives her a shake.

"Oh, yeah! Who wouldn't!" He beams and throws his arms around her. "I like you, Lily."

"I like you, too, Caleb." She holds him close, as close as she can without hurting him. His arms squeeze her, hard, and he lays his head against hers, his nose in her neck. They are melting into each other and although she tries not to, tries as hard as she possibly can, she begins to cry. She is being buried in a loosed avalanche of her own ungiven love.

Caleb leans back, his arms still hitched around her neck. "Are you sad, Lily?"

She gets a grip on herself and smiles. "No, I'm happy. Happy to be with you. Grown-ups sometimes cry when they're happy. It's silly, isn't it?"

He looks at her seriously, as though he doesn't buy it but he'll allow that he does. A five-year-old politician. "Silly. Silly Lily."

"Silly Lily. That's me."

Through her distorted vision, she sees Danny coming quickly toward them. She raises her head to him and his eyes are all over her face. He mouths *It's okay.* He gently extricates Caleb, picks him up and puts him down outside the sandbox. As soon as he is removed from her, Lily starts to weep in earnest.

"Caleb. I see Billy and Kristin and their mom over at the pirate ship. Why don't you go play with them and let me and Lily talk for a while, okay?" He keeps Caleb's back to Lily, pats his tush, and steers him off to the other side of the playground.

The thoughts he had about her on the street that day, they weren't wrong. Someway, somehow, she has lost a child, he's sure of it. From twenty feet away he could see the neediness in her eyes when she looked at Caleb, he could feel the tremor in her hand as she touched him. Now she's kneeling, her hands over her face, tears leaking through her fingers onto the sand.

Danny takes hold of her arm and pulls her to her feet. He puts his arm around her and leads her out of the sandbox. She leans against him. He is acutely aware of the warmth of her body, the sleekness of her skin. Her hair gives off a scent of citrus.

"Sit down." He lowers her onto the bench and withdraws his arm. His receding fingers trail along the back of her bent neck and the ends of her ponytail sweep across his hand.

"Tissues . . . a box in my car . . ."

Danny goes to her BMW, comes back with the box of tissues, and puts it on the bench next to her. He doesn't say anything. He lets her cry until the soggy wad in her lap finally stops growing.

"I'm sorry. You must think I'm a madwoman. I'm so embarrassed."

"No. Don't be." He pries the tissues from her hands. He tosses them into the garbage can behind the bench. "Lily, can I ask you something?"

There is a mournful cast to her eyes as she looks at him and nods.

"Why don't you have children?" He waits and watches as she begins to gnaw at her quivering lower lip.

Lily hears no threat in Danny's question. She sees no desire in his eyes to unearth her private agonies and her regrets and force her to warp and mold and polish them until they shine like fake gold and everyone can pretend there's nothing ugly beneath the pretty surface. She hears and sees only Danny's desire to understand, to help ease her pain. And she knows he can. His own loss has attuned him to hers with an emotion far beyond sympathy.

"Because my first marriage was not a real marriage, and my current husband is a selfish, insensitive man who never once asked me what I wanted or listened when I tried to tell him," she says. The confession pours out of her. "I'm so angry at Paul I can hardly bear to look at him."

She tells him everything then, from Paul's caveat the night he proposed to Rick's dropping the bomb of the adoption at her feet. By the time she's done, the tissue box is empty and Danny has gone to the Volvo for the emergency container of all-natural, unscented baby wipes.

They sit quietly on the bench for a few moments. Strands of Lily's hair have freed themselves from her ponytail. Danny moves a little closer and smooths the errant wisps back into place. As he brings his hand from her head, she captures his fingers in hers. Her head is down and she's not looking at him, but she holds on tight to his hand.

"Have you ever told Paul how you really feel about all of this? How you feel now?"

"I didn't even know that this is how I feel until a few weeks ago." She shakes her head. "I can't talk to Paul about these things. I just can't. I never could. He doesn't want to hear them. He's so ... difficult and ... scary." Lily laughs at herself, as though that might lessen her fear of her own husband.

For her sake, Danny laughs with her. "So, I guess that means you have a thing for difficult and scary men?"

Lily darts a glance at him and laughs and snurfles at the same time. "No. But I have a thing for him."

Danny considers that he should let go of her hand before he asks his next question, but it requires more of an effort than he can muster. "Do you still love him?"

Their twined hands are resting on Danny's leg, half on his khaki shorts and half on his golden-brown thigh. The fine blond hairs on his arms and legs have been stripped of color by the sun and adorn his skin like a layer of transparent glitter. Lily feels them everywhere their arms and hands touch. She feels his heat crawling along the backs of her fingers. She draws her hand from his and brings it to her lap. She tucks both her hands beneath her legs.

"Yes. I still love him."

Danny puts his hands in his pockets.

Lily sighs. "Here comes Caleb." He's making his way to them, his journey interrupted every few steps by the urge to explore something on the ground. "Where did he get those adorable ears?" Caleb's ears come to soft points at their tops. They stick out from his head just a bit. "He looks so much like you, but those are not your ears." She turns and smiles at Danny.

He returns her smile, then gazes off to follow his son's slow progress. "Those are Tara's ears. Her little elf ears. I love them."

There is such longing in his voice that Lily is tempted to take his hand again. She keeps her hands safely under the bend of her knees and takes in his profile instead. The muscles of his jaw tensing beneath his beard, the prominent curve of his cheekbone, the long pale lashes and thick pale brow, the lines radiating from the side of his shockingly blue eye, the roughly cut fair hair longer than when she first saw him, growing now over the neck of his shirt in back, trailing across his forehead in front. He's become beautiful to her. Lily's eyelids drift down and shut him out. She turns her head, opens her eyes, and follows his gaze.

"You had Caleb very quickly."

"Yeah, you could say that. Tara was already pregnant when we got married."

"He was an accident? You didn't plan him?"

"No, he was planned all right. By Tara."

Lily is stunned. "How could she do that? What if you hadn't wanted to marry her, or wanted a baby so soon?"

He shakes his head. "No. I wanted her, and I wanted kids, and she knew it. The problem was that I'd broken up with her."

"But why?"

"Because I was a moron," Danny says blithely. "Even very smart, nice men can do stupid things they don't mean."

Lily acknowledges his oblique reference to Paul with a little push against his shoulder. "You're no moron. Why did you break up with her?"

"I didn't believe she really loved me and I let her mother convince me that I was right. Tara was so young, and I was the only guy she'd ever been with. I couldn't get past thinking that I was just some rebellious fantasy of hers that she'd get over any minute. In eight months she never even told her parents about me. When Eve found out, she paid me a visit. If you think your husband is scary, you should meet my mother-in-law. She knew just where to stick it to me. She looked at me like I was dirt and she told me I didn't belong in their world, that there could never be a place for me there, that I would isolate Tara and drag her down and one day she'd realize it and dump me. I was so afraid Eve was right that I broke it off.

"We didn't see each other for two months and then one night she appeared at my house. I couldn't have sent her away if Eve had been standing there pointing a gun at me. Two weeks later she told me she was pregnant." Danny's voice is sturdy, but his body seems to have gone weak. "We were going to have a whole bunch. We thought we had time."

Lily dangles a baby wipe in front of his face. "I saved you one," she says. Danny sits up straight and explodes with laughter. Lily smiles gently and looks at him with luminous eyes. "You'll have more children, Danny. You're a man, and you're young. You have time. You'll have another chance. At everything."

But I won't. Her words of kindness are laced with sorrow. Danny wishes he could tell her she's wrong, that there's time for her, too. It wouldn't do her any good to know that no matter what chances his future holds, he believes his time has passed as well.

Caleb runs the last few yards and clambers up onto the bench. "I'm hungry, Daddy. Let's go home. Lily, you come, too." He's into bossing people around today.

Caleb starts to climb onto Lily's lap, but Danny pulls him onto his own lap before he can get too far. "I'm taking you to Grandma and Grandpa's tonight, remember?"

"I know, but we're having dinner home first." He explains to Lily, "They're going to the club to eat shrimp because on Saturday night you can eat all the shrimp you want and Grandpa loves them and he can eat a whole ton."

"If you're a sushi lover, I guess you like shrimp, too?"

Caleb wrinkles his nose and shakes his head. "They're yucky. I like cocktail sauce, though. We could have some for dinner. . . ." He leans back against Danny's chest, licks his lips and bats his eyes at her.

Danny gives Lily a *can't fool him* look. "Lily may have other plans, honey," he says, but with a questioning raise of his brow.

She could. She has no other plans. She could go with them, help Danny make dinner, take Caleb onto her lap and eat cocktail sauce with him, watch his lips turn red and his pale lashes flutter against his baby-soft cheek. "I can't. Not tonight. Maybe one night during the week." She can't.

19

DANNY TAKES HIS COFFEE and his cell phone and goes outside. Tara's journal is tucked under his arm. He settles himself into a chair on the shady side of the porch, away from the morning sun, puts the mug and phone on the table beside him, the book on his lap. His mind idles on the fact that the Volvo could stand to be washed. He picks up his phone and calls Lily. When he hears her voice, he unconsciously sinks a little lower into the pliant wicker.

"Hey. Good morning. What are you doing?"

"Hey yourself. I'm in my rose garden, battling Japanese beetles."

"Good luck. You missed an interesting dinner last night. Cold cereal with a side of macaroni and cheese. Caleb was having a feisty day."

"Makes my organic salmon sound downright drab. What are you doing?"

"I'm sitting on my porch. I'm going to do a little reading before I go to work." He lays a hand on the book. "I just wanted to tell you how terrific it was to be with you yesterday."

"Yes, it was. It was wonderful."

"I'll give you a call later, okay?"

"Okay. I'll be here. After the beetles come the weeds."

Danny turns the phone off. He drains his mug. His fingertips trace little circles on the notebook's leather cover. He turns the pages until he finds the place where a week ago he had to stop. He closes his eyes, takes a few breaths. If he falls off the wire this time, there is a net to catch him; Lily is just a phone call away.

Then was the fall of my senior year. Danny had been home since July, returned from France the day of his father's heart attack, but I was working at Princeton that summer and there was no one to tell me. On the few weekends I came back to Stone Creek it was to see my parents and let them take me to the club. They wanted to show me off, their Princeton girl, the future ambassador to France, or wife thereof, graduating in June summa cum laude, accepted into the master's program in International Relations, hand-picked for summer employment by the director of the Princeton Institute for International and Regional Studies. They were so proud of me I couldn't tell them that I felt the world closing tighter and tighter around me. That I didn't want what they wanted for me and I dreamed of being a poet. That I didn't want who they wanted for me, either, and I dreamed of a boy I'd met when I was ten, an inappropriate boy whose name meant nothing to them or anyone they knew.

He'd stayed away for seven years. The last time he saw me I was thirteen and had braces on my teeth. He didn't know me. And what I knew of him was what a child knows. I didn't know him. But I couldn't forget him. Every boy I met was compared and found wanting. But seven years is a long time, long enough for a dream to tatter and stop looking and feeling like reality.

*It became harder and more frightening to keep asking af-
ter him at The Kitchen. Arlene would make me a strawberry
milkshake and tell me, He's still in England; oh yes he has a
girlfriend. He's gone to Japan, can you believe it? He's living
in the south of France; oh yes he has a girlfriend. He's grown a
beard. He was getting older and more and more of his life was
happening elsewhere. I was so afraid I'd come in one day and
Arlene would tell me that he was never coming back, that he'd
married Brigitte or Mylene or Françoise. But on that weekend
in October, I was in great need of a strawberry milkshake. I
went to The Kitchen and Arlene told me he was finally home.*

*I almost didn't go to see him. Ten years of fantasies. Seven
years of his life unobserved, unknown. What if he wasn't the boy
I'd dreamed of, remembered for all this time? What if he was
and he didn't want me?*

*He was staying in the old family house while he renovated
it, driving his father's old van. It was parked in his driveway
and the front door stood open. I followed the rhythmic sound
of a hammer hitting wood. He was on his knees in the dining
room, laying down a new oak floor. He sensed my presence in
the doorway, looked up, and got to his feet. His hair was shorter
and a little darker, his reddish-blond beard made him look a
little rougher. But he was wearing blue jeans and a white T-shirt
and the body beneath them was chiseled and his eyes were blue
lasers and his quizzical smile was sweet. He hadn't changed and
I fell in love with him all over again.*

"Hi, Danny."

*He came toward me. "Hi. Uh . . . are you with the real es-
tate office? I already told someone the house wasn't ready to be
shown yet."*

"No. I guess you don't remember me. I'm Tara Jamison."

He stared down at me with a bemused look and his eyes widened in disbelief. "Oh my God. Tara! I would never have recognized you. You've . . . grown up." He laughed and a flush swept across his cheeks above his beard.

"I've been away at school." I couldn't take my eyes from his face. "I just heard that you were home, and about your father. I wanted to tell you how sorry I am, but how glad I am that you're back. I wanted to say hello."

His smile grew more gentle and his eyes lost their bemusement and I knew he was remembering me, infatuated little Tara Jamison. "Thank you. I'm glad to be back, too. And it's good to see you. It's so nice of you, to come here like this."

He didn't know what was about to happen to him. I did, and it wasn't just because I'd believed it for so long and wanted it so badly. There was an infinitesimal change in his breathing, and the sense of something held down in him rising. "I have to go back to school tomorrow. Would you have dinner with me tonight?"

I could see his thoughts behind his eyes, all his reasons to say no. But I could see his uncertainty, too, and his generosity, his inability to hurt someone when it could be avoided. He said yes.

I wore my red dress. He took me to The Farmhouse and toward the end, hours after we'd first sat down across from each other and begun to weave the unbreakable web that would bind us, he finally asked me did I want the same things for myself that my parents wanted for me. He was being polite, he thought his question was about me, but it wasn't. He already had to know the truth of why I had come to seek him out. So I told him.

"I want to marry the man I love, live quietly in a kind, small town, and raise happy children."

I think he knew what I was saying. That he was the man I loved and wanted to marry and whose happy children I wanted to raise. That it was that day in June and my childhood tumble into his eyes that had pushed me off the straight path of my life.

But he sat back in his chair, looked away from me, and said, "That sounds like heaven. I hope you get to do it someday."

When we parted, I let him tell me why we shouldn't see each other again. But before he turned away, I stepped into him, put my hand on his chest, and kissed him.

I drove back to school that night. I couldn't stay in Stone Creek. I hung suspended in a world reduced to an agony of waiting. Ten days later he called me, and the next weekend he came to Princeton to see me.

Danny reads the pages three times through. With each reading the booming in his ears ebbs until there is but a single lucid sound—the sound of her voice reciting words of love dedicated to him. The fog in his eyes and his brain lifts. He remembers those bits of conversation; they were exactly as she wrote them. He remembers everything.

He stood by a window and watched her walk across the lawn to her car after she'd asked him out. She stopped to look back at the door where she'd left him. She clutched herself, arms crossed tightly over her chest, closed her huge dark eyes, and turned her face up to the sky. Unseen, he observed her silent prayer, drank in the lusciousness of her ivory skin and pouty lips, and he warned himself not to forget where she came from or how young she was. He told himself to be careful with her. As she drove away and he turned from the window into the interior of the empty house, he told himself to be careful with himself.

He agonized over what to wear, where to take her. He pawed through his closet and finally chose the nicest pants and shirt he'd bought in France; nothing else seemed good enough for her.

She wore a sleeveless red dress that curved where she curved and clung everywhere else. Red high heels that showed off her dancer's legs. She asked to see the house, so he took her through it, explained what he'd done, what he was going to do. She floated through the rooms, her trailing fingers admiring his handiwork, and he was breathless as he walked behind her.

They lingered after the other diners had gone, as one by one the tables around them were cleared and stripped down, the chairs turned upside down and set upon the tables, the floors swept. They went out onto the deserted veranda. The first hint of an autumn chill was in the air. Laughter and the sounds of a saxophone and a piano sifted through the shut windows from the bar area. She smiled and swayed to the music, held out her arms, and invited him to dance with her. He was afraid to touch her. He put a timid hand on her waist, tried to keep her at a chaste distance, but the music itself seemed to coil around them and push them together. She came against him, taut and soft and shivering. Something was happening, but it didn't yet make sense to him that it could be happening with her. He didn't see the place where their different worlds overlapped and merged. He couldn't believe that it was she he had come home to find. He put her away from him, put her in his father's van, and drove them back to his house.

He didn't let her come in. He stood with her at her car and said, "Tara, you're just a kid. And I'm no Yale or Dartmouth man. You may think that's not what you want, but, believe me, I wouldn't be good for you."

"You're wrong. I'm not a kid. And you said you wouldn't judge me by my parents' choices. I want to see you, Danny. I'm going back to school tomorrow. I won't be here again until Christmas. It's a three-hour drive to Princeton. My number is on your kitchen counter."

"Tara. Come on. I'm flattered, but I don't fit into your world." He attempted a smile. "You'll outgrow me by the time you're twenty-one. Anyway, I'm seeing someone else."

He watched her face, lit silver by the moonlight, as she stared at him. "My number is on your kitchen counter." And then, without warning, she stepped close, put her hand on him, and kissed him. It was just her mouth on his, and her hand light on his chest, but he felt her everywhere as he'd never felt anyone.

He called her. It wasn't ten days later, she was wrong about that. It was eight. He's sure of it. Because he remembers becoming unrecognizable to himself as, day by excruciating day, his resistance crumbled and his resolve to stay away from her failed. Until by the ninth morning there was nothing left to protect him from the lure of her questing dark eyes locked on his, from the superheated spark of life in her that jumped to him and seared him when they touched, and burned still on his lips. He was a mere mortal, but she was elfin; she was magic.

It's been two hours since Danny's first call and Lily has been chased from her roses and her weeds by the broil of the midday sun. She has drawn a chaise into the shade of a copper beech tree and is lying there, reading.

"Have you vanquished your beetles?"

"No, I gave up. It's too hot. I'm sitting in the shade reading. You inspired me. Are you still on your porch?" Lily puts her book down and cuddles the phone to her ear.

"Yeah. But I'm finished with my reading for the day. I'm going to go over to The Doorway house and see what I can get done. I don't have to pick Caleb up till eight."

There is an unmistakable melancholy in Danny's voice. "Danny, are you okay?"

He doesn't answer immediately, and although she hasn't seen his house Lily imagines him staring off into thick woods while he ponders her question. "No. Not really. How are you?"

"So-so."

"I'd like to get together again, soon. I'm busy the next few days, but can I inspire you to go hiking with me Thursday?"

"Yes. I love to hike but Paul doesn't. If he can't *get* somewhere in half an hour, he doesn't see the point." She knows she's being unfair. It's not that Paul can't see the point of a walk in the woods, it's that he's always so wound up he doesn't know how to enjoy it and she doesn't know how to teach him, how to get him to slow down.

"Impatient man. He should learn the benefits of pointlessness. How about we pick up Caleb afterward and you'll come have dinner with us. He's going to nag me to death if I haven't made a date with you before he gets home tonight."

"We wouldn't want that. Your plan sounds lovely and I eat everything."

"Good. I'll see you Thursday. I'll call you in the morning."

Lily is about to lay the phone down and go back to her book but a crawl of guilt in her abdomen stops her. She and Paul haven't spoken since Thursday, and she hasn't yet been the one to call. It would be better if she waited until the evening, but it seems safer in the brightness of day. She calls him.

When he answers, she hears a strange man's voice yelling, "Damn! I sliced it left again! What the hell is wrong with me today?" then Paul's voice saying, "Excuse me a minute, Mitch. The wife . . ." and then, "Hi. Lily. Hi."

"The wife? Is that what I've been reduced to? Why not the ball and chain?"

"That would have worked. I'm in Denver, they're a little down home here, if you catch my drift. I can't talk too long. What's doing?"

She did indeed call at a bad time and he sounds distracted. But since there's nothing doing, anyway, she doesn't have much to say to him. "Nothing's doing. I just wanted to say hello, find out how things were going."

"Same as when you asked on Thursday. It's a little early to tell."

He doesn't ask how things are going with her *little job*. They did that already and although he listened dutifully, she imagined she could see his eyes glaze over with boredom through the phone line. She hears Mitch again. "Come on Paul. You're holding us up."

"Yeah, yeah, I'm coming, hang on. Lily, I have to go."

"Of course. I'm sure the truth is waiting for you on the ninth tee."

"Hey, come on. I'm working. I'm not out here for fun, believe me. For all I know the truth *is* waiting on the ninth tee. I'm doing what I have to do."

"I know. I'm sorry. I didn't mean to sound like that. I was just joking. Call me later?"

After a short pause, Paul says, "I will. I love you."

"Love you, too."

She knows Paul hates playing golf, although of course he's good at it. He says he'd rather be strapped into a chair and forced to watch paint dry, at least then he wouldn't have to make small talk with chubby men in plaid pants. He does it only for business. So why did she have to make him feel bad? Why did he make her feel that although he hates it, he would rather be playing golf than talking to her?

20

E VE AND CALEB ARE ON the two-seat swing set on the lawn downslope from the house, enjoying a last bout of play before dinner and Daniel's arrival. They are pumping their legs in unison, but Caleb is swinging much much higher than Eve. So high that the chains attaching the wooden seat to the metal frame buckle slightly as he tops his forward motion and a tiny sliver of air appears between his shorts-clad behind and the wood. She envisions him flying off the swing or the chain breaking or the swing going out of control and sailing over the top bar and Caleb plummeting to the ground. She has to compel herself to not beg him to stop. She tells herself he has never fallen, he knows to hold on tight. He is unafraid. Unlike his grandmother, who is riddled with fear for him.

They went to church. They went to Splashdown, the waterpark in Fishkill. They did not go to the cemetery. Weeks ago, Daniel asked her to allow Caleb to decline to visit Tara's grave or to look at photos of her without being made to feel as though he had done something wrong. As though it is *she* who is wrong to want him to remember his mother; as though she would ever do anything to hurt or upset Caleb. It doesn't worry her, however. Caleb is young and there will be time for the cemetery and the photo albums and the knowledge that he once belonged to someone whose love for him will remain forever unmatched. What is important now is that his attachment to her be absolute. In his mother's absence, it is Eve he truly belongs to and it is only her love that will ever rival the love he lost.

Caleb stops pumping his legs. The swing slows its pendulum motion and he drags his feet in the dirt hollow beneath him until he comes to a complete halt. "I'm ready to go in, Grandma. I'm tired."

"You should be. You must have climbed that big slide a hundred times."

He slips off his swing. "Maybe a million times. Can you carry me?"

"Perhaps a zillion times. Of course I can carry you."

Eve rises and hefts him into her arms, sets him onto her canted hip. He is getting heavier every day. He is growing and changing too fast and Eve's fear grows alongside each pound and inch. Sometimes she places her hand on his head and imagines a crack widening, blood seeping, a bulge forming where no one can see it. She imagines the seeding of the next moment of destruction, waiting to level her life to rubble once again. He snuggles against her and she puts her lips to his forehead. He is hot.

"Caleb. Are you feeling all right?"

He pushes his head against her. "Yeah. My head hurts a little. Daddy said maybe I was getting a cold."

For a second Eve cannot breathe. She stops walking so that she will not stumble. "Has your head hurt all day, sweetheart?"

"Yeah. Kind of."

"Yes. All right. I'm going to tell Daddy that he should take you to the doctor. Little boys should not have headaches. It may be something more serious than a cold. I'll tell him to take you tomorrow."

He arches back from her and says, "Am I sick, Grandma?" His eyes are frightened.

She calms herself and pushes his hair, still too long, away from his face. "I'm sure it's just a cold, Caleb, but we have to be cautious. We can't be too cautious."

As she expected, Daniel was maddeningly unconcerned. *He's probably getting a cold, Eve. Half the kids at camp have colds. If his snot turns green, I'll take him to the doctor.*

He is so conscientious with his wood and his varnish and his paints and his brushes and his stupid tools but he is careless with the people for whom he is responsible. The boy has a *headache;* why isn't Daniel rushing him to the doctor? He has repeatedly refused to have Caleb tested, and that Dr. Marcus is of no use whatsoever. Daniel doesn't want to face it and of course Dr. Marcus says what he wants to hear.

Eve shuts off the kitchen light and goes into the den. She picks the remote off the side table by Lester's chair and clicks off the television.

"Eve! I'm in the middle of *The Sopranos*!"

She sits down on the couch. "It is repeated constantly all week. You can record it. I want you to arrange for Caleb to have an MRI or CAT scan or whatever it is he should have. He has to be tested."

Lester sighs. "Eve, darling, you know I can't do that. Why don't we talk to Danny and Dr. Marcus again and see if this time we can convince them. I'll get one of our specialists to come with us. All right?"

"It is pointless! They are both fools! They will never agree!"

Eve cries and springs to her feet. "Oh, for mercy's sake, go back to your program!"

She walks across the grounds to the swing set. She tries to swing but she is too upset to sit. She wants to scream. She is so utterly helpless. It was unfair of her to yell at Lester. It was unfair of her to pose the request at all. Of course he can't do it. No one would perform such tests without the permission of the boy's father. She knows that.

It has never occurred to Eve to have herself tested. She is not worried for herself. The lethal flaw in her daughter's brain did not come from her side, from her family. Generations of Fosters have been envied for their wealth, longevity, and robust good health. So have the Jamisons, for that matter. She doesn't worry about Lester collapsing of a brain hemorrhage any more than she worries about herself, but that is irrelevant. Tara did not inherit the weakness in her brain from Lester. She did not inherit anything from Lester. And if Daniel and Dr. Marcus and the physicians at the medical complex knew that, if they knew what she knows about Tara and Caleb, the secret she can never tell anyone, they would not refuse to look inside the son for the weakness that killed the mother.

Eve fits easily onto the child-sized wooden swing. She grasps the cold chains. She shudders in the damp night air and wonders if there will come a day when she will pick up a *People* magazine at the hair salon, or be browsing through Lester's *BusinessWeek*, and read that Terry Jones, visionary founder of DreamStar Animation Studios, who made his first million before the age of thirty, or more sadly one of his beautiful blond children, died tragically young at home in northern California of a ruptured brain aneurysm. Tara's weakness did not come from Eve or Lester. It came from her father. It was a poisoned gift, the only defect of perfect Terry's perfect genes; it was Eve's punishment for loving him.

21

CALEB INSISTS ON RIDING HOME with Lily so Danny transfers the car seat to the back of the BMW. Lily follows the truck as Danny takes a shortcut that she doesn't know from Caleb's camp to Old Stone Creek Road. She waits by the side of the road while he stops at a farm stand for fresh corn and a fruit pie. Caleb is beside himself with excitement. He is babbling nonstop, except when Lily moves her eyes from the road to the rearview mirror to look at him and reaches back to stroke his swinging leg. She has never had a babbling child strapped in a seat in the back of her car before and she needs to look at him and touch him every couple of minutes. Each time she does, he falls momentarily silent, rests his head against the seat frame, and rewards her with a beatific, infatuated smile.

As they pull into the driveway Caleb flattens his nose against the window glass. "Lily, Lily, look at the mailbox! Daddy made it but I *designed* it. And I helped paint it."

Lily saw the mailbox coming from a dozen car lengths away. Danny had warned her about it. "That is one awesome mailbox.

I've never seen anything like it. You're going to be making your own things soon, just like your dad."

Lily parks next to the Volvo. Danny's house is as he described it, as she imagined it would be—simple and elemental. She was worried that she would feel closed in and isolated by the engulfing woods and the absence of nearby neighbors. She is so used to the long, open vistas from atop her property and to the inescapable crush of human life in the city. But as soon as she steps out of the car the peacefulness of Danny's environment settles over her. She thinks that she could stay here, invisible to the world, forever.

Caleb unstraps himself and tumbles from the car. He tugs at her shorts. "Let's go in."

"Shouldn't we wait for Daddy? Or do you have your own key?" she teases.

"I have a key!" he cries. "See?" He displays a splay-fingered hand. He runs up the porch steps and opens the door. Obviously, Danny doesn't lock his house.

Danny has come in through the kitchen and is unpacking the corn and three-berry pie onto the tile counter.

"Your son is too clever for me," Lily says.

"Tell me about it. I'm going to go take a shower. Do you need one?" He smiles at her innocently. There are sweat stains on her SAVE THE MANATEE T-shirt and her hair is bedraggled and damp. An uneven coating of trail dust powders her arms and legs.

"How tactful of you." Lily laughs. "God, yes. That hike was a killer."

"Daddy, let's take Lily down to the creek."

Lily is about to say how heavenly it sounds, a dip in the creek. But Danny's smile has frozen on his lips and he looks sickly, as if he's just been told to shoot his dog. She understands without having to think about it; he used to swim in the creek with Tara. She turns to Caleb and says, "You know, I didn't think to bring a bathing suit. Maybe next time, sweetie, okay? You want to show me where the bathroom is?" She picks up her bag.

Twenty minutes later Lily steps out into the hallway just as a naked Caleb, his skin pure white in all the places where the sun hasn't been, streaks from Danny's bedroom into his own. A second later Danny steps into the hall, his shirt still only half on. Lily turns her head away from the sight of his bare torso and wet hair.

"You didn't warn me that your son was a flasher," she jokes as she walks toward the living room. There are doors to three more rooms standing open down the other end of the hallway. Rooms that were meant for Danny and Tara's children.

"He has informed me that he is dressing for dinner."

"Is there anything I can do to help?"

"How about making a salad? Use anything you can find in the fridge. I've got lamb chops marinating, and we've got the corn. I'll go light the grill."

They move and hum around his kitchen as though they've been preparing meals together for years. Lily glides by Danny on her way to the sink to rinse the lettuce; he swivels as she passes and moves toward the pantry; they raise their glasses at the same moment and sip at their wine. Lily has the sense that they are dancing, a languid and stately pas de deux. Paul doesn't cook. He makes good coffee and cocktails and is adept at the grill, but he's never cooked anything more challenging than toast and eggs. Before he married Lily, he ate out or had meals delivered to him. Lily and Paul have never moved together in their kitchen like this.

"Where did you learn how to cook?" Lily asks. His refrigerator has no junk in it. Just real food, fresh food, bowls and plastic containers with interesting-looking remnants of recent meals. "Most men of my acquaintance are kitchen averse."

"I had to. When my mom was sick, if I hadn't fed us my father and I would have starved. I'm sure you cooked a few meals for your dad."

"A few. But I had just married Rick when my mother got sick, and my father had the means to hire someone to keep house for him. They needed a different kind of help from me."

"They needed your calm compassion."

They are both standing at the counter, not far from each other, but not too near. Lily looks over at him and says, "Danny," with an embarrassed laugh. He raises his hands and his brows as if to say, *It's only the truth.* They go back to their dinner chores.

"You know, the first time I saw you was actually early in the summer, in Dreiser's. I thought you didn't notice me, but now I think maybe you did." Danny is shucking the corn, his focus fixed on finding and removing every single strand of corn silk. "You seemed to recognize me that day you looked in the window of The Kitchen."

"Right before July Fourth weekend." Lily is shredding lettuce into a bowl, paying meticulous attention to making each piece the same size. "I noticed you. At the end of the cereal aisle."

She lifts her head and he lifts his. Their hands fall still.

Caleb comes prancing noisily into the large, open room, through the living and dining areas into the middle of the kitchen. He plants himself in front of them with his arms open wide and an intoxicated, self-satisfied grin on his face. "Look at me! Daddy, Lily, look at me!"

Danny and Lily look at him. They cast swift glances at each other and immediately drop their eyes to the floor so they won't burst out laughing. There is no word in either of their vocabularies for how atrocious his outfit is. When he goes spinning out into the living room to show himself off to the furniture, they turn away and succumb to a moment of hysterics.

"Are you feeding that boy LSD or something?" Lily says when she can finally talk. She hasn't laughed like this in months. "I didn't know clothing came in that many colors."

"Oh, man. This is your fault, you know. He wants to impress you."

"Well, he most certainly has."

Caleb spins back into the kitchen and gloms onto Lily's leg. For the rest of the evening, he stays close to her. He touches her clothes, he examines her watch, he drags her into the living room to play Ring Around the Rosie. He introduces her to Zilla and when she says "Oh, he's a pteradactyl!" he patiently corrects her, "No, they're not called that anymore, Lily. He's a ptera*don*!" He sits on her lap after dinner and plays with her hair and lets her rain kisses on his cheeks and his head. He tries to follow her to the bathroom, but Danny grabs him and tells him to stay put. He demands that she put him to bed. She helps him into his pajamas, takes him into the bathroom to brush his teeth, then sits by his side on the bed and reads *The Cat in the Hat* to him, and he falls asleep with one hand on her knee. She hears Danny moving around the kitchen, clearing away dinner, cleaning up. He is letting her know that he doesn't need her help; she can sit with Caleb as long as she wants. She strokes Caleb's fingers and watches his sleeping face until Danny is done.

"Thank you for taking me to Anthony's Nose. You were right. The view over the Hudson River from up there is spectacular. No wonder so many artists have painted here."

Danny and Lily are on the porch, in the wicker chairs beside the small glass-topped rattan table. The last of the wine is in their glasses. The cicadas and katydids are going crazy, the creek is splashing off in the distance, but there isn't another sound to be heard.

Danny's elbows are on his knees. He's gazing off into the woods. "It was one of Tara's favorite spots. It always inspired her writing."

"I didn't realize she was a writer. What did she write?"

"Poetry mostly. She had just gotten her MFA from a low-residency program at a college in Maine. She was starting to write children's books, too. But her poetry . . ."

Lily hears the same melancholy quality in his voice that she heard over the phone days ago. He's been reading her poetry.

For just a second Lily puts a hand on Danny's forearm. She feels a tiny spasm in the muscle. "Why in the world does your mother-in-law hate you? You're such a lovely man."

Danny turns to her and smiles. "I appreciate your outrage. But Eve does not find me lovely. It's not complicated. . . . I wasn't good enough for Tara. Both Eve's and Lester's families have pedigrees back to the *Mayflower*. They have money. Position and reputation to uphold. As you can imagine, I'm an embarrassment. Everyone prefers to pretend I don't exist. Also, for all her wealth and heritage, Eve isn't really very worldly. I don't think she knows how to see past what seems alien and disreputable to her. She's always distrusted me."

"Couldn't she see how much you loved her daughter?"

"I haven't a clue what she sees when it comes to me. But now it's the same crap over Caleb. She's waiting for me to ruin his life, too."

"I can't even imagine how stressful that must be. I never had in-law problems. My parents loved Rick, and his loved me. They couldn't stand each other, but that was hunky-dory with us. They couldn't gang up on us about producing grandchildren," she says sardonically. Danny laughs. She grins. "Paul and my father, Max, and his wife, Sylvia . . . they definitely do not understand one another. But Max and Sylvia live in Florida so they and Paul don't ever have to see one another. And Paul hasn't seen or spoken to anyone in his family in more than thirty years, so no problem there."

Danny sighs. "It would be something special to be part of a big, happy family, though, don't you think?"

"Yes, I do think." Lily drops the flip tone. "And I always thought I would be. I don't understand what happened."

Danny looks out over the porch rail. "Yeah," he says on a long exhalation. He takes a deep breath in. "You have a bathing suit in your bag. I saw it when you were looking for your trail mix." He turns back to her. "We should have gone down to the creek. It was a great afternoon for it. I have to get over things like that, I know it. I'm sorry."

"Don't you dare apologize. You'll get over it when you get over it."

After a moment he says, "I don't think I'm ever going to get over it. I don't believe I'm ever going to be happy again. I can't say that to the people who've known me forever. I couldn't stand to look at Will for the rest of our lives if I had to think that he was worrying about me every minute."

"Is that what you really believe, Danny? That you're never going to be happy again?"

"Not the way I was with her. And I know that if you ask me ten years from now if I'm over her, no matter how good my life is the answer will still be no and it will feel just as bad as it feels now."

Lily's response is a breathy grunt.

"What about you, Lily? If I were to call you ten years from now and ask if you were over never having had a child, what do you think your answer would be?"

They are covered in shadow, the pattern of the open-weave drapes staining them like primitive body painting, but they can see each other clearly.

"My answer would be no." She offers him her hand. "So what do we do about it? Isn't there a way to still be happy even if we can't get over our losses and regrets?"

Danny takes her hand. "I haven't got that quite figured out yet."

"Me neither." She presses his fingers. "I should go, Danny. It's getting late and you look as tired as I feel." The stress of twelve idyllic hours spent a mere hairbreadth apart has taken its toll and left them both exhausted. "Come. Walk me to my car."

Now they are wholly in shadow, facing each other, eyes straining in the semidarkness. Lily tries to say good night but the words don't come. Danny leans forward to open the car door for her. As his tilted body breaks across the plane of her upright body, they simultaneously explode into motion as though at the pop of a starter's gun and lunge for each other with desperate clumsiness. Lily's arms fly up to wind themselves around his neck and she falls against him. Danny thrusts one hand into the thick tangle of her hair while the other finds itself flat and hard against the small of her back. He pulls her to him. They are both off-balance, their positions awkward, and the collision of their bodies sends them careening into the side of her car. He crushes her to the black metal. She practically chokes him with the ferocity of her grip. If there were any room for thought to survive, even the tiniest sliver of space, they might separate immediately. But they have left no room for anything but the feel of each other. Their bodies soften and shift as easily as silk sliding on silk and they melt seamlessly into each other, fit themselves one into the other like two complexly notched pieces of a jigsaw puzzle. Their mouths meet, lips and tongues yield and search for one another.

The warmth of him is like the searing summer sun. It saturates Lily's skin and sets her afire. She feels that cleaving of her heart, the same heavenly rending pain as when Paul first kissed her on the terrace. No man but Paul should ever make her feel like that. She turns her head aside, moves her hands to Danny's shoulders, and pushes him away. She sidles along the car as he retreats toward the house. They both look up at the starry sky and after a stunned second start to laugh, Lily with her hands over her mouth. It is laughable, after all, that anything so adolescent should happen between them, so what else can they do?

"Oh, my God," Lily gasps between her snorts and chortles. Behind the hard armor of her mirth she is disintegrating, stretching her arms for him again.

"Ooooh-kay. Well, we got that out of the way." Danny's arms are raised in the air. He looks like a drunken hold-up victim, laughing because he's too plowed to realize something dangerous is happening to him. He has withdrawn toward the house as far from her as he can get without tripping over the porch steps. "I guess we needed to do that."

"Well, I guess so. But we really can't do it again." Lily wags a finger at his disappearing form.

"No. Of course we can't."

Their laughter trickles away and they are back where they started, trying to say good night and not doing it. They are snared in moonlight and shadow, enchanted and paralyzed. Danny takes one step toward her, into the light, and stops. She doesn't move. They stand, rooted and stolid as tree trunks, and look at each other.

"Okay," he says quietly. "Seriously. Friends, yes? No harm done?"

"Oh, no, no. Of course friends." Her gaze is unblinking, but her voice wavers and her hands are crossed over her breast.

"Good. Um . . . look. Caleb and I are leaving tomorrow to go camping for the Labor Day weekend with the Pollacks. I'll call you when we get back?"

"Sure. Rick is coming up for the day Monday anyway. We'll get together next week."

He backs all the way up onto his porch steps, lifts his hand in a gesture of farewell, and goes inside. When the door closes behind him, she gets into her car and drives away.

Danny comes back out onto the porch. He watches the taillights of the BMW fade into the woods. His chest is heaving. He can feel the press of her pelvis against his groin. The flame they ignited burns in his throat. He knows she couldn't see him where he stood inside the dense shadow of the house, couldn't see his greedy eyes eating up the shape of her in the darkness. But she looked in his direction, her eyes surprised and ingenuous, and crossed her hands over her breast. He can still see her standing there, exposed and silhouetted by the moonlight, like a lone woodland creature who had lost her way and stumbled into the open. He lowers himself onto the two-person wooden glider suspended from the ceiling but he doesn't glide. He sits hunched over, his head in his hands, trying to steady his breath.

Of course they can't do that again, she didn't have to say it. He knows it. He knows it, but he doesn't believe it, because there has been a conviction growing in him since the moment he first saw her, grown stronger now than his remorse at betraying his love for Tara. It is a conviction that has taken hold of his brain, his gut, his heart, of every thinking and pumping inch of him: that Lily is his salvation. Now that he's kissed her, he's sure of it. He's sure that if he could make love to Lily, he would be rescued from the dark, narrow fissure that opened beneath his feet and swallowed him up the night Tara died. She would lift him back up into the light and leave him standing on the surface, his life, though forever changed, made possible again. He doesn't know if he's been made delusional by despair and loneliness, he only knows it's what he believes.

But there is one thing Danny both believes *and* knows to be true. Lily loves her husband. She is afraid of him, she is hiding from him, their marriage is foundering on the rocky shore of their emotional dishonesty, but she loves him. And if their marriage does fail, Danny doesn't want it to be because of him.

Lily is motionless before her bathroom mirror, mesmerized by the sight of her lips. They look swollen. They're not, of course. They couldn't be, not from just one kiss, however fierce. But they feel swollen to her, they feel hot and full from his lips and his beard—soft, as she knew it would be—brushing against the tender skin around her mouth. Her eyes travel down the length of her reflection. Her whole body feels hot and swollen.

What is she doing with him? Does she love him? Perhaps. He is such an easy man to love. She could love him, if every single thing in her life were different. But as it is, although her desire for Danny is starting to feel like her old desire for Paul, which realization fills her with despair, and although Paul is a difficult man to love, she knows that it is Paul she belongs to, as he belongs to her. Beneath all the anger and the blame and the disappointment, it is Paul she loves. He's the one she's meant to be with; she knew it the night they met.

Then what is she doing with Danny? Because as certainly as she knows that Paul is the one, she knows that Danny has come into her life, and she into his, for a reason. Is she meant to experiment on him, burrow into the tragedy-soaked core of him, get so close to him that she can finally feel what it is to trust someone with her deepest emotions? So that she can rehearse, in a place of safety, the ultimate performance of revealing herself to a man who has not given her reason to trust him? Because although it is Paul she loves, she has never trusted another man as fully as she does Danny. Not even Rick. Danny has allowed her—no, not merely allowed, required her—to bind her emotions to the exposed receptors of his own, lock and key, yin and yang.

He is so damaged. Perhaps she is what *he* needs. Now, at this moment. Perhaps she is meant to help heal him, be the bridge over which he can pass in safety from his past to his future. But what if she's wrong? What if she's wrong about everything and they both end up with a greater burden of hurt and regret than they already carry?

Lily turns from the mirror, shuts off the bathroom light. She crosses the darkened bedroom and curls up on the window seat. She looks out, over treetops rippling in the warm summer breeze under a blanket of moonlight. There are too many questions and too few answers. When she and Paul spoke yesterday, there had been no hostile exchanges. He even made her laugh with a funny story about the utter bizarreness of Amarillo, Texas. Yet their conversation left her feeling pummeled, like one of those blow-up punch toys that is expected to keep rising up for more. They chatted as if there was nothing terribly important to talk about, and when they hung up Lily felt as though she'd spent fifteen minutes on the phone with a stranger.

What if she has done what Paul said she could never do? What if she has displeased him so much with the poorly hidden, messy manifestations of her dissatisfaction and distrust that he doesn't want her anymore? She can't undo what she's done. It's too late for that. Lily touches her fingertips to her lips. Even if there was a way to make herself invisible again, deflect Paul's attention and hide herself from his unforgiving judgment, she knows she wouldn't. It's too late for that, too.

22

RICK ARRIVES IN TIME FOR LUNCH and Lily takes him to The Kitchen. She's been back there twice since her lunch with Danny and she doesn't think she'll ever go to Rudy's again. When she parks in the post office parking lot and leads him across the street, Rick looks off to his left in consternation and says, "Hey, isn't Rudy's back that way? I like Rudy's. Where are we going?"

"We're going to The Kitchen. You'll like it even better. A local friend took me here. It's been around forever, the food is great, everyone's friendly, and it's dirt cheap."

Lily is talking over her shoulder as she reaches for the handle to The Kitchen's screen door. She nearly falls headfirst into the restaurant when the door swings inward before her hand touches the worn metal. Strong fingers wrap themselves around her arm and steady her.

"Look where you're going, lady."

"Danny!"

He is holding her arm and smiling down at her. She smiles back and for a second there is only the two of them, just like the first moment they saw each other at The Doorway, like the moment in his driveway. Rick comes crowding in behind her. She feels his eyes on her face. She frees her arm, steps around Danny into the space between the door and the long Formica counter, and makes room for Rick to follow.

"Rick, Danny. Danny, Rick."

Danny's face takes on a neutral expression and he does what she can't find the strength to do—he unlocks their eyes, casually moves his from hers. Short weeks ago it was hard for them to look at each another and now they can't look away. Lily's pulse rate slows as the men say hello, nice to meet you, as they check each other out, offer their hands. She's quite sure she sounds normal when she asks Danny, "What are you doing here? I thought you were camping for the weekend."

"We had to come home last night. Will managed to find the only patch of poison ivy in the campground. He's very talented that way. I've got to run. I'll call you later?"

"Okay. Call me tonight, after six." Rick will be gone by then. He'll be bucking the end of Labor Day weekend traffic; his ER shift starts at ten and he can't be late.

It's Arlene's day off. Nancy shows Lily and Rick to a booth. As he follows close behind her, Rick asks, "Is that the local friend who turned you on to this place?"

She keeps her face turned away from him. He's too smart by half. Her cheeks are hot and she doesn't want him to see. "Yep."

When they sit down, Rick looks at her across the table with almost fearful, yet amused, concern.

Lily raises her chin and glares at him. "What?"

"Lily." His tone is gently chiding, as though she is trying to hide something they both know he will uncover. He leans forward and whispers, "Lily, are you fucking that guy?"

"Oh, for crying out loud! Jesus, Rick. No. Why would you even ask something like that?" She's not sleeping with Danny, but she's lying to Rick, nonetheless. From head to toe, inside and out, guilt pricks at her.

"Well, because he's hot, for starters. He's got that irresistible bad-boy look." Rick's eyes narrow and he grins. His expression is merely a diversion, a bit of mischief, quickly gone. "But, seriously. I'm asking something like that because there is definitely a major vibe between you—and don't try to deny it, please, I have very accurate sex-on-the-brain radar, even when it comes to straights. You and Paul are not exactly cooing these days—and don't try to deny that either. Is this why you're up here for months on your own? Have you found yourself a boy toy? My good sweet Lily, are you finally being a bad girl and having a fling with the local hunk?"

Even when he's being pushy and offensive, Lily can't get angry at Rick. He only means her well. "Dream on. I'm not having a fling, get your mind out of the gutter. Danny and I are friends. We met through this Doorway project I'm involved in. Stop being a pain in the ass."

"Well, my dear. What's a gay ex-husband good for except to be a pain in the ass? Okay, I will remove myself from your posterior. But tell me about your friend Danny with the killer eyes. He doesn't look like someone you'd have much in common with."

Lily plays with the corner of her menu. "He's more than what you'd assume to look at him. He's a talented woodworker. He makes exquisite furniture; I saw some pieces in his house. He's smart, he lived overseas for years, he speaks French. He likes to hike. He cooks. He knows how to relax. He makes me laugh." She shrugs. "I don't know, Rick. We enjoy each other's company, what more can I say?"

"I thought Paul made you laugh."

"Not lately." She spits out the words too quickly and immediately wishes she could take them back. She opens her menu.

Rick opens his menu. He peruses it and with his head down he casually says, "Danny sounds like quite a catch. He's not married?"

Lily drops her eyes to the sandwich section. "He's a widower."

Rick looks up and plucks at his left earlobe. "Kids?"

Lily looks up. "A five-year-old son."

He leaves his ear alone and stares at her thoughtfully. He licks his lips and sighs. "Okay. I'm going to get up your ass one last time and then I'll shut up."

"Must you? I was just getting comfortable." She tries to deflect him, but it doesn't work.

"Lily. For a forty-six-year-old woman who's been married twice, you remain one of the most naïve women I've ever known when it comes to people of the male persuasion. You just haven't had enough useful experience with the species. Paul is one sort of dangerous man—the self-conscious, aggressive seducer who leaves a woman no room to maneuver. But this Danny is another sort—sad and sensitive, totally *un*self-conscious, the kind who draws women to him like hooked fish without even trying. You could find yourself in bed with him before you know how you got there. Despite what you won't say to me these days, I know you're not happy, Lily, and you know I would never judge you if you found something you needed—look at me for Christ's sake. All I'm saying is, please be careful."

"I'm not sleeping with him, Rick." Even if Lily were able to talk to Rick the way she used to, she wouldn't talk to him about Danny and what she needs, because what she needs now is for Danny to remain light-years away from the rest of her sorrowful life. Danny is for her and her alone. "And that ends the annoying portion of our program." She smiles at him. "Okay?"

He laughs. "Okay."

This is already another terribly sad and lonely making conversation, but Lily knows the worst is yet to come. She knows why Rick has chosen to spend three plus hours in the car for a five-hour visit with her. He's come to talk about the baby. Lily loves Rick and she doesn't want to ruin his happiness just because this is too hard for her to handle. She can do that for him. She puts a smile on her face and her menu to the side.

"Tell me. Your baby is here. Yes?"

He lays his hand over hers. "Yes. It's a little girl. Two and a half weeks old. She was promised to another couple, but they changed their minds when they saw the color of her skin. The mother is Caucasian but obviously the father wasn't. The agency in San Antonio put her into foster care and then called us. We'll be able to go get her in about ten days."

"Oh, Rick. A little girl." Something inside Lily shifts, and then something else comes to life. It's a sensation as of a cover being drawn from the opening to an unused passageway and a ray of sunlight hitting what is waiting there. She thought it had to be a boy. With Paul's long lean body and black hair or with Danny's blue eyes and easy smile. But it didn't. It doesn't. It could be a girl. A girl to whom she could have taught everything she knows about what it means to be a girl. "You're going to have a little girl."

Rick grins. "Yeah, we are. I think I'm more excited now than Alan. I don't know, now that it's really happening . . . I just can't wait."

She is doing an admirable job holding herself together, but the reservoir behind her eyes is starting to push against the faulty dam. "Have you thought about a name yet?"

"Sophie. Sophie Stone-Milstein. I'm letting Alan get top billing. Do you like it?"

Sophie. Curly hair, dusky skin, saucer eyes. Sophie. "Yes. It's a beautiful name." She's already real. She's sitting next to Rick in a booster seat, chocolate ice cream smeared all over her mouth. "I have to go to the bathroom. Take a look at the menu while I'm gone; I know what I want. And save room for pie." She sidles out of the booth. "I'll be right back." She kisses Rick on the top of his shaved head. "I'm so happy for you."

She locks the bathroom door, sits on the closed toilet seat, and lets the dam crack apart. She is back in Paris, in the bathroom of their suite at the San Regis, trapped in a bottomless pit of disbelief, crying in secret while Paul sleeps.

But she couldn't stay there then and she can't stay there now. She has to go back to Rick, have lunch, spend a few hours lounging around the pool. She can cry after he leaves. She splashes cold water on her face, pats her eyes with it, lets it run over the insides of her wrists. She puts drops in her eyes. She unlocks the door and returns to the booth. There is a metal canister on the table, a glass on each of their placemats filled with chocolate milkshake.

"I thought we could share that," Rick says as she sits down.

His voice is so full of love that for a moment Lily's eyes brim with tears that she can't fight down. "Why did you have to be gay?"

He smiles at her. "So that we could be friends forever."

Danny calls at six thirty. Lily has been weeping for twenty minutes and she makes no attempt to stop when she answers the phone.

"Lily. What's going on? What's the matter?"

"Rick and Alan are going to have a baby girl. Sophie. Isn't

that a beautiful name?" She sobs into the phone and dabs futilely at her cheeks with an already sopping tissue. "How is this happening?" she cries. "It's not fair."

"No, it's not fair but it could be a good thing," Danny says gently. "Lily, she could be your girl. It won't ever be the same as having your own, but it could still be wonderful."

"I know, I've been telling myself that all summer, but it hurts too much, it feels too hard." Her sobs abate some as she listens to his voice, pictures him on the other end of the line.

After a long pause Danny says, "Lily, you have to talk to Paul. Maybe even at some point about adopting a baby yourselves again. This isn't just about you."

Lily takes a fresh tissue and blots her eyes. "I really hate you right now." She sniffs the last of her tears away and laughs.

"Yeah, well, the truth often sucks, what can I tell you. So, I seem to have a quart of fresh peach ice cream here. Caleb and I are going to eat the whole damned thing if someone doesn't stop us. You want to come over for a little while? Or would that just makes things worse?"

Lily looks around her living room. She loves her house but the thought of sitting there alone for the rest of the night is too much to contemplate. She knows that she is borrowing a life that doesn't belong to her every time she's with them, but Danny and Caleb are what she wants and she so wants to have what she wants.

"Maybe for a little while, if I won't be in your way. I know Caleb is starting school tomorrow."

"Yep, and I think he's a little scared. And he's got to get up earlier than he's used to. So actually, you'll be a good diversion and you can help me get him to bed. He'll do whatever you tell him. I'll kick you out by nine, no matter what."

And he does. After they've eaten too much ice cream, played with Caleb and put him to sleep, watched two early episodes of *Seinfeld* on DVD and laughed for an hour. All the time mindful not to sit too close, not to look too long, not to touch each other. They don't talk about Tara, or Eve, or Paul, or Rick, or Sophie. They just try to have a little fun.

23

THE WEDNESDAY AFTER LABOR DAY finds Paul in Seattle. Two weeks down, two to go. This trip is going to pay off, he can feel it. He's applied his persuasive charm and his subtle investigatory skills to a succession of nervous or aggrieved people and one of them is going to give him what he wants, motivated by either remorse or revenge. He's betting on the former.

The grueling schedule and constant intellectual fencing have calmed him. He hasn't used the pills much since he's been away, except for the days he speaks to Lily. When he's not in contact with her, he imagines coming home and finding their marriage the way it was before it changed. When he talks to her, and the strain is palpable and he doesn't know what to say, he realizes that something has to happen to *make* it the way it was before it changed. He doesn't know what that something is and that's when he takes the pill to quell the anxiety. That's when he imagines her leaving him.

It's 8:00 a.m. He's having breakfast alone in the Westin's restaurant, going back over some earlier interviews in preparation for his day of meetings at the offices of the law firm of SynTech's board VP. Halfway through his bowl of granola, fruit, and yogurt, his cell rings. He sees RESTRICTED scrawled across the readout, no number. Maybe it's his remorseful whistle-blower come looking for absolution.

"Hello. This is Paul Spencer."

"Hi, Paul, it's Rick. Hope I'm not disturbing you?"

Paul likes Lily's ex-husband and has never had a problem with Lily being so close to him. He finds their friendship perplexingly admirable—he's never had a friendship like theirs with either a man or a woman—and he finds Rick a funny and interesting guy. He hasn't pursued an independent friendship with him, however, because he doesn't want to intrude on Lily's territory. Rick is about the last person Paul would expect to be calling him.

"Rick? What's the matter? Has something happened to Lily?"

"No. No. I'm sorry, I didn't mean to startle you. I'm calling to ask a small favor of you. If it's not a good time, I can call back later."

Paul's heartbeat thumps from his throat back down to his chest. "No, I can talk now. I'm just eating some breakfast. What can I do for you?"

"I know it's not what your firm does, but I was hoping you might know a good family lawyer you could recommend."

"What kind exactly, a divorce lawyer? An estate lawyer?"

"No. Family law, custody, adoptions, that sort of thing."

"Oh. Is this for Alan's sister?" The divorced sister with the dirtbag ex.

"No, Paul. It's for me and Alan."

"For you and Alan," Paul says slowly. He pushes his unfinished breakfast away. "I'm a little confused here. *What* for you and Alan?"

"For the baby we're adopting from an agency in Texas. Or that *Alan* is adopting since Texas doesn't allow gay couples to adopt, and therefore we want to talk to a good lawyer about how and when I can, et cetera." Rick says, even more slowly.

"You and Alan are adopting a baby."

"Yes. You didn't know? Didn't Lily tell you?"

"No. She didn't. How long has she known?" Paul's voice contains about as much inflection as a lump of granite.

"That we were planning to, since July Fourth. And I told her Monday that they'd found a baby for us. That's why I went up to see her, to tell her in person."

"You went up to see her Monday." They spoke Tuesday morning. She didn't say a word about it. She's known for two months and hasn't said a goddamned word.

After a moment of deadly silence, Rick says, "You sound angry, Paul. You didn't know that either, that I was up there."

"No."

"Well, forgive me for saying so, but I'm kind of relieved to hear this insofar as now I don't think you're a total prick for never saying anything to me."

Paul grabs on to Rick's deliberate taunt. He forces out a laugh and says, "No, but I'm sure you have other reasons for thinking I'm a total prick. Uh, look, call my office later, ask for Bob Whiteman. I'll have him find someone for you."

"Thanks. I appreciate it. Listen, Paul, I'm sorry this came as such a surprise to you. I understand you're maybe a little freaked that Lily didn't say anything. But, you know, this is really hard for her. She won't even talk to me about it. So, don't get angry at her, just give her a little room, okay?"

Paul is more than a little freaked. Tiny explosions, like light-bulbs shattering, are going off in his head. Tiny explosions of fleetingly illuminated memories of him and Lily and various un-pleasant things having to do with babies and adoption and tears and anger and pleading and refusal. And mixed in there, bright-er than them all, memories of staggering happiness. Paul hears Rick's nervous breathing as he waits for him to say something.

"Paul? I'm not trying to tell you what to do, but . . ."

"I'm glad to hear that, Rick."

"Okay. But, listen, you maybe want to meet for a drink in a few weeks, when we're both back in New York?"

Paul and Rick have never met for a drink in the nine years of their acquaintanceship. Paul recognizes Rick's invitation as his kind way of saying that he knows something's gone wrong, that he knows things about Lily that Paul doesn't and is willing to share what he knows with Paul to help Paul make things better. Still, the invitation offends him. That he should admit to requir-ing help, that he should expose himself to someone who knows more about his own wife than he does, is just not possible.

"Thanks, but I'm going to be very busy for a while."

"Right. Well, it was just a thought. Thanks again for the help."

Paul calls his office and leaves a message for Bob Whiteman. He finishes his reading. He signals the waitress for more coffee and the check.

Paul's not stupid. It takes him all of a nanosecond to match the true beginning of Lily's pulling away to their return from Paris, to the end of all discussion about their having a child. He's not stupid, but he's still no good at living with emotional upset, his or anyone else's, and he's even worse at self-criticism. He ignores Rick's good advice. While part of him suspects now that he did something bad, the stronger part is saying that the real problem is that Lily just wouldn't let it go. They were so happy. Why did she have to ruin it? He can't yet see that Lily's wanting a baby is like his wanting her love: it's something she can't make herself stop wanting. All he sees is that her wanting it means that he isn't enough for her. She said he was, but she lied. She lied about being okay with not having kids, too. But the real lie is that she doesn't love him the way he loves her. She is enough for him; why isn't he enough for her? And now he's being punished for it. She's punishing him for not needing anyone but her. Of course, he's been punishing her, too, these past few years, but that he doesn't see. He doesn't see that every time he makes some small, insignificant demand of her, tells her where he wants her to shop, what he wants her to wear, what car he wants her to drive, he is threatening her with his displeasure. That's how he's punishing her for having let him down, for not having given him what he doesn't even know he wanted. He's keeping her wondering if she might indeed displease him enough that he would toss her away.

24

Until he is fully adjusted to his new routine and his new school, Daniel wants Caleb to spend Sundays with him, so Eve and Lester have their grandson just for the Saturday after Labor Day weekend. Eve understands. Caleb *is* a little agitated and it is best for him to be in his own home the day before he goes back to school. At least for a while.

They take him to the club in the morning and Caleb spends two hours in the children's pool with his friends—not the kiddie pool, not the adult pool, the *children's* pool—racing furiously from side to side or climbing out and jumping in over and over again, his nonstop action punctuated frequently with "Did you see that, Grandma?" or "Watch me, Grandpa!" He eats an excellent lunch, sitting like a grown-up in his chair on the dining room's patio overlooking the golf course. Eve lets him drink a Coca-Cola with his peanut butter sandwich and they all three grin at one another and swear not to tell Daddy. After lunch Lester takes him to the practice putting green with his miniature putter and he chases his ball for an hour before taking Lester's hand and saying, "Grandpa, I want to go home. I think I ought to lie down."

Eve probably should have kept him home in the first place. Daniel told her Caleb might tire from the antibiotics he has been taking since Thursday. What Daniel thought was an incipient cold turned out to be mild allergies, which Daniel himself suffered from as a child, and a fledgling sinus infection, already clearing up. She probably should not have let him go into the pool, but Caleb loves to swim and there are only a few weeks left for him to do it. She made sure he wore his nose plugs and he was happy and lively all morning. But now he is listless. He asks to lie down on the sofa in the den. He asks Eve to cover him with the red and black throw that she crocheted. He arranges Zilla so that the pterodon's long-jawed head is next to his own on the pillow brought in from the bedroom and explains to Eve that Zilla says his head feels heavy.

Although Daniel took him to Dr. Marcus, Eve is not satisfied. Since a few weeks before the anniversary of Tara's death and ever since, her worry over Caleb's health has become obsessive. She must be sure, at every second, that he is all right, that boy-sized cysts are not growing in his kidneys, that an abnormality is not forming in a blood vessel in his brain, that his head does not hurt. It torments her that she cannot be the one to watch over him every day and every night. As she sits at the end of the sofa, her hand on his tucked-in foot, and looks at his sleepy face, she reasons that if she cannot physically be with him at least she can instruct him in how to take care of himself. She pulls gently on his toe and smiles at him. He wiggles his foot in her hand and smiles back.

"Is Zilla feeling any better now, sweetheart?"

Caleb turns his head and confers with his dinosaur. "Yes.

He's feeling much better. He likes to lie on the sofa with you."

"I am very glad. Please tell him we can lie on the sofa any time he wishes." She clamps her hand onto his foot and holds it still. "Caleb. I want you to listen to me very closely, this is very important. It's about your mommy. Are you listening?"

He sucks his lips into his mouth and his eyes turn into little blue plates. He nods.

She runs her hand up his leg and holds onto his thigh through the cotton throw. She leans over him. "One night, your mommy had a very very bad headache. She didn't say anything and your father didn't notice and he didn't take her to the hospital in time and she died. So you must promise me that if you ever have a very bad headache, or if you feel very very bad in some other way, you tell your father right away and tell him he *must* take you to the hospital. If he says no, you must insist, or tell him to call Grandma. Do you understand? Do you promise me?"

The slash of Caleb's mouth grows even thinner and his eyes larger.

"Caleb. I am serious now. Do you promise me you will do as I say? I'm not telling you this to frighten you. It's so that you will know what to do if necessary, all right?"

He goggles at her and bobs his head rapidly up and down.

Eve caresses his leg. "My good boy. My darling boy. Grandma loves you so much."

When Daniel comes to get him at six o'clock, Eve says, "That must be a very strong antibiotic, Daniel; he has barely had the energy to speak all afternoon."

25

CALEB, ARE YOU ALL RIGHT?" Danny is a little concerned. Caleb is not eating his dinner. His head is down and he's pushing his cut-up pieces of chicken cutlet around his plate. He's hardly spoken or looked at his daddy all evening.

"Yes."

"Are you sure? You can tell me if something's wrong."

"No, nothing's wrong. I'm not hungry. Can I watch a movie?"

"You have to eat something first."

Danny waits a couple minutes more, while Caleb methodically buries his chicken beneath the untasted mound of mashed potatoes and kicks his feet against the underside of the table. Finally, Danny pushes his own plate away, gets up, lifts Caleb from his seat, and takes him onto his lap. Caleb slumps against Danny and puts his arms around his neck.

"Caleb, look at me."

The boy refuses. He twists his head to the side and digs it into Danny's shoulder. Acid fear fountains up and leaves a metallic burn in Danny's mouth. Danny knows his son. Caleb is not having side effects from the medication. He's upset. Eve has done something.

Danny hasn't felt this particular fear—his fear of her—in weeks. It rushes through him after its brief absence, and with sickening clarity he sees how terrified he's been since Tara died that Eve would not be satisfied with undermining his relationship with Caleb, but that she would try to take Caleb away from him. That she would convince Lester to return to the South, use their families' judicial connections to push Danny's rights aside, and get custody of their grandson. He sees how much the years of compromising himself and ingesting Eve's venom have weakened and reduced him, to the point that he could imagine himself so powerless against her. And while he knows he's not, the fear remains.

Danny breathes in the scent of Caleb's hair. He shifts in his seat so that he can hold him a little tighter. Caleb doesn't move. After a moment, Danny kisses the top of his head. "Honey, I think you're really tired. It's a little early, but how about we put you to bed. We'll watch a movie with Lily tomorrow. Tonight we'll read for a bit and I'll stay till you fall asleep. You want to be all rested for Lily, right?"

Caleb doesn't object or complain. He gets into his pajamas, brushes his teeth, and climbs into bed without a fuss. Danny knows he isn't going to learn anything directly about whatever it was Eve did this time. It will reveal itself sooner or later as it always does, through something Caleb will say or do in the days to come. Caleb picks out a couple of *Babar* stories for Danny to read to him, and by a quarter to nine he's asleep.

*   *   *

Danny is dreaming. He's dreaming that he's walking in Paris with Tara, crossing the river over the elegant Pont Alexandre III, and they stop to look down at the Seine and the Seine is full of boulders and bordered by trees. It rushes beneath the bridge and sparkles in the sunlight. Tara steps into his arms and draws him close. She says, "This is our home, Danny. Let's stay forever." She's wearing a red dress and Danny touches it and says, *"Oui, pour toujours. Tu es le monde. Je t'aimais, je t'aime, je t'aimerai."* A siren wails from the Left Bank and Danny turns his head to see what it is. There's nothing there but the sound grows louder and louder and. . .

"Daaaddeeeee! Daaaddeeeee!"

Danny jolts awake. His heart is pounding and there are spots jumping in the air before his eyes. He'd fallen asleep reading, propped up in bed in his clothes, and for a second he doesn't know where he is or what he's hearing. Caleb's screams come closer, his footfalls are in the hallway, and Danny leaps off the bed, crunching on his book as he hurtles toward the door. He's one step into the hall when Caleb comes flying at him. He hurls himself at Danny, slams into him so hard they both fall back into the bedroom.

"Daddy! You have to take me to the hospital!"

Caleb's face is red and soaked from crying. His eyes are rolling with fear. He grips the waist of Danny's pants with the unnatural strength of hysteria and starts dragging Danny out of the room.

"Daddy! Now! You have to take me now!" His frantic demand gurgles through a mouth full of tears.

A terrible panic floods Danny's guts. He manages to get a hand on Caleb's forehead for long enough to confirm that he's cool. There is no unexpected fever. "Caleb. Calm down. Tell me what's wrong. Does something hurt?" He tries to hold the boy still, but Caleb is writhing about like a speared eel, tugging on Danny, trying to move him into the hall.

"My head! My head hurts! Like Mommy's! I'm going to die if you don't take me to the hospital! Daddy, don't let me die like you let Mommy! Please!" He is sobbing wildly; his voice is shrill with fright.

"Oh, no!" It's a shouted moan, ripped from within that fountain of fear. It's out of his mouth before Danny can stop it. He feels Eve's knife sink into his back and he goes numb all over. His hands lose their shifting hold on Caleb's squirming body and they both stagger backward, Caleb toward the bathroom doorway and Danny toward the edge of the bed.

Caleb regains his balance and comes at Danny again. This time they fall back together onto the bed. Danny's brain feels pricked as with pins and needles as blood and thought start to flow through him again. He gets his arms firmly around Caleb, struggles them upright until he is sitting with Caleb sprawled across his legs, wriggling.

"Caleb, stop. Stop. You're not going to die. I'm not going to let you die. We don't have to go to the hospital, there's nothing . . ."

"Yes we do!" Caleb shrieks. "Grandma said! I don't want to die, Daddy! Grandma said. Call her, call her!"

"I know what Grandma said, but she's wrong." He doesn't know what she said, but he can imagine. He doesn't think he wants to ever know what she said. "You have to listen to *me* now. You are not going to die. I did not let Mommy die, that's not what happened, and I'm not going to let you die."

Caleb is shaking all over and his tears are coming in buckets. "Grandma said," he wails. "Daddy, I'm scared. I want to go to the hospital. Pleeeease!"

"Oh, Jesus."

Danny doesn't know what to do. His shock is turning to rage and he doesn't trust himself to make a good decision. Maybe he should take the boy to the hospital, maybe that's what Caleb needs him to do so that he can feel safe. But he knows there's nothing wrong and he doesn't want Caleb put through pointless exams and tests. He doesn't want him exposed for even one minute to the icy fear that fills the hospital's every room and corridor. And Danny feels his guts rebel at the thought of stepping through the hospital's doors. But he has to do something.

"Okay. Caleb. I'm going to call Dr. Beth and have her come here and examine you. If she thinks you should go to the hospital, we'll go. You trust her, don't you?"

Danny glances at his watch. It's 12:15. He's pretty sure she'll be home and awake. He's pretty sure that tonight's one of her every other Saturday nights on duty at the medical complex. She would have left there at 11:15. He prays he's right.

Caleb wriggles around until he's kneeling on Danny's thighs. He squashes Danny's face between his hands and leans in until they're nose to wet nose. "Call Dr. Beth, Daddy. Tell her to hurry. Tell her I'm sick and I might die."

They wait for Beth on the couch. Caleb is a quaking, sobbing bundle, wrapped up like a papoose in the quilt that Danny leaves folded there. His head is a dead weight on Danny's shoulder as Danny rocks him, his hands weak little claws scrabbling at Danny's damp shirt.

"Where *is* she, Daddy?"

"She's on her way, she'll be here in just a few minutes. Everything's going to be okay."

Danny has gone numb again. This time it's not from the hideousness of what came spewing from the mouth of his traumatized five-year-old son. This numbness is of his own making, a form of self-sedation so that his rage won't consume him and then come after Caleb, or Beth, or anyone who steps into the path of it.

"She's here, honey. Her car just turned into the driveway."

Danny feels Caleb's body relax a fraction as Beth walks through the door. She's carrying her old-fashioned doctor's bag and there's a stethoscope draped around her neck. She gives him a look as she approaches, a look that's a mix of fury and affection and hope, but although she deserves more, all Danny can summon in response is a tepid smile.

"I'm sorry, Beth. I didn't know what else to do."

"Nonsense. I have to take care of my favorite patient, don't I?"

Beth crouches down so she is eye level with Caleb and gives him a big, sunny smile. "Caleb, honey, don't be scared. You're going to be fine. Can you tell me what hurts you?"

"My head. My head hurts." Caleb lifts his head from Danny's shoulder, turns his face to her, gives out a wretched sob. "Am I going to die?"

"Definitely not." Beth puts her hand on Caleb's head and moves it slowly all over. "Can you tell me where it hurts, exactly?"

"I don't know." Then he takes her hand and brings it to his face, over his eyes and nose. "Here."

"Ah," Beth says with great gravity. "I see." She nods sagely. "I don't think we have anything to worry about, but let's examine you just so we'll be absolutely sure, okay? Can you sit up for me, there in the corner, by the light?"

Danny releases Caleb and he scuttles across the couch onto

the corner cushion by the side table, into the lamplight. He's keening softly, a heartrending sound, but within it Danny hears a relinquishing of panic.

Caleb sits very still while Beth takes his temperature, then looks in his ears, his eyes, up his nose, and down his throat. She palpates his neck and his belly. She listens to his chest and his back with her stethoscope. After each procedure she writes on her pad and says, "*Very* good." Caleb watches her like a frightened baby hawk, and after each procedure his crying lessens.

"We're almost done. Just one more thing."

She rummages in her bag and pulls out a blood pressure cuff. She fastens it loosely around the crown of Caleb's head. Danny abruptly coughs and clears his throat. Beth flashes him a tiny conspiratorial grin. The turbulent emotions roiling inside him begin to move off, like storm clouds out over the ocean.

"Now, this may feel a little tight for a moment, Caleb. I'm going to measure what's happening in your brain." Beth pumps the sphygmomanometer's bulb a couple of times, puts her stethoscope to Caleb's forehead, and listens intently.

Caleb's eyes are glued to Beth's face but he's having trouble keeping his lids open. He's worn-out from crying and from the unimaginable specter of his own death. "What's happening in my brain, Dr. Beth?" he whispers.

"Well, sweetie, I can't hear anything."

Now Danny does laugh.

"Dad! It's not funny!" Caleb starts to cry again, but these are only tears of exhaustion.

"No, it's not. I'm laughing with relief, that you're all right. He *is* all right, isn't he?"

"Yes, he most certainly is. Caleb, you hurt behind your eyes and nose because your sinuses are still a little infected and you have some water in your ears, nothing more. I'm going to give you something to help unstuff you, and I promise it will all be gone in a couple of days."

Caleb's eyes close before the decongestant hits his tummy and Danny carries him back to bed.

When he returns to the living room, Beth is standing by the front door. She's holding her bag in front of her body with both hands.

"I don't know how to thank you."

"You don't have to thank me. You know that. And Caleb will recover more easily than you. He's just had his first encounter with the concept of his own mortality. It's a terrifying moment for a child."

"I hate to think that he doesn't feel safe with me."

"Of course he feels safe with you. He can fall apart in front of you because he knows you'll make everything all right. You're his world, Danny. You're his daddy. Talk to him in the morning. He's ready to hear about what happened to his mother in a more meaningful way. Keep it simple and straightforward, but honest. It will reassure him better than anything else."

Danny feels safe with Beth. He would like her to stay a little longer, until his eyes close and he falls asleep.

"Of course I'll talk to him. Go home, Beth. You're asleep on your feet."

"In a minute. Danny, what are you going to do about Eve?"

"I don't know yet. I've got to calm down before I can even think about it. I'll talk to Will tomorrow. I'll figure it out."

"You let me know if I can help in any way. And bring Caleb to see me Monday after school. A last bit of reassurance for him." Before she walks out the door, she gestures with her head toward the coffee table, on which has appeared a glass with ice and a short shot of vodka. "For medicinal purposes," she says with a tired smile. "Drink it. Doctor's orders."

Danny is as cold as the glass he rolls between his hands. He stares down into it, at the hypnotic beauty of the lamplight refracting off the ice and the crystal. There is no forgiveness for Eve left in him. It's not enough that whatever she did or said wasn't meant to hurt or upset Caleb; Eve would never consciously do that. But her skewed love for Caleb, her sense of entitlement, her blind disrespect for Danny have finally pushed her to do something unconscionable. Danny will not allow anyone to cause his son nightmares or plant in him a suspicion that it was his father's incompetence that killed his mother and could kill him, too. Caleb can live a happy life without grandparents, and both of them will find a way to live without Tara, but neither of them will survive if their relationship is tortured until it falters and crumbles.

His body is leaden, it feels welded to the couch. This burden has become too much for him; he needs help carrying it. And not the kind of sane, guy help he'll get from Will when he calls tomorrow, necessary and grounding as it will be. He needs someone who can help him bear the psychic weight. He overlooks the one who had been there, helping him, just minutes before. She's too near for him to see. He goes searching instead out into the distant void. He thinks of calling Lily; he knows he could, even at two thirty in the morning. But although Lily is with him in the void, even she is too near. He still needs the one who is so far away that only a dreamer can see her.

26

SUNDAY NIGHT AND PAUL is unmoored in Portland. Eight more days. San Francisco, then LA, then home. It's been years since he was on the road for such an extended chunk of time. He's forgotten this thin-aired, spreading detachment that accrues inside his head after weeks of having a huge life pared down to a nub, nothing but planes and hotels, a passing parade of people, a single focus, and endless hours spent in limbo, alone. It's crept up on him now, this feeling of home having been transformed into an alien place, while he slept, ignorant of the change, in yet another characterless hotel room. He used to find the sensation oddly titillating; he'd float from city to city, meeting to meeting, and during the limbo hours amuse himself with arbitrary fantasies of staying out there somewhere and reinventing himself, as he'd done before, when he'd left home the first time. That was when his life was incomplete. Before he fell in love with Lily.

It's ten o'clock when he gets back to the Heathman. It's too early to go to sleep and he's too wound up to banish himself to his room. He heads for the Marble Bar, the hotel's cocktail lounge, for a nightcap. As he passes through the lobby, a good-looking willowy blonde in her mid-thirties fixes him in her sights. She's sitting in a plush armchair, one long bare leg crossed over the other. She tosses him a frankly interested look as he walks by. She provocatively uncrosses and recrosses her legs. He holds her eye and smiles with a thoughtless, automatic suggestiveness and a nod of acknowledgment. Like riding a bike, some things you never forget how to do. He goes into the lounge and sits at the bar. He asks for a Ketel One on the rocks with a twist. His drink and his blonde arrive at the same time.

She's an immediate comfortable fit, the sort of woman he knew, intimately and often, in his bachelor days. Bold and experienced and looking for a bedmate for the night. She's the female equivalent of the man he used to be. Paul isn't that man anymore, but tonight he's a volatile combination of horny, lonely, and scared. The last time he tried to have sex he couldn't and he's no less rattled three weeks later than he was the night it happened. He's hyperaware of his age; he's getting old. He's sure now that Lily hates him. He's angry about basically all of it, including the culpability he feels for the fact that he's undoubtedly given Lily reason to hate him. This woman doesn't hate him. She doesn't know him. She's twenty years younger than he is and she wants him and at the moment that makes him feel very very good.

Paul doesn't think about what he's doing. He buys them a few rounds. They drink. They flirt. And after an acceptable forty-five minutes of verbal foreplay they get to the point. She tells him her room number. He secures a pack of condoms from the discreet, all-service concierge and follows her. He has sex with her for two hours, all his skill and plumbing intact and working; he screws her senseless, three times. He does what he does to her without an ounce of emotion or any sustained eye contact. He has no problem doing it, physically, which restores his confidence in his ability to perform, but there's a problem nonetheless. He couldn't have proven to himself any more definitively that it's only Lily he wants than by going to bed with another woman. Nothing else could have revealed to him so starkly how much he cherishes the sublimity of what he and Lily become when they come together.

He doesn't consider the sexual act he committed, in and of itself, to be of real importance, it was so completely meaningless. He wouldn't want Lily to know about it, but he's not worried she ever will. What *is* of real importance is what he realizes as he zips his pants: He wants to be the better person Lily has always believed him to be, because that's what she deserves. He wants to become the fully fleshed man Lily loves, but he doesn't know how and he's afraid it's too late. Whatever it was, that bad thing he did while they were trying to have a baby, he fears it must have been so bad that Lily won't want to love him anymore. It's what always happens, after all. He's never known what he does to cause it, but Paul has lived his entire life believing that a woman's love for him comes with an expiration date. So far, anywhere from perhaps fifteen minutes—and he's only guessing there—to nine years. As an ignorant, frightened child and now as an arrogant, angry man, it has never occurred to him that he could ask if he'd done something wrong. Or that he might not have. Or that he might still be loved even if he had.

Paul has had many one-night stands in the past. He had them when he was otherwise unattached, or ending a current relationship, or even sometimes while he was in one because none of his relationships engendered a feeling of commitment or responsibility in him. He never calculated that he had anything of value to lose, so he took what he wanted and didn't feel bad about it. Now he has everything to lose, and his self-respect and any belief he still harbored that he deserves Lily's love are in tatters.

It's after one. Paul is beset by wakefulness; he's pacing around his spacious, sterile, overly air-conditioned suite. He takes the Ambien from his kit bag, pours two of the white oval tablets into his palm. He has a breakfast meeting at seven thirty; he should get some sleep. Not remain standing shivering in the bathroom, unnerved by his woeful desire to call Lily, wake her from her sleep in the middle of the night to tell her he loves her. That he's sorry. Sorry sorry sorry. He returns the pills to the bottle. He's scared to death to be unconscious. He takes a lorazepam and spends the rest of the night upright on the couch, working.

27

Danny waits until the taillights of the school bus have disappeared around the long curve up the road to the right before turning left onto Old Stone Creek Road. He guns the truck's engine and speeds off. Lester will be halfway to Newburgh by now; Eve will be alone. She's a creature of habit. At eight o'clock she will be in the kitchen, finishing a second cup of coffee, clearing away Lester's breakfast.

Danny parks on the edge of the cobbled apron at the foot of the Jamisons' driveway. His eyes travel past the twenty feet of pink-tinged brick, up the length of the pea-gravel drive, to the entrance of the house. Blue asters and yellow chrysanthemums bloom in enormous terra-cotta pots on either side of the front door. How many times in the past six years has he made this turn, driven up this driveway, walked into this house? How many in the past year alone? A hundred? Two hundred? Not once since mere weeks after Tara died has either Eve or Lester turned in at the bumblebee mailbox, driven up his drive, walked into his house. Always, he has been the one to deliver Caleb, to pick him up. The first several times, Eve simply said, *You will bring him here, Daniel*. Without his being conscious of it, she trained him to do what she wanted. It wasn't hard; he was conscious of so little during those first few months.

He has raced to get here, propelled by thirty-two hours of inarticulate fury churning inside him, but now he's having trouble getting out and walking the short last leg of the journey. As he sits and looks at the house, six crows the size of well-fed rabbits drop from the sky like an assault team and land messily on the gravel. They gather into a belligerent group, take a few angry hops toward the truck, and rupture the peaceful morning with their raucous clamor. Danny's fury wobbles in his chest. He closes his eyes and tries in vain to conjure an alternative to this saddening reality. He's a dove. He doesn't want to be here, hovering like a hawk poised to descend on his son's unsuspecting grandmother.

He picks a pebble off the floor well beneath his feet, throws it at the crows. Skittish things, all caw and no bite, they rise as one into the air, shrieking in alarm, and fly away. The digital clock on the dashboard blinks; it's eight o'clock. Danny leaves the truck and walks up the driveway. He doesn't go to the door, ring the bell, or bang the brass door knocker. He opens the wooden gate and steals around the side of the house. Through a kitchen window he sees Eve standing by the sink, as he knew she would be. There will be no surprises today. He lets himself in through the unlocked kitchen door.

Her back is to him. The water is running and she doesn't hear him come in. She's wrapped in a short sapphire-blue satin robe that Tara gave her, the hem at her knees. Her feet are bare. Her calves are muscular, her ankles and feet delicate. Like Tara's. Danny steps away from the door, leans against the wall, dizzied

by anger and sorrow. Will told him not to do this, to leave everything to him. But Danny can't do that. He can't leave this to
someone else.

"Hello, Eve."

She gasps and whirls around. "Oh, my Lord! Daniel! You
nearly scared me to death! What are you doing here?" She turns
to stone. "Something has happened to Caleb."

Quiet terror despoils the modulated elegance of her voice.
Her eyes are stiff in their sockets and her hands are a vise at the
collar of her robe.

Danny doesn't answer. Eve sways minutely and he leaves her
there to twist. She's done this to him, made him into a man who
can take pleasure in another's pain. Tara's voice comes stealing
into his head. *No.* "No. He's okay."

Eve exhales in relief. "Then why are you here?" She peers at
him. "What is the matter with you, Daniel?"

He has no blueprint. He came not knowing what he would
say to her, only that he has to expel her poison from his system
before it's too late.

"Oh, for pity's sake, Daniel! What is it?"

He rights himself, moves away from the wall. "You're going
to be getting a call from my lawyer, Will Pollack, later today. I'm
not letting you see Caleb, at all, for at least two weeks. And after
that, not unless I'm with him. Me or someone I designate."

She sways again, reaches behind her for the support of the
counter. "What are you talking about!" she cries. "You can't do
that."

"I can. You're a danger to my son's emotional health and to
his relationship with me. I can. I can do more than that."

Eve says nothing. She stands erect and stares at him in horror.
He can hear the rasping of her breath.

"You know what I'm talking about, Eve. All those subtle ways you put me down in front of him. Not calling me when he gets hurt and then telling him I'm not needed. Making him wonder if maybe I didn't love his mommy enough because I don't go to her grave all the time. You want him to go to Harmony, you want him to play with kids from the club. You put ideas in his head so you can teach him to look down on me, the way you do. You tell him I did nothing and let his mother die."

Still she is silent. Her chin is up and the horror in her eyes has been replaced by an emotion Danny can't discern. He assumes it to be loathing, understandably, and he's too far down the road now to stop and see if it might be something else, something he hasn't seen there before.

"He woke up screaming Saturday night because of what you said to him." Danny's self-control threatens to abandon him. He tosses his head as if to clear it, takes in an uneven breath. "I can't do this with you anymore, Eve."

"You cannot take him away from me, Daniel. I will engage my own lawyer. I will fight you."

Danny's anger flares. "You do that. I'd prefer Caleb to have grandparents but I'd rather he never see you again than have him battered around between us. He's going to grow up thinking he has to choose one of us over the other, that it's his fault we argue about him all the time. That's going to be worse for him in the long run than losing his mother. You have to stop hating me, Eve. You have to stop blaming me. I didn't ruin her life. I made her happy."

Eve is slowly inching her way toward the archway into the dining room. "You seduced her. She was just a helpless child; how could she resist someone like you?"

Danny wants to shove the truth down her throat, make her

swallow it as he's swallowed her hatred all these years. Everything she says and thinks of him is such a lie and all he can feel now is disbelief that anyone could think it to be true. But it wouldn't do any good. Eve would never accept that it was Tara who seduced him, that he was the helpless one. And her *No* is still echoing in his head.

Danny collapses against the wall once more; that last plume of anger has burned itself out. A trickle of tears wets his face. "Your daughter loved me. And I loved her, more than anything in the world. Why doesn't that mean anything to you? Why do you have to treat me the way you do? I didn't kill her."

"You stole her. She never walked down the aisle. She never wore the wedding dress I had saved for her. You stole her from me." Her hands are at the throat of her robe again, clenched into fists on the silk trim. "Whom can I hate if not you, Daniel? Who is there to blame if not you?" Her voice is liquid, oddly dreamy, as though she is reciting lines of poetry lovingly remembered from her childhood.

The trickle of Danny's tears is spreading, becoming a flood. He feels like a fool, like a child, unable to stem the damning evidence of his vulnerability and his need for her to believe him. "Oh, shit," he moans and covers his face with his hands.

"You can't take him away from me, Daniel."

She has attained the dining room perimeter. Her words travel across the expanse of the kitchen. He didn't expect an answer to his questions. And just as he couldn't recognize the new emotion in her eyes, neither can he hear the one in her voice. He hears what he is inured by years of her contempt to hear. Disdain for his feelings, disregard for his authority. The implied threat of her greater power.

He raises his head. His wet eyes have turned the color of a

storm-bruised sky. "I'm not going to let *you* take him away from *me*. Not in any way you can conceive of. Go get your lawyer. But remember, I'm his father. You're going to have to prove to me that you can be trusted. It's all up to you now, Eve."

Danny leaves the house and walks back down the driveway, and when he arrives at his truck he has no memory of how he got there. His cheeks and beard are wet and his eyes are still running with tears. Abruptly overcome with nausea, he presses his hands to his abdomen and retches into the boxwoods. He didn't eat anything this morning; all that comes up is excess bile, a storehouse full of it. He dry heaves over the shrubbery until his stomach muscles hurt. When he's done, he rinses his mouth with warm water from the plastic bottle stuck between the front seats, spits it out onto the pink stone. He pours more water into his hand and splashes it on his face, dries himself on the sleeve of his shirt. When he swipes his arm across his face, his watch comes into his line of sight. It's nine minutes after eight.

He couldn't have been inside for more than six of those nine minutes. Six minutes of conversation. That's all it took to torch six years of dishonesty and imposed civility. Six minutes and a handful of monstrous words to reduce to ashes Tara's dream of him and Eve learning to understand and love each other as she loved them. He rests his head against the truck's high door frame and nearly cries again to realize that for the past year it has been his dream, too. That he and Eve, the one other person on earth who was as close to Tara as he was, might find a way to share her in death as they couldn't in life.

He climbs into the truck, turns it around, noses it into the road. He wonders if this is the last time he'll ever be here, if that point of no return came and went sometime in the past and he just didn't see it. His stomach gives another lurch as he pulls out. He heads in the opposite direction from whence he came. He doesn't want to go back to his house; it's going to feel haunted. He heads for town, for The Kitchen, for eggs and toast and a glass of milk. For the company of Arlene and Nancy, women who've known him since he was a baby, who love him.

He's driving with the thoughtless expertise of a mechanically competent person doing something he's done a thousand times. Or so he thinks, although the tenderly sun-dappled woods on either side of him are going by more and more slowly. When the driver behind him runs up his tailpipe, blares his horn, and dashes out across the double yellow line to pass him, he's bewildered to realize that he's crawling along at twenty miles an hour, eighteen, fifteen, ten. And that he has taken his foot off the gas pedal.

He's cresting Kensington Ridge Road. The truck drifts onto the narrow shoulder, seemingly of its own volition, then onto the slanted grass verge beyond. It tilts to the right as the passenger-side wheels sink into the shallow grass ditch at the edge of the tree line. He puts it in PARK and shuts off the engine. A doe and fawn, emboldened by the momentary tranquillity, bolt from the woods, leap the road, and trot up the steep slope of the brick driveway on the other side; the fawn's right front hoof skids off the blue plastic–wrapped newspaper lying a few feet in from the road. Even the local wildlife know which is the best property in the neighborhood. The Spencers' house, Lily's house, is directly across from where he's stopped.

Danny's sense of time jumps the tracks. For a moment he's nineteen, part of the proud construction crew building the grand house at the top of the ridge. The older guys demonstrate their affection for their young carpenter by riding him mercilessly. They've nicknamed him Cradle Robber and are all over him about the dark-haired little girl with the heartsick eyes who lives a half mile up the road and bikes by at least three times a week, in the transparent disguise of a curious neighbor, to gorge herself on his every movement. Time implodes and coalesces into the present again and he's thirty-five, trapped in his truck with his eyes fixed on the forbidden gateway to Lily's house. She walks on floors that he helped lay when he was a boy, embarrassed by the presence of the girl who would become his wife, and she was already, still, a married woman. He and Lily have never spent any of their time together here; it's understood that they can't. He hasn't seen the house since the day the interior crew finished its work.

But he knows it well. For weeks he's been picturing her there. In the kitchen in the morning, when the light wood cabinets and red granite countertops glow like gems in the sunlight streaming through the sliding glass doors. In the oak-paneled den in the afternoon, lifting her head from her book from time to time to inhale the fortifying smell of wood and earth. But mostly he pictures her at night, curled up in the big bay window of her bedroom, staring out over the treetops the way he stares into the woods when he's alone on his porch. At this moment he sees her sitting on that big mahogany deck out back. Yesterday, out of Caleb's hearing, he told her what had happened, what Eve had done. She was so upset for him. She knows where he's just been; he can feel her worrying about him. He pictures himself leaving his truck by the side of the road and taking the trail blazed by the deer's bobbing white tails. When he comes around the back of her house, she'll turn her head at the sound of his rustling steps in the grass and look at him with eyes still heavy with sleep. He'll kneel at her feet, lay his head in her lap. Her unbrushed hair will cascade over him and its sweet darkness will blot out the bitter morning.

Only his eyes move. They follow the path of the deer. He takes his cell phone from his belt.

By eight o'clock Lily has done an hour on the NordicTrack. By eight ten she is showered and dressed and in the kitchen. She puts up coffee, cuts up some fruit, takes the yogurt from the refrigerator, the granola from the pantry. She leaves her breakfast waiting, lifts Blinkie Floyd off the counter and together they go out to fetch the *New York Times*. As she opens the front door, she takes odds with herself on whether the paper will be in the driveway or entangled in the privet; the delivery boy has a strong arm but lousy aim. She doesn't know when to expect Danny's call, and so she has her cell phone in her shorts' pocket.

She is still on the bluestone path between the house and the graveled parking area when two deer rise into view above the slope of the driveway. A doe and a spindly legged fawn. Lily draws in her breath and stands motionless so as not to spook them. They stop on the gravel and swivel their long, graceful heads to look at her. They flick their ears. They, too, stand motionless and match her dark-eyed stare. She knows their population is out of control; they carry diseases; they eat her roses and her lilies; Joan says they're nothing but big rodents with hooves, but Lily loves them. She loves to see them cross her property in the early mornings and early evenings, cavalier and careless, as though they know no harm will ever come to them here. She looks at them and whispers, "Yes, you're beautiful." The doe has seen enough; she bounds off across the lawn toward the far woods, the fawn right behind her. Lily's cell phone vibrates against her hip.

"Danny! Where are you?"

"I'm in town." The privet hedges that extend from either side of her driveway are overdue a trim. There's a cracked brick about ten feet up from the road. "Going to get some breakfast at The Kitchen."

Lily glances at her watch. He said he would be at the Jamisons' at eight. It's barely twenty after. "Have you not gone to see Eve yet?"

"Gone and done." He's not ready to talk about it; the taste of bile is fresh in his mouth.

Danny's voice is caustic. It breaks Lily's heart. He feels so alone with this; he *is* so alone. "That was quick." Her voice rises on the last word, as if she were asking a question, inviting him to tell her what happened.

"There wasn't all that much to say. She wasn't about to beg my forgiveness, I wasn't about to beg hers. How long does it take to tell someone you've had it with them."

"I don't like the way you sound. I haven't eaten breakfast yet. I could meet you at The Kitchen. I could be there in fifteen minutes. Do you want me to? Do you want to talk about it?"

"No." He wants to be with her but they're seeing too much of each other. Five times in the last ten days, since the night they kissed. They've been good at pretending it never happened, but every time they meet, the pressure inside him swells a little more, pushes a little harder at his definition of loyalty and his interpretation of right and wrong. "Thanks. I'll be okay once I get a little distance from this. Listen, I'm sorry, but I've really got to work today. I can't go to Woodstock with you." It's not just that he hasn't been with a woman in so long. It's her. He has to get some distance from her. And he really does have to work; he's falling behind.

"Oh!" A hot stab of disappointment pierces her.

"Yeah, I'm sorry, really. Something came up, I've got some appointments . . ." Danny stops talking before he trips himself up and his lie becomes obvious. "But I'll see you Wednesday night, for dinner at the Pollacks, okay? Come over around six, we'll go from here."

"Sure. I'm looking forward to meeting them. And it's all right about Woodstock. I'm disappointed, but I understand." She does understand. They're seeing too much of each other. There has been no repeat of what happened that night in his driveway, but every time they meet the shape and weight and heat of what they need from each other morphs and grows and strains the boundaries of their friendship.

"Thanks."

"Go. Have breakfast. Have a productive day. I'll call you later to see how you're doing, okay?"

"Please do. I'm sure I'll be in a better mood."

Danny's stomach growls, loudly. It pulses with emptiness. He starts the truck, puts it in gear, babies it out of the ditch. At the last moment, he turns the steering wheel hard around and, with a loud protest of the oversized tires, heads back in the direction he came from. He's not going to The Kitchen. He's going home. This is a day that should hurt; it's not a day to be looking for sympathy.

Lily continues on toward the road on trembling legs. She walks the steep driveway slowly, her eyes down. As she nears the bottom, she hears the masculine roar of a big engine and the screech of tires. The sounds startle her and her eyes come up. A moving wall of silver crosses the frame created by the privet hedges. She dashes to the road and watches Danny's truck moving fast in the opposite direction from town. She stands there, uncomprehending, as it gets smaller and smaller and finally vanishes. She is hugging Blinkie Floyd so hard that she flattens his malleable, polyester-filled body, causing his head to fall back. His eyes glint up at her in dumb panic.

Danny wasn't eight miles away when he called, he was right here, at the foot of her driveway, as close to her as he is allowed to come. He needs to be near her as desperately much as she needs to be near him. He lied when he said he didn't want her to come to him, just as she lied when she said it was all right about Woodstock. A shudder of desire shakes her. Not only the bodily desire that smites her at the mere thought of his physical nearness but, even more strongly, the soulful desire to transcend her own life and materialize into his. They spent the day together yesterday, she and Danny and Caleb. The way any other family might spend a Sunday. After lunch they went to the county craft fair and while they were there something happened. She was holding the wood-carved locomotive that Danny had bought for Caleb in one hand and Caleb's hand in the other. Danny was squatting at their feet, tightening the lace of Caleb's sneaker. Caleb leaned lightly against the side of Lily's leg; Danny's knee brushed her shin. She looked down, at Danny's head bent in concentration, at his strong, patient hands tying the lace of his son's shoe, and she was hammered by a lust for him that was not sexual in origin yet was indistinguishable from the sexual lust that possessed her when they'd kissed. It was all she could do to not sink to her knees, let the toy train fall from her fingers so she could touch him—his neck, his back, his leg—it didn't matter where, so long as the circle of the three of them was completed.

Lily puts a hand in her pocket for her phone. She could call him, tell him to come back. She can't let him into her house, but why can't they stand together where she is standing now alone? She could hold him, and he could put his arms around her and they could shelter each other. Why can't they at least do that? She removes an empty hand. Tears sting her eyes and nose. She shudders again, this time from the chill of impossibility, and turns her back to the road. She picks up the paper and returns to the house.

The food she's readied for her breakfast doesn't interest her now; she's lost her appetite. She puts her paper and her bat on the table and crosses to the counter to pour some coffee. The message light on the answering machine is blinking. Her heart contracts as for a second she fears that Paul has called; days can go by with no room for him in her head and then, out of the blue, for a moment, there is no room for anything but him. The call is not from him, though. He's on the West Coast, it's five thirty in the morning there, he's asleep. She hits the PLAY button.

Lily, my love. It's Rick. It's about . . . eight thirty. I'm just starting a double shift, I won't be able to call again, but I wanted to tell you that Alan and I are leaving in the morning to get Sophie. I'm not sure how long we'll be gone, maybe through the weekend. There's a pause and then a sigh. *Um. Listen. I'm sorry about spilling this to Paul when I talked to him on Wednesday. I had no idea you hadn't told him. I meant to call you right away, but then I thought . . . I don't know what I thought. That I should just stay out of it, I guess,*

*let him handle it. I hope everything's okay. I love you, I'll call
you when we get back.*

Nausea makes a fist of her stomach. Lily leans on her hands
against the counter and squeezes her eyes shut. She should have
told him. That night of July Fourth weekend, when he was distracted by work and mellow with sex, and the agony of the cut
had not yet fired every one of her nerves, perhaps she might
have gotten it by him without her misery showing. Why didn't
she? When did she imagine she would tell him? In ten, twenty,
thirty years? Hope maybe he would be too busy to notice? *Rick
and Alan's daughter is getting married? Knock me down with a
feather! I didn't even know they* had *a daughter!* What is she
going to do now? Her scalp starts to crawl and her brain to swell
and she sees Paul standing in the bedroom of the apartment,
livid, demanding that she love only him, that she stop wanting
a child. How can she possibly tell him about Sophie without
revealing that she has been disobeying him all this time? That
she can't exist loving only him and it's cruel of him to ask her to.
She needs to love a child and she wants to love this child and she
doesn't want to do it alone, she wants him to love it, too.

They had spoken, once, since Wednesday and he hadn't said
anything. It's her fault. He knows she's kept this from him for
months, used her silence as yet another act of hostility and withdrawal. This is a conversation he doesn't want to face, either.
They both know too much now and the knowledge has propelled
them further apart than they've ever been. They are cowering in
their distant corners with the word *baby* spelled out in barbed
wire, stretched across the continent between them.

The ringing of the telephone slices through Lily's thoughts,
pulls her upright, opens her eyes. The nausea rushes up into her

throat. Maybe this time it *is* Paul. The caller ID reads a local number and the name TRACHTENBERG. She breathes out "Oh, thank you," and answers the call.

"Hell-oo, Joan." Lily is silly with relief.

"Lily?" Joan chuckles. "You sound stoned."

"No. I just haven't had my coffee yet, I'm a little out of it."

"You've been a little out of it half the summer. I don't think having your handsome husband away for so long agrees with you. Paul better get his ass home soon. He *is* coming back soon, actually, isn't he?"

"Yes, next Monday I think." Lily takes a startled look around the kitchen. She's pushed Paul so far away she can barely imagine him anywhere in the house without feeling intruded upon.

"Well, then. We've got to talk ASAP, before he drags you back to the city. Can you come for dinner Friday night?"

Lily hesitates. What if Danny . . . "Friday's good. Thanks. What do we have to talk about?"

"You and The Doorway. I know, I know, I'm like a dog with a bone. But, Lily, you would be *so* good with the kids. I understand that you can't be here full-time, but we could work out a part-time situation. Let's just talk about it on Friday, okay?"

The Doorway. It's absurd, but nonetheless Lily says, "Okay."

She takes her coffee, her paper, and her baby bat and heads for the gazebo. At the edge of the deck, she turns around and looks back into the house. *Outside, looking in.* The phrase pops into her head. All summer long she has been outside her own life looking in at other lives, through doors that weren't there before but have all at once appeared and opened to her. The door that leads to Rick and Alan and Sophie. The door that leads to Danny and Caleb. The door that leads to The Doorway. There is something waiting for her behind them all. There are families she can be part of. There are children. There is no Paul behind any of those doors. If she walks through one or two or all of them, will he come with her or will she have to go without him? If she lets them all close, there will be no children, no family, there will be only herself and Paul in the still and lonely room where they have found themselves. How long would he stay there? How long would she? Why can't they see the door that leads them out together?

28

DANNY AND WILL are on the back deck outside the Pollacks'
kitchen. Lily and Sue are inside, taking care of the last bits of
cleaning up. The kids have been asleep for hours, Ellen and Jack
in their beds, Caleb on the living room couch. Will is smoking
a fat cigar, luxuriating in an indulgence that Sue allows him no
more than once a week. Dense round clouds of aromatic smoke
sail from his mouth. Danny is upwind of the miasma, leaning
languidly against the deck railing.

He's feeling tranquil, and not just from the several glasses of
expensive Australian Shiraz he drank. Dinner is long over but
Danny continues to feed on the dreamlike pleasure of being here
with Lily. He opens his mouth and with the same sensual delight with which Will inhales his perfumed smoke, Danny draws
into himself the sound of the women laughing and chattering as
they work. It's such a sweet sound, such a wonderfully mundane
sound. Lily's throaty laugh rises above the murmur and Danny
smiles, picturing the way her eyes shine and her face glows when
she's happy. It's not the laugh he's used to hearing alongside
Sue's, but the sound of it thrills him.

Danny reaches his arms up toward the sky with a contented grunt. "This was one of the best nights I've had in a long long time. Thanks. Thanks for making Lily feel so welcome."

Will exhales a plume of smoke. "She's a nice woman." He extends his arm and taps three inches of ash onto the lawn. "I thought I'd let you enjoy your dinner before bringing this up, but Eve and Lester's lawyer called me late this afternoon."

Danny's lungs constrict. So much for tranquillity. "Who are they using? Should I be worried?"

"Should I be insulted by that question?" Will jokes. "They're using James Resnick, one of the partners in a firm with more names than I can remember. Offices here and in Middletown. I know him. He's a good guy. Not the type to do any cockamamie thing a client asks him to. He's certainly not advising them to take any action against you at this point."

"What do you mean *action*?" Danny can't keep the panic out of his voice. "Like their fighting me for custody? Is that what she's going to do?"

"Whoa! No. Danny, calm down. Jesus, man, is that what you've been worried about all this time? Why didn't you say something? Forget that. They'd have to prove you're an unfit father, and that's so ridiculous it's not even worth talking about. Just totally forget it."

Danny paces down his adrenaline rush. "Okay. Okay. Thanks. Stupid, I know, but I guess I needed to hear that. So, what did the lawyer have to say?"

"Nothing much yet. Eve did make it clear that if you try to stop them from seeing Caleb, you'll have a major battle on your hands and Resnick was kind enough to remind me that grandparents' rights suits, successful ones, have proliferated in recent years."

"I'm not trying to do that."

"That's what I told him, but you gave Eve the impression that you might."

"It was not a calm conversation, Will. I'm sure I said some things."

"I understand. Look, as long as we all keep our heads, we'll get through this. Resnick agrees a cool-down period couldn't hurt; he knows you're in the driver's seat here, so let's just wait and see how it goes. You okay now? No more custody crap on your mind?"

"No, I'm good."

Will nods and then gives Danny a strange look. "I'm glad you're good because I don't think you're going to like what I have to say next."

Danny smiles but Will just continues to look at him. Danny says, "What is it?"

Will gestures with his cigar toward the kitchen. He drops his voice to a hoarse whisper. "Danny, what are you doing? It's not like I don't get it, I do, believe me, I'm not blind. But this is the last thing on earth you need. She's a married woman. She's a lot older than you. You are going to get slammed. This is not a good thing. You know it's not."

Danny's good mood has already soured and Will is right, Danny doesn't want to hear this. His hackles rise instantly. "I thought you and Sue liked her. What were you, just being polite?"

"She's terrific, we like her very much. That's not the point."

Will's deliberate calmness only makes Danny angrier. "Oh, come on, Will. Give me some credit, would you? Lily and I are friends, that's it, and it is a good thing. I've already *been* slammed, and so has she. We're helping each other cope a little better than we've been able to on our own."

"That's good. It's fine. But you don't act like you're just

friends, Danny. You don't look at each other like you're just friends. If you think that's what's going on between you, you're fooling yourselves. Please, man, don't go there with her."

"Get off it, Will. I'm not trying to resurrect my dead wife."

But, of course, that's precisely what he is doing.

"Don't be angry with me, Danny. If I'm wrong, I'm wrong, and I apologize. I worry about you is all. I don't want to see you get hurt."

Danny barely hears Will's placating words. His own lying words momentarily deafen him. He *is* trying to resurrect Tara. He is owed this much at least from the universe; to be allowed to go back and prepare himself for the loss of her. To have her again, knowing that there will be no next time. No child who looks just like her. Knowing that she is not his to keep and this will be the last time.

"I'm not angry." Danny puts his arms around Will and hugs him, uses Will's stocky body for support until the strength returns to his legs. "I'm lucky to have you looking out for me." He draws back. "But you don't have to worry about me, honestly. I'll prove it to you. I'll take Lauren to dinner, okay? I'll spend a nice evening with a nice single girl. All right? Happy now?"

Lily waits in the passenger seat of the Volvo while Danny says his good nights. She's praying that Sue's Moroccan chicken tagine isn't going to exit her stomach in the wrong direction. *It was so good to meet you, Lily. And we'll look forward to meeting Paul when he gets back from his travels.* It was a perfectly appropriate thing to say as they hugged good night, and there was no trace of hidden meaning in Sue's voice, but Lily feels the remark like a glass of cold water thrown in her face.

"Do you mind holding him?" Danny appears at the door

with Caleb in his arms. The boy is dead asleep. "It's a short drive. He'll wake up if I try to manhandle him into his car seat."

"Of course not. Give him to me."

Lily takes Caleb onto her lap. Danny pulls the seat belt from the car wall, leans across her and straps them in together. He dips and kisses Caleb's forehead as he backs out and Lily's nose fills with the clean, watery scent of his hair and skin; a faint whiff of smoke from Will's cigar lingers on him. Caleb stirs in his sleep, adjusting himself into his new bed, and when he resettles, his head lies heavy at her throat and one clenched hand lies heavy on her breast.

Lily holds Caleb's exquisite weight full against her; his noisy breath is at her ear, his flyaway hair feathers her neck and chin. She rests her chin on the crown of his head and tracks Danny as he comes around the front of the car and gets behind the wheel; she tracks him with a stare like a coil of steel connecting them. She watches his every simple movement: the twist of his wrist as he starts the car, the turn of his head as he looks down the road before pulling out of the driveway. The shift of his hips and thighs beneath his jeans as he moves on his seat. *I am riding in a car beside a man I love and his child is asleep in my arms.* Reality, which has been playing hide-and-seek with her for weeks, turns a sharp corner and disappears completely. She doesn't know anything anymore, which life is hers or could be hers, which life isn't hers and can't be hers. Where she belongs and where she doesn't. Or where she wants to be. She holds on to Caleb and watches Danny through eyes that can't take in enough of him no matter how voraciously she looks. His beauty and youthfulness choke the breath right out of her throat. Her heart hits up against the promise of him as though he were yet another wall inside her that there is no way around.

They stop for a red light. The atmosphere inside the car is

visible, it's vibrating before her hot eyes. Danny slowly pushes his head through the thick air, turns and looks at her. Their eyes meet; they stare wordlessly at each other. Lily lifts a hand to lovingly cup the back of Caleb's head. The electrifying sound of quavering breath fills the car. Danny and Lily cling to each other with their eyes and by the strength and sameness of their thoughts they mold the silence into the shape of an imagined life. Its diaphanous form hovers in the encapsulated space, begging to be made solid. The light that bathes them changes from red to green and still they don't move or speak. Head-lights flood them from behind as a car comes swiftly over the small rise in the road. A shock of white light slices through the interior of the car and heartlessly illuminates the spot where their gazes are locked. There is nothing there. Danny's head jerks back toward the windshield and he stomps his foot on the gas pedal. Lily takes a breath and swivels her head toward the side window.

Danny feels her eyes on him like a torch burning its heat through his skin, lighting him deep down where there has been no light. His conversation with Will repeats itself in his brain, an angel on one shoulder, a devil on the other. He can't tell which is which, they look identical to him. Will is surely right; this can never be a good thing. But if that's true, if it can never be a good thing, why is he driving home in the dark of night with Lily by his side, his sleeping son snug in her arms and her beautiful dark eyes boring into him, her need as raw and powerful as his?

He drives on. In the periphery of his vision, Danny sees Lily turn away from him and the smoldering embers of his anger im-mediately reignite. He's furious that she's bound to another man, that she isn't young, that now he's totally confused about what it is he really feels for her. Fuck Will. None of it is Lily's fault, but Danny's anger searches her out because if she still loves her husband, she shouldn't be looking at Danny the way she does; and if Danny still loves his wife, Lily's look shouldn't move him the way it does.

"You're busy Friday night, right?" He blurts out the rhetorical question and doesn't wait for a response. "I'm going to take Lauren out. It's time I had something resembling a date."

Lily had begun to turn back to him, but now she stops. She looks down and plucks at the twisted seat belt. "Lauren? The nursery school teacher?"

"Yeah. I made her cry a few weeks ago, so I owe her an apology at least."

"I didn't realize you liked her that way."

"Yeah, well, I don't know that I do. But maybe I could, I don't know. That's no reason we can't just have a nice evening together." Danny cringes to hear himself. He's behaving with all the maturity of a fourteen-year-old, but the pissy tone of Lily's voice, icy tight with undisguised jealousy, fires the rumble of rage in his chest again.

"No. Of course not. By all means start dating, flex your social skills. As long as she knows you're just practicing on her, I'm sure it will be very enjoyable." Her breezy words practically freeze in midair.

They remain silent, pointedly not looking at each other, as Danny pulls up in front of his house, gets out of the car, takes Caleb. As Lily climbs out after him and goes to the BMW. She opens her car door, glances at Danny with a frosty smile.

"That was a lovely evening, thank you. Your friends are very nice."

"You're welcome. I'm glad you could come." Danny matches her cold formality.

They are looking at each other now, standing mere feet apart, stony with tension. Danny's mouth twitches, and he starts to laugh, and then they are both laughing, so hard they fall against their cars.

"What the hell happened back there? Did we just have a fight? Oh, shit, he's going to wake up." Danny sobers and transfers a suddenly active Caleb to his other shoulder, bounces him lightly. "Shhh."

"I think we did. No, he's asleep again." Lily throws her purse onto the BMW's passenger seat and puts her hand on Caleb's back.

"I'm sorry if I said anything to upset you." As he smiles at her, Danny sees himself putting Caleb to bed, Lily behind him, her hand on his back. He sees himself picking her up and carrying her to bed.

"Me, too. Go out with Lauren, have a good time." She gives him a sisterly peck on the cheek. She turns quickly and gets into her car. "Call me. Let me know how it goes."

There's a small package by the front door, a late DHL delivery. The return address is that of a law firm in San Francisco. It's from Paul. Lily holds the bulging padded envelope gingerly and tiptoes down the hallway, as though the package might blow up in her face if she disturbs it overly much. She begins to pull the envelope open but trepidation stays her hand. Whatever is in there, it's going to make her love him and she's too tired and torn to deal with loving him. She is unbearably tired. She lays the package on the kitchen table and goes upstairs. She flips on the

overhead recessed bedroom lights and is pinned in the doorway
by Blinkie Floyd's chastising stare. She has taken to leaving him
balanced atop the pillows, facing the doorway so she will see him
as soon as she walks in.

Lily stares back. "Oh, all right!" she cries, and runs back
downstairs.

He has sent her a pen. A gorgeous tortoise-shell lacquer Dun-
hill fountain pen with a small bottle of blue-black ink. And he
has written her a note.

> *Darling, this pen is a work of art. Like you. I can just see
> it in your fingers. Maybe it will make your hard work for The
> Doorway a little easier. Hope you like it.*
>
> > *Paul*

It worked. As she sits at the table fondling the glowing amber
pen, she rereads his message and aches with love for him. For
the first time since he's been gone the house feels empty without
him. She can see him looming, tall and dark and adamant, behind the yielding lightness with which she's been filling her eyes
and her heart. She can feel him pushing at the seemingly weaker
obstacle, trying to get it out of his way so that he can reclaim her,
but the obstacle stands firm. It worked, but not well enough.

It's eight in California, he's undoubtedly at a business dinner,
but he answers his phone after the first ring.

"Hi. I was hoping you'd call tonight."

She hears the scraping of a chair across the floor; voices and
laughter. "I'm interrupting you again."

"It's all right. I'm wining and dining two uptight ex-SynTech
guys who definitely know where the bodies are buried. A few
minutes alone with a hundred-fifty-dollar bottle of Château

whatever might give them the courage to share the info with me. Did you get my package?"

"Yes, I just came home and there it was. That's why I'm calling. The pen is lovely, Paul. And so is what you wrote. Thank you."

"You're welcome. I . . . I've been thinking about you, I saw it, it looked like it belonged in your hand. I was hoping it might inspire more of those little notes you used to write me."

He is speaking quietly and slowly, the way Lily walked through the house holding the package: oh so carefully. He sounds frightened. It's been a long time since she wrote him little notes and secreted them in his briefcase or sock drawer or under his pillow. She could tell him she'll write him little notes again, but, as perverse and mean-spirited as it may be, the fear in his voice is one of the most gratifying sounds she's ever heard. It takes the ache of her love and converts it to the ache of the hurt he inflicted on her. And the hurt part of her wants to hurt him back, at times badly enough to make him curl into the corner of a cold room all alone and cry.

"I'll find good use for it, don't worry. It's late here, Paul, I'm tired, but I didn't want to go to bed without thanking you. Go back to your dinner, go get those guys to fess up."

"I hope they do. I'm tired, too. I can't wait to get home. I miss you."

She still doesn't know which doors to push open and which to leave shut, and the time she's been given to decide is running out. Tonight she does miss him, but she's not ready for him to come home. And so she says only, "You'll be home soon. Good night, Paul. I really do love the pen."

*   *   *

As soon as Danny walks into the kitchen he's attacked by hunger. He's ravenous. He should still be full from dinner, but he feels as though he hasn't eaten in days. His hunger scoops out his insides, makes a hollow shell of him again. He stands at the refrigerator and gobbles up the last piece of sweet noodle pudding that Lily made Sunday night. It leaves the tang of cinnamon in his mouth, a taste like the smell of the sweet-spicy perfume she wears, like the imagined taste of her. His breath quickens. The pressure in his loins moves to his racing heart and the phantom pressure of the wedding band he doesn't wear anymore pinches the ring finger of his left hand. He slams the refrigerator door shut, goes into the bedroom, and takes the journal from the drawer. Tara tasted like honey.

> *Danny became my air, my food and water, my shelter. My body wasn't my own any longer, it was a part of his as his was a part of mine. We went dormant with the pain of separation every week, then flared to life again on the weekends, when he drove to Princeton to be with me.*

"Oh God," Danny moans softly. He raises his eyes but there are no soothing pale-green bedroom walls before him, there is only Tara, lying naked on her bed in her shared house in Princeton. His hand falls onto the page and his fingers press into the paper.

He knows what part of their story she's going to tell now and he thinks, *What the hell, how much more tortured can I be?* It's not as though he doesn't still think of her that way, because he does, constantly. He's been a ghoul all these months, preying on his memories of their lovemaking, unable to become aroused except when imagining her. His burgeoning desire for the living ought to make him feel less ghoulish but it doesn't.

My virginity survived for two months. I didn't want it, I tried to give it to him, but he wouldn't take it. I begged him. I crawled all over him. I cried and told him I was ready. But he wouldn't do it. He was protecting me, he said. And he wasn't wrong. Once I knew what it was to take him into my body, to move in concert with him, to have him fill me as I came, to feel him erupt and die inside me, my hunger for him became insatiable. But I wasn't wrong, either. There was nothing I wasn't ready to feel for him; it was himself he was protecting.

Months went by and still I didn't tell my parents about him. Every time I flogged myself to do it, I saw my mother standing triumphant above Danny's bloodied corpse. I had done nothing to prepare her for him and for the grief I was going to cause her because of him. Instead, I'd done the opposite. I atoned in advance, zealously, for my inevitable sin and did everything possible to make her happy. I had to, because I love her and I had already caused her a lifetime of grief. With every one of the million soft kisses, tender touches, reverent looks she has bestowed on me, she has told me that I am her deepest sorrow as well as her greatest joy. I don't know why, but I know that it's true. And just as surely, I knew that she would see my loving a man like Danny Malloy as a defection and a betrayal of her love for me and she would do anything to prevent it.

June came too soon and I ran out of time. Graduation was weeks away. I had to tell my parents that I had declined the job at the Princeton Institute and was coming back to Stone Creek for the summer. And I had to tell them why. My mother didn't order me to stop seeing Danny. Instead, she went to see him, and two days later he ended our relationship. "This isn't going to work anymore," he said. "I care for you, Tara, you know that, but what I said that night outside my house, it's all true. Your friends and your family, they're going to chew me up and spit me out. You won't be happy and whatever you think you feel for me now won't survive out here in the real world. I'd rather just call it quits now."

I wasn't angry at my mother; there's no point in being angry at someone for being who they are. And I didn't bother to argue with Danny. In his quiet way Danny is as stubborn as she is. I knew his true desires, but I knew the truth of his fears as well. What I had to do was clear to me. I had to convince Danny that my love for him was lasting and unshakable, I had to place us both beyond my mother's reach, and I had to give her something equal to myself in exchange for my leaving her. I accepted the job and went back to Princeton. I threw away my diaphragm. I took my basal body temperature every morning. In August, when the calendar and the thermometer concurred that I was ovulating, I returned to Stone Creek.

Poor Danny. I showed him no mercy. I arrived before dawn, snuck up the stairs to his bedroom. It was stifling hot; he was sleeping on a mattress on the floor, on his back, naked, nothing covering him but the breeze from the fan whirring furiously in the corner of the room. I peeled off my clothes, knelt at his side. I put my hand on him, stretched out alongside him, and as his eyes fluttered open and he bloomed within my fingers, I whispered, "I love you Danny. Swear to me you'll never leave me again." Neither of us said a word about my missing diaphragm or the unused condoms in his medicine cabinet. When I left three days later, Caleb was surging to life inside me. Two weeks after that the prophecy of my foolish childhood word game was fulfilled and Tara Jamison married Danny Malloy.

I swear. I swear. Orgasm wrenches Danny from sleep. He cries out as he ejaculates, then lies panting and trembling as he comes fully awake, clutching in vain at the fading illusory sensation of her on top of him. He has relived that night, when she came back to him and woke him that way, in his mind while awake and in his dreams while asleep more often than any other of the thousands of memories he has of her. That night changed him. No woman had ever ripped him loose from himself the way she did; sometimes it took days for him to find his way back into the familiarity of his own skin. But after that night he never found his way back to himself, at least not to the person he'd been before. With the first thrust he knew she wasn't using her diaphragm. He didn't pull free of her but he paused, uncertain of what it meant, what he should do. She responded by tightening her arms around him, lifting her hips as though to gather him in, and waiting. He looked down into her adoring eyes, open wide, beseeching him to trust her. She was offering him everything he wanted or could ever imagine wanting. He let it all go then, all the doubt and disbelief that he could actually be the man she would love forever. The thorny knot inside him unraveled, his love spooled out into infinity, and he gave in, sank into her as deep as he could go.

Danny hobbles into the bathroom and in the near total darkness he washes himself. Before his erection has withered, the ache of desire is building in him again. It never leaves him now. He can't have sex with women he barely knows. He rarely masturbates. If he had control over his unconscious he would put an end to his infrequent wet dreams. Those outlets of physical relief were adequate when he was more dead than alive and far beyond the hope of emotional intimacy. But they lost their effectiveness the day he first saw Lily.

He takes the damp washcloth into the bedroom, turns on his lamp, and cleans his sticky semen off the sheet. Tara's journal is on the bed. He takes it with him back into the bathroom and sits on the rim of the tub holding it in his hands.

Eve found him up on a ladder, painting the shutters on the second-story windows of the old Malloy house, which was what the locals were already calling it now that he had sold it. Her eyes were obsidian disks. They revealed nothing of herself. They took in his sweaty, paint-stained half-naked body, his worn work boots, ripped shorts, Gallo Construction baseball cap, sun-blistered shoulders, and like the evil witch's mirror they showed him only the reflection of his own unquestionable miserableness. He barely heard her words. He'd ceded his right to her daughter before she ever opened her mouth. Even now, it's not Eve's demand that he give Tara up that he remembers most vividly. It's what she showed him and what she said just before she got in her car and drove away. She turned to him with a look of enmity so strong it slapped at him from across twenty feet of springy green lawn. *You would leave her in any case, wouldn't you, Daniel?* she'd said. *That's what men like you do. You are not going to do that to my daughter.*

As he sits in the dark and strokes the leather binding, he recalls those words, Eve contradicting herself and condemning him for being capable of doing what she was commanding him to do. The odd quality of her voice didn't register on him then, he was so confused by the contradiction he recognized in himself: acquiescing to do the condemnable thing at the same time he wanted to tell Eve that she was wrong, he would never leave Tara. But he hears it now, that strange, singsong dreaminess in her voice, because he realizes he heard it again the other morning, right before she disappeared from the kitchen.

Danny returns to the bedroom and sits on the floor next to his side of the bed. The sheet is still damp and he won't sleep on Tara's side. He opens the journal and quickly finds what he's looking for. *With every one of the million soft kisses, tender touches, reverent looks she has bestowed on me, she has told me that I am her deepest sorrow as well as her greatest joy. I don't know why, but I know that it's true.* He rereads these two sentences over and over and over and as he does he replays Monday's confrontation with Eve in his mind until the words and the images merge and he's not certain of what he's hearing or seeing anymore.

29

Y OUR PASTA LOOKED GOOD. Did you like it?"

"It was great, I wish you'd tasted it. So was that wine you suggested. I shouldn't have ordered that second glass, but it was sooo good." Lauren is relaxed in the passenger seat of Danny's truck. Her head is lolling against the seat back and she's smiling at him. Her face is flushed pink.

Danny grins at her. "Tomorrow's not a school day, you can sleep late." He pulls into the garden apartment complex a mile out of town where Lauren lives.

"Mmmm. This was really nice, Danny."

"Yeah, it was. I really am sorry for the way I behaved the other day. Thanks for letting me make it up to you." It was nice; nicer and easier than he thought it would be. He'd taken her to see the new Woody Allen movie at the art-house cinema in Middletown, then back to Stone Creek for dinner at Mario's Off Main. They'd found things to talk about: Caleb, her work, mutual friends, books, movies. She was pleasant company and it felt good simply to do something so normal. From the outset he was clear that it wasn't exactly a date, more of an evening out with a friend, and she seemed okay with it. She kind of reminds him of a cousin he used to play with when he was young, before his aunt and uncle moved to North Carolina, with her shyness, her blond hair and light eyes, her tall lanky body.

"You can make up to me anytime."

Her words are a little slurred and her attempt at vamping him is embarrassingly inept.

"You definitely had too much wine." Danny laughs and doesn't look at her. He thought they would get through the evening without this.

"Okay. Here we are." He stops the truck by the cement path to her apartment and leaves the motor running as he walks her the ten feet to her well-illuminated front door. "So. Good night."

Lauren's pale eyes are glassy in the bright overhead light. She's got a goofy smile on her lips. "Do you want to come in for a little while? I could make us some more coffee."

"Thanks, no. I should get home."

"Of course. Sure."

Her lust is coming at him in waves and for a second Danny is paralyzed by it; he stands there and lets it break over him. He sees what she's about to do before she does it, but he doesn't turn away from her fast enough and Lauren, drunk and heedless, throws herself at him, clamps her arms around his waist and back, and tries to kiss him. He's been so conscious all evening not to do or say anything that might lead her to mistake his intentions, but now he's the one who makes the worse mistake: he returns her kiss. It's a purely physical reflex. His body is so deprived of sex it responds before his brain can intervene. He's been empty for so long, his mouth wants to open and suck her in and let her fill him. But she isn't the one who can fill him; she'll go straight through him, be mangled by his sharp, warped insides, and leave him emptier than before. He quickly disengages and gropes behind him to undo her embrace.

"No, Lauren, don't. Don't do that."

Her eyes fly open and she stares at him with dawning horror at what she's done. Her face turns a brilliant scarlet as humiliation crashes down on her. She yanks her wrists from his grip.

"Lauren, I'm sorry, it's my fault. Don't be upset. It's okay, really." Danny tries to touch her arm in reassurance.

She twists away from him and teeters, bangs her shoulder on the door frame. She breaks out into loud, gasping tears, turns her back, paws inside her purse for her keys.

"Lauren, please."

"Oh, God, Danny. Go away! I can't look at you. Just go away!"

His stomach is churning. He doesn't want to leave her like this but she disappears into the dark apartment and slams the door in his face.

Danny trips and cracks his shin against the riser of the porch's top step. He limps inside, rubbing his leg. The house is lifeless. He couldn't get a babysitter—teenaged girls with their own cell phones and three boyfriends are not so easily lured by the prospect of five hours with a five-year-old and fifty bucks—so Caleb is back at Will and Sue's for the night. The silence and lack of human aura are overwhelming. Danny turns on lights in the living room and dining room as he passes through into the kitchen. He had only one glass of wine at dinner but he feels drunk; emotional and physical distress has unpleasantly altered the connection between his mind and body. He's mortified. He used Lauren. He should never have gone near her. But still, the contact with her has left him aroused and full of yearning, despite his lack of desire for her. It's Lily he wants, Lily he imagined in that moment when he closed his eyes and kissed Lauren. Lily would fill him. He would take her in so slowly, in small loving pieces, and she would fill him to bursting. His thoughts skitter between the complicated reality of a living, warm-blooded Lily and the stripped-bare phantom of Tara and he's immediately sundered by guilt.

It would be better if he *were* drunk. He gets the vodka from the freezer and pours a large shot into an unwashed juice glass sitting in the sink, flecks of orange pulp stuck to its sides. Vodka and orange juice, a venerable combination. He drinks half of it in one swallow and the alcohol seems to go directly from his mouth to his brain. He clutches the glass in his hand and walks unsteadily into the living room, kicking off his shoes and turning lights off as he goes. One of the cordless phones is on an end table. He scrutinizes it as he drops onto the couch. He picks up the handset. He sets it down. He abandons his glass to the end table. He studies the phone some more. He's lost her already; her husband's coming home in three days, so what difference does it make? He picks up the handset and calls her.

"Lily. Hey. It's Danny. Where are you? Oh yeah, you're having dinner at Joan's, right, I remember. Just got back from my date with Lauren, you wanted to know how it went. Well, it was a total fucking disaster." He tries to laugh, but there's nothing humorous in what happened. "Why did you lie to me? Why did you tell me to do it?" His voice is low and pleading. "Oh man. I'm sorry. I must be drunk. Forget I said that—none of this is your fault. Ah, fuck. Sorry. I *am* drunk. Listen, call me when you get home? No, you know, don't. Don't call me. Ignore this. I'll be fine. Don't call, really. I'll call you tomorrow. Right. Okay. Good night."

His head falls back on the cushion and he stares up at the ceiling in a daze. Every one of his nerve endings is jumping and throbbing. The slug of vodka has made his head feel like lead but hasn't helped to dull him after all. He groans and fumbles at the buttons of his shirt with his left hand. When the sound and his own breath come back at him he realizes he's still holding his phone, the connection is still open, and he's groaned out her name.

Lily doesn't get home from Joan and Sidney's until after eleven. She pulls up to the garage door but doesn't hit the button beneath the rearview mirror to open it. She hits the DISK 1 button on her CD player instead, and sits in the car listening to the music and thinking about Danny, and a three-day-a-week job at The Doorway. She should be thinking about Paul, about her love for him that she's been afraid to feel and afraid to lose, but what's the point of it? Thinking about him is a dead end. It won't soothe her anger or subdue her fears. It only makes him seem larger and her smaller and the impasse between them unresolvable. For the next three days, until he gets home and she has no choice, she doesn't want to think about him at all. She wants to wallow in Danny.

It's Danny she's been thinking about all night. And his date with Lauren. She purposely didn't take her cell phone with her to the Trachtenbergs. If Danny called she couldn't talk to him and if he didn't call by ten she'd be imagining him in bed with Lauren, which she is anyway, which is why she's putting off going into the house and checking her phone for messages. She sits there until the CD ends.

He called at 9:47. It's nearly midnight now. Lily listens to Danny's message and when it's over, after she hears him breathe out her name, she breathes out his and dissolves in tears. He sounds so awful. And she feels so guilty. She did lie to him. It was a terrible mistake for him to go out with someone he didn't want to be with. And no matter what he said, Lauren would still believe that Danny might like her. Lily knew it, she knew what would happen, and still she lied. Now he's more convinced than ever that he will only harm himself and anyone he attempts to get close to. If she'd said what she knew to be true—*You don't want her. You want me. And I want you. Don't go out with her. Wait. Wait for this to happen again, but with a woman who is free to love you*—she might at least have spared him that. He should be angry with her. He should have yelled at her. But he's not angry, and he didn't yell. That's not the way he asks for help.

Lily doesn't call him. She just gets in the car. As she drives, she tells herself that she can't leave him alone to suffer like that. He needs someone with him and it has to be her. He didn't call anyone else, she's sure of it. No one else knows. When she attains the bottom of Kensington Ridge Road and is about to turn north, it flits through her head that he won't be home, that he's gone to the Pollacks, where Caleb is. But somehow she knows he hasn't. She can feel his distress hunting for her across the ten miles that separate their houses. He's home, alone, hoping she'll come.

It's mid-September and already the imminence of autumn is in the air. The summer is over. The bumblebee mailbox shines in the light of a harvest moon riding high in the black sky. Lily inches down Danny's driveway, slow and quiet. The musty smell of dry leaves and decaying flowers seeps into the car through her open window. The CD is playing, the volume turned down low. It's midnight and Lily is spellbound. She is wandering into the woods, into the dead center of the trap that she and Danny have set for themselves. She pulls into the clearing, cuts the engine, and all is silence save for the ticking of her car as it cools, the whoosh of the breeze in the treetops, the intermittent chirping of crickets, the far-off rush of water. The car's automatic headlights shut off and all is darkness, save for the moonlight. No sound or light comes from the house.

Lily eases out of the car. She walks the way she drove, delicately, so as not to be observed or heard. She's here, she wants to be here, she needs to be here, but the closer she comes to the object of her desire, the harder she tries to go unnoticed by it. Her Pyrrhic caution reflects an internal disparity so entrenched in her that it isn't until she is immobilized by it, frozen on his porch, that she feels it tearing at her the way it has torn at her all her life. As much as she has ever given of herself, and as much as she believes she has ever taken, the amount ungiven and untaken remains the victor. Danny will let her give and let her take everything. She doesn't love or desire him physically any more than she does, or ever did, Paul, and yet she's never wanted to be with anyone as much as she wants to be with Danny. Lily has never met anyone like Danny before. She knows she never will again. He is her last chance at fearlessness.

His unlocked front door is straight ahead of her and the living room windows are ten feet to her right. There are no signs to tell her in which direction to move. She looks at the door and can't bring herself to walk through it. She tiptoes the ten feet and peers into the living room. Moonlight is coursing silver through the clerestory windows and in its eerie illumination she sees Danny asleep on the couch. His head is turned toward the windows. One leg is bent and rests against the couch back. One arm hangs down to the floor; his fingers touch the spine of an upended book. He's barefoot. His dark shirt is unbuttoned and where it's fallen open, his light skin gleams. A glass, half full of clear liquid, is on the end table, beside the telephone.

Lily is transfixed by the sight of him. She's had a sip now of what he feels like, what he smells like, what she feels when she looks into his eyes. As she peers in at him, she is deluged by her longing for it all, for everything she's imagined since the first time she saw him. On shaking legs, she moves sideways away from the windows until she is standing again at his door. She reaches for the knob . . . *and lets herself into his house. She stands quietly in the space between the couch and the coffee table, looking down at him, and then she lowers herself to her knees. As she does, and just as her eyes settle on his face, his eyes open, soberly and calmly, as if he hadn't been asleep at all but was just lying there patiently all night, waiting for her. His eyes are like the moonlight, deep and clear; they reveal everything that lies beneath and she instantly descends into him. He breathes out her name, Lily, smiles sadly, and raises a slow hand. He strokes her face with the backs of his fingers. Her hand falls onto his stomach and slides upward. She pushes aside his shirt. She brings her mouth to the shallow indentation below his breastbone and his skin is smooth and taut on her lips. Her hand continues sliding on him until it is buried in his hair and his hair is like silk. Like cool pale silk, just as she knew it would be. . . .*

Lily lifts her hand from the doorknob and staggers down the steps and to her car. She's crying. She plows down the driveway, nearly hits a tree, swerves out onto the road, nearly hits the bumblebee mailbox. A quarter mile on, weeping too hard to drive, she pulls off the road and stops the car alongside a white picket fence.

*   *   *

Her crying works its way into his brain and wakes him, like the sound of Caleb crying during the night. Danny is instantly alert and sober. He hears a car spinning away down the gravel drive. He swings his legs off the couch, sprints out of the house. The scent of citrus and spice, Lily's scent, permeates the air beneath the roof of his porch. The perfumed air is chilly in his nose as he breathes her in, the wood at his feet is damp. He shivers but not from the cold. He trembles from within, from the raging battle between the murky layers of his guilt and the healing purity of his desire. It's a battle neither side can win. For what seems an eternity, he hangs there, mired in the enigma of how something he knows and believes to be wrong can be so right and so necessary. The seconds pass. They stretch into a mockingly endless moment, horribly similar to the stalled bubble of time in which he's been held captive. He goes inside for the phone, comes back out onto the porch, and calls her.

She picks up the call, but she doesn't say anything. Danny hears the sounds of her weeping, music, the thrum of her car engine, but not the hum of tires on the newly paved road. She has stopped somewhere nearby, unable to drive.

"Come back. Turn around and come back."

Lily can barely talk. "I can't. We can't do this."

"Why can't we?"

"Danny . . ."

"Oh, fuck it. For once in our lives, let's be selfish. We're both so goddamned screwed anyway. Lily, I need you, and you know you can have whatever you need from me. Just for tonight. That's all I'm asking for. Not forever. Just for tonight."

The barking of a dog echoes distantly through the phone

line. Her sobs have quieted. He can hear the music: strings, a poignant guitar, an anguished male voice.

"Where are you?" He glances in the direction of the road.

"I think I'm in front of your family's old house."

He smiles to himself. "You didn't get too far."

She laughs through her tears, pathetically. "No."

"Lily. Turn around. Please. Come back. Just for tonight. Come back here to me. Please, please, please."

Please, please, please. Lily can't answer him. She can't think, all is chaos inside her head. This isn't a decision she is capable of making and yet she has to make it. She presses her palms over her eyes and lets her head fall against the steering wheel. *Hide me, won't you hold my life. Let me have this time. Lie here, while I close my eyes. Hold me through this night.* The music she has been gulping neat all summer pervades her senses. The words fly straight to her heart and the voice she hears is Danny's; then the words surge into her throat and her voice fuses with his. The chaos resolves to calm. She lifts her head and puts the car in gear.

Danny hears her car move. His heart stutters. There comes the crunch of tires at the entrance to his drive and lights slicing through the woods. He turns off the phone.

He waits for her at the bottom of the steps and she comes to him, empty-handed. She leaves her purse, her keys, in the car; everything she has is safe here. She stands in front of him, so near he can feel the warmth of her labored breath like a caress on his face. He doesn't touch her; he is leaving it to her to take the final step. So they'll both be sure this is what she truly wants. Her mouth is struggling to form a smile, just as it was the first time they spoke, and he wants to kiss her, wants it so badly his bones ache, but he doesn't move. They stand as if in a reverie, joined at the eyes. Lily's are boundless as the dark sky. Danny stares into them, wills her to surrender herself to him. Her hand floats up from her side and settles lightly on his bare chest. She rises up on her toes and kisses him. Danny's entire body stiffens and his breath stops; Lily ends the kiss and rests her forehead against his. He instantly relaxes and brings a hand to her face, brushes the backs of his fingers across her cheek. She turns her head and presses her lips to his hand. Danny wraps his arms around her back. Lily snakes her arms around his neck. There's no clumsiness, no desperation. This time they bring their bodies together slowly, deliberately, inch by inch, and they stay, her mouth at his ear and his at the side of her neck, and they hold each other, closer and closer until their cores meld into each other and stillness is no longer possible.

Danny's lips sweep along Lily's neck and she lifts her head upward to offer her throat to him. He kisses the vulnerable hollow at its base, tastes it with his tongue, the citrus-spice taste of her on the soft skin. *He would take her in so slowly, in small loving pieces, and she would fill him to bursting.* His lips glide along her jaw and he tastes the skin and the bone there; he finds her ear and tastes that, too. A soft scream escapes her. Her strength deserts her and she sags against him. His arms swiftly tighten around her. He wants to devour her, but not quickly. He pulls away, takes her by the hand, and leads her inside.

*   *   *

The moon's ambient light reflecting off the bedroom's pale walls is all the light they need. Lily's hands run over Danny's skin as she undresses him, run like silver water poured from the bowl of the moon itself. She stares into Danny's eyes, bottomless as the ocean, as she slides his shirt off his shoulders. It falls to the floor. Her hands travel avidly down the length of his arms and over his chest and stomach and sides. She bends and lays her mouth on the shallow indentation beneath his breastbone, on the pale firm skin over the hard ribs protecting his tender, broken heart. With excruciating slowness, Lily kisses her way down his body, pressing her lips into one solid-soft spot after another as she descends along the line of fine gold hair that trails down his belly and disappears into the thick of his pubic hair. She feels his hands come to rest on her head as she kneels and unzips his pants, pulls them and his briefs over his hips and down to the floor. He steps out of them, kicks them away. The delicious smell of his sweat and his sex rises to meet her. She explores him without restraint; she's been waiting forever to know the swells and dips of his muscles, the texture of his skin, the racing of his blood. She touches and then licks the tip of his erect penis, takes him fully into her mouth and tastes him. She's been waiting forever to taste him. She straightens and stands before him, pushes her fingers into his hair, his cool silky hair of indescribable color. She grasps his head with her hands and his mouth with her mouth. Lily feels Danny's tongue enter her mouth and she is inundated by the blinding sensation of him coming into her, everywhere. She pulls away and, like a ballerina, lifts her arms up high and presents herself to him.

Feelings that have lain dormant rush through Danny like a rising tide. They rush into his hands as he pulls Lily's sweater over her head and his fingers graze the sides of her breasts. They rush into his lips as he presses them into the swell above the lace of her bra. He pitches the sweater to the floor and it falls atop his pants. Lily sways backward and Danny catches her with an arm around her waist. He takes the lacy fabric of her bra in his teeth and draws it down from her breast. His lips find her nipple and the soft bud instantly hardens in his mouth. He unbuttons her pants, caresses her, feels the slick, secret heart of her blossom like a flower at his touch. He dips his finger into her, brings his finger to his mouth. She tastes of cinnamon. Bittersweet. Lily's legs give out. Danny dances her to the bed, gently lays her down. When they are both fully naked, he lays his quaking body down beside her.

He doesn't want to devour her too quickly, but this time at least he has no choice. There's been a maelstrom swirling and growing within them both, pulling them together, and it drives them rapidly to the brink, to an unpostponable moment of union. He is already deep into her eyes as he starts to enter her but a violent spasm rocks him, stops him. He's trembling uncontrollably from the inner agony of his need to let himself love her and his fear of doing it. Lily holds him closer, lifts her hips a little higher. She cranes up off the pillow and kisses him at the sides of his eyes, one then the other. She kisses his lips and whispers into his mouth, "It's all right, Danny. It doesn't mean you love her any less."

Danny searches Lily's eyes for the truth of her words. She is here, loving him, but it doesn't mean she loves Paul any less. He knows Paul is here with her, just as Tara is here with him. They're in the corners of the room, hiding in the shadows, as sad and frightened as he and Lily. He exhales his held breath and with one long, slow, fateful push he melts into her. They begin to move together. They move in perfect harmony, wonderful and terrible all at once because they have both known what it is to move so perfectly with someone before. Lily comes, and Danny fears he might blow apart when he feels her contract around him. But he can't hold himself back, despite the fear. He opens his mouth to her, and his ears and his eyes, and he lets go. With a sound that hasn't emerged from him in more than a year, Danny lets himself blow apart. As he explodes into the heat of Lily's body, the heavy door of his private prison finally swings open. The release from his loins expands to fill his gut and his chest. Danny feels a stab, like a swift tear in the furiously beating muscle of his heart, and his heart releases. The release continues, traveling ever upward, through his chest and throat, until it reaches his eyes and becomes a flood he can't contain. Convulsive sobs rip from his throat. A deluge of tears runs onto Lily's neck and throat.

Danny's tears fall and sizzle on Lily's electrified skin, then vanish into the layer of sweat that covers her. She lies beneath him, her limbs locked around him. She whispers again into his ear. "You're going to be all right, Danny. We're both going to be all right." She kisses his face, his soft beard; she kisses his tears. He begins to withdraw from her but she won't let him go. She gasps out "No!" and clutches him with her legs. He pushes back into her and stays there while he cries. She holds him close inside her, as she holds him close to her. She caresses his head as though he were a sobbing child, over and over, with soft languid strokes.

The stroking motions of her own hands and the rhythmic sound of Danny's heaving breath at her ear are hypnotic and all at once Lily is floating above the bed, looking down at a beautiful dark-haired woman succoring a beautiful light-haired man. The man is stronger, and he has power over the woman but no more than she has over him. She has the power to heal him. She's the only one who can. A shadow abiding in the corner rises and joins her in the air above the bed. It's as frightened and damaged as Danny and it needs her to heal it. The shadow begins to coalesce into the shape of a man but before it can, Lily drops back onto the bed, back into her body. Danny is no longer inside her; she's empty again. While she dwelled in the air he grew limp and slipped out. He's stopped crying. He has a hand on her mound and his nose and mouth are in her hair. She's still stroking his head. She feels him trickling out of her, cold wetness between her legs.

"Danny, I have to get up for a minute. I have to go to the bathroom."

Danny's hand presses lightly into her belly. "Really?" He raises his head and smiles dopily.

"Danny!" She has to get up. She can't lie there with his wasted semen on her thighs.

"Okay." He rolls halfway off her. "Don't be long."

Lily wriggles out from under him. She climbs off the bed and crosses to the bathroom. She doesn't use the toilet, she doesn't need to, but she flushes so that Danny will think she has. She runs warm water in the sink to wash him away, but she can't bring herself to do it. Wasted or not, she can't wash him away. She turns off the faucet. As she emerges from the bathroom, Danny rises and stands by the side of the bed. She walks toward him and while she is still too far away for him to touch, he holds out his arms for her. In the imperfect light Lily sees Danny's gaze fixed on her face and in his eyes is the same stark look that filled them the first time he ever looked at her. She steps into his arms and he hugs her to him in a crushing embrace, holds her head against his chest. The pounding of Danny's heart becomes a steady throb inside Lily. She falls with him back onto the bed.

The moon has gone and the night's blackness will soon cede to the coming of dawn. They are both utterly spent. Danny molds himself to Lily's back and she nestles into him. His leg falls onto her hip. She cants herself back toward him, threads her legs through his. She pushes her buttocks into his damp groin. His arm comes around her breast; his hand encircles her wrist and holds it. She stretches up her other arm and finds his hand above her head and she twines her fingers through his. They curl together, two exhausted, haunted creatures who have found temporary haven with each other, and they sleep.

Danny wakes to a room filled to all four corners with thick sunlight. The angle and quality of the light tells him that it's late morning, that he has slept for six or seven hours. Without moving. He is still on his right side, pressed into Lily's back. His legs are still tangled with hers, his arm is over her breasts, his hand is at her wrist. His head is still resting on his outstretched right arm. Lily's hand is holding his, up above their heads, but he can't feel it. His arm has gone to sleep, from shoulder to fingertips. He has slept long hours without moving.

Just before he fell asleep, Danny heard the antique wall clock in the living room slowly chime five times and his fading consciousness marked it: twelve months, twenty-nine days, six hours, and twenty-eight minutes from the moment she died until the moment he truly believed that he could live on in a world that doesn't have her in it. Gratitude and relief unfurl inside him and he presses closer to Lily, moves to sink his lips into the warm crook of her neck. He hardens; his leg and arm tense around her. He wants to make love to her again. He wants to make love to her all day, slow soulful love, in the light, where he can see her, and until the light fades and he is with her again in the dark. But before his lips touch her skin, he catches himself. He forces his muscles to relax and he shifts minutely away from her. She doesn't belong to him.

His small movements have woken her. She turns sleepily toward him until she is on her back. Now his leg stretches and holds her across her thighs and his hand rests on her breast. His erection is trapped against her hip. Her breast is hot and full in his palm. They lie frozen, staring into each other's eyes, breathing fast. Danny can't stop himself; he lowers his head to kiss her. She rises to him. This is the moment he knew would come. There is so much here, a mutual desire far more unquenchable than lust and a rare emotional intimacy, more than enough to push them into a relationship that is precisely what, last night, they swore to themselves and to each other they would never allow to happen. There is so much here but not enough to erase the ten years' difference that lies between them, Lily's infertility, and Danny's passion for children. Never enough to erase her love for the man she married. Danny pulls his head back and with a moan Lily falls away from him. He lifts his leg and his hand. When their bodies separate, the air that rushes to fill the space is cold despite the warmth of the sun-drenched room.

"I'm going to make some coffee. Take your time getting up."

With some difficulty, Danny pulls a pair of loose cotton drawstring pants over himself and goes into the kitchen. The digital clock on the microwave reads 11:17. He turns on the faucet and when the water runs icy cold he splashes his face repeatedly until the protrusion of his prick inside his pants subsides. He fills the coffeepot. When he hears Lily in the bathroom, he goes back into the bedroom, gathers their clothes from the floor. He uses the bathroom in the hall, then waits for her in the kitchen.

Lily sees her clothes, placed neatly on the bed, as soon as she emerges from the bathroom. Danny's have been tossed on top of his dresser. She will dress and leave this room, there is nothing else possible to do. But for a second she closes her eyes and gives herself permission to want, one last time, what she can't ever have. *Just for tonight,* they'd said, and now the night is over. She hears him in the kitchen. She opens her eyes and looks down at her pants and sweater, her underwear. The night is over but she's not finished. There is still the one thing she didn't do. She didn't ask, out loud and unafraid, for what she wants. Danny begged her, and she came to him because giving him what he asked for, being selfish with him, was what she wanted, too. But she didn't ask. Her gaze travels to the jumbled pile of his clothing.

Lily halts at the entry to the kitchen. Danny is turned away from her, taking mugs from the cabinet above the sink, spoons from the drawer. She watches the play of his muscles as he moves. His pants ride low on his narrow hips and her eyes trace a path from his bent neck to below the small of his back, down the hard bone line of his spine, to the dimples on either side just above the tight swell of his buttocks, to where his flesh disappears beneath the thin cotton. Drawn like a moth to a flame, she takes a step into the room. He hears her and turns. The look on his face as she glides toward him wearing nothing but his black shirt, unbuttoned and hanging to the middle of her thighs, makes her weak.

"Lily . . ."

She takes his hand and guides it beneath his shirt. "One more time. I want to make love to you one more time. In the daylight, so I can see you."

"Lily." His choked voice holds a warning, but his hand rises to her breast.

Lily hears his warning. There is fear in her, too, of them taking any more from each other than they already have. There is no history here and no future. All they have is this moment they've created, and the longer they keep it alive, the harder it will be to kill it. But still, she has to finish what she started. "You asked me last night. Now I'm asking you. Please." They both smile faintly, remembering his plea. "Please."

She puts a hand to the back of his neck and draws him down to her. As they kiss, she reaches for the loop of cotton that holds his pants closed and she pulls at it. The pants fall open and she has him in her hand, his cock rapidly stiffening and his balls growing heavy with his seed, the seed that made Caleb. He left enough in her last night to produce the houseful of children he wants, but she won't ever produce a child with anyone; her child exists forever only in her dreams. She can't retreat anymore. There's a greater purpose to her being here than having her bad boy at last. She's here to break down the wall of sorrow that has formed around her heart.

"Make love to me like you want to make a baby with me." Her voice is just loud enough to travel the distance from her mouth to his ears. Tears spill from her eyes. "Make me feel it." She kisses him. "I know you can."

This is what he promised: that she could take from him whatever she needed, just as she let him take from her last night. She knows he understands what she is asking, why the love they've already made wasn't enough. She can see his answer in his eyes. As intimately as they plumbed each other, they weren't alone. The shadows never left the room. Danny needs to make love to Lily, not as a substitute for Tara but as though *she* is the one he wants to live and die with. Lily needs to be made love to by a man who isn't afraid to lay his soul bare to her so that she can finally give hers away. They both need to risk being pulverized again, and survive, or the fear will never go away. Lily winds her legs around his hips as Danny lifts her off her feet and carries her to the bedroom.

In the daylight there are no shadowed corners where ghosts can lurk. Lily rises and falls with him, again and again, and in time, together, they find what they need most to find: a place alone in a universe where there is nothing that can hurt them and where everything they want is there before them. But at the end, when Lily relinquishes herself to him, body and soul, and her mind flies free, she is momentarily invaded by a sensation of being Tara. A second later Danny comes and as Lily feels his hot fluid shoot into her she screams, a huge roaring shattering scream. She is lying where Tara once lay, being loved by the man who had loved her, knowing the brutal power of the happiness that Tara must have felt, to have this man to love, to have his love, to share a life with him, to have his child. Lily imagines having all that and she disintegrates into wild weeping.

Danny gathers her into his arms. He pulls them both up, leans his back against the headboard, and cradles her and rocks her as all of her losses and disappointments and despair for her squandered years come gushing out.

*   *   *

When Lily comes back to herself, she is alone in Danny's bed. The light seems unchanged; she hasn't been unconscious for very long. Long enough, though, for Danny to have made coffee. There is a steaming mug waiting for her on the night table. She dresses and goes into the kitchen. Danny is at the counter, slicing bread. There is butter and strawberry jam on the table. Lily sets her mug down. She comes up behind him and puts her arms around him, rests herself against his back. She stays there, feeling the minute shiftings of his skin and flesh. After several moments, she moves away.

"Do you want something to eat?" He talks without lifting his head.

"I can't stay, Danny. I have to go home. I can't stay here any longer."

Danny stops what he's doing. He looks down at his hands, one holding a knife, the other a loaf of bread. He lets them both go, as though they've suddenly become objects whose use he doesn't comprehend.

They stand by her car, as they have done too often over too short and intense a period of time, immersed in each other's eyes. Their private reckonings of what they each have done, to the other, to themselves, flicker in shades of blue and brown. Although the words are right there in their mouths, wholly formed and poised behind their teeth, neither one says *I love you*.

"Call me when you can."

"I will. It may be a while, but I will. We're not going to lose each other, you, me, and Caleb," she says fervently, "I promise."

She reaches up to touch his face but he recoils from her approaching open palm. He grabs her hand in midair and pulls her to him, almost violently. They clasp and cling to each other, then both let go at once.

30

LILY LOADS THE PERISHABLE FOOD into two cooler bags and puts them by the front door. She runs upstairs and packs the few pieces of clothing she wants to take back into the city into a tote bag and lays Blinkie Floyd on top. The clothes she's wearing have to stay here. She takes them off, folds them, bundles them together, smells them, and puts them away on a shelf in her closet. There's nothing she wants from the bathroom, but she goes in there, shuts the door, and turns on the lights. She stands before the mirrored wall and looks at herself. She looks into her moist eyes and sees Danny's eyes. She touches her lips, her hair, her breasts, her belly, between her legs, and feels Danny's hands. She inhales and tastes Danny's breath. She exhales. His shaky breath mists the reflection of her face. She turns off the lights and closes her eyes and in her private darkness she inhales again and holds him in her mouth, in her lungs, until he dissolves into her blood and streams through her veins. She opens the door.

She's calm. Paul's toothbrush is in the cup on the sink, his clothes are in his closet just outside, but Lily feels no guilt or regret. Guilt will come, she knows that. The first time Paul looks at her with his love softening the hard eyes he lives behind, she will want to die from guilt. But she will never feel regret. She refuses. She will not be sorry for having given herself the gift of Danny's love. And she will never regret having given him hers. She remembers what Rick said to her. She made her choice. She took what she needed and she won't judge herself for having done it.

It's turning cold and grey outside. She dresses in warmer clothes and goes downstairs, back into the kitchen to shut off the lights and retrieve her purse. As she's walking out of the room, the telephone rings. She stands still and listens as Paul leaves his message: "Hi. I just wanted to let you know that I'm coming home tomorrow night instead of Monday. A carton full of papers that aren't supposed to exist arrived at the office today. It looks like we've cracked the case. Anyway. That's not important. My flight gets in a little after ten. . . . Lily. Please. Be there when I get home. I'll leave this message on your cell, just in case."

A moment later her cell rings. She can't not answer it; she has to start tearing down the wall, one small piece at a time. Her heart is in her throat as she thumbs on the phone.

"Hi, Paul."

"Lily! I didn't expect to get you. I . . ."

She cuts him off. "Paul, I'm sorry. I don't mean to be abrupt. I don't, really, but I can't talk now, I'm running out the door. I heard your message. That's great news about the case. And yes, I'll be there when you get home."

There's silence, and then Paul says, with the same careful voice he used when they spoke Wednesday night, "Okay. I guess that's all I need to hear. I'll see you tomorrow night."

She isn't lying. She is running out the door. Of course she

will be there when Paul gets home tomorrow night, there's no question of that. But she has to leave Stone Creek today, now. There is another flight coming in and she has to be there for that one, too. She has to be there when it lands. It's coming from San Antonio and it's due at LaGuardia at 5:07 this afternoon. It's bringing Rick and Alan and Sophie home. Even if from time to time it kills her, and she knows it will, Lily has to at least try to be there for her girl.

At three thirty, Danny finally musters the mental stamina to get up off the porch. The sun went in while he and Lily were making love for the last time. An unseasonable cold front has swooped down from Canada and the air temperature has dropped fifteen degrees. He has been sitting there for more than an hour, insensible, wearing nothing but the light cotton pants. Once on his feet, he feels the cold and is possessed by a manic energy. He trots into the bedroom and changes into sweatpants and a T-shirt, a sweatshirt, sneakers. He's hopping and tying his laces as he hurries out the kitchen doors.

Danny runs at a punishing clip, weaving a private, torturous path through the woods on the far side of the creek, through acres of untouched hilly forest that he's known since childhood. Within minutes, he is generating so much body heat that, without slowing his pace, he tears off his sweatshirt and ties it around his waist. His panting breath tails him, an audible misty contrail. His flying feet kick up brown and yellow clouds of fallen leaves. Vines adhere to his ankles; skinny, twiglike branches of half-denuded shrubs grab for his face but he rips past them all, oblivious and uncatchable. Sweat pours from him, soaks through his T-shirt.

An hour later he has found his way back to the creek where it flows behind his house. Dragonflies hover and dart over the surface; tadpoles squirm in the shallows near the banks. The sound of Danny's breath is the sole hint of human presence. He could be the only human being on earth; the first, or the last. Except that she is with him here, always. He sees her in the purling waters of the pool where they loved and played. Frantically, he strips off his clothes and plunges in up to his neck. The cold mountain water shocks his overheated body and bewitched mind. He shouts and thrashes and crashes to earth.

He leaves his clothes on the ground and runs naked and dripping to the house. He takes the quilt from the living room and wraps himself in it. He takes Tara's journal from his night table. He goes outside and huddles on the floor of the porch, against the west wall of the house.

My love,

A week ago I found a lump in my breast. I didn't tell you. I don't know why. I've never kept anything from you. Even my secret intention to get pregnant was no secret. I knew I could rely on you to hear my body tell you what I couldn't put into words. You knew the feel of me so well. You still do, but you couldn't have felt this tiny terrifying pellet, not with the fingers you use when you love me. Today I learned that it's nothing, a cyst, and I still haven't told you. Even with everything you know about the sweetly obsessive nature of my love for you, the things that went through my head these past days are too private for me to say aloud.

You don't believe in God or Heaven, Danny, but you know that I'm not as sure as you. I was raised in a world of faith and there are times when the need for there to be something beyond what we know is just too strong for me to deny. Since the day I first saw you and needed to believe that I would be with you for my life, I have wondered how, if not for His guidance, I could have known when I was only ten years old that you were the love of my life and I was yours. How I could have known that you would be there when I came for you.

Today, in the doctor's waiting room, I needed to believe that there was a power somewhere watching over us. I told myself that it couldn't be cancer, that God wouldn't give us this to deal with so soon, and that certainly He wouldn't let me die. But the waiting was so horrible, and you weren't there, and I almost lost my faith. No matter how unprepared I was, I could get sick, I could die. Illness and death didn't frighten me. What frightened me was that if I died, and there was nothing awaiting us after death, I would lose you. And I can't lose you. So in that needy moment, I chose to believe and I made a pact with God: that he could take me, but only if He would let me love and cherish you forever, haunt you and keep you.

I'll guess I'll have to wait to find out whether He planned to live up to His end of the bargain. But I don't want to wait a day longer to have another baby with you. Tonight, after we put Caleb to bed, I'm going to throw away my pills, and I'm going to make love to you like never before. And I'm finally going to keep this diary the way I meant to when I started it after Caleb was born. I'm going to fill it, volumes and volumes, and one day, when we're old and rocking on the porch and it doesn't matter anymore if you discover that you've been living with a crazy woman all these years, I'm going to give it to you.

I hear your truck in the driveway. I hope I can look at you without crying.

There's nothing more. The rest of the pages are blank. Danny's conscious mind is blank, but he removes her Dupont pen from the leather loop and starts to write. He has never been a writer, was never even much of a talker until Tara pulled his voice from him, but he writes in a blur as words course through him, uncensored words that pour out of him like blood onto the paper.

You made me swear that I'd never leave you, so how could you leave me after what you did to me? Tell me how to forgive you. Tell me you forgive me, because I'm so angry with you I can't bear it. I'm so angry sometimes I imagine that if you suddenly appeared in front of me I would put my hands around your throat and choke the life out of you.

Your damned sometimes God let you die after all. But He honored your pact. You haunt me. But you have to stop now. Last night, for the first time, I made love to a woman in the bed I shared with you. It's so hard to tell you this, but I have to. We both have to accept it, that I'm going to love someone else someday. I won't love Lily. There is no right time possible with her. I want to be with someone who won't come to me from a place of ruin and regret. It's enough that I'll be coming to someone from the terrible place I've been. But Lily helped me see a path through the wreckage you left behind. For the first time since I lost you, I can imagine feeling love again. Not the same love I felt for you. You know that. You always knew that and you always will. I will never love anyone the way I loved you and you will never lose me. You owned me and I will never let anyone do that to me again. I don't want it. If not with you, I don't want it. I just want peace.

I will love you until the day I die and every day I will hope that I'm wrong and you're right and that I will get to love you again in the afterlife or in another life. If there is a Heaven, I know what ours will be. To exist for eternity in that night when you came to my house and woke me with my name on your lips. The night we made Caleb.

The pen slides off the page and his hand falls to the floor, the pen gripped in his fingers so tightly the metal clip gouges his palm. He slowly lets his head come to rest on the rough cedar wall of the house. The sun has reappeared below a bank of clouds on its way to the horizon. Danny closes his eyes to it, squeezes them shut until there is nothing but a shimmering, incandescent wash of red behind his lids, and he cries. He can't believe it; the well of his tears must surely have been pumped dry last night. But as the tears continue to come he accepts what he has known all along to be true, that this pain is not finite. There is no moment awaiting him in a kind future when he will be done with it. It is incurable, and it will rack him again and again through the rest of his days.

When he opens his eyes, the sun is gone, slipped down behind the trees. He uses an edge of the damp quilt to wipe the wet from his eyes and nose. He closes the book without reading what he's written and holds it against his chest, his arms folded across the pliant leather. It took a long time, and it's not going to close the wound, but he's finally done it. He's said good-bye.

31

LESTER DOESN'T FEEL WELL after church, so he and Eve go home and Eve gives him aspirin and makes him some tea and toast. She puts up a pot of chicken soup for their dinner. She sits with Lester in the den until he dozes off, then she has a light lunch and goes to the cemetery by herself. One of the grounds-keepers is raking leaves just inside the entry gate as she drives in. He waves and smiles. They all know her. She makes it a point to talk to them whenever she sees them, these respectful, aging gentlemen who tend to the final resting place of their neighbors' loved ones with such solicitous care.

"Hello, Frank. How are you today, with this unexpected cold?"

"Hello, Mrs. Jamison. A little achy, but this cold feels mighty good after that August we had. You meeting your son-in-law? That why you weren't here earlier?"

"Excuse me?"

"Your son-in-law. Him and your grandson are here. Haven't seen them in some time. Almost didn't recognize Danny without his beard. He said he shaved it just this morning."

"Really. Well, thank you for warning me."

Eve crawls along the mazelike lanes until she sees the Volvo up ahead. Tara's grave is a peaceful distance in from the narrow road. Eve parks half a cemetery block from the Volvo, well off the road so her car is obscured by a tree. She gets out and walks into the field of gravesites on a path parallel to the one that leads to Tara's, but a good thirty feet behind. She stops before she is directly behind Tara's grave and positions herself so that she can see Daniel and Caleb.

They are sitting on the stone bench. Caleb is on Daniel's lap. They are talking. Eve can't hear what they are saying, but from their gestures and the movements of their heads she knows that they are talking about Tara. Daniel's wife, Caleb's mother. Her daughter. Caleb raises his head to Daniel and cocks it at a certain angle. He has asked a question. Daniel says something, touches Caleb over his heart, then on his forehead. Then he touches himself over his own heart, and then on his forehead. *Where is she, Daddy?* Caleb asked, and Daniel touched their hearts and their heads and answered, *This is where Mommy is. This is where she'll always be.* If nothing else, Eve knows Daniel would never point to her grave and say, *This is where she is.* He would never point to the sky and say, *That is where she is.* And he would never, ever, believe or say to his son, *She's nowhere.*

She might not have recognized Daniel at first. He does look different. Younger and softer. He looks boyish, with his worn jeans and his spare body, his disheveled hair and new, smooth cheeks. Caleb lays his head against Daniel's chest and Daniel lays his new, smooth cheek on Caleb's hair. Eve stands stock-still and watches them. If she had been allowed to stand somewhere and watch Tara lay her head on Terry's chest, and Terry rest his smooth cheek on Tara's hair, who would Eve Foster have become? A million times she has asked herself, and a million times found no answer. Eve presses a hand to her heart and fights down her tears. She has been such a fool. She has no right to cry for herself. After a short while, Daniel and Caleb leave. Before they go, they brush the fallen leaves off the grave with their hands, and Caleb places a bunch of wine-red chrysanthemums on top of the headstone.

When the Volvo is out of sight, Eve takes her place on the bench, to tell Tara, once more, the story that no one has ever heard.

32

Lily COMES OFF THE COUCH to the scratch of Paul's key at the apartment door. The reverberations of his footsteps are in the marble-floored entryway, then on the polished parqueted floor of the hall. He's not even in the room, but she's flinching inside at the sight of him. Her eyes begin to hurt. He appears at the edge of the living room and their eyes meet for a mute second.

"Let me just go put my stuff in the bedroom."

Paul glances at her and walks on. There was no emotion in her eyes. She didn't move to greet him. He hoists his bags onto the bed, finds his kit bag, and takes it into the bathroom. He flushes the remaining pills down the toilet, tosses the little amber vials into the trash basket. He washes his face and drags his wet hands through his hair. He has already decided what to do. He's going to cut to the chase and ask the final question, because if the answer is yes, there won't be anything else either of them will need to say.

Lily is nailed to the floor in front of the sofa. She is nearly senseless with dread. What if her love for him has died? What if what she did with Danny hasn't given her the courage to love Paul better, to insist that he love her better, but instead opened her eyes to the ruins of a love she had thought indestructible?

She hears the thump of his suitcase on the mattress, the un-zipping of the heavy zipper, then water running in his bathroom. She is standing where he left her when Paul reappears and halts a small distance away, as if submitting himself for her inspection. She looks at him and this time she sees him. A thick lock of damp black hair cascades over one side of his forehead. His white shirt is unbuttoned at the throat, the sleeves are rolled up over his forearms. His tan has faded a little but the color of his skin is rich and warm. His lean swimmer's body seems broader through the shoulders and slimmer at the hips, his fiery dark eyes set a little more deeply above his angular cheekbones than she remembers. There's no fire in his eyes now. They are dimmed and still. She sees him, waiting for her down in those secret places, and the fear that she doesn't love him takes flight.

He gives her a defeated smile and says, "So, are we finished? You hate me now?"

"I don't hate you."

His smile turns wry. "It's been hard to tell. You didn't answer the first part of the question." He's oddly calm.

"I don't know the answer." Nine years before, she was more afraid to not let herself love him than to risk loving him. But love isn't always enough. It wasn't enough for her and Rick, it wasn't enough for Tara and Danny. It wouldn't be enough for her and Danny. How can she know if it will be enough for her and Paul, to put things right between them?

"What does that mean?" Paul's odd calm tatters. Terror swamps him, makes his body rigid and his clamped-down voice gruff. "Either you want to be married to me or you don't."

The familiar shift to menace in his posture and tone spurs Lily's habitual response. She takes an involuntary step away from him and cowers inside. She fights for a spot in her head where her thoughts can remain clear, and she forces herself to look him in the eye. "I want to be married to you, Paul, but we can't go on the way we've been."

"No. I know. I know." The roller coaster starts back up the incline. "You're angry at me, I know that. All I want is for things to be the way they were. Just say what you're angry about and let's put it behind us."

"Is it really that simple for you, Paul?" Lily's voice is quiet, but it's beginning to bloom with that anger neither of them can ignore any longer.

Paul's eyes dart around the room as if searching out the location of the emergency exit. "I don't see why it shouldn't be, but I'm sure you're going to tell me," he says warily.

"We have to talk."

"Okay. I thought that's what I said. So, talk."

"No, Paul. Not like this. I can't talk to you like this." Pressure is building inside Lily's head from the effort to remain intact, to keep speaking, to not run out of the room and go hide somewhere. Her voice is breathy with fear as she says, "I want us to go see someone."

"Oh come on, Lily. You know I'm not a therapy kind of guy. Just tell me what you want from me."

"I *am* telling you what I want!" she yells, startling them both to immobility. Lily gathers herself and continues before Paul can say anything. "I want us to see a therapist, so we can talk about our problems somewhere I'll feel safe."

Paul looks hurt. "What are you saying? That you don't feel safe here? With me? Lily, we don't need to see a—"

"Don't do that!" She yells again, much louder. Much angrier. Her body pitches toward him as though she's preparing to attack him. Her eyes are stretched open to their limit, her jaw is thrust out.

Paul's head snaps back and he mumbles, "What? Don't do what?"

Lily explodes; she clenches her fists at her sides and screams at him. "Are you blind? This is what you always do! You tell me the things I want are stupid! You use that voice with me! You tell me you won't do what I ask you to do! You trample all over me! Always! Whatever it is, it's always got to be what *you* want!"

Paul stares at her, mute, his mouth open.

She can't stop. Her anger is burning out of control. She imitates him in a mocking voice: "Pekarski's steaks are better, Lily. You want the BMW, not the Infiniti, Lily. You want to go to Venice for our honeymoon, not Paris, Lily. Your little job is idiotic, Lily. I *like* Dreiser's steaks! I liked the Infiniti! I wanted to go to Paris! I love my idiotic job, and I might even want to keep it!"

Paul springs back to life and stupidly latches on to the only thing his flailing pragmatic brain can find to respond to. "What? Why? We live in the city, for God's sake! You can't work up there!"

"Don't tell me I can't!" Her eyes are molten, but with fury, not love.

"Hey! What should I say? That I don't give a shit if we live apart?" Now Paul's yelling, too.

"Why is everything always about you, Paul?! There's something in between 'You can't' and 'I don't give a shit'! *I'm* in between! Why don't you see me? Why couldn't you see how much I wanted a baby!" Lily bursts into tears and Paul's angry stare goes glassy and out of focus. "You ordered me to not want one!

You *ordered* me! What is wrong with you?" she shrieks. She stumbles past him and runs from the room.

The bedroom door slams with such force the floor beneath Paul's feet shakes. The roller coaster plummets. Paul collapses into a chair, drops his head into his hands. For a totally absurd second, he considers getting up and walking out. He doesn't know how to do this; all he's ever known how to do is leave before a woman could make him feel this bad about himself. Except this is Lily, and leaving Lily is not something he can possibly do. Ever. In his heart he knows that she's right about everything. She's the one who is always right about everything, not him.

She is sitting on the bed, her feet on the floor, her knees pressed together, her head hanging down. She is crying quietly. Paul takes a chair from the sitting area, drags it across the room, and sits down across from her. She doesn't look up.

"I've spent every minute of these past weeks missing you so terribly, petrified that you don't love me anymore, plotting how I was going to get you to love me again. And I come home, and I do and say everything wrong. I know what this is all about, Lily. I know why you never told me about Rick and Alan. Even I'm not that dense. But you're going to have to help me. I really really suck at this."

Lily looks up, just to peek at him. "Yes. You do. You really really suck at this." There is no humor or kindness in her voice.

Paul watches her not looking at him. "Is this what I do to you? I make you cry? I make you so frightened that you can't talk to me?"

"Yes, this is what you do. But I let you. Because that's the way I've always been. Afraid of everything." She raises her eyes. "Paul, please. We can't fix this by ourselves."

After a momen he nods. "Okay. We'll go see someone. You

find someone and tell me where and when to show up. Just be discreet. I don't want it getting around that our marriage is fucked up."

"Oh my God. What do you think you're hiding, Paul? *You* are so fucked up!"

She glares at him. He smiles and says, "But I'm not boring."

Lily picks up a pillow and throws it at him. "No. You're definitely not boring."

He catches the pillow and lays it on the floor beside the chair. They look at each other in silence. Paul can't see her love swirling in her dark eyes. If he never sees it again, nothing in his life will have any meaning. Lily's love-filled eyes are the only eyes that have ever made him feel that he's been seen. Truly seen. "I'll more than just show up. I'll do the best I can. I promise. Why don't you get some names from Rick, I'll call Bertram. We'll find someone."

"Thank you." Lily's voice shakes and breaks on the two simple words. Paul can't see Lily's love in her eyes, but she sees his. Her guilt finds her then and grips her hard by the throat, chokes her, brings a gout of blood to her chest and face, a rush of tears to her eyes. She quickly looks away from him.

After a time Paul gets up. He takes Blinkie Floyd from his perch on the recessed shelf and sits down next to Lily. He holds the bat on his leg and plays with his ears, pats his head. "He is mighty cute." Lily is sitting stiffly beside him, looking down at her lap. He kisses her shoulder, bare in her tank top, then puts Blinkie Floyd there. "If you want a baby, we'll get a baby. I'll do anything you want."

Lily doesn't move except to close her eyes. "You don't want that."

"No, I don't. I'm almost fifty-five and I'm the most selfish man who ever breathed. But I love you. More than anything else in my life. And I want to make you happy and if having a baby will make you happy, I'll do it. I'll be a lousy father, but you'll make up for my shortcomings like you do everywhere else."

Lily keeps her eyes closed. She lifts an arm and puts it around Blinkie Floyd. She doesn't say anything. There's nothing she can say. She doesn't know what she wants, and even if she did, she knows that getting what you want doesn't always make you happy.

Paul touches her flushed cheek with the back of his hand. "Lily. I'm sorry. I swear I didn't know what I was doing to you, I don't even know what was going on with me then. But I'm sure that's something we'll be talking about."

Lily rises. She puts Blinkie Floyd back into his cave. She sits in the chair Paul vacated. "I assume you're going into the office tomorrow. Do you know what's in that box or who sent it?"

"I have a pretty good idea who sent it. Serge and Ira took a quick look through it this morning. They said it's pure gold, heads will roll. So yes, I have to go in, early."

They tacitly agree that for now they've gone as far as they can.

"Then we should try to get some sleep. You're on West Coast time. Are you even tired?"

"I am. Do you want me to sleep in the other bedroom?"

Another surge of guilt heats her face, guilt and the irrational fear that if she lies down with him somehow Paul will know that just a day ago she was lying in another man's arms.

Paul misinterprets her renewed flush and her pained look. "Fine. Whatever." He stands and walks stiffly around the bed to his suitcase.

"No. Paul, no. I don't want you to sleep in the other room. But . . . I don't want to make love."

He stops with his back to her. "No, I assumed not. You'll let me know when you're ready."

Thirty minutes later, they're both sleepless, lying without moving on their respective sides of their king-size bed. There's a soft, slow hiss as Paul slides his hand toward her and reaches for hers.

"Is this all right?"

"Yes." She moves her arm so that their hands meet easily.

After a few minutes he says, "Would you let me hold you? Just hold you. I miss the feel of your body."

Lily hesitates, but then she turns her back to him and shifts closer to the center of the bed. Paul spoons her, his front into her back; he puts his arm around her breast. The intervals between Paul's exhalations lengthen. Lily feels each breath as a puff of warm, moist air at the spot where her neck curves into her shoulder, the same spot where she felt Danny's slowing breath as he floated into sleep, just before she floated away after him. In less than five minutes Paul is asleep, but tonight Lily lies awake for a long time, her eyes open into the artificial twilight of the urban night, simultaneously numbed and scourged by the substantiality of Paul behind her. Now she knows the answers to the questions she asked herself weeks ago: Danny's touch thrills her as much as Paul's; his smell is as intoxicating; he fills her and they fit together as perfectly and ecstatically as she fits with Paul. The knowledge does her no good. There's nothing she can do with it. Danny is real, as real as Paul. What happened with him was real, her love for him is real. But even so, he is nothing more than a dream she once had that didn't come true.

33

By the following Sunday, summer warmth has returned for its last lingering visit. Danny awakes early. Without opening his eyes, he moves his hand slowly over Tara's pillow and down her side of the bed as though over her face and body. He lies quietly, his eyes shut, his fingers at the spot where her breast would have been. Soon, another winter will be bearing down on the world, on him. He knows he can't live through another one like the last one. Lily hasn't called. It's been only a week and he knows she's in the city, but he wants her to call. He knows that she will, but he wants it to be soon and he knows it won't be. He's worried about her. He misses her. He misses being with her, talking to her, laughing with her. It was all too brief. Everything. He gets up. He doesn't want to lie there thinking about Tara and Lily that way; he doesn't want what he did with Lily to end up feeling like another loss. He makes coffee and takes his mug out onto the porch, sits down on the steps.

He comes to his feet when he hears a car turning into his driveway. His heart is in his throat as for a second he indulges in the fantasy of Lily's black BMW appearing out of the woods. Of course it won't be her; even if she were here in Stone Creek, it wouldn't be her. It's a beige Lexus that pops out from the trees. Danny's heart drops into his stomach.

Eve parks neatly beside the Volvo, gets out, and stands by the open door, keeping the car between her and the house. She looks at him boldly across the Lexus's roof. Her eyes travel the length of him and come to rest on his face.

"Good morning, Daniel."

In the pellucid morning light, Danny can see that her eyes are puffy and red-rimmed. "Good morning, Eve. Nice dress." It's seven o'clock, the sun has just risen above the eastern horizon, she's standing in the woods, and she's dressed for a cocktail party at the club.

"Oh, this old thing?" She smiles and tosses her head with practiced charm. Her false gaiety quickly dissipates. "I must talk to you."

Danny nods and steps backward up onto the porch.

She comes around the car, stops at the foot of the stairs. "Is Caleb asleep?"

"Yes. For another hour at least."

Eve rubs her arms. "May we go inside, please? And I would love some of that coffee. Black."

Danny pours her coffee and more for himself. From behind the counter, he watches her as she walks slowly around the big room.

"You haven't changed a thing. I'm glad. This is as lovely a house as the day you built it." She trails a finger over the dining room table, the back of a chair, the shelved and mirrored hutch that adorns the side wall. "You really do beautiful work, Daniel."

She comes to the counter, takes up her cup. Eve doesn't drink from mugs. "Delicious. Most people make their coffee too weak. I grew up on muddy brews laced with chicory. Coffee should be strong."

Eve is speaking casually, as though acknowledging Danny's existence, his worth, for the first time is costing her little effort, but Danny can see how tense she is.

"You want to talk about Caleb." He smiles at her. He doesn't want to fight with her anymore and he doesn't think she is here to fight, either.

"Actually, no. At least not directly. I want to talk to you about us, Daniel. I want to apologize to you for the dislike and disrespect I've shown you all these years. You never deserved it. My treatment of you wounded Tara terribly and for that alone I will never forgive myself. And I would not presume to ask your forgiveness." She tilts her head. Her glossy lips form a sad smile. "You look stunned, Daniel. Am I surprising you too much all at once?"

Danny is stunned. He feels as if he's been beamed onto the planet Bizarro, where everything is the opposite of the way it is on Earth and he is being spoken to by someone who looks exactly like Eve Jamison except that she talks and acts human. He blinks several times and then looks at her carefully. He doesn't know if it's because he has changed or she has changed, or if it's because he has read those words, but he imagines he sees the sorrow that Tara saw. He imagines he sees it so clearly beneath her polished facade that he wonders how he could possibly not have seen it before.

"I think I can handle it."

"Good. I'm counting on that. I have a story to tell you, Daniel. You will be the only person alive who will ever have heard it or who ever will hear it. I am going to tell it to you and leave you to draw your own conclusions." She appears steady as a rock, but as she places the porcelain cup in its saucer on the counter divide, next to her purse, it rattles against the hard tiles.

Danny gestures toward the living room. "Do you want to sit?"

"No, thank you. It will be easier if I stand, I think." She wraps her arms around her middle and holds fast to her elbows. "I have hopes that your conclusions will be wise and compassionate ones, because you are a wise and compassionate young man."

He puts his mug down as well and gives her his full attention. "I'm listening."

She draws in a breath and it shudders in her throat as she lets it out. She looks him in the eye and starts to talk.

"In May of 1978 I was twenty-one years old and about to graduate from a small women's college outside Atlanta. Lester was finishing his public health and business degrees at Emory and we were to be married on July fifteenth. We had been engaged for over a year, keeping company for eight months before that. I come from a very puritanical family, as you know, with stern parents and two very protective older brothers. Generations of Fosters and Carlisles had practiced the time-honored Southern tradition of suppressing their females, quite effectively, and I was very well suppressed. Lester and I engaged in occasional sexual activity, not intercourse naturally, but I was too fearful and guilty to enjoy it."

It flits through Danny's mind that he ought to be embarrassed, listening to Eve talk about herself this way, but he isn't. After years of withholding every generous impulse from him, she is now giving him something more than she's given to anyone else: her trust. And trust is something that Danny does not take lightly. There seems no reason for him to be embarrassed for her, in any case. She isn't for herself. She is looking him straight in the eye without the slightest blush or discomfort in her expression.

"On the twentieth of May I attended a party at a sorority house at Emory with a girl I had come out with in Savannah. She very quickly left me on my own to go spoon with her boyfriend. There was alcohol and drugs and sex everywhere and I was too uncomfortable to stay. I was almost at the door, I had nearly escaped, when a boy unexpectedly appeared in front of me. He was so—" She halts. She is looking full at Danny and he can tell from her eyes that she still sees him, but that now it is not only him she sees. "Different. There was a restless, uninhibited energy emanating from him. I could feel it as he stood there blocking my way. He looked at me as though I were a pool of clear cool water and he a man dying of thirst. He wouldn't let me leave. Never in my life have I felt for anyone what I felt for him from the first moment I looked into his eyes. I went upstairs with him and let him do what I hadn't let Lester do in nearly two years.

"His name was Terence Jones. He was a twenty-four-year-old, undisciplined, unpedigreed college dropout from Chicago. He made a careless living as a housepainter and spent his spare time in his parents garage, fooling with those new video games and computers. His girlfriend had recently broken up with him and he'd come to Atlanta to visit a friend and find something to mend his heart. He found me. We made love every day for the next six weeks. I don't know how I managed it. I don't remember having one coherent thought in my head. There was only Terry. I took my exams, prepared for my wedding, saw Lester. . . . But every moment I was falling more deeply in love and dreaming and scheming to run off to California with Terry.

"I saw him for the last time the night of July first. Two weeks later, when I walked down the aisle in my virginal white dress and took Lester as my husband, I was pregnant with Tara."

Danny stares at her in shocked silence. When Eve pulls from her bag a page torn from a magazine and holds it out to him, he is too shocked at first to take it from her.

Her hand is shaking again and so is her voice. Her lids are opening and closing rapidly over her eyes, but they are dry and don't leave Danny's face. "I want you to see him, Daniel. I want someone to see him. His hair is long here, just as it was when I knew him. You can't see them, but he has unusual ears. They are slightly pointed and stick out from his head. Like a little elf."

Danny stops breathing. He takes the paper, extricates his stare, and looks down at the lovingly preserved image of a good-looking man with Tara's impish smile on his lips.

As though reading his mind, Eve says, "But you can see the smile."

He looks up and blurts out, "Holy shit."

"Yes, Daniel, holy fucking shit." For the briefest of seconds, Eve's face contorts but then she tosses her head and laughs. "Ah, my dear, you should see the look on your face. I believe I will sit now." She heads into the living room.

The building pressure in his chest reminds Danny to start breathing again. His eyes trail after Eve. He doesn't seem able to move any other part of him.

"And I would like a drink, please, if I may," she says over her shoulder.

Danny hears her, but he's not sure what she means. He gestures feebly toward the refrigerator. "You mean, some juice or water or something?"

"No. I mean a large bourbon, if you have it, thank you. Don't worry, Daniel, I am not a secret lush. I never got to sleep last night, so as far as I am concerned it is still cocktail hour." She sits primly on the couch.

Danny sets the magazine page on the counter as though it were breakable. He gets the bottle of Woodford Reserve, untouched for more than a year, from the liquor cabinet. He puts ice into a glass and fills it with bourbon. He remembers that Eve likes mint. He has some growing in a pot on the back deck. He cuts a big sprig, crushes it, and adds it to the glass.

"Daniel! How thoughtful!" She takes it from him and liquid spills onto her fingers. She steadies the glass with her two hands and takes an enormous pull.

Danny sits in the armchair. "What happened? Why didn't you run away with him?"

She looks at him with a wicked gleam in her eye. "Oh, did I neglect that part? His girlfriend asked him to come back and he went." Her eyes go dull. She shakes her head. "No. I shouldn't leave you to think that he was callous. He wasn't. He was a good person, and not irresponsible. He cared for me. He did not want to hurt me. But this girl was his childhood sweetheart, and I was a six-week fling. A rebound. He left on July second and I never heard from him again."

Danny slowly gets to his feet. He fetches the bourbon bottle and the page from *People* magazine from the kitchen, then returns to the living room. While Eve quietly sips her drink, he scrutinizes the picture of Terry Jones and his family; he reads the article. By the time he's done, Eve's glass is nearly empty.

"For a college dropout, Terry did pretty well." Danny begins to refill her glass. "DreamStar Animation Studios. He put his youthful interests to good use."

"Just a tiny splash more, Daniel, thank you. He did indeed.

As have you. You can see, I'm sure, the ways, not merely physical, in which you might have reminded me of him."

"Yes. And maybe Tara of yourself at her age."

Eve gently touches the glass to the back of his hand.

"Did you ever think of trying to contact him after you saw this? Tell him about Tara?"

"I *thought* about it, but I never considered doing it. Do you understand the distinction?"

"Yes, I do." He'd had his moments of *thinking* about driving his truck into a tree or taking a long dive off a high ridge in the Gunks, but he'd never considered doing it, although if not for Caleb he might have. He understands the distinction.

Eve drains the last dregs of bourbon and daintily places her glass on the coffee table. "I'm going to leave now, before Caleb awakes. If there is anything more you feel compelled to ask, Daniel, we can talk at a later time. I promise you that things will be different from now on."

Danny fetches Eve's purse, puts the photo of Terry back inside, and walks her to her car. "Are you okay to drive?"

Eve turns to him with a pitying look. "How sweet." She lays her palm against his lightly stubbled cheek. "I like you very much without your beard. You are an appealing man either way, but this is better. You look more like who and what you are."

Eve starts the engine, then rolls her window down and looks up at him. Her eyes reveal her exhaustion. There is no fight left in her. "When can I see him again, Daniel?"

Danny nods. "We'll work it out. He misses you. I'll call you tomorrow."

"And now you will have him tested?"

"No. Not now. He's still too young. But we can talk about it."

Danny leans against the Volvo as Eve drives away. He won't have to ask anything more. She's given him all he needs to understand her unrelenting sorrow and to forgive her for making him the repository of her fear and jealousy and anger. Intolerable, inappropriate emotions she's held inside all these years. No one on earth to whom she could ever confess her sins and her secrets. No answers to her questions. *Who else can I hate if not you, Daniel? Who else is there to blame if not you?* Who indeed, if not him, that-uneducated-atheist-Irish-laborer-your-daughter-married. Who else was there?

He turns to go inside. Caleb is on the porch.

"Did you and Grandma make up, Daddy?"

"We did." Danny looks at his son—his son with the adorable elf ears inherited from a man he'll never know and who will never know him—standing there in innocence, in the sunlight, in his blue fish pajamas, Zilla hanging from one hand, the knuckles of the other digging into his sleepy eye. Danny may not be a man of conventional faith, but still there are things he believes in. One of them is that Caleb will be all right.

"Pancakes for breakfast?"

Caleb compresses his lips. "Mmmm. Pancakes."

Danny takes his hand and they go into the kitchen, and together they raid the refrigerator and the pantry of the necessary ingredients.

"Blueberries?" Danny asks.

"Blueberries."

Danny makes the pancakes and sits and watches Caleb eat them, scrupulously excavating around the berries, saving them with their clinging batter for last. He doesn't make any for himself; he isn't hungry.

"When is Lily going to come to our house again?" Caleb

shoves a too-large forkful of pancake into his mouth. Syrup drips down his chin.

"Careful there, cowboy." Danny wipes away the syrup. "Not for a while, I think. She had to go back to the city."

"Her husband likes the Museum of Natural History. We could go there with them."

"Maybe we can sometime. We'll see." He slides two more pancakes onto Caleb's plate, refills his milk glass. "We'll see."

Danny wonders why he bothered wiping off the syrup; now there's a milk mustache above Caleb's lips and a piece of blueberry skin stuck to the side of his mouth. Danny wonders what would have happened if Lily were thirty-three and single. Or if Lily would even be the Lily who stopped him in his tracks when he saw her if she were thirty-three and single, or if she is that Lily only because she is forty-six, childless, and in love with another man. He wonders whether any of those unanswerable questions matter at all, or if the only question that matters is what would have happened if he'd said *I love you.*

34

Danny backs the pickup to the open doors of the studio. He lowers the rear panel of the truck bed, lays the plank ramp against the edge, and carefully loads onto the thick layer of cloth pads the crate containing the new mantel and surround for The Doorway's ruined fireplace. He pulls the truck around the side of the house and as he takes the wide curve into the long driveway, heading out to the road, he hits the brakes. There is a burst of sun in his eyes, glaring off the rearview mirror, a brilliant reflection of Tara's white Volvo glimmering in the morning light that floods the front yard. Danny stares into the mirror and as the sun moves an immeasurable fraction higher into the sky, the glimmer dies down to dullness and he's staring at a tired, nine-year-old car with nearly 150,000 miles on it that's not going to last too much longer. Before another year passes, there will be a different car parked in front of the house. *Nothing stays the same, Danny, and neither will you.* Danny turns off the engine. The ghost of a thought that he's been chasing in the weeks since the morning of Eve's visit is all at once solid in his grasp.

"Eve, it's Danny." His phone at his ear, he climbs out of the truck.

"Good morning, Daniel."

"Are you busy right now?"

"Terribly. Lester left not one but two English muffin crumbs on the table. Why?"

Danny smiles and shakes his head in wonderment. Eve is funny. "I was hoping you could meet me for a little while this morning." He goes into the house.

"Oh! Well. Yes. I don't see why not. Shall we meet for coffee somewhere? Rudy's?"

Into the bedroom. "No. I thought maybe somewhere more private." He opens the drawer of his night table. "Would you mind meeting me at the cemetery?" Danny's voice breaks on the last word.

Eve's indrawn breath comes through the wireless ether. "No, Daniel. I wouldn't mind. I wouldn't mind at all. Fifteen minutes?"

The sun is shining brightly, but the air is crisp and it's promising to be a blustery October day. Danny grabs his beat-up brown leather jacket from the hall closet and shrugs it on as he hurries back out to the truck. When he arrives at the cemetery fifteen minutes later, Eve is already there, on the stone bench, a cashmere shawl draped over her shoulders. Her straight fall of black hair is swaying in the wind. She is sitting to one side; she's left room for him. Danny sits down next to her, places the small bag he has with him on the ground by his side. He flips up the collar of his jacket against the cold air buffeting the back of his neck.

"Thanks for doing this. Lucky for me Lester is such a neat breakfast eater."

They smile haltingly, both gaze briefly at Tara's grave, then back at each other. They have a very short history of being comfortable alone in each other's presence; it's going to take some getting used to.

"Luckier for me. I have to live with him. I would have come later in the day in any case if you hadn't asked to meet here. I'm here nearly every day."

"I know." In response to Eve's startled look, Danny says, "In the beginning, I used to come more often than you were aware of. Whoever was at the gate, or on the grounds, seemed to feel obliged to tell me I'd just missed you, or you hadn't been yet. Or that you were here. In which case I'd make myself scarce until you'd gone. I guess no one ever figured out that you and I never came here together after the day we buried her."

Eve's lips quiver but she doesn't look away from him. "A great deal of wasted time and emotion. I'm sorry, Daniel."

Danny shakes his head. "No, I didn't say that to make you feel bad, Eve. I didn't want to be here with you any more than you wanted to be here with me. Until last month, I thought we'd die enemies, fighting over Caleb. Fighting over Tara." He reaches into the bag and lifts out something wrapped in a yellow chamois cloth. "I wanted to see you because I have a story, of sorts, that I want to share with you." He holds it in both hands for a moment, then he removes the cloth and places Tara's journal on Eve's lap. "It's not like yours, all inside my head; I'm not going to tell it to you. It's written down, in here, in words more beautiful than I could ever find."

Eve slowly takes her eyes from Danny's face and lowers them to the notebook. She gasps. Her hands have been by her thighs, curled around the front edge of the stone bench. She releases her grip and brings her hands to rest on the red cover. Her perfectly shaped fingernails are the same color as the leather. She uses one to trace what is written there in her daughter's unmistakable, confident hand. As Eve's finger moves over the silver letters, she speaks the name it spells, Danny, then she lifts her hand and covers her mouth. She turns to look at him and her eyes are filled with tears.

"I found it a few weeks after she died," Danny says quietly. "There isn't very much in it, not nearly enough, but still, it's taken me more than a year to read it."

"Oh, Daniel. She loved you so much. Is that what this is, a diary of her love for you?"

"Yes."

Eve looks at him in confusion. "And you're giving it to me? I don't understand . . ."

"I have to share her with someone, Eve. I can't live the rest of my life keeping her all locked up inside me the way I have since she died. I want you to read it, and I want you to know that whatever she felt for me, I felt for her a thousand times over."

"I can't read this, Daniel." She halfheartedly lifts the journal as though to return it to him. "Surely, it's too intimate, I have no right . . ."

Danny gently pushes her hands back down to her lap. "Yes, it's intimate. But no more intimate than what you shared with me about yourself. Not really. It's just expressed differently, and we had six years, not just six weeks. Eve, please. I want someone to see this, and it can only be you. You're her mother, you knew her in ways that I never could. What you told me . . . it wasn't just about yourself, it was about Tara, too, something vital that I hadn't known about her. I want to do that for you. I want you to know this part of her the way I did. You'll understand when you read it."

Eve's tears have disappeared. She stares bravely into Danny's eyes. "Did she hate me for what I did to you?"

"No. She didn't hate you. She could never hate you. She loved you." Danny smiles. "And I'm beginning to see why."

"Didn't I say you were a wise young man?" Eve smiles back. "Thank you. I'll read this, Daniel. I'll try to read it soon, I know you'll want it back, you'll want to keep it close to you."

"Take your time. I'll want it back, of course, but for now I actually would appreciate it if you would keep it for me. I need . . . I need to . . ." Danny can't say it, that he needs to put her away from him, at least until his head and his heart can hold onto someone else without letting go.

"You need to untangle yourself. You need to make some space in your heart for whatever comes next. I understand. I will read this, and I will keep it for you, and when you're ready, you will ask me and I will give it back to you."

Eve leans into Danny's arm, rests her head on his shoulder. "Oh my Lord. She would be so happy."

Danny takes Eve's hand. It's cold. He tightens his hold. They sit on the stone bench, hand in hand, as the wind gusts around them and they watch the brightly colored autumn leaves twirl and leap across Tara's grave.

35

L
ILY AND PAUL EMERGE from the park at Eighty-first Street,
onto Central Park West. They are walking slowly, holding hands.
They're weary, though for a good reason and not in a bad way.
They are seeing a couples' therapist on East Eighty-ninth Street,
twice a week at three o'clock. Paul hasn't once been late or complained about the hours away from the office, although after all
his hard work he is missing part of the rewarding denouement,
the multiple resignations and federal indictments of SynTech's
miscreants. Their therapy sessions have been intense, upsetting,
at times hurtful, but hopeful nonetheless. They have taken to
spending time afterward somewhere in the park before going
home. Today they sat on a bench at Cedar Hill for an hour and
talked, then climbed Belvedere Castle and looked out over the
acres of treetops, at the turning leaves glowing red and gold in
the late-afternoon sun.

They cross the avenue and head downtown. Just south of
Seventy-ninth Street they come abreast of the massive stone edi-
fice housing the Museum of Natural History. Enormous, colorful

banners announcing current exhibitions are draped between the soaring columns and above the high arched entryway. It is nearing closing time and a small crowd of people is making its way down the steps, spilling out onto the street, surrounding Lily and Paul as they stroll past. A father and his little boy, no more than five or six years old, materialize out of the crowd right next to Lily. The man is holding the boy's hand. The boy fixes Lily with big blue eyes and says to her, direct and serious, "Hello. My daddy and I saw dinosaur fossils. They're very big."

The young father, who is looking at Lily with covert admiration, smiles at her. He's blond. His eyes are blue. A tiny, mouselike squeak squeezes through the barrier of Lily's lips as their sides twitch upward in an attempted smile. Father and son move on, leaving before her in their wake the clear and vivid image of Danny's face, his eyes; the memory of his limber body and deft, loving hands; the perfection of Caleb's weight against her breast. *We're not going to lose each other, you, me, and Caleb, I promise.* She's not going to lose them, whatever it takes; she couldn't bear it.

She stumbles and jerks at Paul's hand as he takes his next step.

"Lily?" He quickly turns back to her. "What happened?"

She drops her head to hide her wet eyes and heat-suffused face. "I twisted my ankle."

"Ah. Which one?"

"The right."

Paul squats at her feet and tenderly encircles her ankle with the fingers of both hands. "Is it bad?" He raises his head to her.

Lily looks down at his strong, handsome features, at his dark eyes open wide, asking her to let him love her again. *You're* my bad boy, she thinks suddenly. Not Danny. Women may have broken their hearts on him, but Danny has never been careless with anyone's love. Paul is the thoughtless one with the trail of broken hearts behind him, the untamable one, the irresistible one a good girl like Lily can't stop wanting although she knows he's going to break her heart, too. He did for her what every good girl dreams her bad boy can do: he unzipped her, opened her down to her essence, let his passion for what he saw there reveal to her the power that resided in her every cell, in her every atom. But she needed a good boy, she needed Danny, to give her the courage to use it. Without her courage, she and Paul would surely perish. The jagged edges of her guilt soften slightly, to a tolerable blunted pain.

"Should I carry you home?" Paul is looking up at her with a teasing grin.

"No. But when we get home, I think you should take me to bed." She lays her hand on his head. "You've been so patient with me." A lone tear spills from the corner of her right eye and rolls down her cheek. Her voice drops to a whisper. "I'm so sorry, Paul."

He stands up. "You're worth waiting for." He carefully blots the tear with the pad of his thumb. "I'm afraid to touch you," he says quietly. "That way."

"Don't be. I want us to start over. Can we try to do that?"

After a small hesitation, Paul smiles faintly and says, "You're so beautiful," and he takes her face in his hands and he kisses her. And then, like a teenager shot with Cupid's arrow, not caring who sees them, he kisses her and kisses her and kisses her. He holds her at the waist and steers her down the avenue, stopping a dozen times on the five-block walk to kiss her and he kisses her in the elevator, and in the hallway, and at their door, and by the time they reach their bed Lily is wild and wet and it almost feels like the first time all over again.

*   *   *

Paul is dozing. Lily cautiously disentangles herself from his embrace, gets out of bed, and goes into her bathroom. She stands at the sink and looks at herself in the mirror as she cries. It's not like before. She's not crying for the baby she will never bear, or from the pain of knowing that her love for Paul, profound and enduring as it is, will never be what it once was. She cries purely for herself, for the ache inside that she fears will never leave her; for the impossible wordless longing to turn back the clock, to start over at a place where she could still have it all. Where she could meet someone like Danny when she and Rick end. Meet Paul, but for him to be Danny. She cries because she still doesn't know if adopting a baby now is the right thing to do, and she doesn't know when she'll know or *how* she'll know, not while life with Paul changes day by day. They have been spending their Sundays with Rick and Alan and Sophie, Paul curious but awkward, afraid to hold her, tense and silent when she cries. Lily is aware of him watching Sophie's miraculous face, and watching Lily's face when she holds her. Behind the determined neutrality of his expression she knows that Paul is trying to find his place this time in this new family he's being asked to be part of. He's trying hard.

And she cries for the agony of never knowing what would have happened if Danny had been a little older, if Caleb were all the children he needed; or if those questions would matter at all if she had not stopped herself from sinking to the very bottom of his blue ocean. If she had said *I love you*.

When she returns to bed, Paul is awake.

"Where were you so long? The bed gets so cold when you leave it." He reaches to take her in his arms. "Lily, are we all right now?"

To say yes would be a lie. Lily can live with the lies of omission she has to tell, but she doesn't want to lie anymore to Paul about what's happening between them. "No. Not yet. But I think we will be," she says, because she believes it to be true.

"Okay." Paul caresses her face. "Okay."

"Paul. I want to have Thanksgiving in Stone Creek. I want to fill the house all weekend with everybody we love. Rick and Alan and Sophie, my sister's family, maybe Rick's parents . . ."

"Okay. Great. I like Rick's parents, better than yours," he says drily.

She smiles forgivingly. "So do I." She takes his hand from her cheek and holds it still. "Paul." She moves closer to him. "I made friends this summer. I want to keep them. I want you to know them." Her voice quavers as she attempts to visualize herself and Paul and Danny in the same room and her inner eye goes blind. But as sight fights its way through that darkness, she thinks she sees Paul's long tawny fingers resting on Caleb's yellow head; she clearly sees Caleb and Sophie together, in the oak-paneled den, at the dining room table, asleep on the living room floor. In Danny's kitchen. In the playground, in the sandbox. She fell in love with Sophie the moment Rick put her in her arms, but someone was already there, in that once-desolate place in her heart; a little blue-eyed, blond-haired boy was waiting for the dusky-skinned, saucer-eyed girl to join him. "I want to invite them, too."

Paul gives her a searching look. "Sure. Whatever you want. I'll even let you get the turkey at Dreiser's."

"No way. Pekarski's are better."

Their heads are inches apart, both resting on his pillow. He smiles. "I love you."

Lily stretches her body hard against his and kisses him. She whispers, "Again."

"I'm not thirty-five anymore, sweetheart." But as his body tells her in no uncertain terms that he's up to the task, he says, "However, for you I am willing to pretend."

"So am I."

The reservoir behind her eyes is still full, but now it is full with liquid love. For every drop that falls, a hundred more will take its place and the pressure will never be relieved. It hurts. The pain of all that love hurts; it feels just like the pain of loss.

36

WITH THEIR GLEEFUL, conspiring permission, Danny leaves Eve and Caleb to make chocolate chip cookies without his help. They push him out the kitchen doors onto the deck and tell him not to come back for at least an hour. They're making the cookies from scratch, a lot of them, for the Halloween festivities in town later that afternoon, and with Caleb as his grandmother's assistant, it's not going to be a quick or clean mission. Danny goes into the studio and takes his time sanding and staining the three-foot-long birch-wood boards that will comprise the deck of the sled he is making for Caleb for Christmas. He sketches out the shape of the seat he'll carve out of pliable willow, with a curved, tilted back and side bars to hang on to. He loses himself in the work, but still he hears the muffled sound of the telephone ringing in the kitchen and it startles him, stops his hands and brings his head up. With fixed eyes, he stares at the sliding glass doors and waits for Caleb to come running to get him, to tell him it's Lily. He stares and waits and then goes back to work.

Danny comes in through the mud room just as the oven door is closing.

"The second batch is in the oven, Dad!"

Two trays of cookies are cooling on top of the stove. The aroma of hot butter and chocolate makes Danny's mouth water. "So I see." Gobs of sticky cookie dough cling to Caleb's face, hands, and forearms. "Maybe we should throw you in there, too. You look good enough to eat. What do you think, Grandma?"

"No!" Caleb laughs and swipes at his face with a wet dishtowel.

Eve turns from the oven and smiles. Her face is flushed from the heat and there's pale dough in her dark hair and all over her fingers. "Ah, before I forget . . . Beth Marcus called while you were working, Daniel. She asked how Caleb was—apparently chicken pox is showing up among children in Caleb's grade?— and to tell you that she'll look for you both in town later. She'll be there with her brother and his children."

"I told her we'd be there at five, Dad," Caleb says as he smears the dough all over his face.

Danny takes the dishtowel from Caleb's hand and wipes his face and hands clean. "How about walking with me to get the mail?"

As they walk the driveway, Caleb looks up at Danny and says, "You don't have to grow your beard back, Dad."

They'd made a deal that Sunday morning while Caleb watched Danny shave, fascinated and a little frightened as an unfamiliar face appeared where his father's face had been: if by Halloween Caleb still wasn't used to the way Danny looked without it, Danny would grow another beard.

"You sure? You've got till tonight to decide."

"Yup, I'm sure. You look good. You look like me." Caleb grins.

"No, *you* look like *me*."

They look at each other and smile, both happy about it, whichever it is. Caleb beams up at Danny. It's Tara's smile on his mouth, Terry's smile. Caleb has always looked so much like him, but now, more and more, Danny sees another fair-haired, blue-eyed man in his son's face; more and more he sees Tara.

On his tiptoes, Caleb can just manage to drag the mail from the bumblebee's mouth. There isn't much today. He paws through the small pile, giving a very good impression that he knows what he's looking at, and his eyes open wide.

"Wow, Dad, look!"

Caleb holds up a postcard, picture facing out for Danny to see. Danny's breath catches in his throat. It's a photograph of the huge T-rex skeleton from the Museum of Natural History. Caleb is staring at the written side.

"Dad! It's for me!" He's jumping up and down with excitement. "It's for me!"

Caleb thrusts the card into Danny's hand. "Read it. Read it to me." He starts twirling around in ecstasy.

Danny's eyes don't want to look. "Caleb, be careful, don't go spinning out into the road." His voice is unnecessarily stern.

Caleb stops spinning, stands still before him. "I won't. Daddy, come on, read it to me!"

Danny glances quickly at the signature and immediately the bittersweet taste of cinnamon is in his mouth and there's a hard contraction in his belly. He puts a hand on Caleb's head for a second, ruffles his hair. "Okay. Okay. Here goes . . ." Danny reads aloud:

Dearest Caleb, I'm thinking of you every single day. I promise that I'll call you very very soon and we'll go to the Museum of Natural History, and to the park and the zoo. And I'll see you

in the country soon, too. Tell Daddy what I've written. . . . I
miss you more than I can ever say. I love you.

Lily

"We're going to the Museum of Natural History with Lily! Dad? Dad?"

Danny stares at what Lily has written. He doesn't feel Caleb tugging on his sleeve.

"Dad! Give it to me! I want to put it on my wall."

Caleb snatches the card from Danny's hand and goes skipping past him toward the house, singing, "Lilee. Lilee. Lilee."

Danny stands by the mailbox; his head slowly comes up. His eyes follow the lift of the high ground in the distance until his gaze reaches the pinnacle of Kensington Ridge. Although there's no one to hear him, he says it out loud: "I love you, too."

What he now knows of his capacity for pain, Danny also knows of his capacity for love. His store of love is not finite. But, like pain, love comes in many different shades and textures and strengths, from ones that tickle you to ones that blind you to ones that destroy you.

Danny turns his back to the road and follows Caleb home.

Acknowledgments

T HE AUTHOR WISHES to acknowledge and thank the several singer-songwriters whose music provided the daily soundtrack to the writing of this book. Their rich, honest, passionate, and beautiful songs were a direct-to-the-soul parallel to the battered hearts and turbulent emotions of Danny, Lily, and Paul. The poetry of their lyrics could have told the whole story. . . .

First, inexpressible thanks to the brilliant, incomparable David Gray, whose music has been a constant companion and source of comfort, joy, and inspiration for the past fifteen years . . .

. . . and to Tom McRae, Bruce Springsteen, James Blunt, Frances Cabrel, and Mark Knopfler.

And finally, to wonder women Laurie Liss and Marjorie Braman, my agent and editor, fighters for truth, justice and *Stone Creek*. Thank you for your faith, and for refusing to give up.

Stone Creek

Read on . . .

Reading Group Guide
Topics for Discussion

More About the Author
A Conversation with Victoria Lustbader

READING GROUP GUIDE

In the novel *Stone Creek*, the author, Victoria Lustbader, explores many themes that will be immediately recognizable to the reader. Her portrayal of the participants in this pas de trois of love allows each character moments of revelation and change and allows the reader to relate on an intimate level with all three as they make their way through the nuanced entanglements of adult life and love.

1. All three characters believe they have met the love of their life. Danny thought Tara was the love of his life. Lily and Paul believe they were destined for each other. Do you believe there can only be one *true* love? Or is it possible to love again with the same kind of depth and fulfillment?

2. The book purposely brings up, without judgment, some of the many ways and reasons why people are unfaithful to their committed partners, or to their idea of moral rightness. Do you think infidelity is ever justified? Can it be a good thing under the right circumstances? Do you think it's ever justified to act in opposition to your own sense of what's morally right? What are other reasons, not explored in this book, that might cause someone to take such an action?

3. Each of the main characters in the book experiences a loss that paralyzes him or her in some way. Danny's loss is the

most obvious; what loss do you think each of the other characters—Lily, Paul, Eve—suffer from? Do you think they all succeed in forgiving? Do you think that the act of forgiving, in each case, allows that person to move on with his or her life?

4. At the beginning of their marriage, Lily and Paul seem to have a relationship in perfect balance. How do you think this changes and what does Danny offer that Lily hasn't gotten from her relationship with Paul? Do you think Danny envisions the same intimacy he had with Tara in a relationship with Lily?

5. Danny believes that he and Tara would never have had the problems that Lily and Paul have. Do you agree? Why? What are the differences in the two relationships?

6. Lily wonders which is worse—to lose something vital that you've had, or to have never had it at all. Is one worse than the other, and why? The reactions of the outside world are different in each case—when you lose something you had, the world notices and grieves with you. If you lose something you want but don't get, does the world notice? How does grief for a private loss differ from grief for a public one? Do you think one process is easier than the other?

7. Lily's love for Danny is inextricably bound to her love and need for Caleb. The two of them bring up the two most primal urges in a woman/person: sex and parenthood. Would she have fallen in love with Danny if he didn't have a son, or if she didn't yearn for a child?

8. Danny's feelings for Lily go deeper than her resemblance to his dead wife. What is he responding to in her? Do you think they could have had a future together?

9. Do you think that Danny was right to give Eve Tara's journal? Why do you think he chose to do that? Who do you think it helped more, Danny or Eve? What does his act say about his feelings toward Eve and about his grieving over Tara? What do you think Eve's reaction to what she reads would be? Do you think she will feel differently about Tara and Danny afterward?

10. Lily faces one of the toughest decisions a person can face—torn between loving two people and having to choose one. Did Lily make the right decision in staying with Paul? What do you think would have happened if she had chosen Danny? What do you think are her reasons for her choice?

11. Lily and Danny will see each another again—they are determined not to lose their friendship, and Caleb's happiness. What do you think will happen when they do? Do you think it's possible for two people, who feel the way they do about each other, to remain just friends? Can very strong feelings for a person morph into something just as strong, and yet different?

12. Is this a happy ending?

MORE ABOUT THE AUTHOR

A Conversation with Victoria Lustbader

You were a fiction editor for many years, and worked with many successful writers. You are married to Eric Van Lustbader, a long-time bestselling author. What influence did your previous career and your choice of mate have on your becoming a writer?

Let's have some fun and turn that around! My choices of career and mate were probably influenced by my attempt to *avoid* becoming a writer, although I'd wanted to be one since I was a child. Not that I didn't enjoy being an editor, or don't love my husband, but both my job and my marriage let me take the easy way out, sit on my own ambitions, be a good girl and a good help-mate to those who had the talent I thought I didn't. But often, I would find my sharp, blue editing pencil trembling over a page and dare to think, *You could write this well. Maybe better.*

Being married to a prolific and successful writer was for a long time a deterrent to my attempting to write. I couldn't imagine making the transition from help-mate to competitor, which was how I thought of it: that I would be competing with my husband, and I'd lose. Or worse, I'd win! That was a personal self-esteem issue I had to overcome in my own time. My husband has always been totally encouraging and supportive.

When did you finally start writing, and how? What got you past your fears and doubts?

I started writing for real in the spring of 2001. The underlying psychological theme of the book I wrote first, *Hidden,* is repression, and the damage people do to themselves and others when their true natures and desires are squelched. It's a very personal theme: what "got"me going was that I realized I was seriously unhappy despite having a wonderful life. Unhappiness is surely one of the greatest motivators of change; it's not a state one wants to dwell in. I'd reached the point where I simply had to speak my voice, say what I felt, do what I'd always wanted to do.

Rumor has it you were once planning to be a cellular biologist or some such. How did you end up in the publishing business? What happened?

Calculus happened. And adolescent laziness. Which just goes to prove that being a sluggard sometimes pays off. Yes, the sciences have always fascinated me, and still do—I'm reading up on quantum physics for the book I'm working on now . . . black holes, quarks, fermions, oh my!—but I would have made a terrible lab rat. By my sophomore year in college, I realized I didn't love science enough to do the required work. It was people that really fascinated me. I flirted with psychology, but ultimately became an English major. Pretty much because most of my friends were English majors, and I was still lazy and it was the easiest path to graduation. But as soon as I got my first job, at what was then Harper & Row, I couldn't deny that I'd always loved words, and books, and writing, more than anything. Science, psychology, humanity, history . . . books contained everything. I'd ended up exactly where I wanted and needed to be.

What are some of the challenges and benefits of having the same career as your spouse?

For us, I would say there are mostly only benefits.

Even after working with writers for years, the reality of living with one was an entirely different animal. Eric wrote almost constantly, and seemed "gone" most of the time. Having an intellectual understanding of why, and where he went, didn't help me feel less abandoned. It wasn't until I was writing myself that I understood viscerally what it meant to be partly living every moment in the world you were creating, and to appreciate what a joy that was. And to realize that it didn't make a writer's connection to the "real" world any less substantial.

Now, with both of us writing, there is nothing better than the times when we are in our separate offices, humming away on our books, feeling the creative vibes jumping in the air, each of us knowing that the other is having a good day. They aren't all good days, of course—writing can be a lonely, frustrating, and dispiriting profession. We empathize with one another's ups and downs, down to the bone, and can often help one another. Eric and I write very different kinds of books, have different strengths and weaknesses, and can often complement the other's way of thinking about a problem.

However, being that I'm only human, confident one moment and hopeless the next, it is hard at times not to feel like the family afterthought when I compare my fledgling career to what Eric has already accomplished.

Stone Creek _is your second novel, and totally different from your first,_ Hidden, _which is an historical family saga. How did you come to write two such different books?_
I might have set a story with the themes of _Hidden_ in the present. What people can't express or do hasn't changed as much as we like to think it has. But I chose to set it in the 1920s because it was a period of extraordinary and painful transition. The rules and expectations of behavior and morality were still black and

white for some, while falling to pieces for others. The still-strong Victorian influence and epic historical saga trappings allowed me the freedom to be a bit more narratively melodramatic, and to keep more emotional distance than is possible with a book set in the world I live in.

I love *Hidden*, but by the time I was done with it I knew I was ready to write a contemporary novel. I needed and wanted to write something from which I could *not* maintain that emotional distance. I wanted to write a realer, more "authentic" book, if you will. I'd welcome the opportunity to write a sequel to *Hidden* some day, but novels like *Stone Creek* are my first love.

Lily, the female protagonist of Stone Creek, is childless and married to a powerful, successful man. As are you. So, forgive us, but the obvious next question is: how much of Stone Creek is autobiographical?

A fair, if pushy question!

I realize now, as I'm working on my third book, that everything I write is going to be autobiographical in the sense that the emotional and psychological themes I find myself writing about come from the experiences that have been the most formative in my own life. Those experiences, and the feelings and wisdom they have left me with, are not uniquely mine, by any stretch of the imagination—quite the opposite. That's why I believe they're worth writing about.

That said, whereas nothing in the actual storyline of *Hidden* paralleled my own life, I, like Lily, have had to face the hard reality of not having children. Her story is not mine, she is not me. Paul is not my husband, and—more's the pity!—I never met a Danny. However, the emotional journey that Lily goes through is one I am intimately familiar with. One of the loveliest compliments I've received from readers so far—whether they have shared that exact experience, or some other than engendered similar emotions—is that the book is so true to life they feel I *had* to have lived it to write about it so honestly.

As to the background details, writing a contemporary book after an historical was like being let loose in a chocolate factory. Little fun things got plucked from my life, or the lives of friends. For instance, I actually had a ballet teacher named Miss Ruth when I was a girl; dear friends adopted children the way Rick and Alan do in the book; I spent my youthful summers in a community in upstate New York; we have a mahogany deck around our pool!

If I wanted to write something wholly autobiographical, however, I'd be writing memoirs. For me, exploring and filtering my experiences and observations through the lens of people I create is more interesting; it lets me move beyond myself, into the realm of the universal.

Who is your favorite character in the book, and why?
Oh, that's just not fair. It's like asking a parent of three wonderful kids which one they love the most. So like a parent, but a really really honest one, I'll say, I love *all* the characters, but at the end of the day, of the three leads—Danny, Lily, and Paul—Danny is my favorite.

Lily can't be my favorite, because I'm looking at the world of *Stone Creek* through her eyes; we're too close. And anyway, I like guys too much . . . so . . .

Paul is my cerebral favorite—he's the most complicated person in the book and I love his pretzeled brain and his deep desire to be good.

But Danny is my heart's favorite. He's as close to my perfect fantasy man as I could come without making him feel unreal. He's sexy, passionate, physically competent, emotionally accessible, capable of deep love, and infatuated with his child. As one of my reader friends said, He's beautiful and *he makes things!* He can even cook. And, while Lily, Paul, and Eve all were fundamentally responsible for their current painful lives, Danny had his tragedy thrust upon him. He has an innocent nature, much like his young son, a quality that I find enormously moving.

What was the hardest part of writing this book?

I think the hardest part was expressing Paul's contradictory personality and convoluted psychological makeup, and Eve's rigidity and superficial nastiness, in ways that were comprehensible, believable, and ultimately sympathetic. They could too easily be dislikable characters, and it was essential that the reader come to love Paul, as Lily did, and come to understand, forgive, and like Eve, as Danny did.

Writing a novel is tantamount to working out an enormous, complex puzzle, and figuring out Paul's inner dynamics, especially, was a tough puzzle within a tough puzzle. But, since human psychology is my favorite subject, for all the difficulties he presented, creating Paul was also one of the most enjoyable parts of writing this book.

Another difficult thing was keeping control over the book's language. My writing voice is clean and lucid, somewhat spare but also lyrical and poetic. However, given the huge emotions and passions I was writing about in *Stone Creek*, and my innate romanticism, my language occasionally went veering off into the wild purple yonder, and sometimes I couldn't see it, I was so caught up in the emotions and passions myself. I needed the gentle hand of my wonderful editor to help me tone things down in places.

What do you love most about writing?

That it is a personal, positive, and spiritual experience. I am not a religious person, but like many people who can't turn to existing belief systems or rituals for spiritual comfort, I am searching for it elsewhere: for an inner peace and contentment that makes existence meaningful. Writing is as close as I've ever come to finding that. It takes me out of my mundane self and puts me in touch with an indefinable creative force that exists both within and without.

The moments I love the most are when I'm laboring like mad over a sentence, a paragraph, concentrating so hard everything around me disappears, and then I sit back, read what I've written, and think to myself, *Who the heck wrote that?* I know full well that I did, two seconds before, but the me who wrote those words is not the same me reading them. It's a wonderful feeling to realize there is more to me than even I know.

On a more down to earth level, I love that it's difficult. I love the challenge, and the belief in myself that I can rise to it, and I love when something comes together like nuclear fusion in my head and I'm off and running. Until I fall into the next ditch and lie there bitching and moaning about how I can't do this. Or when I realize I've forgotten to make dinner because the work is going so well that my sense of time and I have parted company.

I think we all need to feel that we've created something from our lives that gives evidence of our having been here. For me, it's turned out to be sharing what I know through my writing.